W9-CYT-017

ILLINOIS PRAIRIE DPL

A65502 090563

Swept Off Her Feet

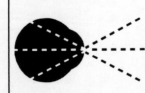

This Large Print Book carries the
Seal of Approval of N.A.V.H.

SWEPT OFF HER FEET

HESTER BROWNE

WHEELER PUBLISHING

A part of Gale, Cengage Learning

GALE
CENGAGE Learning™

Detroit • New York • San Francisco • New Haven, Conn • Waterville, Maine • London

ILLINOIS PRAIRIE DISTRICT LIBRARY

GALE
CENGAGE Learning™

Copyright © 2011 by Hester Browne.
Wheeler Publishing, a part of Gale, Cengage Learning.

ALL RIGHTS RESERVED
This book is a work of fiction. Names, characters, places, and incidents either are the product of the author's imagination or are used fictitiously. Any resemblance to actual events or locales or persons, living or dead, is entirely coincidental.

Wheeler Publishing Large Print Hardcover.
The text of this Large Print edition is unabridged.
Other aspects of the book may vary from the original edition.
Set in 16 pt. Plantin.

LIBRARY OF CONGRESS CATALOGING-IN-PUBLICATION DATA

Browne, Hester.
    Swept off her feet / by Hester Browne.
       p. cm.
    ISBN-13: 978-1-4104-4094-5 (hardcover)
    ISBN-10: 1-4104-4094-X (hardcover)
    1. Chick lit. 2. Large type books. I. Title.
PR6102.R695S84 2011b
823'.92—dc22   2011020725

Published in 2011 by arrangement with Gallery Books, a division of Simon & Schuster, Inc.

Printed in the United States of America
1 2 3 4 5 6 7 15 14 13 12 11

9. 12-11   2.3.24.   Jule

For the Flourish Walls reelers,
belles and trotters,
with love and thanks

ACKNOWLEDGMENTS

I fell in love with Scottish reeling a few years ago, and when I say fell, I mean, *fell.* Evie's encounter with the log basket is based on my own undignified destruction of a similar basket during my first encounter with a truly masterful spinner. I don't know why the Scots bothered with claymores when they could have easily spun the English right back over the border with one flick of their mighty wrists, taking out chunks of Hadrian's Wall as they went.

Now, though — at last! — I have a proper place to apologize to the Charterhall Academy of Scottish Dance for the broken furniture, and to thank its long-suffering teachers for their wonderful hospitality. Kettlesheer Castle, the McAndrews, and the famous table are fictional, but the magic of reeling and turning and skimming across a roomful of kilts and bare arms at two a.m.

7

is entirely real. Thank you so much for inviting me.

I'm constantly grateful to my agents, Lizzy
Kremer and David Forrer, for their encour-
agement and jokes, and to my editor, Kara
Cesare, and the team at Gallery Books, for
their enthusiasm and patience. The writer is
only one person in the Reel of the Romantic
Novel, and I'm lucky to dance it with some
wonderful people.

ONE

Everyone has a weakness. Some people have a weakness for champagne cocktails. Or older men with French accents.

My weakness is old French champagne glasses. Preferably ones that have seen a bit of *après*-midnight action. Or English pub glasses with real Victorian air bubbles, or those 1950s Babycham glasses with the cute little faun.

Any kind of glasses, actually, they don't have to match.

Old *sun*glasses too, come to think of it. Also, gloves (satin evening ones, especially), vintage wedding photos, fountain pens, trophies for long-forgotten tournaments, postcards . . .

Okay, fine.

My name is Evie Nicholson, and I am addicted to The Past.

"A child's teddy bear, circa 1935." Pause.

9

"Missing one eye. And left arm."

Max looked up from the printout the auctioneer had enclosed with the delivery, and fixed me with his best withering gaze. It wasn't the one he used to persuade rich Chelsea wives to buy chaise longues they didn't strictly need. It was astonishing what Max could sell, simply by draping his lanky frame over it and flashing his Heathcliff eyes. Only now they were looking less *Come to bed, Cathy* and more *I'm going to burn down your house and do something unspeakable to your puppy.*

"Would you please explain why you bought a one-armed blind teddy, the stuff of pure childhood nightmares?" he inquired.

"He's a Steiff, and he was going for a tenner," I muttered, picking the bear out of the delivery box.

Up close, he was a bit . . . *mangy.* When I'd spotted him in a box in the salesroom, all I'd seen was his threadbare nose, the fur worn away by thousands of kisses from his sailor-suited owners. I'd seen T-strap shoes and nursery teas and nannies with starched aprons. This brave little bear had once had pride of place in a smart London nursery; I couldn't stand seeing him waved around by some unfeeling porter, unwanted. He was worth *one* bid, surely?

10

"You paid a tenner," repeated Max, "for something even the moths have moved out of?"

I tweaked the bear's wonky limbs into an appealing hug. "Someone's obviously loved him. He deserves a good retirement home."

"Someone loved Adolf Hitler, but that doesn't mean I'd be happy to fork out real money to sell him in my shop. With or without eyes." Max shook the paper again, and it opened up to another three pages. He let out a strangled squeak of horror.

Three pages! I bit my lip, and propped the bear on a bookshelf. I didn't remember buying quite so much. I'd gone in there with my catalogue strictly marked up and sat on my hands for loads of amazing bargains.

"Honestly, it's not as bad as it looks," I said. "I'll pay for some of those myself. I can always eBay what —"

Max's hands flew up as if he were warding off evil spirits. "Don't say *that* word in *this* shop!" he roared.

"Sorry," I whispered.

"Oh, God." He hunched his narrow shoulders and closed his eyes, squeezing his hand over his forehead in theatrical despair. "We're going to have to have The Talk again, Evie. Where shall I begin? With the fact that one man's junk is nearly always *another*

11

man's junk?"

"But —"

"There is a difference between collecti*bles,* and dust collect*ors,*" he began with vicar-like relish. "To succeed in antiques, you've got to ignore the item and focus on the *person* you can sell it to. . . ."

I clamped my lips shut. This was a major bone of contention between Max and me, but for the purpose of filling in the ten minutes until my sister, Alice, galloped to my rescue, I decided to let him do his routine. Antiques for me were all about the lives they'd once been part of. I loved the whispers of the past they carried, the proof that those period films had once been real life. Max, on the other hand, was all about the money. He obsessed about the covert movement of valuables from one wealthy family to another like someone studying the Premiership football-team transfer market, but with Sheraton dining sets instead of soccer players.

His shop in Chelsea, where I worked and he flounced about, provided a small taxable income, most of which was snapped up by his ex-wife, Tessa, but Max's real work was discreetly acquiring treasures from the impoverished English aristocracy and finding new homes for them in Cheshire, New

England, or the millionaires' mansions on the outskirts of London. A bit like Robin Hood, except he was the only one who made any money, and I was the one who wore the tights.

"Your problem is that you only ever buy for *yourself*," he droned on, "and you're hardly the most discerning —"

"That's not fair!" I protested. "I spotted some Chanel costume brooches for Mrs. Herriot-Scott. Big camellias, genuine, in an old biscuit tin — no one else bothered to check it."

I didn't add that *I'd* only opened it because I was a sucker for lockets concealing wartime sweethearts, and you only found those by trawling the depths of general house-clearance boxes. And biscuit tins.

Max ground to an abrupt halt at the mention of Mrs. Herriot-Scott, one of his favorite clients. We loved her, and her insatiable desire for expensive plastic.

"Ah, well, that's different." His black eyes glittered as he calculated the markup. "What about that Georgian card table Jassy de la Mara asked us to look at?"

I glanced at the door and surreptitiously checked my watch. Max was on the second page, when my bidding had got a bit . . . well, emotional.

13

"The card table wasn't right. Reproduction. But I picked up some nice cranberry glass," I said.

Max's face was crumpling alarmingly as he read on.

"And I got some Weymss piggy banks," I added, my voice rising. "For Valentine's presents? It's that time of year?"

"My God," he said, his voice cracking with grief. "Are you trying to break me? Is Tessa paying you to destroy my credit rating as well as my credibility?"

Too late. He'd obviously reached the photo frames, my Achilles' heel.

"I don't know what you mean," I said in a small voice.

He thrust the list at me. "Evie, Evie, Evie, not wedding photographs *again*." Max clapped a hand to his head. "Do I even have to look at them? What freaks have you snapped up this time?"

Damn, I thought. Max would choose this one afternoon to roll back in after lunch. The one afternoon Lots Road Auctions decided to deliver late. He never noticed half my purchases normally; I was an expert at buying, staging, and reselling before he even noticed the shop looked different.

"They're good old frames!" I argued. "And if they're already filled with wedding

14

photos, it'll give people looking for wedding presents the *buying feeling!*"

"*Hello?!* These freaks would put anyone off getting hitched!" Max reached into the box and shoved the top frame under my nose with such urgency that his leather jacket squeaked. "Four eyes and not one of them looking in the same direction!"

If I was being honest, the frames weren't that special, but I felt so sorry for someone's great-grandparents, dressed up in their finest and looking so happy, being sneered at and passed over. Chucked onto the unsold pile. What was twenty quid a go?

Plus hammer tax.

Plus VAT.

I swallowed, and wished Alice would hurry up. I had a bad feeling about where this was going.

Max regarded me with a mixture of frustration and despair. "I'm beginning to think I should start going to auctions myself."

"Yeah, right," I scoffed, before I could bite my tongue.

Max hadn't been to an auction within fifty miles of the shop in five years, on account of his chaise-longue-lizard reputation going before him, and the prices rising accordingly as all the dealers in the room abandoned their bickering and clubbed together

15

in order to see off Max Shacks, the House-wife's Choice. That was the whole point of having an assistant to do his bidding. Literally.

"It's all perfectly salable." I swiped the list of out his hands before he got to the moth-eaten sampler that had made me go all Jane Austen. "If I wanted it, someone else will."

"That's the trouble, though, isn't it? You've got more of my stock in your flat than I have in here." He paused in his ranting and asked curiously, "Speaking of which, did you ever manage to get that knackered Chinese silk dressing screen up your stairs?"

"Yes," I said, lifting my chin. "It's giving my boudoir a very Edwardian ambience."

Max snorted. "You are still living in that sixties block of flats round the back of Ful-ham Palace football ground, aren't you?"

"It's not where you are, it's . . . what you have around you. It makes me *feel* Edward-ian."

He sighed and looked down at the list. "Evie, this really isn't the week to be filling the shop with tat because you feel sorry for it. I've got the accountant coming in — we're living in hard times. . . ."

I'd heard this one before as well, and was easily distracted by the doorbell jangling.

16

The deliveryman had returned. He was backing in under the weight of my final mercy buy, and when he turned round, giving me a full view of what I'd bought, I blanched.

"I know, I know. Why don't you sit down, and I'll make you some coffee?" I gabbled, hustling Max toward the tiny office in the back.

Too late. Hearing the bell jingle, Max turned round and staggered back against an Arts and Crafts bookcase in shock.

"Where'd you want this, mate?" the deliveryman asked, weaving slightly beneath the weight of a massive oak-mounted stag's head. The stag had seen better days. One glass eye was drooping, as if he'd had a dram too many, and both antlers bore traces of tinsel from some recent Christmas party at the auction house.

Max turned to me and widened his eyes until I could see the whites around the bloodshot bits. "Why?" he demanded.

"It looked so noble!" I pleaded. "It just screams *stately home!* I'll find a buyer for it, Max, I promise."

"Who?" We'd reached monosyllables. Not a good sign. Max generally loved the sound of his own voice.

"Um . . ." I racked my brains. "Um,

17

animal lovers? People with hats?"

The deliveryman swayed, but wisely stayed silent.

Max sank onto a mahogany dining chair and put his head in his hands. Then he removed it, and demanded, "How much?"

"Um, I think it's a good price for —"

"How *much,* Evie?"

"Two hundred pounds," I said in a very small voice.

"Nnnggghhh." Max shoved his hands into his hair and gripped tightly. Along with his suggestive mouth and cavalier way with priceless heirlooms, his hair was one of his redeeming features, being thick and black and tinged with gray, in a sort of rakish Shakespearean-actor fashion. In idle moments, I sometimes pictured him in a doublet and ruff, complaining about the price of lampreys.

Sadly, the hair and the mouth did not make up for the foul temper, the inability to work a credit-card machine, or the biting sarcasm that he liked to think was Wildean but usually made him come across more like a petulant geography teacher. He also habitually wore a long leather coat — the trademark he hoped would eventually get him a gig as a TV antiques expert.

"You are paying for that out of your own

money," he informed me, emphasizing each word with a stab of his finger.

"Fine," I said, a bit too brightly. "Why don't you take it out of my —"

"No." This time his voice was very distinct. "No, you're already down to a hundred and ten quid for the month, thanks to that filthy Edwardian wedding dress that even Miss Havisham would have used for dust rags. I want the money in cash, in my account, by the end of the month."

"But it's *February,* it's a short month! And I've still got Christmas to pay for," I protested as the deliveryman inched his way backward out of the cluttered shop. He gestured toward the stag and made *I'm not taking that back* gestures.

I ignored him.

"Keep them, sell them, I don't care," Max went on. "But I want the money. For the freak-show photos, the deformed teddy, the moth-eaten stag, everything. Now, not over time. It hurts me to do this, Evie," he added, less convincingly, "but it's a lesson in business. You are here to learn, are you not? Or am I running some kind of flea market?" He paused, then frowned, distracted. "What's that?"

A long streak of something red had appeared at the window and was peering inside.

"Sweet Jesus! Has that postbox moved?" Max demanded. "I have *got* to stop drinking with Crispin at lunch —"

"No," I said, getting up to let Alice in. "It's my sister. And don't be rude about that coat — it's her style statement for this winter."

"Alice? I'll go and make some coffee," said Max and slunk off.

Alice was one of the few people I knew who could carry off a bright-red maxi coat. She was very tall and always gave the impression she was wearing a cape, even when she wasn't. She was, by profession, an "interiors consultant," and her swishy efficiency extended from her cowed clients to her enviable wardrobe: Alice spent a fortune on one dramatic item per season and wore it everywhere, referring to it constantly in the fashion singular. Once everyone had fallen under the spell of her "key piece," she "retired" it (i.e., passed it on to me) and moved on to the next.

Max had once tried to argue that his leather coat was a key piece, but as Alice pointed out, rather brutally, it was more of a meanness issue than a style one. He'd had it so long that on a pay-per-wear basis, it now owed him money. Alice didn't show her clothes any loyalty, whereas it would take pliers to get that thing off his back.

She swept in, chestnut hair swinging like in a shampoo ad, and I could tell by her eyes, skittering from box to box, that she was itching to tidy up.

"Evie, don't tell me anything, I want to guess why you SOS-ed me," she said by way of greeting. "Has Max got the call from *Antiques Roadshow*? Has he *finally* schmoozed his way to fame?"

Alice threw one hand dramatically onto her hip and knocked over a Chinese vase with her sleeve.

"Oh, bollocks!" she squeaked, making a grab for it as the vase teetered, then fell off the shelf.

That was the saving grace to her otherwise majestic attitude. Like me, she was chronically clumsy, on account of being nearly six feet tall. Something to do with having longer legs and arms than normal and a center of gravity that seemed to shift with the tides. When we were children, our mother never let us go into the china department of any major department store without fastening our arms inside our duffle coats first.

I made a grab for the vase at the same time she did, and between us we managed to knock it onto a bedroom sofa Max had taken in as part exchange for a Tiffany lamp. It lay in the cushions, looking winded.

"Sorry," breathed Alice.

"What's going on?" yelled Max from the back room.

"Nothing!" I yelled back. "Alice was just thinking about buying a vase!"

"Tell her we don't do mates' rates in this shop!"

"Don't mind him," I said. "He has no mates."

"I heard that!" bellowed Max.

"Can you lend me some money?" I whispered. "I went a bit overboard at the last sale, and Max is making me pay for everything myself. I know I can sell it. It'd just be a loan."

"Again?" Alice looked pained. "It's not that I mind lending you money, but —"

"Okay, then," I said, trying a different tack. "Would you like to buy the sweetest little Steiff teddy bear? You could start a collection!"

"I thought *you* were starting a Steiff collection." She eyed me beadily.

"I was. I'll throw in the three I've already found," I replied, mentally retrieving the tatty teds propping up my collection of first-edition Beatrix Potter books in my spare room: I'd been going for a '30s nursery feel, but to be honest, I'd have been equally happy with a Victorian parlor look. "There, you see — you've already got four, and it'll give Fraser something to buy you for Christmas instead of fishing rods and waterproof waders and all that outdoors stuff you've dumped in my garage."

"No," said Alice firmly. "I am totally anti-collections. As you well know."

"You've already got a collection of unused huntin', shootin', and fishin' gear," I pointed out. "Can I sell you a stag's head to complete the set?"

"I'd rather give you the cash." She paused. "I'll give you double if you don't tell Fraser that fishing rod's in your garage."

"Done," I said. "And I'll give you the money back when I've eBayed my purchases for a massive profit."

"I've heard that before too." Alice reached into her gorgeous silver leather bag for her checkbook.

It was a shame Alice was so phobic about possessions, I thought, eyeing the collection of Art Deco cigarette cases in the cabinet behind her. She was the only person I knew who could actually use the cases for business cards, or mints, or —

"Stop it," she said, looking up over her

lashes. "I know what you're thinking. I'm this close to calling Mum and telling her to Simplify your flat." She held up her finger and thumb, then thought for a second and made the tiny space even tinier. "You know she's itching to do it for a magazine?"

I shuddered.

Our mother, Caryl Nicholson — or Carol, as she'd been as recently as 2004 — was something of a lifestyle guru in the leafier parts of south London, thanks to her business, Simplify with Caryl Nicholson, which basically dejunked houses so they sold faster. Mum's spring cleaning had always started just after Christmas; she had to ration her housework so she didn't run out of stuff to do by midweek. Woe betide Barbie if she got so much as badly cut hair; we didn't have a dollies' hospital so much as a sinister Gestapo-style toy abduction squad that spirited away any ailing toys, never to be seen again.

When Alice and I moved out, our father had offered Mum's ruthless tactics to friends who had the real estate agents coming round, mainly so he could read the paper instead of having it yanked from his hands and ironed. Ten years and three hundred skips later, she ran her own "life laundry" business, and wore a lot of Joseph basics while charging rich ladies top whack to march around their executive residences, barking at them to get rid of anything that hadn't moved in six months, up to and including husbands and heavy-shedding family pets.

Ironically, the property market collapsing had only made her more popular, and now she had a whole team working for her, including Alice, who was her central London manager. Both their houses looked like something from interiors magazines, even if — privately — I did think the extreme tidiness was a bit At Home with a Serial Killer.

"She won't want to make over my flat," I said confidently. "She doesn't understand my need for ambience. She said my fifties-diner kitchen set made her want to cry."

"I know," said Alice.

"What do you mean, you know?"

Alice rolled her eyes. "I mean, she mentioned it. And told a journalist from *Good Homes* that you were her last remaining challenge. She has you in her sights, Evie. Consider this your advance warning. There."

She handed me a check for five hundred pounds, and I felt an invisible flock of birds lift my careworn shoulders.

"Wow! Thanks, Alice, I was only going to

ask you for a couple of hundred!" I blurted out. "Here, let me throw the teddy bear in!"

I pressed the bear into her hands, and she shrank away as if it might be a carrier of some rare disease, like untidiness.

Then she looked back at me without speaking, and her meticulously groomed eyebrows knitted a couple of millimeters closer together. "Evie," she said out of the corner of her mouth, "there is something *else* I wanted to talk to you about."

That's when I knew the tip-off and the cash weren't going to be interest-free.

"Coffee?" Max appeared, bearing an old pub tray with three unmatched porcelain cups, a battered hotel percolator, and a packet of HobNobs. "And would you like to explain, Evangeline, how you offered to make coffee, and I end up making it?"

I noticed he'd smoothed down his wild hair and was looking noticeably more dapper. I squinted. He'd added a red silk scarf. *My* red silk scarf.

Alice's steely gaze skated around the shop until it alighted on the stag's head. Suddenly she flashed a dazzling smile. "Max, this . . . big deer thing is *just* what I've been looking for, to give my boyfriend for Valentine's Day!"

"It is?"

"Ooh, what a great idea!" I exclaimed. Fraser would appreciate the noble stag, even if Max didn't. "You see? I *knew* it would be a perfect gift for the man who has everything! And *Fraser* can start a collection!"

"I've told Evie I want it," she went on, shooting me a glare. "We just need to talk about a price."

"Well, I had it marked down at three thou —" Max began, but I cut him off.

"It's one of the items I was going to pay for myself," I reminded him. "Out of my own money. So really she should be negotiating with me."

Max looked foxed.

"I know Evie can't do negotiations with an audience," Alice went on. "Do you mind if I insist on discussing this with her outside the shop?" She glanced at her watch. "Oh, look, it's nearly four already. By the time I bring Evie back, there won't be much time left for you to close up. Tell you what, why don't you just let her go now and then you can start in the morning with a nice big sale?"

"But . . . I . . ." Max spluttered.

"Brilliant, thanks so much! Evie, is that your bag? And where's your coat?"

Obediently, I picked up my bag (Alice's last-year's "patent hobo") and my coat

27

ILLINOIS PRAIRIE DISTRICT LIBRARY

(Alice's last-year's "deconstructed cocoon") and my hat (my own last-year's Marks and Spencer beret), and let her march me from the wrong end of the King's Road toward the much smarter end she frequented.

I was allowed to bask in the warm glow of having acted on my antiques instincts for about ten minutes, before the reason for Alice's sudden generosity was laid before me like the wrong side of a bodged-up table.

Two

Alice took me to No. 11 Cadogan Gardens, a discreet hotel round the back of Peter Jones. It was a warrenlike townhouse with lots of discreet nooks and crannies; she and Mum liked to take clients there to tell them that their lifetime collections of *Vogue* magazines and paper boutique bags had been recycled. No one could hear you scream in No. 11.

"I've got some good news for you," she said, pouring me a cup of tea from the tray that had appeared on the table in front of us within moments of us arriving. "It's a favor."

"For me, or for someone else?"

"For you *and* for someone else." Alice broke a biscuit in half, nibbled it, and got out her phone. "Fraser's mother's neighbors —" She looked up. "Evie, stop looking at the cups."

I put the saucer down guiltily. I couldn't

help it. Cups and saucers were one of my collections. Especially hotel ones, the older the better. I liked to imagine what sorts of people had drunk out of them — movie stars, duchesses, eloping couples —

"Are you concentrating?" she demanded. "Because this is complicated, and I've got to be somewhere at six."

"Sorry," I said. "Go on. Fraser's mother's . . . neighbors?"

"You know Fraser's parents live on a farm in Berwickshire?" When I looked blank, she added, "You know — Berwickshire? The Scottish Borders? Very beautiful, heathery moors, grouse, dramatic North Sea cliffs, steeped in mindless Anglo-Scottish violence, et cetera, et cetera."

I nodded. Alice had been invited up to stay with Fraser for New Year (or Hogmanay, as apparently no one called it). They'd been seeing each other for two years, so Mum and I had held our breath until about the third of January, waiting for Big News; but Alice had returned from Scotland with only a lot of salmon and a very bad cold — and a look on her face that made it clear there was nothing she wanted to discuss.

"If you'd told me about the heathery moors instead of the cobwebby loo, I might

unspectacul
made half m
on eBay last
people like
clients to chu
how it was p
related to eit
on the Interr
those "baby-s
Yorkshire area

"I've got th
Alice went o
"Why don't y
and discuss it?

"Duncan?" I
terms already?

She ignored
voice. Alice wa
And tears.

"Duncan an
Actually, why d
pretend to be y
a decent day ra
for the chance
She started scri

I decided, glo
down to Alice
reminded me o
just organized m
less than a year

have remembered," I pointed out.

"I didn't *see* them, I was too busy not freezing to death. Anyway, Fraser's family are old friends with the people who have the big house next door, the McAndrews. It's a castle, really, called Kettlesheer," she added in a terrible Scottish accent. "You'd love it — Sheila says it's crammed with random junk. Some forefather was one of those Victorian collectors, shot everything he saw, then stuffed it in cases to gather dust for eternity. We drove past at New Year — it's all turrets and bats' nests. The problem is that the McAndrews need to raise some cash to fix the damp, or the roof, or something. Basically, they need an expert to advise them about what items to sell."

"And you volunteered me?" My heart thumped in my chest; it sounded *amazing*. I'd always dreamed of getting into one of those big houses, opening the ancient cupboards, peering into the rusty suits of armor, maybe finding Maharajah's diamond, wrapped in cloth and hidden for years in a trinket box. . . .

Something shifty in Alice's expression stopped me as I was mentally waltzing down the ancestral portrait gallery.

"Is there a reason why they haven't got in touch with one of the big auction houses?"

I asked. "Bonhams and Christi[e]s who you might meet up
branches in Edinburgh."

"Ah," said Alice. "Well, they a hard stare. "Please tell me
one discreet. And very good," ation isn't going to end up at
split second too late. "Reading; again. I do not need you and
lines, they don't want it gettin[c]romanage my life. I am not a
sherry-and-shortbread circuit nawed hoarder."
having to flog off the family e you're not!" she protested.
Max has a whole book of privat[o]ng do you want to work for a
love random junk, doesn't he?" s to send you to do his bidding

"If by junk you mean priceles because everyone else thinks
—" I started.   than a weasel's backside? You're

"Evie," said Alice, dropping to be able to build your own
routine. "He buys random junk[h]ile you're running round after
aristos and sells it on to lottery

don't know better."   on the battered silver teapot —

"Right," I said instead, and af the big hotels on Park Lane,
biscuit Alice had left.   and tried to work out why half

"Besides which, Mum and I wooning and the other half was
talking," she said ominously.   , mutinous.

*Please, not the broadening hori*cker for a turret, let alone a suit
again.   nd I did want Max to take me

"I don't want to give you a le usly. But I wanted to do it my
Alice in her most lecturing tone, tly, Alice and Mum had started
a great chance for you to make ut me — *while I was there,* I
contacts of your own. Broaden — like some sort of renovation
zons. Step out of your comfort z if stripping bits of my life out

She spread her hands and sm ng the rest a professional neutral
fully, like someone on QVC de l a spacious, airy new Evie.
a life-changing garden-sprinkl rty, not sixty; I had a regular if

when Mum dressed us in matching smocks, we were so alike that people often mistook us for fraternal twins. Yet these days, apart from sharing the same chestnut hair/lanky limb combo, we were totally different. She was better dressed than me, more sociable than me, just more in focus altogether. If she weren't my sister, I'd probably hate her.

But she was my sister, I reminded myself. And no matter how bossy she came across, she did genuinely have my best interests at heart. My messy life bothered Alice a whole lot more than it bothered me.

"Do you fancy going for some supper?" I heard myself ask. "We could get an early-bird deal somewhere?"

She stopped writing. "Um, I can't," she said. "I've got to be somewhere at six."

"Late appointment?"

"No, it's . . ." She stopped and gazed up at me, her brown eyes full of dread. "You're going to laugh."

"I won't."

"You will. Think of the very last thing either of us would want to do on a Friday night."

"Taxidermy?" I suggested. "*Star Trek* convention?"

"Worse. More mortifying."

"Oh! You're having that colonic Mum

booked for your birthday present?"

Alice bit her lip, then silently opened her bag to show me the contents.

"You're not serious," I breathed, turning white at the same time her nose turned bright red. My whole soul crinkled at the edges in sympathy as our shared childhood humiliations flooded back. "Not . . . what I think it is?"

She nodded. "Yup."

Our eyes met, and in an instant we were both standing in a freezing gym, two fed-up herons in a flock of pink-tighted cygnets.

"I am going to a *dancing* lesson," she spat.

For me and Alice, dancing was on a par with normal people getting dressed up as a pantomime horse. Hilarious for everyone else, but mortifying, overheating, and potentially dangerous for those actually inside the horse suit.

Our tiny, matchy-matchy mother was horrified that she could have produced two gangling girls routinely referred to as Big Bird and King Kong even by their teachers. In her infinite wisdom, she decided that dancing would somehow neutralize our uncoordination, and so from the ages of about six and five respectively, Alice and I were launched on a program of enforced lessons.

have remembered," I pointed out.

"I didn't *see* them, I was too busy not freezing to death. Anyway, Fraser's family are old friends with the people who have the big house next door, the McAndrews. It's a castle, really, called Kettlesheer," she added in a terrible Scottish accent. "You'd love it — Sheila says it's crammed with random junk. Some forefather was one of those Victorian collectors, shot everything he saw, then stuffed it in cases to gather dust for eternity. We drove past at New Year — it's all turrets and bats' nests. The problem is that the McAndrews need to raise some cash to fix the damp, or the roof, or something. Basically, they need an expert to advise them about what items to sell."

"And you volunteered me?" My heart thumped in my chest; it sounded *amazing*. I'd always dreamed of getting into one of those big houses, opening the ancient cupboards, peering into the rusty suits of armor, maybe finding Maharajah's diamond, wrapped in cloth and hidden for years in a trinket box. . . .

Something shifty in Alice's expression stopped me as I was mentally waltzing down the ancestral portrait gallery.

"Is there a reason why they haven't got in touch with one of the big auction houses?"

I asked. "Bonhams and Christie's both have branches in Edinburgh."

"Ah," said Alice. "Well, they need someone discreet. And very good," she added, a split second too late. "Reading between the lines, they don't want it getting round the sherry-and-shortbread circuit that they're having to flog off the family jewels. And Max has a whole book of private clients who love random junk, doesn't he?"

"If by junk you mean priceless antiquities —" I started.

"Evie," said Alice, dropping her polite routine. "He buys random junk from skint aristos and sells it on to lottery winners who don't know better."

"Right," I said instead, and ate the half-biscuit Alice had left.

"Besides which, Mum and I have been talking," she said ominously.

Please, not the broadening horizons lecture again.

"I don't want to give you a lecture," said Alice in her most lecturing tone, "but this is a great chance for you to make some new contacts of your own. Broaden your horizons. Step out of your comfort zone."

She spread her hands and smiled forcefully, like someone on QVC demonstrating a life-changing garden-sprinkler system.

32

"Who knows who you might meet up there?"

I gave her a hard stare. "Please tell me this conversation isn't going to end up at speed dating again. I do not need you and Mum to micromanage my life. I am not a sad old cat-gnawed hoarder."

"Of course you're not!" she protested. "But how long do you want to work for a man who has to send you to do his bidding at auctions because everyone else thinks he's slimier than a weasel's backside? You're never going to be able to build your own client list while you're running round after Max."

I focused on the battered silver teapot — from one of the big hotels on Park Lane, maybe? — and tried to work out why half of me was swooning and the other half was feeling, well, mutinous.

I was a sucker for a turret, let alone a suit of armor. And I did want Max to take me more seriously. But I wanted to do it my way. Recently, Alice and Mum had started talking about me — *while I was there,* I might add — like some sort of renovation project, as if stripping bits of my life out and painting the rest a professional neutral might reveal a spacious, airy new Evie.

I was thirty, not sixty; I had a regular if

unspectacular turnover of dates; and I'd made half my annual salary selling my finds on eBay last year. Most of it was "junk" that people like Mum and Alice had forced clients to chuck out. Sometimes I wondered how it was possible that I was biologically related to either of them; I'd even checked on the Internet to see if there were any of those "baby-swap nightmares" in the North Yorkshire area round the time of my birth.

"I've got the McAndrews' details here," Alice went on as if I'd already said yes. "Why don't you give Duncan a call tonight and discuss it?"

"Duncan?" I said. "Are we on first-name terms already?"

She ignored the heavy sarcasm in my voice. Alice was good at ignoring sarcasm. And tears.

"Duncan and Ingrid. Very nice people. Actually, why don't I call them for you? I'll pretend to be your assistant. I can negotiate a decent day rate. I bet you'd do it simply for the chance to poke around their attics." She started scribbling.

I decided, gloomily, that my mutiny boiled down to Alice — or rather, myself. Alice reminded me of what I could be like if I just organized myself a bit better. There was less than a year between us, and in the days when Mum dressed us in matching smocks, we were so alike that people often mistook us for fraternal twins. Yet these days, apart from sharing the same chestnut hair/lanky limb combo, we were totally different. She was better dressed than me, more sociable than me, just more in focus altogether. If she weren't my sister, I'd probably hate her.

But she was my sister, I reminded myself. And no matter how bossy she came across, she did genuinely have my best interests at heart. My messy life bothered Alice a whole lot more than it bothered me.

"Do you fancy going for some supper?" I heard myself ask. "We could get an early-bird deal somewhere?"

She stopped writing. "Um, I can't," she said. "I've got to be somewhere at six."

"Late appointment?"

"No, it's . . ." She stopped and gazed up at me, her brown eyes full of dread. "You're going to laugh."

"I won't."

"You will. Think of the very last thing either of us would want to do on a Friday night."

"Taxidermy?" I suggested. "*Star Trek* convention?"

"Worse. More mortifying."

"Oh! You're having that colonic Mum

35

booked for your birthday present?"

Alice bit her lip, then silently opened her bag to show me the contents.

"You're not serious," I breathed, turning white at the same time her nose turned bright red. My whole soul crinkled at the edges in sympathy as our shared childhood humiliations flooded back. "Not . . . what I think it is?"

She nodded. "Yup."

Our eyes met, and in an instant we were both standing in a freezing gym, two fed-up herons in a flock of pink-tighted cygnets.

"I am going to a *dancing* lesson," she spat.

For me and Alice, dancing was on a par with normal people getting dressed up as a pantomime horse. Hilarious for everyone else, but mortifying, overheating, and potentially dangerous for those actually inside the horse suit.

Our tiny, matchy-matchy mother was horrified that she could have produced two gangling girls routinely referred to as Big Bird and King Kong even by their teachers. In her infinite wisdom, she decided that dancing would somehow neutralize our uncoordination, and so from the ages of about six and five respectively, Alice and I were launched on a program of enforced lessons.

36

We stuck out like a pair of sore thumbs, making even the kids with "left" and "right" written on their mittens look like Liza Minnelli.

We begged — *begged* — Mum to let us pack it in, but with her steely ability to superimpose her own version of reality over everyone else's, she managed to see miraculous improvement in us, and always clapped far too loud when we shambled on at recitals, clouting some unfortunate classmate or denting the scenery in passing. This went on for eight agonizing years and numerous dance styles, during which time I developed an allergic reaction to leotards and Alice was banned from all tap classes within ten miles of Harrogate.

Alice and I had made a solemn pact never ever to so much as conga knowingly, and we'd stuck to it through university balls and other people's weddings. For me, the one good thing about not having a regular boyfriend was knowing there was no way I'd be hauled up onto the dance floor at wedding receptions. Alice did have a boyfriend, but luckily Fraser wasn't much of a snake-hipped disco-demon himself, and if forced onto the floor, she usually managed to bark something about safety regulations and drag him away.

All of which made the presence of a book about Scottish reeling and a pair of flat dancing shoes in her bag baffling.

"Are you *trying* to split up with Fraser?" I demanded, waving them around. "Has he *seen* what you can do to a grown man's foot?"

Alice squeezed her eyes shut. "Fraser invited me to a ball up in Scotland. He made it sound amazing, white tie, champagne, candlelight. . . ." She opened one eye. "It's at Kettlesheer, the house I was talking about? Apparently he only missed last year because he was in Paris with me."

"Champagne can make up for a *lot* of dancing," I said, already suffering a twinge of envy. Alice's social life was significantly more upmarket than mine. "Especially when served in a castle."

"Yes, well, I thought it would be like the balls you get in London — you know, lots of standing around the Dorchester, drinking kir royales and slagging off everyone's bolero jackets."

"And it's not?"

"No," she said flatly. "It's not. It's full-on dancing, ten till three in the morning. Six different reels to learn. Like one aerobics class after another. Tickets are like gold dust — you have to know someone on the committee. Soon as Fraser got ours, he made me go to this reeling society he belongs to, in Chelsea. With *experts.*"

"Oh, my God," I breathed, intrigued and horrified. *"Experts."*

"This is my sixth session, and I still have no idea what's going on." Alice's voice was rising dangerously. "I feel like someone's taken my feet off and put them back on again the wrong way round. Everyone keeps shouting *one* and *two* and *set* and *turn,* and I'm just like . . ." She mimed someone coming round after a major operation.

"But what *is* reeling?" I asked. "It must be the only class Mum didn't send us to. Is it like Morris dancing?"

Alice struggled for the right words. "It's like rugby, but without a ball," she managed. "You have to move into the right space at exactly the right time, then the man spins you, then someone else catches you, then you swerve around the next person. And if you're not in the right place at the right time, it all goes tits-up, and everyone yells. Just to put you off, the whole thing's accompanied by *accordion music.* Oh, God. I can't explain. You have to be there. Worse than *Riverdance.*"

"No," I mouthed. Nothing had been worse than the one Riverdance workshop we'd ruined.

"And it's on *Valentine's weekend!*" Clearly this was the final straw. "I mean, honestly! I wanted to have some romantic minibreak in Venice or somewhere! Or Paris! I thought —"

"Calm down, Alice," I said sternly. "You're getting mad eyes."

She pressed her lips into a line, and vulnerable, panicked Alice vanished beneath the streamlined house-stylist once more. It was like watching one of those séances where the host body reasserts itself over the gabbling spirit.

"I've said I'll go," she said. "And I will. It's not like Fraser doesn't know to bring padding. I've already given him a wrist sprain and a gimpy leg."

"But I bet he's said you're doing a *marvelous* job," I said reassuringly.

Alice's expression softened, and she nodded. "Even when I pulled him over last time, he still said I had an admirable grip."

That pretty much summed up Fraser Graham: polite, even in the face of personal injury. He was one of those courteous men who automatically offered women ("ladies") his seat on trains, and was bewildered when they accused him of thinking they were pregnant. He always had a hankie, wouldn't let you buy a coffee. That sort of man.

I had been nursing a clandestine crush on Fraser for ages. I could totally picture him at a ball, offering his arm to ladies while fetching them ice water and sweeping them around a dance floor.

"Well, if Fraser's there, you'll have a nice time," I sighed. "Bet he looks divine in white tie."

Alice was shrugging her red coat back on and leaving money for the tea. "No white tie for him. He'll be wearing a kilt this time," she said. "It's that sort of do. Full-on Scottish."

"A kilt?" I croaked as Fraser's sturdy calves in thick white socks flashed before my eyes. My cup and saucer gave a telltale wobble.

Alice stopped adjusting her beret and fixed me with a gimlet eye. "You know what? He's going back up there on Sunday for his week in the Edinburgh office — why don't you drive him up? He can show you where to go, and fill you in properly at the same time. Yes, that's a good idea. . . ." She got out her phone.

Just to explain, Fraser worked for a very top-drawer wine merchant with a branch in London and one in Edinburgh, so he and Alice spent half the month together, which

41

was why he probably still thought Alice was a sunny, non-control-freak sort of gal.

"Is there any point in disagreeing?" I asked.

Alice shook her head, and her bob swung emphatically.

I hadn't really thought there was. Luckily, I now had the image of Fraser in a kilt to soothe the pain.

THREE

I don't know if you've ever tried to drive with your knees clamped together and your stomach pulled in while trying not to worry about getting so much as a fly on the windscreen of your boss's precious car, but I can tell you it's exhausting. By the time Fraser and I crawled onto the M1, my inner thighs were on fire, and not in a good way.

Fraser, of course, had no idea of my silent agonies. He was too busy making lovely conversation. The checkered history of the Scottish Borders, why chardonnay is the chameleon of grapes, my work (which I'd upgraded as much as I dared), etc., etc. Fraser could talk the hind leg off a donkey, unlike many men of my acquaintance, but — and this is a crucial difference — he always remembered to ask *the donkey's opinion.*

". . . really very kind of you to drive me up," he was saying, as I tried to change gear while somehow clenching my triceps. "Alice does seem to get everyone organized."

"It's genetic," I said. "Mum's so organized we have to give her our Christmas lists in July so she can buy our presents on sale. Dad has reminders on his phone for mowing the lawn and pruning."

Fraser laughed as if this were some kind of joke. It wasn't.

"Did she tell you much about Kettlesheer?" he inquired. "Or the McAndrews?"

"Just that it was cold." I sighed. "I *love* stately homes. They're my secret passion. I like to walk round and imagine what everything smelled like."

I would have been more scintillating, but there was a taxi driver right on my tail, and the stag's head in the back was obscuring my rear view. Max had heaved it into the car personally and wrapped the antlers with Fraser's clean socks for protection; Fraser, as I'd guessed, adored it, and had already christened it Banquo.

"Well, you'll love Kettlesheer, then. I wonder if they'll give you the bed Sir Walter Scott's meant to have had pneumonia in. Mind if I have a travel sweet?"

"The bed that . . . ?" I momentarily took my eyes off the road, saw the cluttered glove box open and Fraser holding out a tin of hard candies. My heart gave an illicit bump.

Even in jeans and a cable-knit sweater, Fraser Graham looked like a Regency gentleman. The thick blond hair, the wide mouth, the accent that sounded like expensive dark chocolate — and what really swung it for me, the charming, totally unaffected manners.

He grinned affably, and I melted a little further. Fraser had actually opened *my* car door for *me* when I'd picked him up at his flat in Notting Hill. It was a constant struggle not to imagine him galloping around on a horse, tipping his hat to the ladies. He was absolutely wasted on Alice, who kept trying to make him wear long-sleeved T-shirts and get a trendier haircut.

"Yes, help yourself," I said, before remembering that we were in Max's car. "Oh, actually, be careful that —"

Too late. He was opening the tin and frowning at the contents.

"Ah," said Fraser, quickly slamming it back into the glove box before I could see what was in there. "Perhaps not. Where was I? The McAndrews — lovely people, Duncan and Ingrid. They used to stay at Kettlesheer in the summer when Duncan's uncle Carlisle had the place. Now, *he* was a one. His wife, his horse, and his dog all had the same name — to save effort, apparently."

"He sounds mad." I *loved* bonkers posh people. No one wore a jaunty hat and matching cape for breakfast like a minor British aristocrat.

"Oh yes, dangerously so. I don't think Duncan was expecting to inherit, but then, you don't expect a ninety-year-old man to disinherit his two perfectly good sons and take up mountain biking, do you?"

"Not in my family," I said. "There are rules about mud. So come on, give me the gossip. Alice went all discreet on me."

Fraser settled back into his seat and crossed one long leg over the other, revealing a flash of red sock. "Well. Up until two years ago, Duncan was a deputy head teacher at some prep school in Kent, and Ingrid was the school secretary. Nice house in Wimbledon, his and hers Jaguars. Suddenly Carlisle falls off his bike, and bang! Duncan's got his own tartan and grouse moor, and poor Ingrid's having to learn fifty ways with cocktail haggis. Mum says she went round in a trance for the first month, virtually begging someone to tell her it was a huge practical joke."

The traffic had slowed down, so I sneaked

46

another sideways glance. "But . . . surely you have an inkling that you're going to be left a *castle?* It's not like being left a train set."

I didn't add that if there'd been any chance of *me* inheriting a castle, however remote, I'd have been fantasizing about complicated lawnmower accidents at family gatherings involving anyone standing between me and the keys to the drawbridge.

"Ah, well. Family tradition. Duncan inherited because there's this ye olde McAndrew superstition that the castle can't be left to an unmarried heir, and both of Carlisle's sons were divorced. Well, one was divorced, the other misplaced his wife in Thailand."

"I don't understand. Why can't they inherit?"

"Because bad things happen." He made a *Whooo-oooh* gesture, wiggling his fingers and jiggling his eyebrows up and down in Scooby-Doo ghost fashion.

"Like . . . what?" My imagination filled up instantly with walled-up nuns and hauntings.

"Oh, just the usual bad things that happen when a man doesn't have a wife to run his castle," said Fraser. "Grill-pan fires. Unflattering trousers. Tax inspections." He gave me a wink. "Not such a bad policy, if

47

you ask me."

I felt my cheeks go hot, but then had to snap my attention back before I hit the car in front, which had slowed to join the back of the traffic jam ahead.

Banquo bounced reproachfully in my rear-view mirror.

"So is your mum showing them the ropes?" I said, trying to regain my composure. "Does she know the castle well?"

"Like the back of her hand. She grew up running around the kitchens. Her family's always farmed on the estate, and my granny was a lady's maid at Kettlesheer, when they had a full staff to run the place." Fraser discreetly turned off my turn signal to stop the man behind beeping at me. "It's a lot for Duncan and Ingrid to do on their own," he went on, little knowing how my stately home fantasy was now bubbling into full color with each word, "keeping a house that size watertight and clean, as well as fulfilling the social obligations, of course."

Social obligations!

I realized I'd said it out loud.

"Absolutely. Duncan and Ingrid have got to host the local ball once a year, throw sherry parties for the local hunt, sit on endless committees. And of course, it all costs money." He paused, and his voice turned

48

serious. "Which is where, as I'm sure Alice explained, you come in. If you could find one or two things they could sell, to the right people, it would solve a few problems."

The traffic had stopped again, and I allowed myself to look properly across the car, my best take-me-seriously face at the ready. I liked Fraser's solemn expression. It spoke to me of illicit conversations in drawing rooms and carriages.

"I'm sure there's plenty up there that they could sell," I said. "Max seems to think it's a real treasure trove."

That was a direct quote, incidentally. When I told Max why I needed a week off work and the loan of the Duchess, his prized Mercedes, since my own battered Polo wouldn't have made it past Luton, he'd come to life in the most spectacular fashion.

"Kettlesheer?" he'd breathed, spreading out his bony fingers as if playing an invisible piano of longing. "That is number four on my top ten stately homes to get into. It's *crammed* with stuff, and practically no one knows it's there. How the hell did you manage that?"

"Oh, contacts," I'd said.

"Well, it can't have been through your social diary," he went on with a waspish pout. "The McAndrews don't socialize."

Max spent many hours indulging in and recovering from other people's hospitality in the name of stalking antiques. He claimed his hangovers as a tax deduction and had a file of drunken notes scribbled on loo paper.

"So, what should I look out for?" I'd asked.

"Everything. Scottish silver, oils, Italian marbles dragged back from the Grand Tour . . . Every four generations there's a McAndrew who makes a bloody fortune. Then the next three spend it." From the distant look in his eyes, Max was gamboling around Kettlesheer with a pricing gun. "If they can't buy it, they marry it and reel it in that way — they bagged an American heiress at the turn of the last century, must have brought some quality gear with her. For years, Derek Yardley's been saying there's a table up there worth a mint. But no one's ever seen it, so I don't know. . . ."

I was still on the American heiress: I loved Edwardiana. And Victoriana. Any -ana, really.

"What sort of heiress?" I'd said. "Like Edith Wharton's Buccaneers?"

"Bucktoothed, probably. But very rich. Try to keep that tiny mind of yours on the antiques, not the photo albums, Evie." Max had smiled with all his teeth and both eyes.

I preferred him when he was shouting. "Don't forget, if you need any help, just give me a call and I'll come straight up. In fact, wouldn't it be better if —"

"No!" I hadn't meant it to sound so emphatic, but the thought of having to deal with Alice and my mum checking up on me to see how my comfort-zone breakout was going while Max fingered the valuables and engaged in industrial-strength sycophancy was just too much.

Fraser coughed, and I realized my knuckles were white on the steering wheel and the cars were moving again around me.

"So, will you be holding valuation audiences? Like on television?" He mimed the *Antiques Roadshow* Mask of Fake Middle-Class Surprise. " 'This dusty old vase? Worth eight *million* pounds?' "

"I definitely will *not*." I cringed. "I can't work with an audience, it . . . spoils the vibrations. Speaking of which," I went on, keen to get off the topic, "how's the Scottish dancing going? Has Alice injured anyone yet?"

"No, no! She's very good!" Now Fraser's good-humored expression faltered, then reengaged manfully. "Takes a while for the penny to drop with reeling, but I'm sure she'll get there."

"By this weekend?" I couldn't help it.

"Well . . ." His mouth twitched, and I felt as if we were sharing a secret. A warm, slightly guilty flower of excitement bloomed in my chest. "I've got a couple of practices lined up for the end of the week," he confessed. "Just to put her at ease. But she's really tried hard, and I appreciate her making the effort for me. She keeps saying she won't let it beat her."

"No," I said. That was Alice all over. I would have learned to reel backward over hot coals for a proper man like Fraser; Alice would learn so no one could accuse her of not being able to count up to eight.

"I've stocked up on arnica," he added, spoiling the effect a bit. "My brother, Dougie, swears by it for bruising, and he's always falling off horses."

"I'm sorry, it's a family failing, clumsiness." I sighed. "I once gave someone a black eye just shaking hands."

"If that's the worst family failing you've got, then I'm a lucky man!" Fraser replied gallantly, and I temporarily forgot how adolescent it was to nurse a crush on your sister's boyfriend.

Luckily, a big lorry slammed on its brakes next to Max's precious bumper and gave me something real to worry about.

We made reasonable time on the motorway, especially after I relaxed my core muscles and Fraser spelled me at the wheel for a bit. By five-thirty, dusk had fallen and we'd wound through Berwickshire's beautiful rolling countryside, dotted with gray sheep and neat stone villages, and were nearing Rennick.

I slowed down to take in the local detail as we passed the *Welcome to Rennick, Home of Rolled Oats* sign. It was a pretty town with a terraced main street, a post office, an off-license, and a gun shop. Fraser directed me past the sturdy Victorian town hall and down a hedged side road to the Grahams' farm, Gorse Bank.

The car's wheels crunched into a circular drive, and when the security light came on, I could make out a modest sandstone Georgian house, double-fronted, with lovely symmetrical sash windows. The sort of place the quiet but respectable gentleman usually lives in Jane Austen novels. There was a mud-spattered Mitsubishi 4x4 outside, which wasn't so Jane Austen, and when Fraser opened his door, I got a brief blast of pure North Sea air and a distant snatch of spaniels going nuts inside the house.

"Do you want to come in for a coffee?" he asked, heaving the stag's head out of the boot. One antler had shifted in transit and the eye had rolled to one side. "You can advise me where best to hang Banquo."

I shivered; the temperature gauge on the dashboard read nearly freezing. It might have been spring in London, but it felt more like midwinter up here. "That's very tempting, but I'm supposed to be arriving at Kettlesheer for tea. I'm already ten minutes late."

"Well, tell them it was my fault for not navigating properly. I hope you'll let me take you out for lunch this week?" Fraser was leaning into the car now, close enough for me to smell his cologne. Acqua di Parma. I knew that, because Alice bought it for him. "Least I can do to say thanks for the lift."

"That'd be lovely," I said, mentally punching the air. Lunch with Fraser! In a cozy country pub! With a log fire and dogs and haggis and oatcakes or whatever the Berwickshire specialty was.

"Marvelous. I'm around this week — we're supplying all the wine for the ball, so I'll be copping a day or two off keeping the client happy, right? Now, listen, to get to Kettlesheer, you need to go back to the

54

main road, take the next left through the village, then there's a sign to the right, and you go up a long drive. You could walk there from here, across the field, in ten minutes if you want to leave the car. Evie? Did you get all that?" he added.

"Um, yes," I said. I hadn't been listening. I'd been imagining our lunch unfolding like a movie in my head. We were at sticky toffee pudding and witty banter. A dog had appeared at our feet and was gazing up at us lovingly.

"Main road, left, then right," he repeated.

I made a thumbs-up sign and began turning the car round. In my rearview mirror, I watched Fraser shoulder the stag's head as if it weighed nothing and weave his way to the front door.

I noted as I sailed confidently down the track that Alice hadn't let him put Banquo in his London flat. I would have done. It could have been "our" stag.

Of course, I got lost.

Totally lost.

The lost you can only get in the middle of nowhere, on a dark winter night, where there are *no* streetlamps and *no* signs because everyone navigates according to whose cows are in which field.

I was nearly back in Berwick before I finally worked out where I was, using Max's free-with-petrol atlas, and by the time I stumbled onto Kettlesheer's twisty drive, I was wailing actual curses on the whole stupid countryside.

They dried up instantly when I turned the final corner.

"Blimey," I breathed out loud, as I fell deeply and instantly in love.

Kettlesheer rose magnificently against the wooded hillside like an eccentric grande dame, trailing ivy and turrets and weather vanes, with two crenellated wings sweeping back from a proud main elevation. Right on cue, the clouds shifted away from the moon, bathing the stone façade in white light and glittering in the pointy windows like jewels.

I held my breath and drank in the view, my heart swelling in my chest. I *dreamed* of houses like this. Kettlesheer was exactly the sort of moss-covered ancient pile I'd always pictured when reading about Border war rescues and romances and skirmishes and shotgun weddings. It had a drive that cried out for the thunder of horses' hooves and the rattle of a carriage pulling up posthaste from London. Turrets built for leaning out of, to catch the serenade of bagpipes.

I gripped the steering wheel and wished

violently that I'd been witnessing this romantic splendor from the window of a landau, not through the fly-smeared windscreen of a very boring Mercedes estate wagon. As a small sop, I abandoned the local radio station and tuned to some classical music for the final stretch of the drive.

As I got nearer, I realized actual lights, not moonlight, were illuminating the long downstairs windows, and an array of cars, mostly of the rugged agricultural type, were parked on the gravel circle. Either the McAndrews had a big family, or they had company.

I pulled up next to the shabbiest available Land Rover, and checked my reflection in the mirror. I wasn't that happy with what I saw. I'd planned my "casual weekend look" for Fraser's benefit, but I'd intended to stop in a lay-by to change my jeans for something more befitting a Chelsea antiques expert before I arrived at the house. Now I was late, shiny-nosed, *and* dressed for an afternoon's light furniture removal.

My wheelie suitcase was in the boot. I could drag on a pair of tights and a skirt. . . . It was dark. No one would see me, if I was quick.

I leaped out of the car, and gasped as the evening chill bit through my shirt. The air was nose-stingingly cold.

I amended my plan to putting on a better pair of boots and covering the whole thing up with Alice's mad but fashion-forward cocoon coat. That should give me enough time to arrive, get my wheelie case upstairs, and change into something more appropriate — what exactly, I hadn't worked out yet.

I leaned against the car trying to pull my boots on. Suddenly the front door opened at the top of the stone steps, spilling yellow light onto the mossy verandah; before I could speak and draw attention to myself, a man strolled out onto the verandah and let out a sigh of frustration that ended on a screech.

Damn. I hopped, hopped again, and with a crashing inevitability toppled over behind the car.

FOUR

Once I'd picked myself up, I peered through the car window at the tall man by the door. He was so busy muttering to himself he hadn't even noticed my messy crash to the floor, which was a small comfort.

Was that Duncan McAndrew? I hadn't even spoken to him; Alice — my "agent" — had sent me a very bare set of notes, mostly about percentage fees.

The man looked about thirty years too young to be Duncan; from his Converse sneakers and jeans, he seemed about my age, maybe a few years older. He certainly didn't look very Scottish or lairdlike. If anything, he reminded me of the IT programmer in the flat below mine, Trendy Will, who had one remote control for his entire flat and kept blowing our communal fuse box with his multiple gadgets.

The man shuddered and rubbed his arms through his hoodie, muttering something about the bloody cold in a very English accent. His face was shadowy in the light from above the door, and it made his cheekbones stand out even more. He couldn't see me, and I gazed at him in a way I wouldn't have been able to had he been looking back at me. He was very handsome. Dark eyes, *big* dark eyes, and a strong nose. His hair was dark too, and fell into his face; Alice would have marched him off for a haircut.

I wouldn't.

I breathed out and carried on hopping into my boots. He obviously wasn't Duncan, just a guest. Maybe staff? Fraser hadn't said there were *no* staff, just not a full household. It was okay. I still had time to sort myself out.

I stood up just as he turned my way, and being nearly six feet tall in my boots, I must have given him a shock, suddenly appearing above the roof of the car like that.

"Jesus!" he gasped.

"Hello," I said, stepped out from behind the car, hugging my coat tighter round myself.

He stared at me for another moment, and then for some reason his expression changed into one of warm recognition. "Hey!" he began, pointing at me, but didn't get any further before a girl with a dark braid and an attitude came barreling out behind him.

"Robbie," she snapped, grabbing his arm. "Don't just walk off when I'm talking to you! We need to discuss the set reel with Mummy and Ingrid. It's really important for us to be —"

She registered him looking at me, and then registered me, and stopped. The look on her face would have frozen the blood in my veins, if it weren't halfway there already.

It's very bad, I know, to judge people by their clothes, but she was wearing a green tweed miniskirt, green tights on long legs, Ugg boots, and a sheepskin vest, with a resigned-looking Jack Russell terrier stuffed under one arm like a handbag and a long silver chain over her green cashmere poloneck. Make of that what you will.

He was still peering at me through the darkness with that unsettlingly familiar glint in his eye. "Why didn't you *say* you were coming tonight?" he demanded, now jogging down the steps with outstretched arms.

Now is the time to come out with some appropriately country-house-ish repartee, prompted my reeling brain. *Now. Anytime now.*

"Um . . ." I began.

I didn't get the offer of embraces from handsome men so often that I could afford

61

to pass them up, but even so, I began to panic. What exactly had Alice said when she was setting this up? And who was he? Had I met him somewhere?

I'd definitely have remembered brown eyes and sharp cheekbones like that. I never got *that* drunk. Butterflies shoaled up in my chest as he got nearer and I could see the hollow of his throat framed by the V of his hoodie.

The girl's eyes narrowed. She'd been very heavy-handed with the eyeliner to begin with, and this made her eyes nearly disappear. "Robert, aren't you going to introduce us?" she barked, but he was ignoring her, and before I knew what was going on, he'd crossed the remaining gravel in a couple of long-legged strides and enfolded me in a bear hug.

My spinning brain noted three things: He had nice strong arms. He smelled delicious — not just aftershave, but that weirdly familiar smell you encounter once in a blue moon. He was also hugging me in a manner that suggested hugs had been taken before.

I couldn't help it. I squeezed him back and, to my amazement, I felt him lift me slightly off my feet.

No man had ever attempted that, let alone

managed it.

"Robert!" From somewhere deep inside Robert's shoulder I could hear Uggs marching on the gravel, and suddenly Robert disengaged and a cross face appeared between us.

"I'm Catriona," she snapped, and I pulled away with a start. "Catriona Learmont."

She shot out the hand that wasn't carrying the dog, and I shook it vacantly, still reeling from the whoosh of hormones swooping round my chest.

"This is Alice Nicholson, Fraser's girlfriend," Robert announced, at the same time that I said, "I'm Evie, Evie Nicholson."

Robert and I stared at each other. I knew I was blushing — the heat from my cheeks was the only warm part of my whole body.

He took a step backward.

"Oh, my God," he said. "I'm so sorry, it was the coat — I've never seen a coat like that anywhere else, and I thought . . ." He squinted at me. "I assume Alice *is* your sister?"

"Yes, she is! Happens all the time, honestly, don't worry about it," I babbled. "Quite a compliment, actually! Ha-ha! Sure it wouldn't go down as well the other way round. . . ."

Catriona stared at me as if I were talking

Welsh, then gave Robert one of those *Don't make me say it* frowns Mum flashed at Dad when he tried to buy full-fat milk instead of skim in Waitrose.

"You can't just slope off when you're the host, Robbie." She turned back to me with a smile only slightly warmer than the wintry air. "Lovely to meet you, Alice, or Evie. But I have to drag Robert off, I'm afraid. We hadn't finished discussing what he's wearing to the ball!"

"Yes, we had." Robert raised his hands. "I thought I'd made it clear. No kilt. No sporran. Sorry. But no."

Her eyes narrowed.

His eyes narrowed.

Five excruciating seconds passed, during which I was literally frozen to the spot. I was about to make some random comment just to break the tension and get myself inside to thaw out, when Catriona grimaced and swung her braid like a scorpion's tail.

"You're tired. So am I. We'll talk tomorrow. *Good night.*"

She beeped a Range Rover open, threw the obedient Jack Russell in, then leaped in herself, showing a lot of green leg. With a roar of the engine, she backed round, nearly clipping Max's car, and set off down the drive in a squirt of gravel.

Robert and I were left staring at her vanishing taillights.

After a moment, he turned back to me and held out his hand. "Shall we start again? Robert McAndrew. Friend of Fraser's. And Alice's."

"Hello," I said. "Evie Nicholson. Sister of Alice. Friend of Fraser. Hello."

Stop saying hello, I told myself. But my brain had gone into slow motion, to save energy for the butterflies careering around my stomach. Good-looking man, glamorous castle, freezing cold, fancy dress ball — I didn't know what to focus on first.

Besides, it felt a bit awkward to go back to shaking hands after I'd been so recently pressed up against the soft bit of his neck.

I wondered if Robert was feeling as jangly as I was, but he didn't show any outward signs of it. In fact, he was moving straight into polite chitchat, as if the hug, the spat, and the sudden departure hadn't happened.

"Are you here to Simplify us?" he inquired. "I'm not surprised Alice sent reinforcements ahead. I think the junk in this place would defeat even her fearsome skills."

"Oh, it's not *junk*," I began. Max's clientele were always so self-deprecating about "tatty old rugs" used to line dog baskets, which then turned out to be priceless

65

Persian treasures.

"*Junk*'s maybe too strong a word," he agreed. "How about . . . *museum-quality bric-a-brac?*"

"Robert? Robert, are you out there?" hissed a woman's voice before I could retract my dropped jaw. The voice sounded as if it were coming from deep, deep inside a well of despair, but in fact it was coming from the porch. "Janet's *asking* for you! And I need *help!* Your dad's about to offer everyone the carrot schnapps!"

I spun round and saw a small woman peering out into the darkness. The light above her head was turning her silvery blond hair into a halo of frizz, and she was wearing a sequined cardigan with dangling bell sleeves that she kept shoving nervously up to her elbows. It looked too big for her, as did the majestic porch itself.

I rushed over to the source of heat. "Evie Nicholson," I said, shaking her tiny hand. "Is it Ingrid? I've come to value your antiques. I'm so sorry I'm late. I didn't realize you were having a party."

"Oh, we're not! I mean, I didn't realize we *were* until they started arriving just as I was putting some tea on. . . ." She shoved the sleeves up and they slid down her arms almost immediately. Underneath the glitz

66

was a rather Sunday-night T-shirt.

If I was being brutally honest, she wasn't *quite* what I'd pictured as the chatelaine of a house like this. I'd been thinking more . . . Princess Margaret crossed with Helen Mirren. With some tartan.

Suddenly she pulled herself together and gave me a sweet, if deranged, smile. "Sorry, come on in. You must be frozen!"

As she spoke, a man hove into view behind her, and he was much more what I'd been expecting. He was sporting a pair of red tartan trousers, a pink golf sweater, and a tie adorned with golden stags' heads. The comedy Scotsman look was accessorized with a large crystal tumbler of some orange liquid, and a shock of pale red hair that — I peered as discreetly as I could in the weak light — was either a very bad wig or just very unfortunate.

"What's going on here?" he inquired with a genial beam. "Catriona with you? And that antisocial son of mine?"

"Evie, my husband, Duncan," said Ingrid. Did I detect a touch of *froideur,* or were we all just freezing? "Duncan, this is Evie Nicholson. The antiques consultant."

"Evie!" Duncan set his tumbler on a nearby stone eagle, and clasped my hand in both of his. I normally hated golf-club

67

handshakes, but frankly I was grateful for any warmth I could get. "How marvelous. Do come in. Come in. . . ."

He started to usher me inside, then paused and peered over my shoulder. "You too, Robert. In. Now. Don't go sloping off. You've been spotted. And there are people you need to talk to."

Robert muttered something, but I wasn't lingering outside to catch it.

By some impressive trick of Scottish architecture, it was almost colder in the entrance hall than it was outside. The huge fireplace, big enough to roast a horse in, lay empty apart from a stone jar stuffed with dried thistles, and the draft whistled a merry tune direct from the Russian steppes through the leaded windows. The hall was stone-flagged, and littered with large oak chairs and hulking carved boxes that might have contained the remains of Jacobite rebels or spare cannonballs.

I could see glass display cases everywhere — ships in bottles, fossils, iridescent shells, barometers — and what wasn't oak was hung with tapestries. My pulse quickened. The hall wasn't breathtaking just because of the cold. It took my breath away because I could totally see ghosts of old McAndrew warriors and damsels floating through the panels in ancient kilts, trailing long tartan sashes and melancholy and *history.*

Not literally, but you know what I mean.

"We've just got a few people round for Sunday night drinkies," Duncan went on, sweeping me, suitcase in tow, through a section of hall bedecked with disembodied antlers and medieval weaponry as far as the eye could see. "Hope you don't mind. Bit of a local tradition. Well, a new tradition. One we've started!"

"Let me take your coat, Evie," said Ingrid heavily.

"Um, I might just hang on to it for a while," I said, picturing the moment when I'd have to reveal my jeans to a drawing room full of cocktail party guests, probably all wearing bow ties and possibly toting cigarette holders. I racked my brains for the etiquette; were cocktails more or less formal than dinner?

It didn't help that my eyes kept flitting from the amazing tattered old Scottish flag hanging over the balcony to the lamp in the shape of a giant brass fish to a huge emerald witch ball suspended above the balustrade.

"If it's not too rude," I went on, dragging my attention back to the matter at hand,

"maybe I should go and freshen up before I
—"

Duncan grabbed my elbow and steered
me toward a closed door. "No, what you
need is a drink and a warm-up by the fire.
Ingrid? Tell Mhairi to take Evie's case up to
the Gordon Suite."

Ooh. The *Gordon Suite.*

I glowed at the thought of my case being
whisked away by staff, just like in a Merchant Ivory film, until I remembered exactly
how heavy it was. Not having spent much
time in stately homes outside National Trust
opening hours, I'd fallen back on my exten-
sive knowledge of period dramas and packed
for most eventualities, up to and including
some impromptu shooting and light cro-
quet.

As Ingrid went to take it from me, I
stepped back protectively. I'd sat on it for
hours to get that "traveling light" look.

"There's no need," I said. "I'll take it up
myself."

"No, no!" said Duncan, and I remembered
too late that you weren't supposed to porter
your own luggage in posh houses. I hoped I
wasn't being scored on this.

"Now, do come through. So many people
are dying to meet you," Duncan was saying,
while Ingrid telegraphed something to an

invisible maid over the top of his head.

"What do you mean, 'so many people —' " I began, but he'd pushed open the door and shoved me inside ("Come on, come on, don't let the heat out!"), slamming the door behind us, nearly trapping my heels in the process.

At once, conversation ceased as all eyes swung my way.

I blinked hard. There was a lot to take in.

Twenty or so guests were gathered in the green-and-maroon drawing room, most wearing tartan trousers or cashmere twinsets or, in a couple of cases, both. All were standing as close as they could to the big marble fireplace, in which a modest basket of firewood was burning valiantly, and were clutching tiny sherry glasses.

A normal drinks party, in other words, give or take the palatial setting. But what really sent a shiver of ice down my spine were the other things most guests were clutching.

A carriage clock. A Clarice Cliff teapot. A violin case. And, in several cases, plastic supermarket carrier bags.

It was a drive-by valuation party. And I was trapped.

FIVE

Some people have nightmares about retaking their A-level school exams stark naked. I had a recurring nightmare about being forced to do on-the-spot valuations in front of a room full of expectant people clutching fake Lalique vases. The trouble was, unlike nude exams, it did sometimes happen in real life.

For me, a party wasn't a party until someone demanded I value their earrings. Max warned me about it: as soon as you mentioned you worked in antiques, everyone was emptying their handbags to show you the silver Edwardian letter opener their granny gave them that they now used to counterattack muggers in Clapham.

I mean, it *could* be a great icebreaker, as Max himself proved time and again with many horse-riding ladies of a certain age; but the trouble was, unlike him, (a) I didn't have the auction prices of every single item in the whole world at my fingertips, and (b) I wasn't great at pretending I did.

Now, faced with a room full of guests, I took an involuntary step backward toward the door, but Duncan was already pressing a lead-crystal glass of some liquid into my hand, and ushering a strange-looking man toward me.

"Here you go, Evie, chin-chin! Now, have you met Innes Stout? Innes, this is Evie Nicholson."

Innes looked like the kind of man who spent a lot of time in the open air, "tending" to vermin. He wore an army-surplus sweater under a tweed jacket, and a tie. At least he wasn't wielding an Arts and Crafts barometer.

I extended the hand that wasn't gripping my drink. "Hello, Innes."

Innes responded by reaching into his jacket pocket and pulling out a flintlock pistol, causing the woman earwigging next to us to let out a loud shriek and stagger backward into a red velvet sofa.

Luckily for Innes, people were always pulling unexpected things out of their jackets at Max's shop. I'd seen *much* worse. My grin fixed more rigidly on my face.

"Calm yourself, Sheila!" Duncan barked over my shoulder. "It's only Innes's dueling pistol! Gets it out all the time at the golf club! You *must* have seen it before."

Ingrid appeared from nowhere and began tending to the winded Sheila, all the while shooting murderous glances at her husband.

I hoped she didn't think I'd asked him to do that.

Meanwhile, Innes and Duncan were carrying on as if nothing had happened. "My great-great-great-great-grandfather shot four Englishmen wi' this." Innes proudly stroked the barrel. "Not at the same time, mind." He looked at me as if I were going to run some kind of bar-code scanner over it and beep out a value. "D'you need to hold it?"

"Um, I won't, thanks," I stammered. "Four Englishmen, eh?"

"Aye," said Innes. "All stone deed. I've a couple more at home. Not implicated in fatalities, mind."

"Go on, it won't bite," urged Duncan. "Have a feel!"

What else was I meant to do? I could feel several pairs of eyes pretending not to look in our direction.

Gingerly I took the pistol from Innes. It was heavy, and I got an odd dark feeling from it.

I didn't ever put it in so many words to

Max because he would have laughed like a drain, but I had a bit of a sixth sense when it came to the history of the antiques I bought. Maybe it was my fertile imagination, overcompensating after growing up in a wipe-clean house full of brand-new furniture, but memories seemed to bubble into my head when I held old things, like the faint trace of perfume on a coat, or cigarette smoke in an old cocktail bag. I never bought repro at auctions, even when it was skillfully done; it never felt right in my hands.

"It's a dueling pistol?" I asked cautiously. It had a dark feeling about it.

Innes nodded. "One of a pair."

"How *interesting*," said Duncan, his shoulders bouncing up and down with excitement. "What d'you say they'd be worth, eh, Evie? In your professional opinion?"

I swallowed. I could hardly say I didn't know, not when I'd come up here under the guise of being an expert — but I *didn't* know. I didn't come across a lot of firearms in my day-to-day business.

"You'd need to go to a specialist appraiser for something like this," I gabbled, hoping Innes hadn't just had them valued. "I'd hate to mislead you about something with so much . . . family significance."

That was a good phrase. Max used that a

lot, when he had no idea whether something was worth millions or buttons. "I can give you a number for an *excellent* dealer," I went on, feeling more confident. "I certainly don't come across anything as unusual as this every day."

"Ah'm not planning to *sell,*" objected Innes, cradling the pistol dangerously to his bosom as if I'd threatened to grab it then and there.

"Of course not!" Duncan beamed genially. "How interesting, though! Rough value?"

"Oh, I wouldn't like to . . ." I demurred.

"Roughly?" Duncan persisted.

I tried a polite laugh. "I couldn't . . ."

He carried on looking at me with his boggly fish eyes. Hard. "Ballpark?"

"A thousand pounds?" I guessed. It was a figure that usually went over well.

Duncan raised his eyebrows in a belated display of discreet appreciation.

"Evie!" Someone grabbed me by the arm. "Have you met Sheila?"

I turned and saw Ingrid McAndrew standing behind me with Sheila the shocked lady, now more flushed and embarrassed than shocked. Sheila was twice the size of Ingrid, and her bright red cheeks were being offset nicely by her bright red twinset; with her white hair on top, she had a bit of a Mother

Christmas look going on, right down to the general air of jolliness and the faint aroma of tangerines.

"No, I haven't," I said, holding out my hand. "Hello."

"Fraser's mother," Ingrid added, but she didn't need to: Sheila's wide-set blue eyes were exactly like Fraser's, as was the welcoming, open smile.

"It's lovely to meet you, Evie." At last, a proper Scottish accent! "I've heard so much about you and your family."

"Really?" I couldn't imagine what Alice had found to tell the Grahams about our family. We had the shortest Christmas letter in existence. "All good, I hope?"

"Och, yes. Alice says you've been working with one of London's best dealers since you left college," Sheila said, glancing at Ingrid.

"Ha-ha-ha!" I stopped when I saw how anxious Ingrid looked. "Oh, um, yes. Max is . . . very well-known in his field."

"There you go, Ingrid, you're in good hands!" Sheila nodded reassuringly, and Ingrid managed a nervous smile, which faded as quickly as it had come.

"You really do have an *amazing* house . . ." I began, but ran out of words.

Amazing didn't really do justice to the sheer magnificence of it all. If this was just

77

the drawing room, what was the rest of the place like? My eyes roamed greedily around the room, taking in the many knickknack-piled tables, huge sofas, and paneled walls that probably swung round to reveal hidden passages down to the secret chapel. Mum would have passed out at the sheer surface area of dust-attracting furniture, but I was struggling not to rush round touching everything.

I tried not to stare too obviously, but everyone was pretending they weren't staring at me. Over by a towering brass urn filled with aspidistras, Duncan and Innes had been joined by a bony lady cradling a teapot in one arm like a baby. When I looked round, all three stopped talking, and Duncan raised his tumbler in my direction. It was nearly empty, unlike everyone else's glasses, which remained noticeably full.

A thought occurred to me. Max often rhapsodized about the bizarre social habits of the rich, especially rural types, and this lot looked good and eccentric. One woman had a tiny spaniel draped over each shoulder, and there were a pair of identical white-haired men, both smoking pipes.

It might not be a valuation party at all. They might just be . . . doing some kind of predinner show-and-tell? After all, my handbag contained a powderless powder compact and a jade frog, for no other reason than I liked having them around.

"Do people often bring dueling pistols to parties round here?" I asked Ingrid hopefully.

"Just for English guests!" said Sheila. "Only joking!" she added, patting Ingrid's arm as Ingrid squawked in horror. "I think someone's trying to catch your eye, Evie."

I looked round, and immediately everyone's eyes dropped. Most of the guests seemed to be roughly the McAndrews' age — midsixties or so — but there were a couple of younger women standing by the grand piano. They were doing that party isolation thing, blocking off a conversational victim from the rest of the room, using their shoulders as a sort of vest-clad velvet rope. I wondered who they were talking to with such intensive flirtiness.

The taller of the two shifted as she made some tipsy gesture with her drink, and I spotted who it was: Robert McAndrew. He must have slunk in through one of the other doors. It was the sort of drawing room that boasted more than one entrance, so unseen staff could swoop in and out with trays and suchlike. He looked even more handsome in full light — but he seemed very uncomfortable — irritable, even. He kept fiddling with the silver-framed photos on the piano, rearranging them as if they were in his way.

Fraser was *much* more heirlike, I thought to myself. He'd have been leaning on that piano, holding forth about the relatives in the photos with charm, not looking as if he'd like to sweep everything off with one whoosh of his arm.

Robert lifted his glass to drain it, and caught me staring at him. He raised one eyebrow at the items cluttering the piano, as if to say, *See? Junk!* I made a big show of looking appreciatively at the oil next to me, a pile of dead pheasants next to an apple. It was a bit grisly, now I examined it closely, but I tried not to let that show.

Sheila made a low gurgling noise. "Ah, I'll just . . . refresh my glass. Excuse me, Evie."

"Sheila, no! Don't — oh, thanks," hissed Ingrid, just as Duncan approached with a lady who was far more what I'd had in mind for the chatelaine of the castle. She had a long nose, swept-back dark hair, and a silver Celtic knot brooch on her fluffless navy cardigan. She made it look like some kind of badge of state.

Ooh. Maybe it was.

"Evie, meet Janet Learmont!" boomed Duncan, presenting her to me with a flourish. "Janet's the chairwoman of the Kettlesheer ball! What she doesn't know about reeling isn't worth knowing! Janet, this is Evie Nicholson, our antiques consultant."

"The famous ball!" I said. "I've heard so much about it already. It sounds magical."

"Yes, it is," said Janet, without any shred of modesty. Her accent was so posh the Scottishness was almost undetectable. "The Learmonts have been on the committee for years, so it's very much in the blood. My mother, and her mother, and her mother before, have all done their bit. And I'm hoping my daughter will be taking over soon enough." She cast a meaningful look in Duncan's direction. "It's good for Catriona to learn the ropes now, before she has the rest of Kettlesheer to worry about!"

Ingrid let out a faint squawk.

"It *is* a responsibility, I know," said Janet condescendingly. "Catriona's had a wee bit more training than you, Ingrid. You're doing very well." She left a microscopic pause before adding, "Considering."

"Thanks," mumbled Ingrid, and I wished Sheila would come back.

Janet angled her long neck over our heads. "Where is Catriona? Now I've got you two, we should have a quick chat about the set reel. And Robert's outfit."

81

"I think she might have left already," I said, trying to be helpful. "And it sounded like a no on the kilt front."

"I managed to get him to agree to white tie, though," blurted Ingrid, as Janet's face darkened. "It was quite a struggle. Robert hates formal dress. He says it makes him look like a waiter. Not that there's anything wrong with waiters."

"Oh, I don't know, these London types. . . . Let's get him over here to explain himself," said Duncan. "Where is he?" He turned round and searched the room.

Robert had vanished.

"I do think he's being a bit pigheaded about this." Janet's voice was clipped with disapproval. "He has a very important role to play as the heir. They're first couple in the opening Reel of Luck," she added to me.

"What's the Reel of Luck?" I asked.

"The first dance of the night," said Ingrid. "Traditionally, it's supposed to bring good luck to any courting couples in the room, and —"

"It goes back many, many years to the great Sir Ewart McAndrew," Janet began, as if Ingrid hadn't spoken. "He founded the ball in order to find wives for his seven sons. Traditionally — correct me if I'm wrong,

82

Duncan! — the favored girl of the McAndrew heir was invited to dance this first reel in front of all the assembled McAndrews, alongside his family."

Duncan opened his mouth to agree, but Janet swept on regardless.

"The story goes . . ." Her voice hushed, and her catlike face assumed a distant expression, the type you see tour guides adopt when they're trying to convey the solemnity of Westminster Abbey to a group of non–English speakers. "Wild Cullen McAndrew was the heir to the estate, and his partner was the most beautiful girl in the Border counties, Louisa Bell, incidentally a distant relation of mine. They danced upstairs in the great ballroom of Kettlesheer, without a single step out of place. And when they were done, the bold Cullen was so smitten with Louisa's fine footwork, he gave up his gambling and mistresses and called for the local priest to marry them on the spot. And they were wed in the chapel on the grounds that very night."

I was spellbound. I could totally imagine the whole thing: pipes, reels, flaming torches, discarded mistresses, the lot. "How romantic!"

"And since then —" Ingrid began.

"And since then, there's never been a ball

83

that hasn't resulted in a proposal," Janet carried on as if she hadn't heard Ingrid. "So long as the reel is performed without a hitch."

"And Robert and Catriona dance this on their own?" I asked Ingrid. It only seemed polite to direct one question to her, as the hostess.

But Janet leaped in. "Oh, *no!* No, dear, you need eight people for a reel. Four couples. Everyone else watches while this reel opens the ball."

"No pressure for the others, then!" I joked.

Janet let out a little laugh, while Duncan and Ingrid turned ashen. "Did you hear that, Ingrid? No pressure for you and Duncan at all!" Her voice took on a metallic note. "I hope you've been doing the practices I gave you?"

"Yes, Janet." Ingrid nodded.

"And have you —"

"Robert!" Duncan suddenly shot out a hand and pointed at Robert, catching him in the act of sidling out. His teacher's eyes in the back of his head clearly still worked. Reluctantly, Robert came over.

"Your mother tells me you've said no to a kilt! For God's sake, lad! You can't turn up in those jeans of yours! It isn't a nightclub, it's a big occasion!"

Robert's eyes slid toward me, then returned to Janet, who was pretending to be embarrassed at Duncan's mentioning it. "I don't want to pretend to be something I'm not," he said. "I'm not Scottish. I was born in Merton."

"That doesn't matter!" said Janet. "You're part of Kettlesheer now! Catriona will be wearing *her* clan tartan. Everyone will be expecting you there in your full regalia."

"We'll see," he said politely. "Would you excuse me? I've got to take a call back at the lodge. Work. Sorry."

"Always working, that boy," said Duncan as Robert weaved his way through the furniture to the door. I couldn't tell whether he sounded frustrated or disappointed, or both.

"Still no date fixed to move up here properly?" asked Janet.

"Soon, I should think, Janet." Duncan winked. "Depending on how this reel goes, eh?"

I was so overwhelmed by the Jane Austen nature of this exchange that I took a theatrical sip from my glass, and nearly choked.

It was like drinking petrol flavored with carrots. Suddenly I understood why no one had been touching theirs.

Just to compound my embarrassment, an old lady suddenly thrust a butter dish into my hands, and I had to spend the next twenty minutes doing off-the-cuff valuations. Pottery spaniels followed a silver snuffbox; then came a carved elephant with a missing tusk, about which I managed to get quite emotional after its owner explained it had belonged to his twin sister who died in the Second World War.

At a quarter to seven exactly, I was in the middle of pronouncing on a Spode teapot when I became aware of a marked thinning-out of the guests. It was as if a plug had been pulled out of a bath, and they were all circling toward the door, half against their will.

In the hall I could see a dour woman in a plain black dress, evidently wielding some kind of invisible social tractor beam. She was handing people their coats from a portable rack that had also materialized, and they were dazedly bundling up in fur hats, scarves, and lots of Barbour jackets.

"Mhairi's a wonder. Her family has looked after the house for years, her father was the last butler," murmured Ingrid, appearing at my elbow with a full tray of unfinished drinks. "Do you know, everyone round here leaves parties when they're supposed to?

And they arrive on time, not an hour late!"

We both gazed at Mhairi. Something about her didn't encourage dawdling.

"Do you have a lot of staff?" I asked, envisioning rows of black-and-white-clad parlormaids in starched caps, lining up by the stairs.

"Just Mhairi. I don't know how I'd cope without her." She looked down at her full tray. "Actually, it was Mhairi's idea to let Duncan serve his carrot schnapps instead of sherry. She doesn't like parties to go on after half seven."

"This is carrot . . . schnapps?" I asked.

"Home brew," said Ingrid. "Duncan's very . . . keen. Anyway, I should go and . . ." She made a vague gesture toward the door, as if she were still getting the hang of her own house.

"Oh, yes, absolutely. I'm fine here," I said. Actually, I was eager to go poke around the silver wedding photos on the piano, for a start.

Once Ingrid had fluttered out, I stood back and tried to take it all in. McAndrews through the ages glowered back at me from the burgundy wallpaper: the floppy hats, wigs, and tiaras varied, but the strong nose and shrewd Scottish eyes stayed exactly the same. The young Regency buck posing

87

against a tree stump had the same brooding good looks, if not the same breeches, as Robert McAndrew.

It must be incredible, I thought enviously, to *see* that you were part of such a long chain of people. We had one album of family photos. You'd think the whole Nicholson family fell out of the sky fully formed in 1974, the year my parents got married. I'd have been happy for a snap of a relative in a bowler hat, let alone a suit of armor.

One blond head stood out in the crowd of swarthy swaggerers: a full-length portrait of a young woman hanging by the bay window. Something about the mischief in her pretty face made me sleepwalk over for a closer look, trailing my hands across velvet sofas and threadbare cushions as I went.

She was younger than me — about twenty — but she had a grown-up sophistication about her half-smile and knowing blue eyes. I didn't recognize the artist, but I could tell he was good: he'd captured the pre-party sparkle of anticipation that glowed around her and the golden softness of her swept-up curls, the luminescence of the pearls in her delicate ears. Going by the nipped waist and floaty off-the-shoulder neckline of her gown, I estimated it must have been painted sometime before the First World War. The last hurrah for languid society beauties and their untroubled lives of house parties and never-ending afternoon teas.

Ooh, I thought suddenly. Was this the heiress? Was I gazing into the eyes of the American buccaneer who'd steamed across the Atlantic to save this ancient castle from financial ruin?

"Jolly well done, Evie," said Duncan, appearing next to me with a side order of cold air still hanging around him. "Who knew Jock Laing's toy cars were worth more than his real one? Ha!"

"Who's this?" I asked.

"My great-grandmother Violet. Painted just after she got engaged to Ranald, that chap there." He indicated a companion portrait on the other side of the fireplace: another dark-eyed McAndrew male, this time in shiny-buttoned regimental uniform, with a thick mustache and rather luscious brown eyes that hinted at a devilish streak beneath the stern exterior.

"What a handsome couple," I said, instantly imagining them holding court in this very room, sitting on those big sofas. Yes, I could picture Ranald warming himself beside the fire after a brisk hunt through the rolling moors that surrounded the house. And Violet in a sumptuous day dress, arranging flowers from the hothouses round the side of . . .

"Do you have hothouses here?" I asked. "Or an orangery?"

Duncan frowned. "I don't know. There was some form of piggery during the war, I think. Now then, dinner!" He rubbed his hands together. "Mhairi will show you to your room. Dinner at half past?"

I'd have liked to hear a bit more about Violet and Ranald — how they met, what her fortune was made in, all that — but Mhairi had now appeared and she didn't look in the mood for reminiscing. I replaced my barely touched sherry glass on the silver salver and followed her out into the bone-chilling hall and up the stairs.

It was almost impossible not to feel as if I were stepping into one of my own most colorful daydreams.

SIX

I trailed behind Mhairi as we tackled the glorious oak staircase in silence, my eyes widening with each step. My attention skipped from one intriguing glass case to another, and more McAndrews, draped in their distinctive orange-and-black tartans and posed standing on dead things, even the women. I ran my hand up the thick banister and wondered how old the tree was that had made it — it must have seen Henry VIII, at least.

"Mind the halberd," said Mhairi as we ducked beneath a scary pike thing. She had a proper Scottish accent, like deep-fried haggis.

"It's magnificent," I breathed, walking backward to take it in, but not wanting to get left behind.

"Aye. It's a pain to dust."

At the top of the stairs, we headed down a book-lined corridor, and Mhairi pushed open a solid oak door with an enameled coat of arms. It gave out a proper haunted-house creak.

"Your case's in here." Mhairi delivered each pronouncement as if words were strictly rationed.

"Thank you!" I squeaked.

She reached around for the brass switch, and a low light flooded the room. "There's a bell if you need anything."

My eyes widened.

My overnight wheelie case was lying open, embarrassed, on the counterpane of a real four-poster bed, the sort monarchs chose to die in, all crimson velvet hangings and gold swags. There was more crimson and gold at the bay window, a marble fireplace with a selection of ticking clocks, and a rococo dressing table that wouldn't even have fitted through the door of my flat.

That was the headline furniture. Alongside that were assorted mahogany chairs, gilt mirrors, a chaise longue for swooning onto, a wardrobe big enough to house Narnia plus any other mystical universe, and a linen chest with a vast Japanese Imari dish containing silver and gold glass balls.

I gazed in delight at the dressing table, with proper silver brushes with which to brush my hair before dinner!

I turned to ask Mhairi how far up the scale the McAndrews dressed for said dinner, but she'd already gone, leaving me free to explore my room like a child in a sweet shop.

Needless to say, once I was sure I was on my own, I lost no time in holding on to the bed frame and imagining a maid lacing me into a very tight corset. Mhairi's great-grandmother had probably hauled tight enough to make even the whalebones squeak for mercy.

The bathroom wasn't so much a mere bathroom as a whole other room, and it took me nearly fifteen minutes to run enough tepid water into the cavernous roll-top bath.

Still, it gave me time to admire the magnificent brass taps, and the curly iron rack for holding your book and wine while you soaked. And the paintings of artfully draped ladies, and the stuffed pike, caught in the estate lake in June 1909.

Just before half seven, I left my room looking smart but feeling frozen. I'd opted for a silk wrap dress and heels that I hoped would be grand enough. Two steps down the staircase, though, and — mentally, at least — I was in a whispering silk crinoline and heavy tartan sash.

One didn't just walk down these stairs, I thought, my pace slowing the better to savor each step, one *descended.* As if someone were waiting for you in the hall, with tragic/urgent news from London, maybe even toting one of Innes Stout's dueling pistols.

"Why, my lord!" I murmured in my head. Well, more or less in my head. "The bagpipes? I simply *adore* them!"

There was no one around, so I tilted my head to show off my swanlike neck to an imaginary admirer, trailing a hand along the banister, worn smooth by generations of hands. Big, claymore-wielding hands, and delicate embroidering ones, resting where my fingers were now.

"Lord Dunmore, the Dunmore of Dunmore? For dinner? How unexpected!" I paused at the corner of one flight, and pictured the hall beneath thronging with ladies in diamonds and men in wing collars, waiting as their cloaks were taken before the ball. I imagined the tarnished gas lamps polished up and blazing, and the empty grate filled with logs, the air heavy with gossip and flirtation and woodsmoke.

This was exactly why I loved antiques: Kettlesheer was crammed with proof that those Regency romances had once been everyday life. I paused, and smiled down into the dim hall, imagining everyone gazing up at my arrival, the mysterious chestnut-haired beauty from London. My hand lifted, and I found myself giving a small royal wave.

And Fraser Graham, the handsome eldest son from the neighboring house, was waiting to take my hand and lead me into the —

Alice's hand. Waiting to take *Alice's* hand.

Guiltily I rejigged my vision.

I could almost see Fraser Graham, the handsome young heir from the neighboring house, and his *unattached brother Douglas* —

There was a discreet cough from the stairwell.

I jumped so hard, my foot slipped on the worn carpet and I had to grab the banister to stop myself from falling. Luckily it was made of sturdy stuff.

Robert McAndrew was standing just round the corner by a wall-mounted sword, his arms crossed over his gray hoodie. He hadn't bothered to change for dinner, I noticed. He hadn't even changed out of his *jeans.*

"Are you all right?" he inquired.

"I'm fine, I didn't see you there," I stammered, cursing the stupid shadows and the lack of modern lighting. At least he couldn't make out my red cheeks as I scuttled down the remaining stairs.

"You don't have a camera crew with you?" he went on.

"No!"

"It's just that you seemed to be making an entrance." He paused, and gave me an inscrutable look. "And you were talking to yourself."

"Absolutely not," I said, concentrating on not slipping. That never happened in *Jane Eyre,* Jane skidding down the stairs on her bustle. "I was examining a painting. Am I late for dinner? Were you sent to find me? I'm sorry — it took a while to run the bath."

"A bath? I'm surprised you're not still up there — it's quicker to fill a moat." Robert gestured down the corridor. "Don't worry about it. I'm late too. We can be late together. After you," he said, and I stepped forward.

"Chop-chop," he added. "Uncle Carlisle set up those Scrooge lights that go off before you've had time to see where you're going. We've got thirty seconds to get down the east wing."

"It's a wonderful house," I said, dragging myself past a cabinet full of Roman frag-

96

ments. "Everywhere I look, I want to stop and make notes, and just . . . breathe in the history. But I suppose you're used to it by now."

"Nope," said Robert, somewhere behind me. "Mum and Dad only moved up here a couple of years ago. Takes a bit longer than that to get used to living in Scotland's biggest attic."

"You live in the *attic?* Aren't there enough rooms?"

"Metaphorically speaking." He laughed. At least I think he did. "It's like they never threw anything away — they just stuck it in a case. If you think this is bad, you should see what's actually *in* the attic. I keep telling Dad: just because it's old doesn't mean it's *important.*"

This time I knew Robert wasn't being faux-modest; he sounded genuinely repulsed. In fact, he sounded a bit like Alice: she was always threatening to start a localized fire in my garage to "cure my hoarding."

"Well, one man's junk is another man's priceless collectible, as a wise man once said to me!" I replied. "It's all part of someone's life, isn't it? And those people are part of your life."

We'd reached a dimly lit corner of the

paneled corridor, and I hung back, waiting for him to hit the next light switch. I couldn't resist tapping a dark oak panel with my knuckles. Then the one next to it.

"Sorry, what are you doing?" he asked.

I looked up. "Tapping the panels. To see if there's a hidden passage."

"And what sort of noise would one of those make? Out of interest."

"I'm not sure," I admitted. "I've just seen them do it in films. You tap the oak panels and one of them . . . swings back." As I said it, I realized how ridiculous I sounded.

"To reveal what?" Robert raised his eyebrows inquiringly. "The slide down to the Bat Cave? Or the chute for the discarded servants?"

"You never know with houses like this," I said. "You read about noblemen hiding chests of gold pieces during enemy raids, and then dying in battle so they're undiscovered for centuries." My eyes widened. "Wouldn't that be fate?"

Robert sighed and raised his hands. "Fine, let's get this out of the way before dinner," he said. "As far as I'm concerned, there is no buried treasure in this house. No unburied treasure, either. Kettlesheer is a giant white elephant, full of someone else's colonial supermarket sweep. I'm *embar-*

rassed by some of it, frankly."

My mouth dropped open. "But there are some wonderful historical things here that —"

Robert held up his hands. "So give them to the Museum of Scotland. A house this size is a massive drain in this day and age. It's ruined at least three recent ancestors, and I don't want to watch my parents dragged down by the stress of keeping it going. Selling little bits here and there for the roof, to do the electricity — waste of time. Personally, I'd sell it tomorrow." He made a chopping gesture in the air.

"But it's your family home!" I protested, swamped with disbelief that he could dismiss it so coldly. The spectral McAndrews around us must have been clutching their jabots in shock.

Robert ran a hand over his face. "Our family home was a perfectly nice villa in Wimbledon, by the common. Big garden, tennis court, ample parking. No bats. No sculptures in the bathroom. I'm not saying this *isn't* beautiful — it'd make an amazing hotel, or a nursing home, or something. But it's not a *home* home."

"It *is!*"

"It's a *museum.* To tat and kleptomania."

I couldn't believe I was hearing this.

99

"But you can *see* it's a home everywhere you look," I protested, my voice so high even the aforementioned bats could hear it. "It's just a bit more . . . scaled-up. You've got portraits instead of photos. I mean, that worn-down foot-scraper by the door, and . . . and . . . this mirror here — can you *imagine* what that mirror's seen over the years: the changing costumes, and the hopes, and the romances —"

"There's nothing *romantic* about a house that costs forty thousand a year just to heat."

"Log fires are the most romantic thing *ever,* and you've got your own forest out there!"

Robert started to say something, then stopped himself. It seemed to be taking a fair bit of self-control. "We may have to agree to disagree on this one," he said. "I'm only telling you now because every meal we have when I'm home turns into a row. Dad has fallen for this place, and he thinks I should too. But I'm a businessman, and he's not. I don't want you to be embarrassed about whose side to take. He's your man to talk about romance with. Just don't ask him how much the insurance costs, because he hasn't the first idea."

"Fine," I said, scrabbling to make amends.

"Tell me what I can talk to *you* about, then?"

He looked at me quizzically.

"Dogs?" I suggested. "Ibizan clubs? Rhubarb?"

The corner of Robert's mouth twitched, but the rest of his face remained impassive. "I'm sure we'll find something to chat about." He gestured toward a spiral staircase leading downward. "I'll go first, give you something to fall on."

"Oh, wow! A spiral staircase!" I said before I could stop myself. "Aren't they meant to go clockwise, so noblemen could sword-fight up them? Or was it down them?"

Robert looked up from three steps down, and I felt the shrewd McAndrew eyes taking me in. I couldn't quite read them.

If I'd met him in a bar in town, I'd have put Robert well out of my league. His clothes were casual but expensive, his general aura urbane and confident. Whatever he did for a living, he was in charge. His only obvious flaw was rather wonky teeth. But there was a funny vibration about him — not nerves, not awkwardness, just a sort of . . . not quite wanting to be there — that made a tiny chink in his polish.

"They go left so the chambermaids can

hold the chamber pots in their right hands."

"Really? I suppose it does make sense —"

"No," he said. "I just made that up."

We clicked down a stone corridor lined with cobwebbed servants' bells for various bedrooms, studies, games rooms, bathrooms, nursery.

"Are those still in use?" I asked, thinking of Mhairi's instruction to ring if I needed anything.

"You've an electric one."

I thought it was a bit odd that we were dining in the cellar when there was bound to be a perfectly good baronial dining hall, but maybe they'd done up the kitchens as a big basement diner.

We passed several butler's pantries before we came to the kitchen. I assumed it was the kitchen, anyway; it was the only room with a thin sliver of light beneath the door. I wrapped my cardigan more tightly round myself as Robert pushed his way in.

"Punctuality costs nothing," said Duncan, tapping his watch. "Not you, Evie, you're very welcome."

I did a double take.

No gleaming candelabra. No dining table. No butler.

Instead, round a long scrubbed pine table

sat Duncan and Ingrid McAndrew and Sheila Graham. Sheila was still in the same twinset and skirt, but Ingrid was wearing a mushroom-colored tracksuit, and Duncan had changed into a blue velvet smoking jacket and a hat with a tassle.

If you didn't count Duncan's bizarre hat, I was the only one who'd dressed up. My expression froze, along with the rest of me.

"Good Lord, Evie, you must be a warm-blooded girl, wearing a dress like that!" barked Duncan. I was still thinking what on earth to say to that when he turned to Robert and added, "*She* obviously doesn't feel this terrible cold you're always whining on about."

"I'm not whining," said Robert — heading for the chair nearest the Aga, I noted. "I'm just pointing out that there are parts of this bloody freezing house that you probably couldn't legally keep animals in."

They didn't dress for dinner! Robert could have *said* something when he saw me, for God's sake. He could have *told* me that everyone else would be bundled up to the nines when I still had time to go and get several cardigans. We were eating in the *kitchen!*

"Evie, that's a beautiful dress," said Sheila, noticing my discomfort. "And orange and

black to match the Kettlesheer tartan —
did you know?"

Ingrid's face dropped. "Oh, Evie, you
needn't have bothered," she said. "We never
dress for dinner. I mean, we dress in that
we put more clothes *on*. . . ."

"This? Oh, it's nothing special," I lied. "I,
er, have thermal underwear underneath."

"Jolly sensible," said Duncan. "Be prepared."

"Come and sit here, where it's warm,"
Ingrid said, getting up to give me her own
seat. "And let me get you a drink," she went
on, pushing a glass in front of me. "Red?
White?"

"Wow, are these Georgian?" I forgot my
annoyance in a nanosecond. The table
might have had generations of servants who
sat round it, but the place settings were fit
for a duke: big porcelain plates with gold
rims and purple thistles flanked by heavy
silver cutlery.

Like the kitchen, it was a funny old mixture of fancy and plain, but I was completely
charmed. It had atmosphere, with its worn
stone flags and polished brass pans sitting
next to a very modern KitchenAid mixer.
There'd been some hustle and bustle in here
over the years, I could feel it.

"You tell us, Evie!" Duncan said at once.

"We've got about a hundred upstairs — worth much, do you think?"

"Dad, Evie's already valued half the tat in Rennick tonight," said Robert. His voice was light, but his eyes were warning. "Give her an hour off, will you?"

"Tat? Tat!"

Duncan glared at Robert and I was reminded of the painting in my room of two stags glowering at each other in a handbags-at-dawn standoff.

Sheila Graham offered me the bottle of wine just as Ingrid McAndrew closed her eyes and reached for her glass in one practiced movement.

Normally, I didn't drink much in new places (I had a bad habit of getting rather mystical about people's valuables, which was embarrassing if they'd only just bought them), but the sudden frost in the air had nothing to do with the conditions outside, and I pushed my glass toward Sheila. She filled it with an almost inaudible sigh and a conspirational wink.

SEVEN

I was woken the next morning by a strange smell — the sort of burning-rubber whiff you get when you don't take the plastic off a microwave-ready meal properly.

I pulled the four-poster's heavy curtain aside, ready to face the bright Scottish sunlight streaming into the room, and found myself staring into the eyes of a burly black Labrador bearing a silver teapot on its back.

I squawked and jerked backward into the pillows, nearly knocking over the water jug on the bedside table.

Once the room swam into focus, however, I realized that the dog was stuffed, and a solid mahogany breakfast tray had been placed on a small table behind it. I wasn't surprised that someone had come in and left it without me noticing; the drapery was so thick the Scots Guards could have piped the breakfast in without disturbing me.

I sniffed warily. The smell was coming

from beneath a silver dome. Next to it was a battered silver pot of coffee, and some milk, and a bowl of solid oatmeal that you could stand a spoon up in. There was no sugar, just a small bowl of salt. Proper Scottish porridge, in other words.

And — I leaned over and lifted the dome with some trepidation — kippers.

To be perfectly honest, kippers were one of those things that I always liked the *idea* of more than the reality. These looked as if they'd been freshly scraped off the outside of a trawler. But on the other hand, they were sitting under a silver dome on a crested porcelain kipper plate. With kipper knives and some kipper implement I'd never even seen before.

How often did you get the chance of a breakfast-in-bed that crossed over with the life of Queen Victoria? *Not* very often.

Gingerly I maneuvered the tray onto the eiderdown, and poured myself a cup of coffee in readiness for the fishy challenge ahead.

It was a gorgeous cup: fine porcelain and crested with a thistle wrapped in little flowers. I sipped more delicately than I usually did with my first coffee of the day, and admired the Labrador, which had obviously once been a much-loved family member. It still had its collar on: Lord Bertold had been its name. I felt a twinge of sympathy; I kept our cat's old collar in a treasure box, having retrieved it from Mum's merciless tidying of Cleo's basket after The Long Dark Trip to the Vets.

Between the romantic Reel of Luck and their inability to throw anything away, including deceased pets, I was starting to think the Clan McAndrew could be one after my own heart. Or maybe I was just a thwarted aristocratic collector trapped in the body of an underpaid London singleton.

Then, with a deep breath, I tackled the first kipper.

Once I'd finished the porridge and coffee and forced down half a kipper, I pulled on as many layers as I could manage, then headed downstairs with my breakfast tray, ready to tackle the castle and all its hidden nooks and crannies.

In the kitchens I was greeted by the sound of Duncan bellowing some rousing Scottish song in the worst Scottish accent I'd ever heard. Mhairi was washing up at the big Belfast sink, wearing fur-trimmed fuchsia washing-up gloves with giant plastic solitaires and gazing impassively into the bubbles, presumably praying to be struck deaf.

"Good morn, good morn!" he roared as I appeared at the door with my tray. "How'd you find the kippers? Put hairs on your chest!"

"Um, I couldn't finish them as well as the porridge," I lied. "Delicious, though."

"I had one when we first moved in here two years ago, and it's still repeating on me," said Ingrid. She was sitting at the kitchen table with a pile of notebooks and pens around her, and yellow Post-it notes fluttered from every surface as she flapped her hands around, looking for something. "Give me muesli anytime. Duncan, how many loo rolls do you think three hundred people reasonably need? Barring accidents?"

Duncan didn't answer. Instead, he rubbed his hands together and advanced toward me. "Now, the guided tour!" He beamed. "As my noble kinsman, Merry Ivan McAndrew, famously commented in 1564, 'There's aye fashing in mickle muckle.'"

He adopted a strange hunched, one-eyed posture as he said it, and I smiled nervously. Was that a question or a statement? I had no idea.

"Duncan, don't forget Janet Learmont's coming over at eleven for the committee meeting." Ingrid sounded as if she were talking about a dental appointment. "Please don't tell her about your sporran."

"It's in hand," said Duncan cryptically.

"I meant to say," I started, "thanks so much for the breakfast in —" but Duncan was ushering me out and up the spiral staircase, outlining the history of the castle as he went. I managed to insert a question every now and again, but it didn't seem to make much difference to the general narrative theme: the McAndrew passion for *stuff.*

He marched me through the oak-paneled hall, where my eyes were drawn to the bloodthirsty decoration. Where other people might have a nice Canaletto, the McAndrews had wall after wall of grisly medieval weaponry. It looked as if someone had put an enormous magnet next to the Battle of Bannockburn.

I made a mental note to ring Max and ask him if we had any bloodthirsty clients with a *Braveheart* fixation.

"Were these family weapons?" I asked. "Or were they . . . collected?"

"Probably picked up off the field of battle," said Duncan cheerfully. "Or found in the gardens. It's always been a lively area, Berwickshire. Sometimes English, sometimes Scottish, with reivers — or bandits, I suppose you'd call them — mounting raids over the Border on both sides, Scottish lords trying to control the northern lands. Lots of to-ing and fro-ing. Marrying, slaughtering, pillaging. And that's just the prince Bishops! Nothing like that now, of course! Well . . ." His face went thoughtful. "The Ball Committee has its ups and downs, but that's Janet and Sheila for you! Old habits die hard!"

"Ooh!" I said, intrigued by a massive parchment painted with a family tree, the red lines surrounded by thistles and ferrets rampant. "Is this the McAndrew line? Wow! How far does it go back?"

"All the way to 1269!" he said proudly. "There I am. And Robert, of course." Duncan peered and pointed to himself, right at the bottom. The line of succession swung wildly from generation to generation as unmarried heirs failed to grab the prize and other brothers' urgently produced children sprouted like grapes on a vine. There were also a lot of nuns.

I *loved* a family tree. I'd tried to persuade my parents to help me do ours, but they couldn't see the point. And looking at this, I could sort of see why: there were McAndrews here when the Spanish Armada was passing by, whereas all I'd discovered was that most of my dad's male relatives were called Ernest.

I tried not to touch the glass with eagerness. There was Ranald Claude Duncan, born in 1879, and Violet Esme, born 1884, married in 1902; their five children, Clarence, born in 1903, James in 1904, Beatrice in 1907, Carlisle, 1915, Lachlan, 1916 . . .

"Robert'll have to get a move on," observed Duncan. "Don't want to run out of space! Still, fingers crossed things are moving in that direction at last! Wink, wink! Now, up we go! I thought we'd start upstairs."

"Oh, aren't we going to begin in the main living rooms?" I asked, thinking of Max's mysterious table. If I could find that, it'd be a good start. "I —"

"No, no!" Duncan interrupted. "I'd rather you had a look at some of our — how shall I put it? — surplus furniture first." He ushered me onward, past a cabinet full of Venetian glass and up the main staircase. He moved pretty quickly for a big man in tight trousers, and I found myself jogging up the stairs to keep up.

"We pop a lot of stuff out of harm's way before the ball, you see," he explained, stopping by a thick door. "Gets a bit *raucous,* if you know what I mean: people swept away by the party spirit, champagne flowing all night . . ."

"Really?" I breathed.

He had to put his shoulder to the door to get it open, and I flinched at the ominous cracking noise. I couldn't tell whether it came from the door or Duncan.

"Yes, well, between that and the reeling, the blood fairly gets going! It's a marvelous night. Dinner beforehand's a family tradition, started by my grandmother, Violet. Bit of an entertainer in her day, brought a full Limoges dinner service for sixty people over from New York when she married and made Ranald promise they'd use it once a year. Ingrid's got a hard act to follow, bless her." He stepped back triumphantly as the door swung open. "Now, I'm confident you'll find at least ten wonderful items in here."

I took a deep breath. China-blue walls with white molded swagging were just about visible behind the stacks of brown furniture and lumpen china. It was as if the furniture had gone feral and bred indiscriminately — tables with chairs, sideboards with linen racks, and everything covered in crocheted antimacassars. I could barely imagine the carpet, let alone the historical scenes that had once taken place in here.

"And this is just *one* of our spare-furniture

rooms!" Duncan guffawed. "You should see the attic!"

I couldn't see where to start. I gazed around, but all I could see was brown. Brown wasn't great, when it came to finding cash-convertible antiques.

Was Max's table in here? It could be. But so could a whole stuffed polar bear, for all I could make out.

"Take your time, pull out the drawers, do whatever it is you experts do," said Duncan, tenderly wiping the dust off a glass case containing an owl making short work of a stoat. "Would it help to hear a few of the amusing anecdotes about Kettlesheer? Such as the time Uncle Carlisle had the pest controllers in to get to the bottom of the rattle in the attic, and ended up calling the parish exorcist! Turned out to be the ghost of . . ."

I was torn. Part of me was longing to hear some rip-roaring tales of country-house antics, but the larger part of me needed to get on with the task at hand. It was a bigger job than I'd anticipated. Much bigger. Plus I wanted to poke around in the hundreds of drawers on offer and really lose myself in the deliciously dusty atmosphere.

"Maybe we could do both?" I said. "But I do need to get online. Where's the best place for me to connect to the Internet?" I gestured to my laptop bag. "I might need to e-mail some photos back to my partner in London, for a second opinion."

"Internet?" Duncan raised his eyebrows.

"You do have broadband, don't you?"

"Broad *band*," repeated Duncan. "No, I don't think we do." His face brightened. "There's a fax machine in my office, if that's any good?"

"No Internet?" I croaked.

"If you ask me, you young people are too reliant on it." Duncan actually wagged a schoolteachery finger at me. "You need to use this!" He tapped his head, then his eyes. "And these!"

"Right." I swallowed. "So, tell me about your childhood here! Did you fish for salmon and that sort of thing?"

"We did indeed." Duncan began edging his way between the sideboards toward the leaded windows, his hands behind his back like Prince Philip. "I remember learning to make butter from the cows that my grandmother kept down in the field behind Robert's house, churning it in the old dairy and — Oh, dear."

I looked up. Duncan was staring out at something, panic visibly freezing his eyebrows. He swiveled round, nearly knocking

115

over a Chinese dragon, and started to squeeze his way back out.

"Something the matter?" I asked. "Please, do go on."

"No, no! No, I've just noticed that Mrs. Learmont has arrived. For her Ball Committee meeting." Duncan grimaced. "And I haven't quite finished the, ahem, list of tasks she . . . Would you excuse me?"

And, like one of the ferrets on the family tree, he wriggled off.

Curious, I tiptoed onto the landing, and heard the front door open. Voices and a chill draft drifted up.

". . . *yes,* Janet, I have. . . . Yes, I've *done* that. . . ."

It was an excellent balcony for eavesdropping. I leaned farther over the solid banister, at which point my eye was caught by a morose Regency-period nun, who could almost have been hung there on purpose, to deter nosey parkers. I jerked backward, and crept back into the Room of Writing Desks.

I spent nearly two hours dutifully going through every item, taking photographs and trying to put dates on things so Max could value them. The whole lot would fetch about two grand at auction, and to my immense disappointment there weren't even any love notes or interesting trinkets left in the drawers, just old newspaper linings, which were fascinating — the adverts! the news! — but definitely not the valuable table Max had wanted me to find.

I sat back on my heels. I was going to need more help.

But when I got my phone out of the bag, I discovered the castle was even more resistant to modern life than I'd thought: there was no reception.

I tried climbing on a desk, then standing near the window, then leaning out of the window, but still nothing. Even going out onto the landing and leaning out of the window seat didn't help.

Footsteps echoed from the hall downstairs, and I could hear more posh Scottish voices discussing fire exits and "crash zones."

I tucked my phone into my bag and racked my brains. I didn't have time to waste photographing Victorian reproduction writing desks. Max needed something big, and by the sound of it, so did Duncan and Ingrid.

I closed my eyes and tried to listen to my instinct.

If I were the owner of this house, where would I put all the really good stuff? Not in a junk room. Not upstairs.

I'd put it where people would see it. Where it was warm. Where the social business happened.

The drawing room.

To my relief, there was something rather fabulous in the drawing room: a magnificent inlaid mahogany console table that I hadn't noticed behind the huddled bodies of last night's guests.

I laid my hands on it and felt the beeswax polish layered over hundreds of years, the bored rubbing of housemaids' yellow dusters. I could picture tea being served on this, when tea was a real ceremony. I could imagine Violet arranging a bowl of pink roses, fresh from the garden. It was a lovely thing.

The delicate inlay on the top was partially hidden by the froth of knickknackery that covered Kettlesheer's every surface, in this case a cricket ball bowled in the 1979 Ashes series, many small pigs, Ingrid and Duncan's wedding photo (bride and groom both sporting mad '70s flares). I took some photos of the table on my phone, then made some notes. I reckoned it was George III, the quality plain to see in the pale ribbons and swags that rippled out of the polished wood.

As per Max's tuition, I got down on my hands and knees to examine the underside, making sure it all matched up. While I was down there, I must admit I got a bit distracted by tapping along the edges, in search of hidden drawers, and it was only when I saw feet approaching at the other end of the room that I realized I was no longer alone.

The drawing room was so big that it was partially divided by couches and occasional tables. Underneath the console table, I was still hidden behind several rows of other furniture, and as the feet marched across to the couches, I weighed up whether I could inch my way out without looking ridiculous.

It didn't help that they were already talking and, as a result, I was already eavesdropping.

". . . can't tell people where they have to stand, Janet! What are you going to do? Put up sheep pens?"

I recognized that amused voice: Sheila Graham, Fraser's mum.

"Sheila, I have to disagree, dear. It's perfectly possible for a skilled set of reelers to complete the reel and finish beneath the trothing ball." A quick slap of a clipboard against a palm. "Ingrid merely needs to *see* the possible collision zones and pad accordingly!"

I shuddered. I recognized those nasal tones too: Janet Learmont.

"I'm still not one hundred percent reassured about the fireplace," said a querulous man's voice. "It's a potential fatality."

"Gordon, no one in the two hundred years this ball has been taking place has had a problem with the fireplace," said Sheila impatiently. "Unless you count the time Janet's brother-in-law managed to get his —"

"That was a reaction to his medication," snapped Janet.

I peered round the side of the table, and saw the Ball Committee arranging themselves on couches around a large tray of coffee and biscuits.

Sheila Graham was on one side, her firm jaw set as if she'd had it wired shut, and facing her was Janet Learmont. Between the flared nostrils and bared teeth, she was giving off a very Dragon-y vibe. Catriona perched on the sofa arm behind her, clutching her little dog. They were like clones, only Catriona had her long braid draped over one shoulder and Janet had an Hermès scarf patterned with bridles. Both wore natty tartan trousers and sheepskin vests.

Sitting nervously to one side was a tall, thin man with white hair holding a file marked *Health and Safety,* and in the middle was Ingrid McAndrew, who virtually had *Tense Nervous Headache?* stamped across her forehead.

Janet, and Catriona, and Catriona's evil-looking terrier.

No, I thought resignedly. *I am definitely trapped beneath this table now.*

EIGHT

The Ball Committee wasted no time on pleasantries and got straight down to the main business, which, it seemed, was the Reel of Luck, starring as it did two actual committee members.

"Now, while we're on the topic of the first reel . . ." Janet's voice trailed away, leaving a long pause. Then, when no one took her bait, she added, "What do we think?"

I held my breath as Janet stared pointedly at Sheila and Ingrid; Catriona was stroking her braid and pretending they weren't talking about her, and Gordon was jabbing at his calculator. Whatever it was, it clearly wasn't his problem.

"I suppose what I'm saying *since no one else will*," sighed Janet, "is . . . are they up to it?"

"Don't worry, Mummy," said Catriona. "Robbie'll make an effort on the night. He knows how important it is."

"I wasn't talking about Robert, darling. I mean, he really ought to have dragged himself along to those practices, but I'm sure he knows what he's doing. If you'll forgive me, Sheila, I was meaning Fraser and this new girlfriend of his. Alex, is it?"

"Alice," said Sheila.

The skin on my arms went goose-bumpy.

"It's the highlight of the evening, and all eyes will be on them," she went on in her clipped accent. "Sir Hamish and Lady Morag obviously have years of experience. You and Duncan should be fine, Ingrid, and if you're not, then I only have myself to blame, a-ha-ha." The tinkly laughter stopped. "But it's a great deal of pressure for a newcomer."

At that point, I had to stop myself from jumping up and telling the miserable old cow that Alice would, in fact, be the best dancer she'd ever had the pleasure of having her shins raked by; but that would mean giving away my hiding place, and possibly some insider info — and Alice clearly needed that more than ever. So I clamped my lips shut.

"She'll be *fine*," said Sheila Graham, to my relief. "Fraser's organized a run-through at our house on Thursday."

Janet glanced toward the end of the room,

123

and I thought she'd seen me, but her gaze traveled to the door opposite where I was sitting. She seemed satisfied that no one had come in, because she raised her voice to a normal level.

"Does she know what a responsibility it is, though? Being part of the Reel of Luck? I mean" — pause for modest effect — "I'm the *last* person to be superstitious, but it would be such a shame if no proposals happen because a poor wee girl misses her cue, through no fault of her own. Apart from total inexperience, of course."

I blanched. The scene was already unfolding in my mind's eye. The hush. The shocked faces. The awkward arrival of the First Aid stretcher . . .

"Och, Janet, you're making problems where there are none," insisted Sheila. "I've met Alice, she's a fine strong girl, and Fraser's been reeling since he could walk. And for heaven's sake!" She snorted. "If no one got married because someone muffed the first reel, then we'd be wall-to-wall spinsters. Have you seen how much wine gets put back before the horn sounds?"

"Well, far be it from me, but I've spoken to my Laura, and she wouldn't mind stepping in."

"Laura hasn't wanted to dance with Fraser

since they were at school," said Sheila firmly. "And that was fifteen years ago."

Janet smiled, but without showing her teeth, which were presumably grinding. "Well, we'd all like the reel to be particularly lucky this year. Even if there is someone *English* in the eight!"

"Och, dear," mumbled Gordon. "English in the eight. Dilution!"

I dropped my head into my hands. Well, that was *that* for Alice! Inexperienced, not Laura Learmont, and now . . . English.

Through the gaps between the furniture, I could see Ingrid had been fiddling with her pen and Post-it notes, but now she could contain herself no longer. "I'm English," she squeaked. "And Robert's half-English! And Duncan might as well be English — he grew up in Manchester!"

"You're Scots now, dear," said Janet, patting her hand. "And the heir to Kettlesheer's a Scotsman through and through, regardless of where he grew up."

I wasn't sure that was the point Ingrid was making.

The Ball Committee agenda moved on to matters pertaining to the dress code, and — now firmly trapped under the table until they left for lunch — I listened, so entranced

125

by the details that I barely noticed my leg going to sleep. Okay, not by the Portaloo dilemma so much, but by the serving of breakfast at three in the morning, and who would divide up the dancers into sets, making sure no crashes occurred.

Even the lack of Internet was quite romantic, I told myself. It was nice not to be checking my phone every other minute. This castle was like a lost time bubble of Edwardiana, and I was getting to live in it for a few days.

There was a gentle tapping on the window behind me. I ignored it. The wooden frame of my four-poster bed had tapped and cracked all night because of the cold; the first few taps had made me sit bolt upright in terror, but it had gone on all night and I'd gradually tuned it out.

"Now, after last year's entirely avoidable contretemps with Katie MacDonald, I am proposing a dress inspection team at the door," said Janet. "In my experience, spaghetti straps and a vigorous Duke of Perth reel are *not* a family-friendly combination."

The tapping continued.

I glanced behind me, and jumped. Robert was standing outside the window. He must have been in the flowerbed, because his eyes were just visible over the windowsill. He was

wearing a thick peacoat and a woolly hat —
not the usual Barbour jacket and flat cap
beloved by Fraser — and he still looked
frozen.

He mouthed something at me, and
waggled his fingers. He was wearing red-
and-blue stripy wrist-warmers.

What? I mouthed as Janet began to list
the types of dresses to which she would
refuse entry: inadequately anchored strap-
less, above ankle level, anything in animal
print, anything in potentially flammable
material (Gordon's suggestion) . . .

Robert waggled his fingers again, then got
out his iPhone, showed it to me, and mimed
typing on it.

I still had no idea what he was on about. I
raised my hands apologetically, and he
boggled in mock despair at my slowness,
making the corners of his dark eyes crinkle.

I turned to a new page in my notebook
and scribbled, *Can't talk — the Ball Committee is in the middle of a meeting.* I held it up
toward the window.

Robert mimed horror, then jabbed away
at his phone and held it up. He had one of
those fancy scrolling apps that sent the message large across the screen.

*That's why I'm out here. Dad says you need
the Internet? I have broadband in the lodge.*

I gave him a thumbs-up sign, then grabbed my pen again and wrote, *Thanks! I'll be right out.*

Robert's head disappeared from view, and I focused my mind on how I was going to sneak out now without being detected. There was a fair distance between me and the nearest door, and it wasn't open.

"Fraser will be coming on Thursday, with a hundred cases of champagne to start chilling — he's arranged for the flutes to be delivered at the same time, and some special ice sculptures, which sounds fancy." Sheila looked up from her notes. "Now, Gordon — what's happening with the piper?"

"I've sent off for special high-visibility bands for the ends of his pipes to prevent any accidents in the dim lighting," Gordon began, and went into a health-and-safety spiel about "having people's eyes out" but I tuned that out, enchanted by the romantic image unfolding.

Champagne! And a piper! I leaned forward instinctively to hear more, and in doing so managed to dislodge something on top of the console table. I could hear it rolling, then, frozen with horror, watched it drop in front of me.

It was the bloody cricket ball, no longer balanced on the presentation square of turf.

It crashed to the floor with a resounding crack, and rolled some way down the carpet toward the couches. My armpits prickled as the whole Ball Committee leaped out of their seats as one, looking round for the source of the noise.

"Ohmigod! What was that?" Catriona gasped as her Jack Russell was catapulted onto the sofa. She made a grab for him as he started barking right at me. "Stay! Stay, Nipper!"

"Is that the ghost?" Ingrid squeaked. "Duncan keeps talking about a ghost!"

"There *is* no ghost, Ingrid," said Sheila.

"Now, that is what I *mean,* ladies!" insisted Gordon. "We need to cover this place quite literally in plastic wrap or else face the consequences of loose antiques!"

The dog's neck had gone all bristly and it was growling. Oh, God. Any minute now it was going to *launch* itself at me.

I was about to come crawling out with my hands up, but Sheila's voice cut through the twittering. "Calm *down.* It's probably just old Carlisle turning in his grave at the thought of Janet making the lassies wear cardigans. Now, if no one else is going to eat it, I'm going to have the chocolate biscuit. . . ."

Any genteel shock about ghosts was instantly forgotten as the committee members squabbled over the two good foil-wrapped biscuits in the selection, and I grabbed the opportunity to slide out from under the table and scuttle toward the door.

Outside, the air had taken an even chillier turn, and I hugged Alice's coat tight around me as I gazed at the wuthering landscape around me. The sky was a washed-out gray-blue and even the box hedges seemed pinched. Robert was on the phone, several windows down from the committee meeting. He was deep in conversation, and I hung back, not wanting to interrupt.

"No, I can't get back till Monday earliest," he was saying. "I'm sorry, but it's a family commitment. And I'm on holiday, all right? I don't need to say where. . . ."

He turned round and saw me. "I've got to go," he said. "E-mail me the details and I'll try to look at them tonight. Okay, cheers."

I walked self-consciously down the steps, trying not to slip on the moss clinging to the ancient stone. Under different circumstances, I'd have indulged in an imaginary jaunty cloche and an imaginary Daimler waiting for me at the bottom, but Robert's expression nipped any flights of fancy in the bud.

"Why didn't you just come in?" I asked. "You don't need to lurk around in your own flowerbeds, surely?"

"What were *you* doing under a table?"

Touché.

"I was inspecting the dovetail joints." I could feel myself turning red.

He glanced at me, amused. "I'll take your word for it. I didn't come in because I don't have a spare hour to talk about kilts, and to be honest, I don't like Catriona's dog." He pointed across the gravel drive toward a path into the woodlands around the castle. "And Nipper doesn't like me."

"Probably senses the competition," I said as we set off down the drive at a brisk march. Robert had long legs, but then again so did I.

"There is no competition. Catriona's made it clear to both of us that we're equals in her affection. I might even be slightly behind. You have a dog?"

"No," I admitted. "We had a cat, Cleo. Mum never forgave her for shedding. Fish only after that."

Robert laughed. "Round here, if you don't have a dog, you might as well have a tattoo saying, 'I'm disreputable.'

"Has Janet tried to bully Major Muirhead into checking that the men in kilts have come adequately underdressed? There's always one Young Farmer who slips through her net."

"Do you mean — oh!" I squinted, unsure if he was teasing me, and not wanting to look stupid. "I thought that whole. . . . *no pants* thing was just a rumor put about by the English."

Robert lifted his eyebrow. "Alas, no. Janet was all for getting one of those mirrors on a pole, like the bomb squad used to use for checking under cars, but Mum drew the line."

My mouth dropped open with genuine shock.

"Joke," said Robert. "You really will believe anything, won't you?"

"Can you blame me?" I protested, flustered. "My social life rarely extends to dress codes beyond 'No sneakers, please.' Anyway, we didn't get to the men," I went on, picking up my pace. "She was more concerned about the ladies."

"Any new rules I should know about?"

"Cardigans. She'll be applying cardigans to girls who turn up with exposed clavicles and visible tattoos. Your mother has been deputed to scour Rennick's charity shops for appropriate cover-ups."

"Janet would like to go back to the old

days when girls were only allowed to wear black or white and tiaras," said Robert.

"Why not?" I said. That sounded gorgeous, a ballroom full of monochrome and sparkle. "I don't get to wear my tiara enough as it is. You'll be in your kilt, I assume? I mean, I know you're putting up a fight, but it *is* a kilt occasion."

Robert made an *Ugh* noise, and motioned me off the main drive and onto the footpath that led down into the woodlands. "I'll be wearing a pained bloody expression."

"Is that that knife you stick down your sock?" I asked innocently.

"No, it's —" He stopped, then tilted his head to check if I was serious.

"Joke," I said. "Duh."

Robert let out a little huff of acknowledgment. "The only thing I'll be sticking down my sock is a tiny flask of brandy," he said. "And that's because the local shop's out of cyanide capsules."

"Oh, *stop* it," I said. "It's a *ball!* With champagne and a piper! What's not to love? It's like time travel!"

"Right, *now* I get it." He paused to wag his head cynically at me. "You're one of those weirdos who go around saying, 'What would Jane Austen do?' and picturing every man you meet in a wet blouse."

"No!" My eyes boggled with the effort of denying it.

If I were being honest, modern life's lack of breeches was a constant disappointment for me. There were too few opportunities for men to display the little touches of gallantry I lived for. Could you blame me for wanting to superimpose top hats and carriages on the limp, BlackBerry-twiddling specimens I met at the speed dating Alice ushered me to?

"You are," he said heavily. "Oh, *God.*"

"No! It's just that . . . I've never been to a ball," I went on. "I'm imagining candles, and white gloves, everyone bowing to each other. . . . But what's a modern one like?"

"Exactly like that," said Robert. "Give or take the odd tattoo. The men have to get trussed up in either formal dress — kilts with dress coats — or white tie and tails, if they're English. Or red hunting jackets, if they ride with the local hunt."

"Really?" I tried to suppress the flutter of excitement. "That's so . . ."

I didn't want to say *amazing* or *romantic* or any of the other words that bubbled to the forefront of my mind; there was nothing wrong with a romantic soul, but Robert clearly had me down as a deluded bonnet-junkie already. And yet I just couldn't stop picturing myself in an Empire-line gown, curtsying modestly in front of the gold rococo mirror in the hall.

In my imagination, of course, my bosoms were not spilling out inappropriately, and I'd somehow acquired ringlets and balance.

"*So . . . ?*" Robert's prompt cut through my shimmering vision, and I scrabbled for a word befitting a London antiques expert.

"So . . . historical. And" — I couldn't stop myself — "magical."

"That's one way of putting it. The committee does its best to take any actual magic out of it. Is Gordon still bellyaching about the potential stab hazards of the pencils on the dance cards?"

I stole a sideways glance to check his expression, but his face was straight, concentrating on the uneven path ahead. We were striding along at a blood-warming pace, and I was sure from his deadpan delivery that Robert was using our lack of eye contact as a chance to wind me up. "Dance cards? As in . . . may I have this dance, Miss Bennet?"

"Yup."

"You're joking!" I paused. "You *are* joking?"

He shook his head. "You need a different partner for each reel, so to save embarrass-

135

ment, there's a free-for-all over dinner to get the evening booked. And before you say, *'Ooh, how romantic,'* in reality it's brutal. I've seen men get ditched right over the crème brûlée when a better dancer walks past."

"You love it, really," I said, tingling. "You know you're the first one to get bagged."

Robert raised his hands in pretend amazement. "Why, yes, Miss Nicholson! It's every man's *dream* to dress up in an orange, yellow, and black skirt, and tag-team wrestle to the sound of a fiddle being scraped with a cat. While trying to make small talk with some random woman who keeps hinting about settling down and what sort of horse do I have? When she knows full well I don't even *have* a horse."

We'd been walking along the leaf-covered track for several minutes, with green thickets on each side that rustled (rabbits? mice?), but now we'd reached a gate that opened onto a smaller stone path, leading deeper into the woods. Robert opened it for me with an old-fashioned flourish that might have been him taking the mickey. He definitely inclined his head as I thanked him. I wasn't complaining, though: I'd had more doors opened for me in the past twenty-four hours than I had had all year.

"What a trial for you," I went on. "Forced to suffer an evening of candlelight and champagne in your own ballroom. Boo-hoo."

"Don't get me wrong. Candlelight and champagne — fine," he said. "It's the dancing and the social machinations that aren't my thing. Are you a keen dancer? Have you reeled?"

I laughed out loud. "God, no! I'm a *shocking* dancer. I make wardrobes look like slinky movers. I'd cause some kind of pileup if I ever tried reeling."

"You wouldn't. It's not as hard as it looks, especially not for the girls. You just have to resign yourself to being spun from one place to the next. Fun for you, bloody hard work for the men."

"From what I've heard, I'd break myself and probably someone else. I have issues around coordination."

Ahead the trees thinned out, and in the clearing I saw a neat lodge behind a small cottage garden, a perfect chocolate-box house with a slate roof and a squat chimney and a weather vane in the shape of a fox.

"This is your house?" I breathed.

"No, Snow White lives here, I'm renting a room. Of course it's my house." Robert patted his pockets, looking for his keys. "Girls can get away with being rubbish in the reel, but you wouldn't believe the criticism men get. I'm so bad, last year Lady Duffield commiserated with my mother about my 'awful riding accident.' Turns out she thought I was Dougie Graham — and he'd broken his leg in three places and was wearing a cast under his trousers."

I'd heard this sort of thing before, usually before dancing classes where the "terrible dancer" turned out to be the tap and modern champion of East Sheen.

"Yeah, *yeah*," I scoffed. "I bet you've never managed to split your own lip doing the Charleston."

Robert turned round and looked straight at me.

"Do you want me to demonstrate?" he asked. His eyes had a twinkle in them that made my stomach loop suddenly up to my chest. I wanted to look away — and frankly, I should have, because I wasn't completely sure what my face was doing — but something made me hold his gaze.

Robert pocketed his keys and held out his hands. He had nice hands, with long fingers under the wrist-warmers. "Come on, let me show you."

I hesitated. The man had no idea what he was risking.

"Plenty of room out here," he went on, glancing at the bare trees around us. "Not much to crash into. I can't do the exact music, but if I screech a bit, it should give you an idea."

If I hadn't felt such a disorienting tremble inside, I'd have grabbed his hands without even thinking. If it had been Fraser, or even Max. But even though I'd already felt Robert's chest against mine and his arms around me — albeit mistakenly — I was swamped with self-consciousness about touching him again.

"Impressive period blushing, Miss Nicholson," he observed.

Stupid cheeks. Stupid pale face. Alice never blushed; she had special foundation that ensured she looked pallid and steely at all times.

I offered my hands, not even sure how I was supposed to hold them. "Um, is this the right way up? I honestly know nothing about —"

Robert reached out, turned my hands sideways, and circled my thumbs with his crossed hands, his fingers warm against my skin. "Grip my thumbs. That's it."

I'd been expecting some delicate drawing-room fingertip grip, and this robust physical contact made me swallow with surprise.

"The main move in reeling is the set and turn." Robert started to lift our joined hands, pulling me nearer with a controlled force. "The man has to spin his partner round, then put her opposite her next partner. Whether she likes it or no."

Through years of practice, my body recognized the opening moves of a Dance Step and went stiff. I was within breathing distance now of his thick jacket, and he was still pulling me closer. We were about as close as I'd hope to get at the end of a good date, and we'd known each other less than twenty-four hours.

"Just relax and . . ."

He was increasing the pressure on my thumbs, and I gripped his tighter too. "I don't relax when I'm dancing," I gabbled. "It's dangerous for everyone if I stop concentrating."

Robert grinned and leaned back. "Lean into it," he said. "And turn . . ."

"And what?"

He raised his arms and started to turn me round. My arms went rigid with panic, and his phone rang inside his jacket pocket.

"You'd better get that," I gasped.

"No, I'm on holiday," he said. "Just move where I'm putting you."

Twigs and leaves cracked beneath my

boots as I shuffled on the woodland floor, and we performed a weird cat's-cradle sort of thing with our arms.

This is not *making me look good,* I thought, filling up with regret.

The phone carried on ringing. And then *my* phone began ringing — we'd obviously wandered out of the reception black spot hanging over Kettlesheer and reentered the modern world.

Robert looked at me over our joined hands, which felt like the one warm spot in the whole forest. He didn't let go, and I didn't want to look rude by dropping his.

Okay, so I didn't want to let go. *Couldn't* actually let go. My sleeve was sort of caught on the button of his jacket.

"I can't let go," I explained. "I don't want to rip your sleeve."

We jostled awkwardly, trying to free ourselves, and by the time we'd got loose the ringing had stopped.

"Excellent," he said, looking straight at me. "Now you have to do that ten times as fast and in heels."

"I should think getting caught on a kilt's a real recipe for disaster," I said, and his mouth twitched.

"Depends who's wearing the kilt."

My cheeks flamed with a sudden blast of

warmth as he winked at me.

An old-fashioned phone inside the house started pealing, and the moment was broken.

"Someone's really trying to get hold of you," I said.

"All the more reason to ignore them," he said, and got out his keys again. He unlocked the front door and marched in, grabbing the phone from a table by the front door.

"Hello? . . . Oh, hi. . . ." The playfulness had gone from Robert's voice, replaced with a very businesslike clip.

I gave myself ten seconds to shake off my daze, and then I followed him inside.

NINE

The outside of the lodge might have looked like a gingerbread cottage, complete with ivy round the door, but inside it couldn't have been more modern: clean and bright, and still smelling of new paint.

Robert was talking into an old green Post Office phone, which sat on a stunning glass sideboard that Alice had dragged me to worship at Heal's in London. I couldn't remember the name of the designer, but she'd had tears of pure joy in her eyes as she'd lovingly opened and shut the drawers in the manner of a game-show hostess. Robert had nothing in the drawers besides a Yellow Pages.

It looked perfect in his hall. But then, the hall was as sparse and tasteful as the showroom.

He motioned for me to go on in as he squeezed his forehead with his spare hand and tried to get a word in edgeways with whoever it was on the phone. I stepped through the perfectly cream hall (no pictures, no stags' heads, not even a teeny claymore) and into the open-plan kitchen, marveling as I went at how empty it was, compared with the main house.

I'd picked up enough of Mum's " 'Less is more' *costs* more" principles to know that the simple oak kitchen units were probably handmade and extortionate, along with the impressive array of matte black appliances, most of which didn't even have visible controls. I did like the kitchen table — an old thing amidst all the newness, with two long benches and a wooden bowl full of apples in the middle.

I set my laptop bag down on it and checked my own phone, which had sprung to life in the fertile technological atmosphere of Robert's modern house.

Seven new voice messages, four new texts.

I clicked onto my voice mail, keeping one eye on the hall, where Robert was saying nothing but tapping his finger on the sideboard as if he wanted to drill a hole through it.

Sunday, 10:07 p.m.: Alice, wanting details of the journey up.

Monday, 9:10 a.m.: Max, demanding details of the table.

Monday, 9:21 a.m.: Max again, looking for the "other" receipt book. And telling me he now had a bet on with Charlie Sykes about the table being part of Bonnie Prince Charlie's "lost" furniture.

Monday, 10:37 a.m.: Alice, furious that I hadn't already called with details of the journey up. Reminding me to remind Fraser about some dinner party or other.

Monday, 11:10 a.m.: "It's Caryl, your mother. We need to talk, darling." No, we didn't.

I hung up as Robert finished his call and came in.

"Sorry about that," he said. "No peace for the wicked."

"Work?" I asked.

"If only." He flicked on the kettle.

"Pleasure?" I hazarded.

But Robert wasn't so easily cracked as Max. Something had flicked a switch in him. He wasn't unfriendly, just closed off.

"Tea? Coffee?" he asked. "Dad said you needed to e-mail some photos back to London — be my guest. I've got Wi-Fi and a signal booster for mobile reception."

"So I see. Tea, please." I opened my e-mails and plugged in my camera to download the photos I'd taken of the drawing-room table. "What is it you do for a living

145

that you need all this technology?"

Robert paused, kettle in hand, as if I'd asked an odd question, then said, "I'm in storage."

"What? Like . . ." My mind went blank. "Cupboards?"

"I run storage facilities, long-term, short-term, specialist." When I nodded blankly, he elaborated, "ParkIt? The big red warehouses?"

"Oh, ParkIt! My mum's always on at me to move my flat into a ParkIt bay," I exclaimed. "It's her weapon of mass decluttering — she gives clients one packing box, and everything else has to go into storage, and she 'allows' them half a box at a time, while she supervises. That's you, is it?"

"It is." Robert put a white mug down in front of me. He'd done tea-bag-in-a-mug tea, despite having about three million china teapots back at the house. "Clutter is the biggest hurdle to productivity, at home and at work. It's one of the reasons I find Kettlesheer such a colossal headache — I just want to *shove* it all into boxes."

He made frantic shoving gestures, then paused and looked embarrassed. "I'm sorry about last night, by the way. I didn't mean to sound so negative about the place. It was

146

a combination of stress about this ball, and work, and Dad's revolting carrot schnapps."

"Don't worry. You couldn't put me off Kettlesheer if you tried," I said. "And if I can find some things to sell, won't that make you *and* your dad happy? Cash *and* some clear space?"

"That'll be the first thing we'll have agreed on since he moved up here," he said.

I picked up my tea and peered at him over the edge of the mug. "Are you not running the place together? I thought that was how these things worked. Father and son, working side by side at the country-house coalface."

"Maybe a hundred years ago." Robert squeezed his tea bag meticulously in his cup. "Dad and I are too different. He's a teacher, I'm a businessman. We can't even agree on how to get the accounts sorted out, even though I've got a bookkeeping qualification! Basically, he thinks I should still be going back to law school, despite the fact that I've run my own companies since I was twenty-two."

I raised an eyebrow at the sharp edge in his voice. "Well, perhaps that's why he wants you to take an interest in the castle."

"Sorry?"

"Because this is something you *have* got

in common: your family. It's not something money can buy, belonging to a house like this." I realized I'd probably overstepped the mark, so I added quickly, "My dad's a bit like that — not understanding why I do what I do, I mean. He's always on at me to get a proper job, with a career ladder. He and Mum aren't into antiques. Alice and I are officially the oldest things they possess. Even our house is newer than me."

Robert's tense forehead uncreased slightly. "My dad can't get his head around the fact that ParkIt also stores computer data. He wants to know what sorts of boxes it goes in."

"Have you tried showing him?" I asked. "I once took Dad to Christie's, thinking some of the excitement might rub off. He got into a row with the auctioneer when he grabbed the phone off a proxy bidder and told them not to waste space on the Duchess of Gloucester's old Meissen tea service when they could put the same money into a savings account and get a guaranteed return and not have to dust it." I sighed. "Sometimes I think there must have been a mix-up at the hospital. Somewhere out there, there's a rock star with a daughter desperate to be a dental nurse."

"Can't be. You look just like Alice," said

Robert, and I felt quite flattered.

"Is that how you know Alice, through Simplify?" I asked. Some things were falling into place. Robert wasn't really my type, but he was much more Alice's frequent-flyer ideal. He even wore the sort of expensive but fashionable clothes she was forever buying for poor Fraser and his rugby-playing neck.

"I'm how Alice knows Fraser, actually. I handled Simplify's storage account for a while. I invited her to a party where she met Fraser, whom I've known since we were kids, and the rest is, as they say, history."

"But you don't deal with Simplify anymore?" The more I looked at Robert's cheekbones, the more baffled I was as to why she hadn't mentioned him when she sent me up here. Unless she didn't *want* me to meet him. . . .

"Alas, no." He opened and closed some cupboards, then turned round with a sardonic look. "Well, I say 'Alas.' Alice nearly broke the sales director with her negotiations. Should we be braced for some paint-strippingly honest plain talk from you too? Does it run in the family?"

"No." I sighed. "I wish something interesting *did* run in our family, but the only thing we all have in common is freakishly long feet."

"Well, I envy you," said Robert. "There's nothing worse than going out for a pint round here, and having total strangers coming up to you and saying, 'You must be the McAndrew lad' just because of the way you look."

The tension had returned to his face, so I thought it best to change the subject.

"How long have you been here?" Judging from the sparse furnishings, Robert was either very tidy or had everything still packed up in cases somewhere.

"A year, on and off. I've been tied up in London with work. My idea was to renovate this place, then rent it out to provide some income, then maybe do other cottages on the estate as holiday rentals." He paused. "And, of course, it gets me out of the main house."

"The clutter must have been driving you mad up there," I said. "You've got a very distinctive style. Very . . . tidy. Very chic."

"Oh, I can't take credit for this, Catriona did it all." He waved a vague hand around. "She gutted the place, pulled out the old range, the hooks in the beams, stuck in new floors. But that's her job, interior design, so it was a weekend project for her."

"Right." I hesitated, not wanting to sound nosy but at the same time burning with curiosity. "And . . . she doesn't live here?"

"No," said Robert. "She lives with her parents. They've got a similar sort of country pile, about twenty miles north. Her dad's a property developer. They've got a helipad where the old tennis court used to be."

He said it in a way that put a stop to any more Catriona questions.

I looked round the kitchen, trying to picture what it had looked like before the makeover. It was hard to imagine any scullerymaids here now, with the halogen strip lights and chrome fittings. It was smaller than the kitchen in Kettlesheer, but nowhere near as cozy, somehow. "Who lived here before you?"

"My great-grandmother. She was shunted in when Carlisle took over the main house — with his *wife*, of course."

"Was that Violet?" I asked eagerly. "The blonde in the drawing-room portrait? The American heiress who married the army officer?"

Robert looked slightly unsure. "Er . . . yes?"

"Robert," I said, pretending to be reproachful. Well, sort of pretending. "Haven't you *studied* the family tree in the hall?"

To give him his due, he only rolled his eyes, and didn't bite my head off. "You've probably noticed, there's a lot of McAndrews to get my head round."

"Poor Violet, though," I said with sympathy. "Being pushed out of that wonderful house! After she'd lived her whole married life there!"

"Well, that's the way it goes. Son inherits, mum's booted out. She seems to have brought most of its contents with her, anyway. I've got *three* livable rooms." He gestured toward the open-plan sitting room, cream-colored and empty apart from two low sofas and some Art. "Kitchen, the sitting room, and a bedroom. The others are packed — and I mean *packed* — with boxes. Carlisle never let anyone in to sort it out after she died, and I've never had time. Someone really needs to go through all that stuff."

"Ooh!" I couldn't help it. My imagination rippled at the tantalizing prospect of a whole life in boxes. "What sort of stuff?"

Robert saw my eyes gleam and raised a hand in warning. "Don't get your hopes up," he said. "Just stuff, okay? Clutter. Photographs. Clothes. Old newspapers. No mysterious cases containing priceless diamond tiaras — anything valuable stayed up in the big house."

I would have *fallen* on anything belonging to any member of my family pre-1960. Fallen like a ravenous *beast*.

"But that *is* the really valuable stuff!" I protested. "Especially since you don't know anything about her. You're not curious to get to know your great-grandmother, see if she left any letters, any secrets about her own family? You've got a whole other side of the family in America, haven't you?"

"I guess so," Robert sighed. "I'm not into all that research-your-ancestors stuff. All I really care about is what I do now, not what someone else did a hundred years ago. I find it quite tedious."

His eyes had gone guarded, his mouth a tight line. But seeing my face fall, he batted the question back to me. "Don't tell me — you've researched your whole family back to Merlin the wizard."

"I wish," I said ruefully. "I started, but we peter out mysteriously in Pickering just after the Boer War. Dad reckons there must have been some name-changing shenanigans, refused to let me research any further in case we were career criminals and it got out round the bowls club."

"But what's so interesting about other people's marriages and lives and divorces?"

153

Robert looked at me, genuinely bemused. "It's like Kettlesheer, full of other people's stuff. Wouldn't you rather have your own things?"

"No! I *love* holding little bits of other people's lives. It's almost as if they haven't died if their locket or their tea set's still being touched and used." I closed my mouth, surprised by the way that thought had just popped into my head out of nowhere.

"Well, I find it absolutely suffocating," he admitted. "Can't get that through to Dad in the right way — it's not a criticism, it's just the way I've lived my life, doing my own thing." Robert paused, as if he were actually considering what I'd said. "But I can see what you're saying. It's a nice sentiment."

I wanted to say something witty, but I couldn't. I couldn't stop looking at his extraordinary brown eyes. They were huge, and they seemed to look right inside my mind.

Luckily, Robert pulled a face and ruined the moment. "Good job for me that there's money to be made from people's inability to have a good clear-out."

At that, my breath rushed out in an embarrassing half-gasp, half-laugh. I hadn't been aware that I was holding it.

"Are you okay?" he asked.

I nodded and pretended to cough.

Robert's old phone rang in the hall — it sounded weird in the modern kitchen, like history calling to reprimand him for what he'd just said.

"That'll be the original owner of the phone," he said, as if he'd read my mind. "Calling to check up on me."

"And that was . . . Violet?" I shivered.

Robert nodded. Then frowned and shook his head. "I mean, no. That's either someone from work, or Janet Learmont. *Again.* Would you excuse me?"

As he left the room, my own phone rang: Max, calling back, I hoped, with a comprehensive list of cocktail party gossip about the McAndrews and their valuables, plus his considered opinion on the photos of the George III console table I'd just e-mailed to him.

I grabbed my pen and notebook, keen to get my brain back into professional gear. My hands, I noticed, were shaking.

"Hello?"

"Good work on the table," said Max. It was incredible how quickly he could drop the louche act when money was involved. "That's the bobby. Worth about ten, twelve grand on a good day. I know a lady in Altrincham very keen for a table like that. Was

155

there a second one?"

"Not that I saw."

"Check for a pair. Bumps up the price."
He paused. "Table? Found it?"

"Which one? There are about a million!" I
said. "I don't know where to start. Give me
a clue."

I heard the click of a lighter and a tense
exhalation at the other end. My stomach
clenched. Max only smoked when coffee
wasn't getting his heart rate high enough.

"I'm not in the mood for games. I've just
had that penny-pinching weasel Daniel
Finch round."

My heart sank. Daniel Finch was Max's
accountant. They had the sort of love/hate/
fear relationship normally found in Meat
Loaf duets.

"What did he want?" I asked warily.

"Blood," groaned Max. "My liver. My
firstborn son. I mean, he's *welcome* to Jas-
per. Please. It would get me out of paying
for his driving lessons —"

"What did Daniel *want?*" I repeated.

"Let's just say that we seem to have
slipped behind with our rent, as well as
some other payments on account, and
friend Daniel seems to think that an assistant is one of life's luxuries I should be
casting by the wayside, along with decent

wine and soft loo paper."

I grimaced and looked for something to crush, silently. This was a worrying echo of last year, right down to the buck-passing syntax.

When Max's business was failing, it was "we," up to the point where "Daniel" insisted that Max sack me. He'd spared me at the last moment, thanks to Alice getting him into some old dowagers' bridge club in Chelsea; but last year Max's turnover had been three times what it was so far this year, *and* I owed him money. Times were hard, and I didn't doubt Max would cut me loose without much of a backward glance, especially if I couldn't pull in a big deal from a house apparently full of saleable items.

"Fine, I get it," I said. "How much would we pay for a herd of escritoires? Because that's all Duncan's steered me toward so far."

Max made a rather fruity comment about the escritoires. "Find this bloody mystery table! It can't be that hard, even for you. Have you tried the dining room? It could be a dining set — ow!"

"What?" I stopped writing.

"My head," said Max in his pathetic "hurt bear" voice. "Daniel has induced a migraine. Where've you put those super-strength headache tablets your most obliging sister acquired for us?"

"They're in the tea caddy in the kitchen. Don't take more than one at a time — they're illegal in the EU."

I could hear Robert talking on the phone in the hall. His voice was rising, and I strained my ears to hear what he was saying over the sound of Max's whining.

"And that's another thing, when are you planning to come back?" Max demanded. "I've got a shop full of your tatty flotsam and jetsam staring me in the face, and I honestly cannot bring myself to sell it. I have a reputation to consider. I do not want to be seen flogging grotesque wedding photos like some antimarriage counselor."

"I'll be back by Friday," I said, hearing the old-fashioned jingle of Robert hanging up the receiver. "If you're really not feeling well, see a doctor. And don't forget it's Valentine's Day on Saturday."

"You sound like my ex-wife."

"I am nothing *like* your ex-wife, Max," I replied, then turned round just in time to see Robert standing at the door. One eyebrow shot up, and it occurred to me that it might sound a bit wrong, out of context. "Put all the teddies out, throw some confetti over them, and I'll see you on Friday," I added, and hung up.

"Trouble at home?" Robert asked as I slammed my notebook shut before he could see my despairing asides about his family furniture.

"No, no, just my boss. He needs his hand held sometimes."

"What . . ." Robert left a meaningful pause. "Literally?"

"Oh, no! God, no! No!" I shook my head, hard. "He wears a leather coat. *No.*"

"Ah, it's that maidenly blush again," Robert observed.

"That's not blushing, that's . . . the cold."

Robert checked his watch. "I don't mean to hurry you out, but is there anything else you need to know about the Wi-Fi, or the house? That was Cat — I've got ten minutes before she and her mother appear to make their last plea on behalf of skirts for men. You're welcome to stay and finish what you're doing, but there won't be much peace and quiet."

"Is it an extension of the committee meeting?"

He sighed. "There's an agenda, yes."

Then it was a meeting I didn't want to be at, eager though I was for more ball detail.

"I'd better leave you to it. But I suppose they just want it to be perfect," I said, packing up my laptop. "Don't you feel like the leading man? The Kettlesheer heir surrounded by the most beautiful girls in the Borders?"

"More like a lamb to the slaughter," he said, then added, as I opened my mouth to protest, "I know you think castles and reels and tartans — ooh, romantic!" Robert mimicked my breathiness so perfectly, I winced. "But keeping places like this running was never *romantic.* It was more about political strategizing and mergers. Cold-eyed business."

"Maybe in the *very* old days —" I began.

"Oh, come on." He looked at me as if I was being hopelessly naïve. "It wasn't *that* long ago that Ranald McAndrew needed a strategic overseas investor to refloat his expensive castle, was it?"

"I'm sure it wasn't like that," I protested, not wanting to think of the vivacious girl in the drawing room steaming across the Atlantic as some sort of . . . *human checkbook.* "And if it is just business, surely you're more qualified than anyone to take over? Because you *don't* love it?"

"Ouch." Robert's face softened, and we regarded each other frankly, neither wanting to concede the other had a point.

"It can't be *all* misery," I said. "You're

160

hosting a white-tie-and-champagne ball at the weekend. Please. Humor me here."

Robert leaned on the kitchen table, dropping his eyes, then raised them to mine. His face was open and honest, and a bit weary.

"I'll tell you what it's like," he said. "It's like being given a job you didn't realize you'd interviewed for. And then being told you've got to judge Miss McWorld on top of that, while everyone points at the family tree in the hall and gossips about your sex life because you haven't got married yet. And then introduces you to their daughter. And you're, like . . ."

Robert illustrated it with a manic grin, and for a moment the storage-focused businessman fell away and he looked like any of the other panicky blokes herded in my direction at the singles dinners Alice and my mum dragged me to.

In a flash, I felt sorry for him. Sorry, in fact, for all the other male McAndrews who'd been frog-marched to face a selection of capable local girls they didn't fancy as much as their fathers fancied the land the girls came with.

"I still think it's amazing to belong to a house like Kettlesheer," I said.

"But that's just it. I belong to the house, not the other way round." Robert raked his

161

hand through his already tousled hair, and frowned at his cold tea. "What I want doesn't seem to come into it." He glanced up. "Sorry. I know, boo-hoo for me. You don't need to hear all this."

"Why not? I'll be off on Friday. Looong before you have to staple your party face on for the Reel of Luck."

Robert laughed. "You should stay for the ball. See for yourself."

"Thanks, but I hear you have to have exact numbers," I said ruefully. "I don't want to spoil Janet's battle plans."

"I know the organizers," said Robert, with a jokey tap of the nose. "I can get you in."

I sighed, because my entire body was screaming *Show me the dance cards!* "I wish. But since we're talking business, I've just had fair warning from my boss that if I don't get back to London on Friday with a selection of priceless gems for your father to sell through us, I might as well not bother coming back at all."

"Oh dear."

"So if you know where the collection of Fabergé egg spoons has been hidden, now is the time to tip me the wink."

"I wish I did," said Robert. "Even if I think it's a waste of time to sell them, I'd hate us to be the reason you lost your job.

You'll let me know if there's anything I can do?"

He looked directly over the table, and again the shrewd brown eyes stalled my brain. Something fluttered in the air between us for a moment, and then it was gone.

"I should get back up to the house." I hoisted my laptop bag onto my shoulder.

Robert pushed his bench back and got up to escort me to the door. "If I think of anything, I'll let you know. And if you need the Internet, text me."

"I haven't got your number," I pointed out.

"Hang on, I'll get my phone — I'll ring you."

I lingered in the cool hall passage as Robert turned back to get his phone from the kitchen table, and my attention was drawn to a tarnished brass door handle.

My imagination gave a little fizz, picturing the housemaids in starched white headbands who must once have polished that, dreaming of the underbutler at the big house. Was this the old drawing room? Full of Violet's stuff? It was a bit nosy, maybe, but a quick peek wouldn't hurt. . . .

I pushed the door open as quietly as possible, and my heart skipped: the room was jammed with trunks, tables, standard lamps, some storage boxes, photographs stacked in silver piles, all smelling of lavender and leather and another time.

Violet's life, from New York childhood to Kettlesheer widow, all waiting for someone to explore.

Ten

Without thinking, I began to inch into the room, heading for the tempting packing crates like a sniffer dog, my mind full of Violet and her gilded life.

These rooms must have felt tiny after the airiness of Kettlesheer — after whatever splendid New York townhouse she had left. I spotted a photograph of Ranald, darkly dashing in cricket whites, the brooding McAndrew eyes burning over a luxuriant mustache; and an old gramophone, a lady's sewing box with a beautiful tapestry lid, and a rocking horse with a dappled mane and faded ribbons.

Against the far wall was a painting of a dimpled blonde in tennis whites, a white band crushed against her curls and a racquet over one shoulder. Older than the portrait in the drawing room, a woman in her thirties now, but still the same mischievous glint in her smile. I got a familiar shiver of something exciting, and valuable. I wanted to know her. I felt like she was inviting me to explore her life.

I picked up a beaded evening handbag sticking out of an old banana box. It glittered with jet beads and gold links —

"I know. Where to start, eh?" said a voice from behind me.

I dropped the bag and jumped back.

Robert was standing a few paces away, holding his phone. He sounded more amused than annoyed.

"You're welcome to have a look," he said. "I've been meaning to sort it out for months."

"Really? You don't mind?" I asked. I was already edging back inside, running my gaze over the various boxes and crates with the quick "junk or gem" scan I used at auctions. Obviously, what I was really craving were photo albums. Photo albums were *people*. Parties. Weddings. Moments in real lives, like mine. What were Violet's?

"Be my guest," said Robert. "Phone number?"

I rattled off my mobile number almost without thinking as I opened the nearest box. It looked like the contents of a lady's desk: notebooks and letters in faded ink, stiff wedding invitations, calling cards belonging to Lady Violet McAndrew.

Reverentially, I lifted the top card — an engraved order of service from Ranald and Violet's wedding in London.

"Oh, they were married at St. George's, Hanover Square!" I exclaimed.

"And?"

"It's where all the smart society weddings were held. Look, they had the most beautiful hymns. . . ." Images swam in front of my eyes from other society photographs I'd pored over, the French lace veil, the gold-buttoned guard of honor outside, the masses of crisp white blossom —

There was a knock at the front door. The sort of firm knock designed to travel through ancient hallways without doorbells. The knock of a horsewoman.

"Oh, God," said Robert, "they're here."

"Who're here?" I asked, still entranced with bridal Violet, now boarding the steam train to Berwick in my mind's eye, the station platform at King's Cross piled with her Louis Vuitton trousseau.

"Catriona and Janet. Listen, take that box if you want, and I'll have a look through here later, see if there's anything that might help you."

"Thanks." I stepped back into the hall. I could see two bold shapes through the door glass. "You should . . ."

"Right, yes." Robert marched forward and opened the door to reveal Janet and Catriona on the step, now in matching quilted jackets and fur-trapper hats, each with a clipboard under her arm.

"Good afternoon!" barked Janet, her breath pluming in the cold air.

Catriona didn't look thrilled. "Oh, hello, Evie."

"Evie was just going," said Robert, ushering me safely past them. "Ring me if you need . . . help." He made a phone sign, his finger and thumb held up to his ear. It seemed a very London gesture, set against the backdrop of snowdrops and stone walls outside.

"I will." I squinted against the sun. Robert was perfectly framed by his contradictory house: cream and cool behind him, mossy and old round the door.

I raised a hand in farewell to all three of them and set off back to the big house, the contents of Violet's desk tucked under my arm, taking deep lungfuls of the clean Scottish air until my jittering pulse returned to something nearer its normal rate.

The forest path to the big house seemed much shorter on the way back — or maybe that was because I'd picked up my pace, eager to get back to sift through the box under my arm.

I saw the walk back through Violet's eyes now. Through gaps in the trees, I could make out grazing fields beyond the woods, sweeping away toward rolling gray hills on one side, while the woodland thickened on the other. Had she and Ranald ridden down here when she was still mistress of the big house? Did she look back with regret, once she'd been moved out? There were hoof prints here and there, in the dried mud. My fertile imagination immediately provided a chestnut horse, a sidesaddle riding habit, a large hat . . . with a veil?

I was startled out of that particular dream by a pheasant rattling unexpectedly out of the undergrowth and surging straight up into the taller trees. As I squeaked with shock, a couple of rabbits bolted out of the hedge and bounced across the fields, their white tails flashing against the grass.

I was the anti–Snow White. Wildlife didn't flock to me so much as make a run for it.

I shouldered my bag and pushed open the wooden gate onto the main track. After a few minutes' brisk marching, Kettlesheer's turrets rose up through the trees ahead of me. The sun had set now, though it wasn't yet dark, and one by one the lights went on in the downstairs windows like friendly beacons guiding me home.

For such a dramatic house, I thought, it had a surprisingly intimate pull. But then I felt like I'd been given a glimpse behind the tapestries, and now I didn't just see Kettlesheer's stately rooms, I was starting to see the people who had lived in them.

Inside, the hall was deserted, apart from a pile of post on the dark oak sideboard, a file marked *Cloakrooms,* and the keys to several Land Rovers.

Since there was no one about to herd me back to the junk rooms, I slipped upstairs to leave Violet's box in my bedroom for later, then get looking for Max's table.

It took all my self-control to leave the box on the bed and not leap into it, right then and there. But, I reminded myself, Max hadn't been joking. He would sack me if I didn't come back with the table, and now was my chance to get a proper poke around without Duncan at my shoulder, waving African hunting horns at me.

I wandered down the passageway, trying not to look directly at the suits of armor lined up against the walls. They were real Scooby-Doo specials, the sort that usually came with narrowed eyes flickering from side to side in the slits, only these had huge medieval swords attached. I wasn't sure what the obsession with military hardware said about the family. Was there a ruthless streak running deep in the current McAndrews, under their soft English accents?

I shivered, imagining Robert in a boardroom, his eyes flashing with the wild-eyed courage that had once defended the Kettlesheer estate from English —

I caught my own moony reflection in a framed photograph of the staff, circa 1880, and pulled a face. I really had to get a grip.

Kettlesheer was a *big* house. It had a lot of rooms — and they all had tables. Downstairs, I passed a couple more drawing rooms and a library, and each one made me want to stop and close my eyes and just breathe in. The stately house atmosphere was infectious. My shoulders straightened as I walked past huge mirrors; my neck seemed to arch as if all my hair were piled on top of my head in an elaborate bun.

I paused next to a double door in a long corridor decorated with painted crests and imagined myself about to sweep in, announced by a discreet butler.

"Lady Evangeline Nicholson." I inclined my head, eyes closed, half-smiling in acknowledgment.

Well, there was no one around.

"Lord and Lady Fraser Graham —"

And then voices floated into my mind. Actual voices! I couldn't make out what they were saying, just the low murmur of conversation, but they were definitely coming from behind the very door I had my hand on, as if my warm fingers had set something back into motion. A shiver ran over my skin.

The house really was coming to life around me. This was the spookiest, most spine-tingling —

"Ah, Evie!" A hand descended on my shoulder, delivering a pat that sent me staggering against the doorframe. "I wondered where you'd got to! Carlisle amassed the most fascinating collection of hyacinth glasses that I think might prove to be worth a pound or two!"

It was Duncan.

"I went down to the lodge," I said. "I needed to send some photographs to my boss, and Robert was kind enough to offer me his Wi-Fi."

Duncan's jolliness dropped a level or two. "Wi-Fi? If you'd said you needed music, my dear —"

"No, Wi-Fi. Not hi-fi, sorry, was I mumbling?"

"Modern technology's rather wasted on me, as Robert will tell you." Duncan sounded a bit baffled, but perked up when he realized there was a room he could show me. "Are you coming in?" he inquired, nodding at the door. "Rather splendid, our dining room!"

"Oh, er —"

"Let's see what's going on." He pushed open one of the doors, ignoring my bleats of panic, and immediately pulled it shut again. "Ah," he said. "Maybe not."

"What's in there?" I gasped, my mind crowding with spectral diners.

"Ball Committee," he mouthed. "Ingrid, Sheila. That old woman."

"But Janet's down at the —"

"Not Janet. Gordon. More of an old woman than all the others put together. No, best leave them to it," he went on. "Come with me to my study — I'd love your opinion on some pocket watches my grandfather left me. . . ."

And with that, I was swept reluctantly back down the hall.

That night, I got dressed with a vengeance. I wasn't going to make the same wardrobe mistake for dinner twice. I piled on as many layers as I could fit under my clothes, and made my way down to the basement with an extra cardigan, just in case.

In the kitchen, Ingrid's blond head and Sheila's white roller-set curls were bent over something in the middle of the table. It looked like a board game, with ivory counters in pink and blue. Sheila had a pencil behind her ear, like a builder. There were wineglasses the size of buckets, but no sign of Duncan.

He was, Ingrid explained, at a meeting of the Rennick Winemakers. The glass she pushed toward me had, she promised, *nothing* to do with him.

"Duncan's always been into home-brewing," she explained. "All the teachers at St. Theobald's were. You name it, he's mashed it up and added alcohol to it. It's just got worse, now he's got access to his own water supply and hundreds of outbuildings to store the revolting stuff."

"Like what we were drinking last night?" I asked.

"Yes," said Ingrid. "And I'm very sorry. The first time he served his home brew at one of those soirees, Dr. Murray called to see if we'd had a campylobacter outbreak, there were so many patients needing his attention the next day."

"You'll have us teetotal yet," said Sheila

cheerfully. "Imagine that! What was the nonsense Jock Strathmorris was telling me about Duncan making whiskey in the stables? He's not serious, is he?"

"I'm afraid he is." Ingrid took a big slug of chardonnay — I noticed the bottle was the house white from Fraser's wineshop. "Duncan thinks that Kettlesheer turnip vodka they made at Christmas could be a moneymaker. God knows we need one. I've got the gas bill and the electricity bill, and I can't decide which to hide first." She sighed, making the silk ruffles on her blouse flutter sadly. She wore one of Duncan's old cardigans over the top for warmth, which diminished the glamour somewhat. I admired her for trying, though. "I love this house, but I think the boiler runs on liquid gold, not oil."

"If the water's unusual, mightn't a microbrewery work?" I asked, wanting to be positive. "Lots of big houses have breweries. You've got the space."

"Evie, hen. I'm a Scotswoman through and through, but even I think there's a place for turnips, and it's not in a glass," said Sheila.

"Well, what about bottled water?" I persisted. "I bet Robert would know how to market it to London shops. He could do a business plan, and Duncan could . . . um, design the label? If you put the castle on, I bet it'd sell by the lorryload!" I beamed at Sheila. "*Fraser* could sell it! It could be his shop's house water!"

Ingrid and Sheila exchanged trepidatious glances.

"I'm not sure Robert and Duncan quite see eye to eye on business matters," said Ingrid. "I sometimes think Robert feels owning a castle *spoils* his business credibility. No, what we need is a quick lump sum, even if it means prying some valuable out of Duncan's hands." She grimaced. "You might have some trouble persuading him to sacrifice something. It's all very personal to him, you see."

That I could understand, but I thought of what Robert had said, about not wasting time selling little bits here and there. "If I can't find the right thing," I said cautiously, "has Duncan thought about putting the whole castle on the market? I mean, if it costs so much just to keep going every year —"

"Duncan will never sell." It was the first time I'd seen Ingrid definite about anything. "Absolutely not."

"Ingrid, he might have to," said Sheila. Her tone was gentle, but realistic. "People do, you know. It's no shame, these days. No one's got the income. Well, apart from Nigel Learmont. . . ."

Something flickered in Ingrid's face, and my drama radar pinged. I wasn't quite sure why, though. An old crush, maybe? A refusal to see Janet lord it over her? Something to do with Robert and Catriona?

"Duncan won't sell," she repeated, shaking her head. "He's always said how it's the family's duty to keep this place going. His father drilled it into him and his brothers that if they ever got the house, they had to move heaven and earth to stay here. He got that from *his* mother. She used to sit them down in the nursery and tell them grisly tales of how their ancestors chopped off people's heads to get Kettlesheer, and that it was only fair to those poor headless people that they didn't let it go."

"Oh, *Violet,*" said Sheila. She smiled. "Yes, I can imagine her doing that, especially after Ranald died. Wanting to stay, no matter what."

"But she was American," I said. "Didn't she want to go home?"

"No! No, she *loved* this place. She was more Scottish than he was by the end," said Sheila. "She was buried with him out on the grouse moor with her shotgun and her saddle, like one of those Saxon queens."

"That's what Duncan wants," added Ingrid. "I've told him no. I fully intend to be cremated back in Wimbledon. I'm not spending my twilight years watching telly by candlelight under four blankets, just so we can be buried in a field together, like a pair of dead family pets."

I didn't point out that McAndrew family pets were more likely to be stuffed and kept in a spare room.

"Fraser said on the way up that your grandmother was a lady's maid," I said to Sheila instead. "Did she tell you stories or was she terribly discreet?"

"Oh, she had a tale or two, after a glass of sherry. But it was common knowledge how much Violet loved this place. How much she loved Ranald too." Sheila's comfortable face softened and she looked almost girlish. "It was the big fairy tale when we were wee girls, like Liz Taylor and Richard Burton. We all wanted to be swept off our feet like Violet McAndrew."

I leaned forward, my elbows on the table. "What, romantically?"

"No, literally," said Ingrid. "Ranald ran her over on his bicycle in Regent's Park, playing bicycle polo with his cavalry division. Something about — oh, go on, Sheila, you tell this better than me."

"Och, no . . ." Sheila pretended to be polite for a second, in a way Janet Learmont hadn't, and then launched into the story with relish.

"*Well,* Violet had sailed over from New York with her sister Lilianne to do the season and to find a nice titled Englishman to marry," she began. "She was very, very rich — her Papa had made a lot of money on the railroads and wanted to set his girls up properly, like a lot of wealthy Americans did then. And the story goes — Violet told my granny this, and everyone else, actually — that she was strolling in the park with Lilianne and their chaperone when suddenly something knocks her flying. When she gathers herself together, there's a brown-eyed gentleman holding his hankie to her forehead, and when she sees how handsome he is and how lovely his Scottish accent is, being a practical sort of girl, she promptly invites him to a ball she's throwing in Park Lane."

"That is romantic," I breathed. "And practical!"

"Luckily for her, he turned out to have a castle and a title, and was as mad about her as she was about him. They got married six months later. Ranald brought her up here, all the staff lined up outside in their uniforms, and she fell in love all over again, this time with Kettlesheer."

"I can see why," I said. "It must have seemed like something out of a storybook."

"Well, in those days, it was," sighed Sheila. "They had a household of about fifty, and her daddy built a railway extension from Berwick straight to the house, so guests could travel direct from London. All overgrown now, of course. And they did everything together, Violet and Ranald, which was really unusual then. She rode out hunting with him, went fishing on the Tweed with him, handled a shotgun like a lad. . . . And of course, she loved reeling. *Loved* the Kettlesheer ball."

"Have you been up to the ballroom yet?" asked Ingrid. She'd pushed back her chair while Sheila was regaling me with Violet's life story, and was moving around the kitchen, stirring something on the Aga and slicing fresh bread.

I shook my head. "I've barely even 'done' the main drawing room."

"Oh, you'll love it," said Ingrid with a knowing nod.

"It's in some architectural study," said Sheila. "Violet spent a fortune remodeling it; then she invited the Prince of Wales — big shooting friend of Ranald's — to the first ball there. He led her into the Reel of Luck, and he *never* danced at these things. If you look at the carvings, there are violets entwined with the McAndrew thistles in the paneling, and the heraldic feathers of the Prince of Wales and American eagles. There'll be a photograph somewhere, won't there, Ingrid? Of the royal party?"

Ingrid waved a bewildered hand in the general direction of the house. "Somewhere."

How could it be *somewhere?* I thought wildly. I'd have had it on display! I made a mental note to find it, to take it down to the lodge where it belonged.

"So it was a real love match?" I said. "Not just a financial arrangement?"

"God, no! I mean, it helped that Violet had so much money, but they were devoted to each other. They were known for it — the only couple round here that insisted on *not* being separated at country-house parties." Sheila laughed. "My granny used to get all sorts of teasing from the other staff at those. No breakfast tray scandal for Violet and Ranald!"

"Were they married a long time?" I asked, trying to remember the dates on the family tree.

Real sadness crossed Sheila's kind face,

and I felt an instinctive panic for the young lovers.

"Ah, now, that's the sad part," she said, and I put down my glass, already braced for the worst.

ELEVEN

"What happened?" I asked. "Was it the war? Did something happen then?"

"Not directly, but everything changed, one way or another. Two of Ranald's younger brothers were killed at Ypres in the First World War, and half the estate lads were killed together at Passchendaele. They'd volunteered together, you see — Violet turned the house over to be a hospital for the Border Regiment. And then before the Second World War, her family money ran out. Not that we were meant to know," Sheila added. "From what my granny heard, Violet's father lost every cent he had in the Depression. Shot himself, poor man. And Daddy was paying the bills."

Sheila looked anxiously over at Ingrid. "It's never been a rich estate, not many farms, and Ranald was no businessman. His youngest brother got into trouble in London, needed to be bailed out — that took

183

most of his inheritance. Then when he was only fifty, Ranald had a heart attack while out fishing and died there, on the bank. Poor Violet — she was devastated, and with the house and death duties and five children to look after. All on her own."

"When was that?" Coldness crept over me, thinking of a love like that, a gilded, easy life, suddenly snatched away. And to be alone in a strange country, surrounded by everything she'd loved, but with her heart broken forever. Even I felt cheated, and I was just *hearing* the story.

"Ooh, nineteen thirty-something? But you know what? She got herself through it." Sheila tapped the table for emphasis. "She spent three days in bed, refusing food, company, everything. Then, the day after the funeral, lawyers came round with an offer from a family in Edinburgh. Always liked the house, apparently, wanted to take it off her hands. Granny didn't want to let them in, but Violet swept downstairs and told them, in front of everyone, that she might have lost her beloved Ran, but while she was still in his house, part of him was still alive in her. And that she'd never sell."

Sheila's eyes were glistening. Mine were too. Ingrid had stopped stirring. "God knows how she did it, with next to no money," Sheila finished, "but she managed to keep the big house going, *and* nearly all the staff who worked here, *and* the tenant farmers."

"Were a lot of stately houses sold off?" I asked.

"Och, yes. Who had the money to run them? Ollerslaw, that castle by the main road?" Sheila jerked a thumb toward the window. "That was sold to a hotel chain to pay death duties. And Edderburn, *beautiful* castle, been in the Dean family for centuries, that was turned into a reform school, then an old folks' home, and now it's executive apartments and a spa."

"Nigel Learmont was the developer on that," Ingrid added. "They've done a lovely job, bought some fishing and shooting rights too. Catriona runs a lot of outdoor functions there."

She put a plate of thick Scotch broth in front of me. "Sorry it's just soup," she said. "I'm on a diet. Sheila's altering a ball-gown for me, and there are only so many pairs of Spanx a girl can wear at once. It's tiny. Vintage clothes always are, though, aren't they? Malnutrition."

She sounded almost envious.

"Is it one of Violet's?"

"I should think so." Sheila moved the

185

board and ivory counters to one side. "Made by Worth. Beautiful frock, lace like spiderwebs. You'll look stunning, Ingrid."

"So long as it passes the Janet test."

Sheila made a disparaging noise.

I sipped the Scotch broth. It was very good: homemade and thick with barley. "Did Violet remarry?" I asked, picturing the lovely young girl downstairs; it was hard to imagine her shrouded in widow's weeds. "Surely she must have had offers, if she was so popular and beautiful?"

"Oh, plenty!" Sheila shrugged. "But she didn't want to. There was only ever Ranald for her. She stayed here on her own until she finally managed to get that big idiot Carlisle married off to a girl with some money, and she was well into her sixties by then."

"She could have reeled in some rich old toad and just stowed him in the attic," said Ingrid. "There's enough room. They had soldiers invalided here during both wars — bet they barely noticed."

"But she was too devoted to notice another man," I breathed.

"Well." Sheila winked. "As Granny used to say, it's one thing saying you don't want to remarry, but that doesn't stop you hosting the Kettlesheer Ball looking like Grace

Kelly in your diamonds and letting all the old fellas hope. She always kept the last dance marked for Ranald on her dance card."

"That is so sweet!" I said. Well, mouthed. I was a bit choked up.

"Can you move the placement thing so I can put the bread down? Carefully, mind — I cannot face the idea of starting again with that," Ingrid said.

"What is it?" I asked as Sheila lifted the board with great delicacy so the ivory buttons didn't move.

"A placement arranger. For the dinner we host before the ball. You assign each guest a little token and then shuffle them round until you get a table plan that works. That one was made especially for the table upstairs," said Ingrid. "What it doesn't come with is instructions for how the bloody hell you're meant to seat sixty people, all of whom have some pressing reason not to sit next to or opposite anyone else, which of course I have to *guess,* because there's no way you could *know* Innes Stout once said something unforgivable to Janet Learmont's mother at the Edinburgh Tattoo in 1976."

She gasped crossly, running out of breath, and put the bread down.

187

"This is a small place," said Sheila, buttering a roll serenely. "We have to make our own entertainment. People get married and divorced a lot, and get up to all sorts of shenanigans out hunting at bridge."

But I was picturing a long table, dressed for dinner and glowing with soft candlelight and silver candelabra, glittering with reflected diamonds and tinkling laughter. Everyone around it in elegant evening gowns and starched shirtfronts, batting witty conversation and gossip back and forth just like in a Merchant Ivory film.

"Will Alice be dining here?" I asked. I bit my tongue on the *the lucky cow* part.

Ingrid nodded. "Sheila's party's joining us. Fraser and Alice, Douglas and Kirstie, Sheila and Kenneth."

"Robert was saying you arrange dance cards over dinner." I hesitated, not sure how much to hint without landing Alice in it. "Alice will be next to some nice people, won't she? Experienced dancers?"

"I've put her between Robert and Douglas," said Ingrid. "And opposite Sheila's Kenneth. She should be fine. Don't you worry. We'll look after her!"

Oh, life was so unfair. While Alice was penciling in her dance card with Scotland's most eligible and polite men at her side, I'd be going home to a Marks and Spencer Dine In for a £10 dinner, all to myself. And I had three vintage ballgowns just sitting in my wardrobe!

"I'll nudge Douglas and Robert," said Sheila. "Men don't always appreciate how important a full dance card is, especially when you're not saving the last reel for your late husband!"

I paused with my spoon halfway to my mouth. "Does Robert know about Violet's story? I mean, does he understand there's a family reason why Duncan's so reluctant to sell? He seems to see it in very . . ." I struggled for the diplomatic word. ". . . black-and-white terms."

"Ah, it'll be different when he's got the right girl and wants to put his own roots down," said Sheila confidently. "He's always dashing about the place, being his own man. That's natural."

"But I thought he'd met the right girl." I looked between the pair of them. "Are he and Catriona not . . . ?"

"Catriona would be a marvelous wife for Robert, running this place," said Ingrid. "She's grown up with it. In fact, she's always giving me little hints about how to deal with drafts. And tradesmen. And Duncan."

"Just waiting for a certain someone to stop dashing about and put a ring on her finger," said Sheila. She tapped her nose. "Which might be why someone else's so keen to get this Reel of Luck nailed at the weekend? Hmm?"

"How long have they been . . . ?" I trailed off.

"I'm never really sure with Robert," said Ingrid doubtfully. "He doesn't really confide in me. But she's always been round and about, you know, with Janet. They've been going out for years."

"McAndrew men are pretty good at avoiding marriage," said Sheila, only half-joking. "They've had mothers firing fiancées at them from all sides since this ridiculous tradition began."

"Right." I nodded and smiled, but I didn't think it sounded very romantic for a twenty-first-century heir. Between Catriona's family money and her way with a draft excluder, she sounded more of a marriage of convenience than Violet and her millions had done.

"And call me a mother hen," Sheila went on with a conspiratorial wink, "but might there be another certain someone who's hoping for some extra luck at the ball?"

"Who? Oh! You mean, Alice?" I hadn't

even thought of that. Maybe that was why Fraser hadn't proposed at Christmas — he was waiting for the ball.

"It's such a romantic evening," sighed Ingrid.

"It is indeed. Even men get a bit giddy after a Hamilton House or two," said Sheila. "Kenneth proposed over breakfast. He said it was a combination of my pas de basques and the best bacon sandwich of his life that did it."

Why did the thought of Fraser down on one knee in front of Alice make me feel so . . . *curdled* inside? Was it because it was *my* private daydream, Fraser in formal evening dress, acting like a gentleman? My heart prickled, and I reached for another roll from the basket. At least I didn't have to worry about fitting into a ballgown.

"So, did Violet's sister marry a duke, or an earl?" I started, but Ingrid didn't answer. She raised her hand, and in the silence we heard footsteps approaching down the flagged corridor outside.

"Brace yourselves," she warned us. "Duncan threatened to bring some samples back with him."

There was a brisk knock on the door, but it wasn't Duncan's frizzy red head that popped round. It was Robert, bundled up against the cold in a big ski jacket and beanie hat.

"All right if I join you?" he asked, unwrapping the scarf from his throat. "I seem to be out of milk at the lodge."

"Really?" said Sheila. "Didn't I see a Tesco delivery van at —"

"Forgot to order milk," said Robert as Ingrid leaped to her feet.

"Of course it's all right!" She planted a kiss on his cheek. "I thought you were working this evening. Didn't you have a conference call?"

"Got canceled." He glanced over at me, and I smiled back, with just a flutter of unease at what he might have heard, had he walked across from the lodge a little faster. "Hello, Evie, Sheila. Hope I'm not interrupting anything?"

"I was just going to tell Evie about your great-grandmother and her magnificent war effort," said Sheila. "How she dug up the rose gardens and planted carrots."

"I'm sure she got someone to plant the carrots for her," said Robert.

I noticed the defensiveness return, but Sheila calmly ignored it.

"No, she did it herself, with my mother," said Sheila. "Most of the usual carrot planters were too busy being shot at in France."

"She sounds like a fascinating woman," I said. "Imagine if she had a diary!" My eyes widened. "Do you think she had a diary?"

"She probably didn't have time," said Robert.

"Did you get your white tie from the cleaners?" Ingrid put a bowl of soup down in front of him. It was twice the size of ours.

"I did. Janet was kind enough to bring it round this afternoon." Robert picked up his spoon and stirred. "Along with a selection of cummerbunds so I match whichever of the three dresses Catriona's choosing from. The kilt issue's still not dead. Despite my stamping on it."

He caught my eye, and I had to suppress a grin at the quick boggle of horror.

"Oh, do rethink the kilt, darling," said Ingrid. "Your father's wearing one."

"God help us all," said Robert. "Nice soup, Mum, did you make it?"

Ingrid launched into the story about the vegetable garden she'd started, and Robert made the right noises about her organic turnips. I let my gaze linger.

Robert wasn't handsome-handsome like Fraser — his nose was quite pointy, and he was lanky, not solid — but there was something about his wide, mobile mouth that made me feel odd inside. Like being in a car when the road's icy, and feeling the wheels move without you steering. Unbalanced. I barely knew him, yet I had the unsettling sense that he knew me.

And his eyes — dark and clever, watchful like an owl's. As I watched him sip his soup, I felt an echo of the butterflies that had filled my chest when he'd caught my hands outside and —

"Evie? More broth?" Sheila was looking at me, and I fumbled with my plate in an attempt to cover up my confusion.

Between Sheila's chattiness and Ingrid's eagerness to hear more about previous years' balls and gossip about the house, the evening passed quickly. Even though the subject matter must have wound him up, Robert let his mother and Sheila tell him off for working too hard and not understanding Scottish accents, only casting the occasional wry look in my direction.

We finished the soup and another bottle of wine, and were on coffee and shortbread, when Ingrid suddenly raised her hand and stopped Sheila mid-scandalous-tale of Pauline Pipe's tasty young gardener who'd run off with her Renoir.

"What was that?"

We froze, coffee halfway to our lips. The crashing came nearer. Then it too stopped, readjusted itself, and continued toward the kitchen.

"I think that's the master of Kettlesheer back from his home-brew evening," said Sheila.

She was right: the kitchen door was flung wide, and there was Duncan, his tartan trews accessorized with a chilled nose and a beatific smile. Something clanked in his Barbour jacket.

"Good evening, one and all!" he bellowed, wiping his nose with a hankie. He missed his nose, but made a good job of wiping his ear. "Do you know, do you, what a splendid vegetable the celeriac is? Can you believe that it makes a delicious aperefic — aperitif?"

He brought out a coffee jar full of straw-colored liquid and placed it on the table. "Kettlesheer Gold, I thought we could call it." He beamed at Robert. "We could sell it! Give the protifs — profits to the local church fund."

"I don't think you could give that away," said Robert. "Not without a license."

"Oh!" Duncan wagged his finger. "Don't be so nga — negative!"

"Listen, I don't mean to be rude, but I need to turn in," said Robert, pushing his chair away. "I've got an early start tomorrow."

"Me too," said Sheila. "Kenneth's got some ewes in the barn, waiting to lamb."

I looked between everyone. I'd happily have stayed the rest of the night hearing more tales of Violet's heroic war efforts, but not if I was going to be forced to drink whatever was in the jar.

Ingrid saved me. "Evie, you look worn-out. I expect you'll be ready for your bed. Would you like some cocoa to take up?"

"Coffee, was that? Marvelous!" Duncan settled himself in the chair next to mine. "Now, Jock swears by a nip of this before bed to ensure a good night's sleep. Evie?"

"I said I'd show Evie something . . . in the hall before I go," said Robert, pulling out my chair. "Night, Mum."

He was pretty strong, I thought, as the chair moved underneath me. That took some brawn.

As Sheila, Robert, and I made our way down the stone corridor, Duncan's sharp tenor began to echo from the kitchen, much like bagpipes but with words. We scuttled in silence until we were safely out of earshot upstairs.

"Now then, Robert, do you need a lift across to the lodge?" asked Sheila, rummag-

196

ing in her bag for her car keys.

"No, I'm fine walking, thanks."

She stopped and looked up at him. "It's bitter out there, you know?"

"Don't look surprised," he said. "Just because I live in London doesn't mean I've lost the use of my legs. It's, what, ten minutes' walk?"

"You'll have heard there's snow forecast for this weekend?" Sheila looked pointedly at both of us. "You want to make sure you've provisions — you in the lodge, and you in your car for driving back." She fastened her scarf round her head, Queen style. "Have you snow chains, Evie?"

I didn't know what they were. "Er . . . I've got a thermos flask?"

"Och!" She exchanged a glance with Robert. "I'll ask Fraser to check the car over for you before you leave. Right, now, I'll see you two later."

I hovered by the foot of the main stairs as Sheila fired up her Range Rover outside, watching Robert rewrapping himself in his many layers.

"So," I said, "what is it you wanted to show me?"

Robert looked blank, then said, "Oh, nothing. Just thought you needed an escape?"

197

I felt a flicker of disappointment. But had I really believed that I'd somehow turned around his attitude to Kettlesheer in one afternoon?

"Thanks," I said.

"That's us McAndrews. Chivalrous to damsels in distress."

He finally reached his hat, and I couldn't really linger much longer.

"Well, good night," I said, setting my foot onto the first step.

"Look at you," said Robert. "You've gone all Vivien Leigh."

"I have not."

"Fiddle-dee-dee! You have! Look at the way you're standing — like you're in a corset."

I frowned at him. "I am *not.*"

"Oh, hang on." Robert put a hand on my arm. "I have got something for you," he said, and reached inside his jacket. "I found it this afternoon in those boxes you moved."

He handed me a leatherbound notebook, with worn edges and a black ribbon holding it together.

"You mean you went back and had a look through the junk?" I said. I was laying the "surprise" on thick, but I *was* quite surprised. Pleased, too.

"Catriona gave me an earful about getting

the decorators into those rooms before the summer." Robert shook his head. "Well? Aren't you going to open it?"

I looked up from the notebook. His eyes were searching my face, waiting for a reaction. I didn't want to say that I was savoring it: feeling the outside first, instead of leaping in.

"Okay. . . ." I undid the grosgrain ribbon, and let the book fall open.

It was a list of furniture with dates and prices and names, noted in flowing handwriting that didn't seem too bothered about minor details like lines. Tissue-thin invoices were also folded carefully into the pages, with a couple of envelopes.

Violet's handwriting. Violet's voice floating through world wars and chauffeured motorcars and flappers and servants and Worth evening gowns, from the lodge to my hands!

"Is this the furniture from this house?" My heartbeat quickened. Provenance made all the difference, as well as giving me some clues about what to look for.

"Yup," said Robert. "I suppose it was for insurance or something like that. There are estimates in there and some dates and what have you. Someone probably advised her to take stock after Ranald died."

"This is incredibly helpful." I tore my eyes from the columns of mirrors and tables to look at him. "It's going to speed things up for me so much."

"Not too much, I hope." Robert pulled up the hood on his sweatshirt, ready to hike back through the moonlit woods. It framed his angular face, casting his cheekbones into shadow.

"I . . ." What did *that* mean?

"Don't want you to let your boss think it's too easy. See you tomorrow." He winked, then let himself out of the heavy front door.

I hung on to the banister for a long moment, drunk on the sheer unreality of what was happening to me. The castle, this unsettling man, this world full of glamor and wealth where the antiques were real household history, not parched items in a shop. It was like walking into my own imagination, and discovering I could touch it all.

Until Friday, I reminded myself. Just till Friday.

Then I totally indulged myself with an invisible crinoline as I swished my way up the stairs to my four-poster bed, eager to dive into that box of priceless scraps of paper.

TWELVE

The last thing I read before my eyes finally got too heavy was so romantic I couldn't sleep for longing to go back in time.

In the top of the box was a stack of postcards, tied with a purple ribbon. They were all of Regent's Park in London, and began in 1903.

One year since the luckiest accident of my life, the first read, in strong male handwriting. *I am the happiest man alive, and still the luckiest. Your R.*

The next was a different view — of the zoo, this time, a year on. *All God's creatures are happiest in pairs. Your R.*

Each of these cards was a different view of the same park, and were dated June 2 each year, obviously a reminder of the day Ranald and Violet met. My tired eyes filled with tears at the simple, dignified notes from a man obviously not given to gushing sentiment, but clearly head over heels in love with his wife.

One in particular made my chest ache with regret that I'd never meet either Ranald or Violet. It was a card depicting the boating lake and an old-fashioned bandstand. *It makes me so happy to see my precious girl in the most beautiful place in the world — darling V, never leave me or Kettlesheer, and we will never leave you.* It was dated 1924, not long before Ranald himself would leave both of them forever.

In the morning, the bedside tray was there again, this time, thank goodness, kipperless.

I drew the curtains so I could look out of the window as I ate my porridge. Clouds hung low over the rolling Cheviots in the distance, while nearer the house white sheep moved slowly against the scrubby green fields. The view was spectacular and soothing at the same time, and I could absolutely see how Violet, so used to Park Avenue hustle and glamour, had fallen under the heathery spell of Kettlesheer.

I'd happily have spent the morning poring over Violet's dance cards and wedding invitations, but I made myself take a closer look at the notebook Robert had brought me. It was *very* useful, if any of this furniture was still here: each piece was carefully listed, with approximate dates of manufacture and any documentation from the estate. It wasn't as fascinating as the glimpse into her real life provided by the jumbled bills and notes, but now at least I had the cheat codes to the house.

Which gave me more time to spend wandering around the house in search of Violet and Ranald.

With Violet's notebook, the house seemed to open up. By eleven o'clock I'd successfully located a decent Orpen oil painting of a stag and a couple of "important" chairs, and had decided that I might just take an hour off to show Robert the beautiful postcards his great-grandparents had exchanged. Maybe a real love story could succeed where plans for a turnip distillery had failed in getting him involved in his inheritance. If he saw how much Ranald had wanted Violet to keep the house, well . . .

But I'd barely got through the herb garden to the wooded path when my phone rang. It was Alice.

"Why haven't you called me back?" she demanded. "I've left *so* many messages!"

"The mobile reception is weird," I explained. "My phone only works if I'm standing facing due north or in the —"

But she wasn't pausing for breath. "How's it going? Good drive up with Fraser? How's the castle? Any amazing treasures? How's your room? Did they give you the four-poster bed with the ghost of the Indian manservant in it?"

"The *what?*"

"But seriously, you should have called me sooner," she said sternly. "There are things we need to discuss. Important things."

"Alice, I've barely had time to think!" I protested. "I've been working nonstop since I got here. Literally. They made me value the neighbors' heirlooms at a drinks party before I'd even got your coat off. And the house! Oh, my God, it's the most beautiful, atmospheric —"

"Yes, yes, priceless treasures, yadda yadda. Great. You're going to make Max a happy man, excellent." And with that, Alice dropped any pretense at being interested in the McAndrew antiquities and got to the point. "Rewind to Fraser. Did he say anything in the car on the way up?"

"Yes, he advised me on some excellent-value claret and explained why supermarket wine offers are a massive con."

It was childish, but I sort of wanted to keep my lovely drive up with Fraser to myself. The two-hour stint where he'd taken over the driving (safe but masterful, especially when passing) and I fed him Fox's Glacier Mints was the closest I'd ever get to being Mrs. Fraser Graham, and I didn't particularly want to share it.

"Did he say anything about the ball?" said Alice, ignoring my snarky tone. "And me?"

"Just that you dance like a wounded cow on a hot plate."

"He said that?"

"No, of course he didn't. He said you were going to be fine. And that he was looking forward to it."

"Did he go with you to this drinks party?"

"No. But I'll tell you who else was there — the son and heir. Although he's not exactly what I'd have pictured as a laird-in-waiting," I added. "Why didn't you mention him?"

"Who? Robert?"

"Yes, Robert."

"Because I didn't think he'd be there. He's usually in London." Did Alice sound a bit shifty? "Anyway, what do you mean, he's not very lairdlike? He's dashing enough."

"He isn't! Dashing is . . . horse-riding, and cricket whites, and blue eyes . . ." I realized I was describing Fraser. "Anyway, for your information, the first thing he did was to mistake me for you and give me a massive hug. Does he hug *all* his clients?" I asked. "Even Mum doesn't do that."

"He's an old friend of Fraser's," she responded. "And if you want to know the truth, that hug was probably an apology, because last time I saw Robert, he —"

She bit off what she was saying, and huffed. I was intrigued.

"The last time you saw Robert, *what?*"

"Oh, forget it," she said. "We don't use ParkIt anymore, so you don't have to talk up Simplify or anything. But tell me if he says anything about Mum or me," she added, sounding more like her usual self. "Write it down. And I want to know what his house is like. He wouldn't let us in at New Year — Catriona was in there, bullying builders. Have you met her, by the way? Bossy girl, black hair? Sounds like she's constantly eating a huge toffee?"

I thought that was a bit rich, coming from Alice, but I let it go. It might have been jealousy, over either Robert or the tidying-up gig. I wasn't sure who I'd put my money on in an Alice versus Catriona boss-off.

"I've met her, yes," I said. "And her mother."

"Hmm," said Alice darkly. "Has Fraser

206

said anything about Catriona? And Robert?"

"Alice, I'm here to value the furniture, not prepare some kind of dossier on everyone! Ask him yourself — you'll be seeing him again soon enough," I said. "When's your train? Thursday?"

"Yes, Fraser's meeting me at Berwick station. He wants to get some last-minute practicing in." I could hear the beginnings of her anxious tooth grind. "I've been trying one of those hypnosis CDs you put on before you go to bed."

"Don't you think you might be better off actually sleeping?"

"I don't have time to waste sleeping!" she yelled, so violently that I had to move the phone from my ear.

I lowered my voice — no idea why, since there were just the trimmed box hedges and some flowerbeds to hear me. "Actually, I heard something yesterday that might be helpful. You know the first reel you're doing? Make sure you start off with your back to the fireplace — Catriona's trying to make sure she ends up standing underneath some lucky artifact so Robert'll have to propose to her."

"She'll be so lucky," scoffed Alice. "Did they tell you how many people will be dancing? Hundreds. Imagine the National Lottery balls set to accordion music."

"Not in the *first* reel," I said. "The one with just the eight of you."

"The one with . . ." There was a pause. "What?"

"The Reel of Luck, the opening one. You and Fraser, the McAndrews, Sir Fergus and Lady Jockstrap or someone, and Catriona and Robert."

The line went silent, and I wondered if maybe Fraser had been keeping this minor detail to himself, so as not to terrify her too far in advance.

"But it'll be *fine*," I went on hurriedly. "I mean, isn't it better if you have loads of room? You won't be knocking into people. And it's right at the start of the evening, so you'll be sober. Well, soberish. You've got to have dinner here first with the McAndrews. And oh, my God, Ingrid's got the *actual* placement arranger from the *actual* table. . . ."

Alice still wasn't saying anything, and that was a very unnatural state of affairs.

"Anyway, no one will be looking at *you*," I said, desperately trying to fill the silence. "They'll be staring at Robert McAndrew. Why didn't you tell me the really romantic stuff about the ball? And the proposal tradition? And the heir? Like Cinderella but in tartan . . ."

A sudden image of Robert McAndrew sprang into my head, leaning against the hall fireplace, his white tie undone and his hair tousled —

— in a very London style. I frowned. Try as I might, I couldn't make Robert's face go historical; it stayed sharp-cheekboned and wry. Too modern.

Helpfully, imaginary Fraser appeared behind him, resplendent in muttonchop whiskers. Fraser through the ages was much easier to conjure. This one was actually in military uniform, not unlike Ranald's —

"You're doing that fading-out-of-reality thing," said Alice sharply. "Come back. Come back now."

"Sorry, sorry. I'm just . . ." I sighed happily. "Totally in love with this house. Apparently someone proposes every year, and they're allowed to get married in the Kettlesheer chapel. I still reckon there's a secret passage from the house. . . ."

I paused as imaginary Major Fraser Graham dropped to one knee in front of the miniature cannon in the hall. There was a slight blurring as to whether it was Alice or me clasping her hands above him, but whoever it was was wearing a flattering

Empire-line gown.

"In fact," I said, remembering what Sheila had hinted at over dinner, "you might think about getting your own proposal face ready, because —"

"Rewind to this reel. How long is it?" asked Alice in a strangely metallic tone.

"I don't know. But if no one botches it up, the whole ball is declared lucky and engagement rings pour forth. Didn't hear what happens if it is botched up. I assume you're not thrown from the turret or anything. Oh, and you're piped in by a piper! A real Scottish piper!"

"Jesus. Bagpipes."

"Shut up, it's like a connection to the spirit of the place, calling out to the wild warrior McAndrews of old. And —"

"Right, now you just sound mad," said Alice. "Evie, I'm going to have to go."

And then she was gone.

Weird, I thought, checking that we hadn't been cut off by Kettlesheer's everfluctuating reception. No, I still had three bars. Honestly. Alice took time management to the most outrageous lengths.

I dropped my phone back into my bag and checked again that the little parcel of postcards was still safely in there. I tingled at the prospect of showing Robert, and watching his reaction. I surprised myself by how tempting that felt, but what a strange squirm my stomach gave.

But Duncan intervened, as usual. As I glanced back, I saw him at the drawing room window, waving some kind of brass instrument at me, pointing and making *How much?* gestures.

I ought to get back and find this table. Might as well get a cover story for my trip to the lodge.

I knew Max would demand to know if I'd got into the dining room next time I spoke to him, so I decided to make that my priority. My quick flick through Violet's notebook of furniture had revealed pages on the dining room; there were bound to be some notes on the side tables, chairs, and so on.

I marched purposefully into the house, only temporarily distracted by the mahogany hall stand: now that I'd held faded notes sent through the local post, my eye was caught by the Kettlesheer postbox set in the side, with the times of day that letters would be collected and delivered by the servants. I paused, my hands on the lid, trying to feel the gossip and the intrigue, but all I sensed was emptiness.

I sighed, and dragged myself away.

As I approached the dining room, I could hear voices coming from within, but this time they were raised so high even I couldn't imagine them into spectral diners.

"No, not there! Douglas, that is an *antique,* not a hay bale, lad!"

I peered round the door.

Ingrid seemed even more birdlike than usual, standing next to the hulking Jacobean serving table, with Sheila in a navy-blue cashmere cardie on one side and Janet glaring at everyone on the other, clipboard clasped to her bony chest. They looked like the oldest, least compatible Scottish girl band in history.

Meanwhile, Fraser and an equally strapping blond lad — whom I took to be his brother, Dougie — were grappling with the dining table that dominated the room, manhandling the extension under Duncan's loud but vague directions.

"Pull it out, yes, that's it. . . . Your end now, Douglas, very good. . . . Ah, Evie, just the girl!"

He stepped away, causing Dougie to drop the table leaf with a strangled roar, and bustled over to the door, beaming all over his red face.

"What do you reckon?" He patted the table. "Nice bit of mahogany, isn't she?

212

Seats nearly sixty, with everyone budged up."

"I hope we won't be 'budging up' on Saturday," said Janet, in a tone that I think was meant to sound jovial but came out peevish. "I will be wearing a crushable fabric."

"You'll be fine, Janet," said Ingrid hastily. "Look, we've worked out the seating plan — here, you'll be near an end, plenty of space."

"Oh! Next to Innes Stout! How . . . lovely." Janet reached for the pencil hanging round her neck. "I might have to have a look at that. . . ."

"Ingrid wanted to check we've got everything shipshape for the grand dinner," Duncan went on as I took in the sideboards crammed with crystal goblets of various sizes and enough crockery to accommodate the whole Border Regiment and friends. Enough for a royal party. "And I'm following Janet's list of items to be moved out of the way. Don't worry, I won't be asking you to step in — Fraser and Douglas have kindly volunteered."

"Have *been* volunteered," muttered Dougie.

"I only came round to check about the wine for dinner," said Fraser cheerfully. "If

213

I'd known we'd be shifting furniture, I probably wouldn't have worn my suit."

I took a moment to appreciate the fact that Fraser was indeed wearing a smart gray suit — he'd taken off his jacket and loosened his tie but still looked like the ideal city wine merchant, one who'd tell you all about the Chablis, and then carry it inside for you. Dougie closely resembled Fraser in countryside mode — square jaw, broad shoulders, thick blond hair — but in jeans and a Rennick Young Farmers rugby shirt, and with more of an attitude. More what I'd had in mind for Robert, actually. More . . . heir-like.

Whereas Fraser had tamed his hair for work, Dougie's fell into his eyes, and when he pushed it aside I noticed he had a black eye.

Rugby? Riding? A fight? I mentally put Dougie in a big white poet's shirt and breeches, and found it worked surprisingly well.

"Would you like to cast your expert eye over it?" Duncan suggested.

For a second I thought he wanted me to inspect Dougie's injury, then realized he was talking about the table.

I felt all eyes turn to me, waiting for the slick routine Max would have wheeled out

— Fraser especially seemed keen to hear me hold forth. I swallowed. The table was, without question, something special. The sheer scale of it was beyond anything I'd ever seen before, but I couldn't say much until I'd had a proper look. And then checked in Violet's notebook.

"I need to get underneath and, you know . . . Maybe I should come back later?" I looked over at Ingrid, Sheila, and Janet.

"No, we're done," said Ingrid, then undermined herself immediately by adding, "We *are* done, aren't we, Janet?"

Janet glanced at her clipboard. "Yes, it looks as though we'll manage for glassware. So long as Mhairi follows my instructions for the cleaning this time."

"I didn't realize you were such an expert on housework, Janet," said Sheila pleasantly.

"I'm an expert on instructing staff, Mrs. Graham." Janet ticked off several things, peered at a candelabra, and scribbled a note. It looked very much like the "important typing" I did when Max walked in on me playing solitaire on the office computer.

I caught Fraser's eye, and he made a funny mock-alarmed face.

"Chaps, if you wouldn't mind applying your biceps to a few items in the hall?" inquired Duncan, sweeping his hand toward

215

the door. "After your good self, Mrs. McAndrew?"

Ingrid flashed me a quick smile, then stepped out. There was some almost imperceptible jostling between Sheila and Janet about who should be next through the door, and I was left alone in the gloomy dining room.

Well, not quite alone. Various strapping McAndrews smoldered down at me from above the paneling. It was an imposing room even without the long table and the carved marble fireplace. Golden sconces punctuated the bits of the wall that weren't decorated with ancestral portraits, and the view from the long windows revealed the rolling greenery of the parkland around the house. I picked up a wineglass and marveled at the weight in my hand. My eyelids drooped as I reached for the memories of candlelit dinners and —

A clock struck the half hour, as if someone were impatient to get me focused on the table.

I slid over to the door and closed it, then sank onto the nearest chair and turned the notebook's sprawling pages, replacing the letters and receipts, until I found an entry for the dining table. And then my jaw dropped.

This wasn't just a good dining table. This was . . . something else entirely. . . .

THIRTEEN

I looked again at Violet's handwritten entry, to be sure I'd got it right.

Dining table, Thos Chippendale, circa 1760, see original letter of commission from Kirkland McAndrew, enc.

I looked at the table, then looked at the notebook again. My heart gave an unhealthy lurch in my chest.

It couldn't be. Surely?

Practically no undiscovered furniture made by Thomas Chippendale himself still existed — if this provenance was accurate and not some family hearsay, it was worth a *fortune.* Even if it had been made by a craftsman, based on a design from Chippendale's book of patterns, it was still worth a lot of money.

But if it was original, Max would hyperventilate. Commission would run into the tens of thousands. He'd actually fainted over Geraldine Hardwick's Fabergé egg, and I didn't think that was entirely for her benefit.

I spread my fingers over the smooth surface, letting the texture of the wood vibrate under my touch. I loved dining tables: they absorbed the happiest memories. How many Christmases, marriages, homecomings from battle and from the Empire, had been celebrated here?

The cobwebby fireplace faded from view as I pictured a dinner-jacketed Ranald at the head of his table, soft candlelight glowing in the polished wood as he stole a glance at his energetic young wife. Violet at the opposite end, her white throat blazing with Tiffany diamonds, drawing out a shy neighbor's conversation about the day's fishing on the —

My daydream broke with an imaginary needle-off-the-record scratch. Something wasn't right. I couldn't *feel* anything in the table: all the warmth was in my head.

This table, which must have had hundreds of hands touch it since it was delivered, was completely still. It *looked* right: the chair held me in a way that was comfortable but straight-backed, and the legs and inlay of the table seemed authentic. But I couldn't *feel* anything.

Maybe it was just out of my league. I'd

never seen anything as valuable as this before.

I slid off the chair and crouched underneath, trying to make out what I could of the underside, where any bodging would be more obvious. That was another of Max's dubious tips: "Get on your knees and have a look at the bottom."

The light in the room wasn't good, but I noted the lighter wood, the neat joinery, the right marks. All present and correct. The wood was old. The shapes were right. And yet . . .

Max would know, I thought, taking photos as best I could. He was pretty good at telling repro from the real thing. He'd seen everything in his time, and in places you wouldn't expect. But I wanted him to say it was the precious real thing. I wanted this to be Duncan's lifeline to keeping Violet's home in the family.

"Please," I muttered, praying to the auction gods. "I won't buy another photo frame for a year if you can just make this real."

"Are you okay under there? Dropped a contact lens?" asked a solicitous voice.

I jumped and banged my head, then slumped to one side in my haste to get out, banging my head again against the gateleg holding up one of the substantial extenders.

"Whoa, careful!"

"Ow!" I put a tentative hand to my forehead. A bump was already forming above my right eye. Lovely. I backed out, knowing I looked like a double-decker bus reversing out of a garage.

When I stood up and saw it was Fraser who'd witnessed my undignified exit, the blood rushed to my face. Why could he never happen upon me doing something . . . elegant? Or dynamic? There were plenty of times he could have come across me staring thoughtfully out of a window.

"Just wondered if you fancied some lunch?" he asked. "Duncan's run out of storage space upstairs. Trouble is, they move everything up there each year and never get round to moving most of it back down again. It's silting up."

"Not *silting*," I said, struggling for the right word. "Just . . ."

"Well, now, there's another suit of armor and two fire screens on top. Sounds like you've been busy," said Fraser. "Any exciting finds?"

Guiltily I swept the notebook into my bag with what I hoped was a devil-may-care yet professional swagger. "Lots."

That would have been quite elegant if the bag hadn't then spilled three pens, my

221

change purse, a timetable, and my keys out of the side, but at least it distracted from my lump.

"Don't suppose you've heard from Alice, have you?" he asked casually as we strolled down the paneled hall toward the kitchens.

"I spoke to her this morning," I said. "Was she supposed to call you?"

"Oh no. No. Well, yes, actually. She usually calls me a couple of times a day, just to check that I'm okay." He paused. "That I've had a protein shake. That I've read whatever it is we're supposed to be reading for our book club. That I'm not sick. You know what she's like."

I did. Dad was the same. If I didn't call him every two days, he assumed I was being eaten by next-door's cats. He wasn't a control freak, but he did have insurance for kidnappings and terrorist attacks.

"And she hasn't called?"

He shook his head, like a large dog that's been given the wrong food. Not exactly unhappy, just . . . perplexed. I was perplexed too. Why would she call me and not Fraser?

"Well, the reception here is awful," I suggested. "I can't get a signal in the house. Have you been here long?"

"About half an hour? She hasn't even texted. Not that I mind," he added quickly.

222

"It's just a bit out of character. I thought something might have happened to her."

We shared a knowing look. Only a very long tunnel or death could come between Alice and her micromanaging phone habit.

"Well, I'm just heading down to Robert's house to send some e-mails," I said. "I'll give her a call and tell her to ring you. She's probably in a shop, narrowing down her outfit options. Have you told her the colors of your kilt?"

"Red and green," he said with a hearty grin. "Plus the full frilly shirt and velvet jacket. As my dad always told us, it takes a real man to wear a skirt and knee-high white socks."

I glanced down. Fraser had good, sturdy legs, the sort usually seen on portraits of Henry VIII or prewar rugby players. Magnificent for gallantry in any period.

"I think you could carry it off," I squeaked.

"And, of course, the obligatory tartan undies underneath! Or not!"

I indulged in a miniswoon; then something occurred to me. "Um, Fraser? Alice and Robert . . . they do get on, don't they?"

Fraser's guileless face beamed. "Oh, absolutely! Two of a kind, those two! Both a bit opinionated, and I must admit sparks occasionally fly over dinner, but I knew when I met Alice at Rob's thirtieth that if he liked her, she was a good sort."

"Childhood friends, eh?"

He nodded. "We had some good summers up here. Rob used to love this place. Bit sad it's not quite the draw it once was for him. But that's growing up, I guess."

"I guess," I said. And I wasn't sure why I felt so sad.

After more Scotch broth in the kitchen, I felt justified in heading down to Robert's, armed with my exciting table news for Max and my secret mission for Violet.

It had turned even chillier, and I swung my arms as I strode down the crackling path, trying to imprint it all on my brain — the crisp, green-smelling air and the masses of skittering rabbits shooting off into the tangled undergrowth as I clomped past.

My mind played idly with a new vision of myself in tweed and a big hat, strolling with Fraser along the hillside, with a couple of spaniels —

No, Labradors. One chocolate, one yellow, trotting obediently by our sides as we —

No, a spaniel *and* a Labrador.

I was still trying to decide on the dogs,

and contemplating a horse, when I reached Robert's house and knocked almost without thinking on the door.

"Hello?"

My head spun round. It wasn't Robert at the door, it was Catriona.

She was dressed in a sheepskin vest and snug jeans, her black hair in a tight plait over one shoulder. Countryside Angelina Jolie, give or take some children. She smiled, but in that polite *Don't come in* way that people use to freeze out political canvassers.

"Um, hello," I stammered. "Robert said I could send some e-mails? There's no broadband up at the house?"

Her expression changed — slightly. "Oh, I know, it's a nightmare. Like living in the Dark Ages! Robert's not here, though. He's in Berwick all day and I'm using his computer." She pulled a face. "Papers all over the table. Can it . . . wait?"

"It's about the house," I said, feeling an unexpected obstinacy dig in. "Furniture from the house. It is quite urgent."

"Oh, well, in that case I suppose you'd better come in." She stood aside to let me through.

I went ahead of her into the kitchen. Robert's table was indeed covered in very neat piles of paper, annotated with different-

225

colored Post-its, as well as several glossy catalogues and a tape measure.

"I'm planning the new kitchen for Kettlesheer," she explained before I could even ask. "It's simply impossible to run proper events like the ball there — it should all be in a museum! The caterers I've got in for the ball were horrified when they saw what they had to work with, so I just said to Robert, I know it's jumping the gun a *little,* but let me get some builders in, and get things moving in time for next year."

"Next year?"

"Well, the next ball. I'm taking over from Mummy. And . . ." She bit her lip coyly. "Well, fingers crossed on something else too!"

"What are you planning to do?" I asked, thinking of Ingrid's cozy basement kitchen with its handy nooks and crannies and its painted china cupboards. And its big teapots, and old range, and tables that I could see plump cooks making plum pudding at.

Catriona widened her eyes. "Rip it all out! Start again. It's the only way. It's like I said to Robert when I did this place, you've got to rip everything out, deep-clean, salt-blast, and then go for modern design." She waved a hand around the kitchen. "This was a trial run, and I think it worked pretty well, don't you?"

That was my cue to nod. I managed a small nod. I felt like running over to her plans and ripping *them* up.

"I mean, this place was worse," Catriona went on. "It took my guys days just to empty it. You know those blancmange molds you get in junk shops? The ones with those lumps that get full of dust?"

"Oh, yes! I've got seven of those!" I said. "Mostly rabbits, but some pretty heart-shaped Edwardian ones that —"

Catriona looked me in the eye. "Have you ever tried to clean one?"

"I've never actually *used* them," I confessed. "But those must have come from Violet's own cook, don't you think? Maybe she brought them all the way from America! Can you imagine the puddings they must have had at the —"

"They all went, all thirty-three of them," she said, making a spit-spot Mary Poppins gesture with her hands. "I'm going through this place room by room when I've got time off from work."

"Are you?" Violet's stuff! Was that going to get spit-spotted too? "You must be very busy," I angled, trying to work out how long I had to convince Robert to go through those rooms. "With the ball. And work."

"I am rushed off my feet," she said happily. "Cup of tea? Herbal okay?"

I nodded. What I really wanted was a coffee, but I didn't think that was on offer.

"I'm scaling back, though. I want to concentrate my energy and expertise here. There's an awful lot to take on with Kettlesheer. It's a big house, but it's got a lot of potential."

"It's a *magical* place," I agreed. "You can feel so much in all the rooms!"

"Yes, *damp!*" Catriona had an irritating laugh. "And spiders and old people! But it's got good proportions. It can support bold interior-design choices. I'm seeing something very much like the lodge, but on a grander scale. Accent walls. Modern art."

I didn't know what to say that wouldn't come out sounding as if it had a horrified question mark at the end of it, so I just smiled and nodded.

The kettle boiled, and she passed me a cup of hot water with a foul-smelling bag in it.

"You know, I've remodeled loads of houses, but Kettlesheer's different. I can plan it as a professional, but with my own wow factor in mind." Catriona pursed her lips confidentially over her own mug. "I've even planned where the nursery will go! Right next to my office and the home gym."

It was hard to look at Catriona in quite the same way after what Ingrid and Sheila had said yesterday about how suitable she was. Suitable for Kettlesheer, not Robert. But were the two one and the same for her? They weren't for *him*.

"Is that . . . an imminent decoration project?" I asked hesitantly.

"God, no!" Again the irritating laugh. "I'm thinking in a year to eighteen months, aiming for a September birth. Give me time to finish the decoration. But don't tell Rob that," she added, with a girls-together wink. "Best if men don't know the gory details, eh?"

I swallowed. That wasn't jumping the gun. That was bringing your own gun and then getting the other person to jump it.

I felt a sudden waft of sadness in the room, like a draft snaking in under the pantry door. It was cold, and sad, and not unpleasant. Sort of . . . foresty.

"Can I plug in my laptop?" I asked, suddenly not wanting to hear any more. "I need to catch my boss before lunch."

"Sure." Catriona put down her mug and started to move some papers — for three nanoseconds, before she gave a little huff of faux-apology. "Is it very bad of me to ask if you wouldn't mind working over on the counter, there? It's just that all this is in order. . . ."

I looked at the tiny area of expensive marble she was proposing, between the espresso machine and a state-of-the-art toaster that looked more like a missile launcher.

"No problem," I said. I didn't fancy hanging around anyway.

FOURTEEN

I woke before my alarm in the morning, aware that there was something odd about the bedroom. Well, odder than a stuffed Labrador.

I pushed the bed hanging aside with a sleepy hand, and my eyes adjusted to the layers of darkness beyond my cocoon. A sliver of silver light was cutting into the room. It was making Lord Bertold's glass eyes sparkle in a demonic fashion and giving everything else an unearthly glow.

I hauled myself out of bed and went over to the window, pulling the curtain right back.

The view was so magical I forgot to breathe. A gleaming blanket of snow had fallen across the gardens like a fat layer of royal icing on a Christmas cake. It rolled out over the stone edges of the terrace, topping each peak with a white hat of frost, and went on as far as the eye could see, untouched and pristine and dazzling.

I'd never seen anything so glorious in my life. A bird had hopped along the window-sill, leaving crisp star-shaped prints behind. It *never* snowed in London like this — even a heavy snow was grimy and pigeon-pocked before I ever got my boots on.

I dressed quickly now that I was awake, and was downstairs in the kitchen before I even noticed it was just gone seven o'clock.

I wasn't expecting to find anyone, but Mhairi was already there, stirring a pan of porridge and boiling a kettle on the Aga while the local radio station babbled in the background. Roads were closed, schools were closed, rescue teams were being scrambled, but she carried on stirring impassively. I had no idea how she'd got there. It wouldn't have surprised me if she slept in a cupboard.

"Morning, Mhairi!" I said cheerily. "Isn't it *gorgeous?*"

The kitchen was cozy and smelled of toast and the linen drying on an ancient rack suspended above the Aga. Messy and friendly, like a kitchen should be. How had I thought it was chilly on my first night? Maybe I'd acclimatized.

"Aye, snow," she replied, without taking her eyes off the pan. "Not good if you're driving. The roads'll be shut round Rennick. Will you have tea?"

"Um, yes," I said. I hadn't thought about the roads. Would it be gone in time for the ball? "Thank you."

"It's in the pot." She nodded at the huge brown pot on the table.

I poured myself a cup and looked round at the dark wood dresser running nearly the length of one wall, filled with blue everyday china. I loved the rows of spoon-dimpled brass pans hanging from the rafters, the hooks for hams and herbs. It was a proper old kitchen, down to the stone flags worn from generations of cooks' feet. It made me almost panicky to imagine Catriona ripping it out and replacing everything with marble work surfaces shipped in from Wandsworth.

I stared at Mhairi's impassive but not unfriendly back, and wondered if she was on the list of fittings to be removed. Even on our short acquaintance, I reckoned she'd be harder for Catriona's men to chuck out than the ancient old range, and twice as disastrous a loss. The last real remaining connection to Violet's once-bustling staff of fifty.

Time to get down to the lodge with my secret weapons of mass conservation, I thought. There was no time to lose.

■ ■ ■ ■

Robert looked the type to be at his desk before most people were awake, I thought as I strode through the unbroken snow on the drive in a pair of Ingrid's spare wellies. I could see him running before work. Or swimming — he had the single-minded look of a morning swimmer — long arms, muscled shoulders, solitary lengths down a deserted pool —

Whoa.

I checked myself. This was turning into a crush, and I didn't want that. I was prone to instant crushes — actors, films, Art Deco powder compacts — and developing one on Robert was a *terrible* idea.

My crush on Fraser was bad enough, but there was something about Robert that wasn't quite so . . . comfortable. He was impossible to pop into my ready-made fantasy sequences — too spiky and unreadable. And he had a girlfriend, and responsibilities, and not one single framed family photograph in his sitting room or interesting curio in his loo.

Apart from that old telephone like yours.

Apart from the old telephone, I conceded. But that was probably only there until he got a new one.

That wasn't Robert, that was the house. *It's the* house *you have a crush on,* I reminded myself. But what was the harm in that, just for a day or two more? I'd be back in the wrong end of the King's Road with Max's leather jacket for company soon enough.

I turned my attention instead to the snow crunching beneath my boots as I reached the little gate that led down through the woods toward the lodge. It was quite hard to see where the track went, the snow was so thick. Someone had already been out, walking a dog — a dog that had been having a right old time of it, by the scampering tracks it had left up and down the bank. Rabbits? Or foxes? Or badgers?

I made a note to check out the stuffed-animal section up at the big house for clues.

Just as the cold began to seep through my two pairs of socks, I saw Robert's house ahead of me, ridiculously picturesque beneath a shawl of snow. It was a shame that smoke wasn't trickling out of that chimney pot, but other than that, it couldn't have looked more fairy-tale if it had been made out of gingerbread.

Actually, now I was here, smoke would

have been good. It would have showed he was up.

I shifted my laptop bag onto my other shoulder. A little voice in my head started nagging that I should have phoned ahead first, to check if it was convenient. What if Catriona was here?

I stopped at the gate and looked down. My footprints were leading up the path — if I turned round and went back now, he'd get a hell of a shock when he opened his front door and wondered what had visited him in the night.

Something from the past. Someone coming home. . . .

Stop being so ridiculous, I told myself, and knocked.

And waited.

Ugh. I blanched as a vision of Catriona opening the door in a towel struck me. What if I was interrupting something?

I struggled with some butterflies, then fixed a smile on my face as the lock clicked on the other side.

"Sorry, is this a bad time?" I blurted out while the door was still being opened.

"It depends what you're here for." Robert ruffled his damp hair. He was wearing a couple of long-sleeved T-shirts, one over the other, and an old pair of battered jeans. His feet were in thick walking socks, and a recently showered smell hung around him. I hadn't realized Robert wore contact lenses, but he was sporting a pair of horn-rimmed glasses that made him look like a rather hot young professor. "Reeling practice? Tax return?"

"E-mail. I know it's early but I'm waiting for my boss to get back to me. And I want to show you something." I paused. I couldn't hear Catriona, but that didn't mean she wasn't there; I didn't want a repeat of yesterday. My conversation bank was down to "the weather" and "Catriona." "I could come back later —"

"Don't be daft, I've been up for ages." He opened the door farther to let me in and I pulled off my snowy boots. "Have you had any breakfast?"

"Yes, the full Scottish. Apart from the haggis. And the black pudding."

I followed him through to the kitchen, where a laptop sat on the kitchen table, surrounded by piles of paper.

"Oh, and the kippers," I added, taking in the half-drunk mug of black coffee, the rack of toast, and the neatly scraped butter next to it.

"So just porridge, then?" said Robert.

"Yup. Could do with some toast, to be

honest."

He shoved some papers out of the way so I could put my bag down, and lifted the cafetière to pour me some coffee. "Coffee okay? You're not one of these decaf wheatgrass girls?"

"Does it look like it?"

He paused, scrutinizing me. "I don't know. Does it?"

"My normal breakfast is two double espressos," I said. "I've got a set of really gorgeous vintage coffee cups from the George V hotel in Paris. For five minutes, I'm Coco Chanel. And then it all goes downhill, but you know, for five minutes . . ."

"Which came first?" he asked, and put the mug down in front of me. "The coffee for breakfast? Or the cups?" He paused. "Or the wanting to be Coco Chanel?"

I opened my mouth to say the coffee, then realized that until I'd bought the coffee cups at auction, I'd had tea, like Max. "Coco Chanel," I confessed. "But the caffeine helps me deal with my boss. His natural state is artificially stimulated. I keep suggesting a detox, but I'm scared he'd just collapse in a pile of dust."

"I'm just the same," he said, refilling his own mug. "Catriona keeps leaving green tea here for me, says caffeine isn't good for either of us."

I got an abrupt, unwelcome flashback to her baby plans. I wondered if he knew.

"But I don't have time for any other vices," he added with a conspiratorial wink. "So the coffee stays."

"Good," I said. "Make a stand for caffeination."

We looked at each other for a moment, and I felt that unsettling familiarity again. It was freaky. I'd barely met him, yet I felt like we'd known each other before. Maybe it was something to do with me looking like Alice, I thought, fiddling with my mug.

"How did you get on with that notebook?" he asked. "Was it helpful?"

"Oh, er, yes. Really interesting. But look what I found in that box I took away." I reached into my laptop bag and brought out a daybook from 1923.

My plan was to start with the super-practical factual side of Kettlesheer life and then, once he was softened up, to hit him with the poetry of Ranald's love notes.

"It's a daybook," I explained, pushing the leatherbound diary across the pine table. "It was Violet's — look, it's got all her notes to give to the housekeeper about flowers and linen, and menus, and details of house parties and which bedrooms to use for which guests." I watched anxiously as Robert took it and began leafing through. "Doesn't it make the house come alive when you see what used to go on in those rooms?"

"Did you know you're sleeping in Ranald's bedroom?" he asked.

"What?" I felt my heart bang in my chest. "Really? Why didn't someone tell me?"

He looked up, his eyes amused. "Maybe they didn't know. I didn't, I just noticed in here. That adjoining bathroom, you've probably seen it has two doors? One each side. The other would go through to Violet's suite."

"Oh, wow," I breathed, suddenly seeing my room in a whole new light. No wonder I felt a presence in there — Ranald and Violet must be watching me unpack their story, reading their notes, in his bed, of all places. . . .

I felt myself blush. They didn't seem the separate-bedroom type to me. Even if it was the convention.

"Don't go all misty-eyed on me," said Robert sternly. "He didn't die in there or anything. And it's been a guest bedroom for years. Plenty of time for the atmosphere to wear off."

I blinked and tried to look businesslike. "I

thought maybe if you decided to open the house to the public, you could use this sort of thing as the basis for an exhibition of country-house life. Violet has *beautiful* hand-writing."

"And a naughty sense of humor. Did you see what she had to say about the Lord Lieutenant and his lady wife?" Robert passed me the book with an outraged expression.

Lord Lieut (snorer)
Lady Lieut (not safe after sherry)
Mick McLennan (park near Lady L)

"Good Lord!" he added. "Who knew you were on the money with your secret-panel tapping? There must be hidden tunnels from bedroom to bedroom all over the house!"

"I'll ignore that," I said, then couldn't resist looking up to see if he might actually be serious.

"I'm joking," he said, deadpan.

But he'd slowed down his flicking to take in each page properly, so I pressed on. "Have you seen how she has all her children's birthdays marked? With each one's favorite meal — blancmanges, and shepherd's pie . . . And her wedding anniversary,

241

and the dates they went to stay with friends for balls in London and shooting in the Highlands . . ." I leaned forward to show him, and our foreheads almost touched over the table.

Robert must have noticed, but he didn't move away. "She had a fair bit to do, I'll give her that," he said. "Have you seen how much coal she had to order for all the rooms? No wonder they had some fireplaces blocked up."

I could feel his breath on my face as he whistled in awe. *Now is the time,* said a voice in my head. *Show him the postcards.*

But I couldn't move away.

Oi! Now, insisted the voice, and reluctantly I leaned back to reach in my bag again.

"And I found these," I said, putting the postcards next to the daybook. Robert was still reading. "Look!" I insisted. "This is more romantic."

"I'm adding up how many grouse they shot," he murmured; finally, when I waved the postcards under his nose, he looked up.

"Did anyone tell you the story of how they met?" I asked.

"*Yes.* In London. During her . . . season?"

"And?"

"There's more?"

I told him as he undid the ribbon and

began to read the backs of the cards. I watched him, hawklike, for signs of tears along his long lashes; but, disappointingly, he was made of sterner stuff than me. Just as he was turning over the fourth postcard, my phone started to ring.

I wanted to ignore it, but as soon as it went to voice mail, it rang again.

Better answer; it could be Max about the table, I thought.

It was Alice. "Hi, Evie, how are you?" she asked. "How are you getting on?"

Alice never usually bothered to start off a conversation that way. "I'm fine," I said, then added, "Alice," for Robert's benefit.

He raised his eyebrows above the tortoiseshell rims of his glasses. Geeky but sexy. I looked away quickly.

"Evie, are you on your own?" Alice went on. "I need to talk to you about something rather delicate."

"I'm at Robert's," I said. "But I don't have to repeat everything you say. I can do yes-and-no answers."

"Tell Alice I'm not listening in," said Robert. "And tell her I hope she's done what I told her and been to see that dancing teacher. I don't want her letting my mate down on the dance floor."

"He says he's not listening —" I realized

how patently untrue this was, and glared at him. He raised his hands in pretend innocence.

"Tell Robert to get his nose out." Alice didn't sound amused. "Can you go outside." It wasn't a question.

"Okay." I pointed at the phone and mouthed, *Excuse me.*

Robert made a *Go for it* gesture and turned back to the postcards.

"How far outside would you like me to go?" I asked, stepping quickly down the hall toward the front door. "How bad is this news?"

"Two-door bad."

That was a family code: two doors between our mother's eagle ears and the phone.

"Right, I'm outside," I said. "Well, not outside. I'm in the porch. I don't want to go outside because it's bloody freezing up here —"

"I don't have time for a weather forecast," said Alice. "Listen, I'm not coming."

"What?" It came out too loud. "What?" I repeated, with less volume but more emphasis.

"I'm not coming to the ball."

That's what I'd thought she'd said. It didn't, however, make any sense.

FIFTEEN

"What do you mean, you're not coming?" I demanded. I stared out of the frosty glass around the door. All I could see was white. "Have you had an accident?"

"I'm really, *really* sorry," said Alice. "But I can't do it. I've left a message on Fraser's voice mail apologizing, so don't try to talk me out of it. It's done. I'm not coming."

"I don't understand. You can't come, or you don't *want* to come?" I racked my brains for a reason. "Is it work? Are you ill? What's the problem? Is it Fraser? He seems fine. He'll forgive you for being rubbish in the reel!"

"No, it's not that." Alice went silent for several seconds. "I can't say. Trust me."

"If you don't say, then how do I know whether to worry about you or not?" I demanded.

"There's nothing for you to worry about,"

she said. "But I do need you to do me a favor."

"And what's that? Oh, *God,*" I said, suddenly realizing. "I'm stuck here with Duncan and Ingrid and Fraser and Sheila all going ballistic because you've ruined their seating plans, their dancing plans, everything! What the hell am I going to say to them?"

"Exactly — that's the favor. You have to go in my place," said Alice, as if this were totally reasonable. "You can't just flake out like you can with cocktail parties. They *need* eight people. And it's too late to invite someone else now — everyone'll be busy. It's Valentine's weekend. You're the only person who'll be free."

"But I *can't* just go in your place," I wailed. "I don't know how to do the dances! And correct me if I'm wrong, but that does seem to be *quite* an important element of the evening."

"Learn," said Alice. "You've got enough time."

I spun round in disbelief, nearly dislodging the ski jackets hanging on the porch wall. "Four days? Get lost! I haven't got the first clue about Scottish reeling!" I felt a tug and felt the long hood of my cardigan catch on a peg. I had to stop to disentangle myself

246

before I broke the coat hooks, on top of everything else.

"Look, they *can* find someone," I went on. "Catriona's sister's name came up — Laura, is it? I wasn't going to mention it, but Janet Learmont was very keen to sub her for you in this precious Reel of Luck."

"No! I don't want Laura Learmont moving in on Fraser! I know what —" snapped Alice, then softened her tone, a fraction too late. "No, it would be better if you go. Don't you want to dance with Fraser?" she added artfully.

Of *course* I did. How could I not? "Well, yes," I said.

"Go on. He's brilliant — you just have to let him put you in the right place. *And* you'll get to meet some of his single friends. Like his brother — have you met Dougie yet? You can broaden your horizons, step out of your comfort zone. . . ."

Oh, that was too much. I almost yelped at the cheek of it.

"Alice, I'm already so far out of my *comfort zone* that I'm virtually in orbit around it! Was this part of your plan?" I demanded. "Are you and Mum and Max in this together?"

"Of course not." Alice had recovered the upper hand. "It's a wonderful night, and

247

you'll love it once you get into it. It's not hard, and you always were quicker at picking things up than me."

"No, I *wasn't.*"

"You were." She sounded almost wistful. "Tap dancing. You got the shuffly thing way before I did."

"After *three years,* Alice! Three years and a hell of a lot of Gene Kelly DVDs!"

"Please. Do it for me. I'll owe you one."

I wavered. Historical Fraser swam back into my head. He was wearing a top hat.

"It'll be so romantic," she went on. "Ballgowns and dance cards — everything you're always banging on about wanting in your life."

I wavered harder. And Alice hadn't even seen what I'd seen. Kettlesheer's woodsmoky, chilly ghosts were creeping into me, and the prospect of the ballroom lit up with lamps and filled with rustling ballgowns was hopelessly alluring. And — I only let the thought flicker around the edges of my mind — I rather wondered what Robert would look like in evening dress. I already knew how Mr. Darcy–tastic Fraser would look. And I'd be the one on his arm. Possibly even in his arms.

It was my absolute dream, actually happening? So what was holding me back?

Fear. Fear of being the one part of the dream that didn't match up.

"Go on," Alice urged. "It could be fabulous, and if it's not, so what? You'll never see these people again."

"Okay," I said. "For you. I'll do it."

"Oh, thank God," breathed Alice.

"But on one condition," I went on. "You've got to tell me why you're bailing out. Is it this first reel? Because if it is, you shouldn't be lecturing *me* about stepping out of my comfort zone."

"No," said Alice, "it's not that."

"Is it Robert?" Whether there'd been a falling-out or a getting-off, I could detect something there. I just couldn't work out what.

"No." She sounded firm.

"And it's definitely not Fraser?"

"No, it's . . . I . . ." She stopped. "I can't put it into words properly. I'll tell you after. But it's a really good reason, and if you love me, don't ask."

"Alice! You know how much it winds you up when Mum does this! Sometimes it's *good* to talk about things," I protested. "Just because we're not allowed to talk about the time Dad went to Manchester doesn't mean it didn't happen."

That was akin to mentioning Lord Voldemort. Nothing ever happened in our family — apart from the time our happily married parents mysteriously split up when I was twelve. Dad went to Manchester for six months, allegedly to oversee some merger, and we were supposed to not talk about Mum dyeing her hair blond and taking up Pilates. He came back, she reverted to a brunette pixie cut, we were supposedly none the wiser. Except from then on, any family holiday was subjected to forensic examination by both of us.

We were both silent. It was one of those moments when I wished Alice didn't slam down her wall of "We're not going to talk about that," and that I didn't just blurt out the first thing that came into my head. It was only because our family life was so relentlessly *dull* that we got away with it as much as we did.

"Shall we focus on the task at hand?" inquired Alice. As usual, she immediately covered the trails of awkwardness with a list of instructions. "I'll get my dress couriered up to you — will you stay at Kettlesheer or move down to the Grahams'? I'm sure it'll be fine with Sheila if you want to move down there — she's expecting me."

"That might be a problem. With the dress, I mean." I polished the pane of glass with my sleeve. My stomach was tightening with suppressing the tension. We got through catering packs of heartburn tablets chez Nicholson.

"Why? We're more or less the same size. If you breathe in."

"No, I mean I don't think the courier will be able to get through. Not for a few days, anyway."

Alice snorted. "Oh, come on, you're just outside Berwick, not in the Orkneys!"

"Hello? We're snowed in. Hasn't it been on the news yet? Mhairi says it could be days until the roads get cleared. Are you okay?" I added. Her breath had whistled in with a very sharp, possibly sweary noise. "In some respects, I guess you *couldn't* have got here by Thursday . . ."

My voice trailed off. A figure was striding up the path toward the lodge. A man. A broad-shouldered, capable-looking man in a flat farmer's cap. I squinted.

Oh no.

"Alice, Fraser's coming up the path," I squeaked. "I bet he's looking for me! What did you tell him?"

"Nothing! I panicked. I thought *you* could come up with an explanation."

"What? Are you mad?" I ducked down

behind the window. "What am I supposed to say?"

"You're the one with the insanely overactive imagination! Tell him I've broken my leg. Or I've got swine flu. Just anything that would stop me dancing at the weekend. But don't hurt his feelings. Don't tell him I've run off with my assistant or anything that might . . . upset him."

There was a wobble in her voice. It sounded as if Alice was close to tears.

"*Fine,* okay," I said. "But you have to buy all those teddy bears and whatever photograph frames Max still has in the shop tomorrow. I *need* my commission. And you have to make it up to Fraser."

"Deal," said Alice as Fraser started to knock on the door. He spotted me crouching by Robert's coat and changed his knock into a confused wave.

I pocketed my phone, stood up, and opened the door. "Hello, Fraser!"

"Evie!" he said, leaning to kiss me on the cheek. "Just the woman I was looking for."

I inspected his guileless face for signs of Alice's phone message. If he was gutted at being stood up by his girlfriend on the eve of the Most Romantic Night of the Year, he wasn't showing it. Fraser's manners really were full coverage.

"You were looking for me down here?" I asked, confused.

"No, been up to the house. Mhairi said you'd headed — Ah, Robert! I see you've got other people answering your door for you now! Taking the laird thing seriously, are we?"

"Tradesmen round the back, if you've come about the wine, Graham," retorted Robert cheerfully.

It was the casual rudeness that spoke of a long, long British male friendship.

"Kettle's on," he continued. "Come in and tell me how I can fill up our entire cellar with your cheapest plonk, so there's no room for any of my dad's Kettlesheer Gold."

"Actually, it was Evie I wanted a word with." Fraser smiled at me, but now I looked closer, his eyes were worried.

Robert huffed and motioned him in. "That's all I seem to hear these days. Get in, you're letting the heat out."

Somewhat awkwardly, given the narrow hall, the three of us walked in formation back to the kitchen, where Robert seemed to sense that Fraser wanted a private word, and excused himself, padding out of the room in his socks like a panther.

"Um, it's a bit awkward, Evie, so I'll come straight out with it," said Fraser. "I've just

253

had a very strange message from Alice about this weekend. She says she can't come, but that you'll be taking her place. Is that right? Have I misunderstood?"

I cleared my throat. "Yes. I mean, no, you haven't misunderstood."

Fraser bit his lip manfully. "I see. That's marvelous, of course, that you're coming, lovely to have you and all that, but . . ." He drew in a breath, let it out, drew it in again, then blurted out, "Is something wrong? Is she ill? Busy? I've tried calling her back, but her phone goes straight to voice mail."

Bloody Alice, I thought as Fraser looked at me, expecting a satisfactory explanation for Alice's vagueness. This was beyond out-of-character for someone who kept a GPS chip in her handbag in case of unexpected abduction by a cabdriver.

"I hope it's nothing *I've* done," he added. "I don't *think* we've fallen out."

"God, no!" I almost hugged him, he looked so worried. "No, it's *nothing* to do with you."

"Have you spoken to her?" He leaped on my apparent knowledge of the situation like a cat onto a doddery mouse. "I mean, if it's a private matter, then obviously I don't want to pry, but . . ."

Pry? About his own girlfriend of over two

years? Fraser was really looking forward to seeing her, the mad fool. He deserved a good excuse. The trouble was, my mind had gone blank.

"She's . . ."

Ill? Busy?

Fraser looked at me expectantly as I juggled the possibilities. I was making this sound even worse than it was. Fraser's face was braced for Bad News, and now Robert had wandered back in.

"What's going on?" he asked. "Everything okay?"

"Alice can't make it, she's snowed in!" I blurted out.

Robert looked incredulous. "Snowed in? There's no snow down in London. I've just been speaking to —"

"No, I didn't mean snowed in. *We're* snowed in. I meant, she's snowed *under*. Snowed under with work." My face was heating up.

"Is that all? Oh, Alice always overreacts. It's only Wednesday," Fraser pointed out, clearly relieved that she wasn't sprawled under a bus. Or under another man. "She'll be finished by tonight. She doesn't *have* to come tomorrow, we just thought it would be nice to get an extra practice in." He made little giddyap motions. "Maybe even go for a ride. Alice was saying she's never been on a horse."

God. Alice micromanaging a horse. It didn't bear thinking about.

"Ring her back and tell her to get a later train," Fraser went on. "I'll check the times on my phone. We'll get her back from the station somehow."

Robert gave me a look so cynical it went straight through my head and out the other side, leaving hot prickles in its wake. "Should I give her a call?" he inquired. "See if there's anything my assistant can help with?"

It had to be something to do with *him*, I decided. Either he knew something about her and might tell Fraser, or she and Robert had had some dodgy business falling-out, or maybe they'd argued over exactly how nice Fraser was, but there was something grim in Robert's face right now, and I knew it was to do with Alice.

"No!" My brain lurched into gear without warning and my mouth started moving of its own accord. "I mean, she's snowed under . . . because she's sprained her ankle. Trying to move a packing case in high heels, you know what she's like, so hands-on if people aren't chucking things away fast enough. . . ."

"It's not one of those *cold feet* sprains, is it?" asked Robert.

I glared at him.

"Technical term," he explained. "You lose all sensation in your toes. It can be a problem for dancers, I hear —"

"She didn't go into detail," I interrupted as Fraser's brow furrowed. "She can't walk on it. But the good news is that she's asked me to stand in!" I glanced between the two men. "I mean, not good news as such, but good news that your table plans won't be wrecked. Alice was very worried about that — she didn't want to spoil the ball."

"But you *hate* dancing!" Robert feigned extreme concern, but his eyes had a mischievous gleam, though his face was straight. "What was that you were saying to me on Monday? When you nearly dislocated my shoulder outside the —"

"Oh no!" I flapped my hands. I knew I shouldn't have been so open with him. I hadn't had him down as a repeater. "No . . . I was just . . . exaggerating. As I said to you, I'd love to go to the ball. The history, the spectacle . . . and so on."

"But you'll be dancing in it," said Robert.

"Yes, I will." I swallowed. "I will indeed. So I'd better get some instruction from someone who knows what they're doing.

And I hear, Fraser, that you're just the man for such a challenge!"

"It won't be a challenge," said Fraser gamely. "I'm sure you'll be fine. We can just bring the practice forward. How about tonight? Robert? Are you and Catriona doing anything? And, Evie, you must come down and stay with us, if the McAndrews have guests arriving."

"That's really kind, Fraser," I said. "I'll ask Ingrid."

"But what about your plans for Valentine's Day?" Robert inquired. "Didn't you say you had a busy weekend ahead?"

I wasn't sure I had, actually. Or had I?

"I'll just have to cancel," I said airily. "Treat 'em mean and all that."

"How funny, that's what Alice says," said Fraser. " 'Treat them mean, keep them clean.' It's her motto."

"One of many," I said, and helped myself to some cold toast.

SIXTEEN

Sheila took the news of Alice's unexpected defection with more grace than most hostesses would, faced with the prospect of a total novice in their midst.

I *thought* I saw her face tighten when Fraser walked me back through the snow and informed his mother that she had three days to teach me six reels; but then again, it was pretty chilly in the Kettlesheer dining room, where she and Ingrid were sitting in hats and quilted jackets, polishing silver cutlery and listening to reports of ten-foot snowmen in Hawick.

"Poor Alice. It's maybe as well," she said when I stammered out a version of "the news" that I hoped matched the one I'd just given Fraser. "A dance floor's no place for a weak ankle." She glanced down at mine, evidently assessing them for strength.

"I thought Evie could come along tonight for the practice," said Fraser. "Duncan and

Ingrid were coming over anyway, weren't you?"

"Oh, thanks," said Ingrid. "I was hoping we might have been let off."

"Mum never lets anyone off reeling practice," said Fraser.

"Not while Janet Learmont's marking you on a scale of ten, no," said Sheila, serenely polishing a steak knife.

And so, that evening, I found myself bumping along the estate backroad to the Grahams' farm. I was in the back of Robert's Land Rover with Ingrid while Duncan bellowed over his shoulder about the interesting "wet dog" notes in a carrot brandy, and Robert kept his eyes fixed firmly on the whited-out road ahead.

Catriona was already installed on the Grahams' sofa when we arrived, listening with rapt attention to Dougie's account of some catastrophe at the last point-to-point steeplechase. Her Jack Russell was parked on her knee in standby mode. Dougie's girlfriend, Kirstie, was perched next to her, texting and chewing her long red braid, and by the door with a bowl of Pringles was Sheila's husband, Kenneth, who looked as if he couldn't wait to get back into the lambing shed.

Sheila plied everyone with large slugs from

the bottle Duncan had brought along (which coincidentally looked as if it had been brewed from actual slugs), and announced that no one would get any supper until I'd learned the Eightsome reel. Cries of "Ten minutes, then!" ensued, mainly from Fraser. I hoped very much that the others had concealed a chocolate bar or two about their persons because, knowing my capacity for instruction better than they did, supper could be a long way off yet.

Fraser and Dougie shoved the furniture back against the walls, Catriona stowed her own and the Grahams' various dogs in the kitchen, and then Sheila hustled everyone into the resulting space, and so began my reeling career.

"The Eightsome. It's really very simple," she said.

"I bet it's not," I muttered to Fraser, who was standing next to me, bending his knees in a Dad-like manner as if he couldn't wait to get started. "If I had a pound for every time someone's told me that just before I've caused a major pileup, I'd have enough cash to buy . . ."

Catriona and Dougie were spinning round behind me as I spoke, and I ran out of words as Catriona finished up with a delicate reverse twiddle maneuver. She was *ex-*

cellent. Even Dougie was skillful, and he looked like he was more at home on a tractor than a dance floor.

"To buy new shoes?" suggested Fraser.

"And buy everyone a very stiff drink," I said glumly.

"Cheer up!" He put a reassuring arm around me. "I've got great faith in you."

That made me feel about thirty percent worse than I already did.

Sheila flexed her fingers. "Come on, Duncan, Ingrid. Let's have you here, opposite Evie and Fraser. And Kirstie, Douglas, you there. And Robert and Catriona, excellent. Now, you're going to start by holding hands and going round in a circle for a count of eight."

Douglas spun Catriona back to Robert with a flourish and an irritating curtsy from her, and took my hand. We all shuffled into a sort of circle and marched round while Sheila counted like Irene Cara in *Fame,* but without the big stick.

"Six, seven, *eight.* And now back the other way. . . ."

Fraser's hand was strong and I could feel him steering me as best he could without making me feel stupid. I tried to fix the steps in my head, but suddenly he'd scooped one arm round my waist and was swinging me into the middle of the room.

"Whoa!" I gasped, but no one took any notice. Instead, Kirstie opposite caught my flailing hand and steered me round as firmly as Fraser, while Sheila carried on instructing from the side.

"And now we form a cartwheel, girls' right hands in the middle, two, three, four . . ."

I was facing the wrong way, baffled. Fraser steered me back, and then suddenly the *men* were in the middle and the girls were wheeling around outside.

"Seven, *eight.* And now you set twice to your partners — Evie, dear, *setting* means hopping from one foot to the other," called Sheila. "Keep counting."

Fraser was doing a sort of casual sway from side to side that I tried to copy. He gave me an encouraging thumbs-up, which I knew wasn't warranted: a glimpse in the mirror over the fireplace confirmed that my setting looked like someone desperately queuing for the loo in Starbucks after four venti lattes.

"And now the men will turn their partners — Fraser, gently, please!"

"We'll work up to that," said Fraser, and took the crook of my arm as if I were a little old lady, moving me round as slowly as possible while everyone else did the spinning-top thing.

I had to admit it: the spinning-top thing looked amazing when the girls let the boys turn their wrists inside out and around, twirling them so fast their hair flicked — even in this sitting room, with no music, there was a controlled wildness about it. Add fiddles, skirts, champagne, candle-light . . .

My wrists clicked as Fraser tried, unsuc-cessfully, to spin me round, and instead got himself caught on my bracelet. There was an ominous ripping noise and we were sud-denly in a compromising tangle, my back pressed right against his chest, his arms partly around me.

"My fault! My fault!" he said, untangling the catch from his sweater. "Don't move!"

"Can Alice spin properly?" I asked, trying not to notice the solidity of Fraser's chest behind me. We were almost hugging, his arm around my chest. Luckily, Kirstie flashed past in a flurry of long skirt and made my heart sink in a different way. Kirstie had a nose stud and still danced like a Celtic princess.

"Eventually," said Fraser. "I mean, yes! She's an excellent spinner! There! Free!"

Poor Fraser. I was going to let him down so badly. And he'd be wearing a set of evening clothes I'd be bound to tangle myself up on. What if I caught him by the kilt? What if I got stuck in his sporran?

"Fraser, be honest," I hissed. "You reckon I can learn to do that before the weekend?"

"Of course," he said, but there was more than a hint of good manners in his expression.

I glanced over to where Robert and Catriona were waiting for Sheila's next instructions. Douglas and Kirstie were doing extra spins for fun, and Catriona seemed to be twisting Robert's arm to do the same, but he wasn't playing. He was checking his phone.

"And now we weave round in a circle, ladies clockwise, men counterclockwise, offering left arm, then right arm, then left arm . . ."

I was lost for a second, but then the rest of the circle caught up with me and I found myself being shoved and pulled round and back to where I'd started. I barely had to do a thing; it was like being stuck in a pinball machine.

"Now then, that's the only hard part," said Sheila. "Next we put the first lady into the circle. Who wants to go first?"

Catriona stepped forward without waiting to be asked, and looked up from under her lashes at Robert, who shoved his phone reluctantly into his back pocket. "Some ladies would take that phone of yours and stand on it," she said. "I hope your sporran doesn't have a mobile-phone pocket!"

"There will be no sporran, Cat," he said, "because there will be no kilt."

She wagged her finger playfully at him. "Or will there?"

I saw a blankness enter his face, a shutting-down. Max did it at auctions or when someone brought something valuable into the shop. Robert was closing himself off.

Catriona dropped the playfulness and put her hands on her slim hips. "But you have to! It's traditional! You have your own tartan! I'll be wearing my sash!"

Robert's gaze traveled over her shoulder, and he caught me watching the pair of them. I looked away, because his eyes weren't quite so unreadable anymore. They were clearly saying *Shut the hell up.*

Sheila's voice broke through the tension. "Now, we all circle round again while the lady in the middle does her party piece for eight bars."

"Party piece?" I repeated. God. Could this get any worse? "What? Like . . . impressions?"

"Whatever you like, so long as it doesn't

involve profanity or nudity," said Sheila. "The committee is very strict on that score, although the Young Farmers aren't."

"And no push-ups, *please*," said Kirstie, nudging Douglas. She had a pretty Scottish accent. "They're *sooo* boring."

The circle moved off, with Dougie and Kirstie squabbling about his biceps, but my eyes were glued to Catriona, who was doing that pointy-toed Scottish dancing you see on commemorative tea towels. She carried on prancing, her eyes cast down modestly, while we changed direction. Only once did she glance up, naturally at the very moment when I was gawping straight at her. She smiled, accepting the compliment I wasn't exactly paying her.

"And first lady sets and turns her partner, then the man directly opposite," called Sheila.

Catriona started jigging opposite Robert, who swayed even more vaguely than Fraser.

"Come on, Robert," said Duncan. "More effort than that! You're the leading couple, for heaven's sake!"

In answer, Robert whirled Catriona round with a deft flick of the wrist that sent her spinning into the middle, her skirt wrapping perfectly around her calves, and suddenly she was staring at me and Fraser, all smoky eyeliner and sparkling confidence.

"And now she sets to the opposite man," said Sheila.

"Do your worst, Fraser Graham," Catriona said with a wink that summed up about twenty years of reeling together. Fraser responded by shimmying at double speed, grabbing both her hands in his, and doing a complicated twisty-turny thing that would have definitely broken both my wrists, if not his.

"And figure eight!" bellowed Sheila as Fraser, Catriona, and Robert set off walking round each other. Catriona was doing a pristine hoppity-skip, while Fraser — to Douglas's approval — swaggered like a cowboy with rickets. Robert walked normally.

As he came within a breath of me, he caught my eye, and I smiled, before pretending to turn to Sheila for instructions. There was something about the way Robert looked directly at me — into me, almost — that made me too self-conscious to hold his gaze for more than a second or two.

We all joined hands and circled again, with Catriona doing her pointy-toed routine again, this time with her hands above her head like something off a music box, and then she repeated the flirty setting-and-turning routine, this time with Douglas and Duncan. I tried to fix it all in my head.

"I don't suppose there's any chance of us wearing numbers, is there?" I asked plaintively.

Everyone laughed, and I had to pretend I was joking. Only I wasn't.

"And we do that over and over until everyone's had a go in the middle," said Sheila. "Right, do you think you have that, Evie?"

"Er, yes," I lied.

"Would you like me to give you my reeling guide?" asked Catriona. "I made booklets for clients who come up here to get married and want reels at their wedding. Very, very simple, with step-by-step pictures." She bestowed a slightly patronizing smile on me. "Even English people get it by the end!"

"Catriona, I'm sure Evie doesn't need you to draw diagrams —" Robert began.

"Please do, thank you," I said. I'd lost my pride years ago when it came to dancing. "I'm more of a visual person."

"It'll make sense when you hear the music," said Sheila. "Douglas, did you set up your Walkman hoojamiflip? What do I press?"

Douglas moved her aside and fiddled with

his iPod, which was plugged into some speakers. A crashing accordion chord blared out, making Catriona gasp with shock.

"So, shall we begin?" yelled Sheila over the din. "Bow and curtsy to your partner, and *round,* two, three . . ."

Before I could even think what was going on, Fraser and Douglas grabbed my hands and began marching me round in a circle. I just about managed the cartwheel business, and the setting and turning, and even the weird ribbonless maypole stuff, but then suddenly I found myself being propelled into the center by Fraser's strong hand in the small of my back.

He was making me be first lady.

I turned, with *No!* written in silent plea on my face. Then, for good measure, I added, "No, please!" aloud, in case he couldn't read faces.

"Better get it over with while it's fresh in your mind," he urged, and set off circling again. The music did *not* help. It was so fast and frantic that I couldn't think, which only added to my mounting panic, trapped in the middle while Dougie and Catriona screeched "Party piece!" at me.

"Do something, dear!" urged Sheila. "Anything!"

"Value Sheila's furniture?" suggested

Catriona.

Everyone laughed, and promptly changed direction and went the other way.

"Nice corner cabinet," I said, trying to follow Sheila as she moved around. "Is it . . . Waring and Gillows?"

"Indeed it is," she said. "My mother's. Now set to your partner."

Fraser grabbed me before I could go past him, put me in front of him, lurched from side to side, then with a twist of his hands spun me round. Even though my arms went stiff and my feet started moving in a different direction to the rest of my body, he still managed to put me back in the middle, pushing me toward Robert.

"Now me," said Robert, reaching out to turn me toward him. As his hand touched my arm, something tingled across my skin. He bowed his head mock-formally as I shuffled from one foot to the other, and then gripped my wrists, and the room was turning — or I was.

I was surprised by how easy he made it. And surprised at how I didn't tense up the way I had with Fraser — I just seemed to flow into the turn as his strong arms gave me nowhere else to go. And then I was back in the middle again, feeling a little stunned, and facing Catriona, who flapped her hands at me.

"Figure eight!" she squawked. "Figure eight! Quick!"

Fraser and Robert started walking round me as if I were a traffic cone, giving me discreet shoves as they went.

Too late. The circle was moving again and I was feeling faintly seasick. The music was so *fast.*

"And *back* into the middle as we all go round!" called Sheila. "Your next partners are Dougie and Duncan, *five,* six, *seven,* eight."

"Oi! Perform!" yelled Dougie.

My eye skated around the sitting room — old Indian rug, sofas pushed back against the wall, large marble fireplace . . . "Mantel clock, Victorian!" I said, pointing to it. Then, as the circle went the other way, I added, "Nice pottery spaniel figurines, I'll give you a hundred quid for them!"

"Ai-yaaaarp!" shrieked Dougie.

Fraser went past and smiled encouragingly, soon followed by Robert, who merely raised one eyebrow like James Bond.

The music changed to a rattling sequence, and Duncan put out a hand to stop me, as if I were a ball in a roulette wheel. He set to me with some wild leaping from foot to foot, but then walked me round very carefully, and I felt a contrary pang that he wouldn't be turning Kirstie and Catriona quite so cautiously.

"I wish I knew how to do this!" I confessed.

"I was a mere beginner a year ago — and look at me now!" he said, guiding me back to the middle, spoiling it only by going back to the wrong place in the circle and having Sheila grab him and reinsert him next to Ingrid.

The only thing I could say was that at least I hadn't fallen over yet. Still, I told myself, just one set and turn to go, and I'd be free to sink into the background while everyone else showed off.

I stepped back to face Dougie, and caught Catriona leaning in to murmur something in his ear. She stopped when she saw me.

"Och, Duncan, Cat's right, she'll not learn if you turn her like that!" snorted Dougie, and reached out to grab my wrists. "Just keep your arms loose," he went on, ignoring the warning quacks from Sheila, "and let me steer you into —"

"Let you what?" I gabbled, but Dougie was already winding me up. Just as he applied maximum force to the spin, my body went rigid, as it always did when threatened with a step sequence, but I carried on backward as if I'd been shot from a cannon.

The music drowned out any shrieked guidance from the others, and then I must have lost my footing on the carpet, because my shoe slipped off, and I was spinning, then slipping, then stumbling backward, arms flailing.

Everything really did go into slow motion, because I had time to think (a) *I am definitely going to fall over,* and (b) *I hope my head doesn't connect with that original Doric-columned marble fireplace directly behind me.*

"Evie, mind the fire!" screeched Sheila, so loud I could hear her over the dueling accordions.

I lurched and crashed into something scratchy, and my feet flew up over my head, revealing (oh, my God) the large hole in my emergency tights that I hadn't planned on wearing, because up until the dancing class I'd had no intention of wearing a skirt. But at least I wasn't on fire, or out cold.

There was a moment's silence before the pain crashed in, and I heard a clunk, which I presumed was my shoe landing on the wrong side of the sofa.

Then the sting of splinters, the ache of bruises, and the burning hum of embarrassment hit me all at once.

"Now, *that* is a party piece," said Douglas. "Right into the log basket."

"Evie, are you all right? Speak to us! Douglas Graham, you are the most stupid boy I have ever . . ." Sheila and Ingrid rushed over, but even from my low vantage point, I could see they were both trying hard to swallow gurgles of laughter.

Frankly, I could have done without the crowd round the log basket. It was hard enough to sort out my skirt and unbuttoned shirt, let alone gather my tatty dignity, without negotiating the hands that now stretched out to haul me back to my feet. I'd made a right mess of the basket. There was kindling *everywhere.*

"I'm fine," I said, bravely dusting myself off, ignoring the metallic tang of blood where I'd bitten my lip. "Honestly, how funny. I hope it wasn't an heirloom. Ha-ha-ha."

The *Ha-ha-ha* didn't ring with authenticity, but it allowed everyone else to stop fighting their hysterical giggles. And how.

While Catriona, Kirstie, and Dougie were clutching their aching sides and rocking back and forth like windup monkeys — and even Sheila and Duncan were patting their eyes — only Fraser seemed absolutely mortified.

"Did you get any splinters?" he asked, examining my skinned palms. "You must think we're a right bunch of thugs, letting Dougie hurl you across the room on your first go."

"Aye, and I thought I'd lost my touch with hammer-throwing," mused Dougie, to mass cackles.

"More like a *caber!*" hooted Catriona. "No offense!" she added.

"Och, she could have been *killed!*" giggled Kirstie. "No, I mean, it's *terrible.*"

My hands were throbbing, but I didn't mind because Fraser was doing some kind of EMT inspection to make sure I hadn't broken anything. It involved squeezing and moving my extremities with the utmost gentleness, and wasn't totally unpleasant.

He was gazing right into my eyes, too. I swallowed, rather thrilled at the sudden attention, then realized he was checking my pupils for concussion.

"I'm so sorry," he said as he flexed my fingers experimentally. "You were doing so well, too. Please don't let that put you off."

"I just need to learn how to do that spinning whatsit," I croaked.

As I said it, I knew I really *did* want to learn how to do the spinning whatsit. For that brief second when it was almost working out, and that briefer second when Robert's hands had grabbed mine and I'd felt him dance with me, I'd wanted to glide with the same poise as Kirstie and Sheila. I wanted to rise to the occasion, and not just because the fireplaces in Kettlesheer were twice as big and twice as likely to knock me out cold.

The shock almost took away the pain in my hands and legs. I *wanted* to dance. And I was going to learn how if it killed me.

"Oh, you'll get it," Fraser assured me. "We all had to learn once. It's just practice."

"I might need some extra lessons," I said.

He smiled, his sunny, perfect-gentleman smile, the one that made me feel delicate and bonneted. "I think that's the least we can do, since you've been brave enough to volunteer."

I heard imaginary strings swelling behind us in *Gone with the Wind* fashion, but they stopped with an abrupt screech when Robert appeared at Fraser's shoulder. He looked amused and modern.

"Nothing broken?" he asked. "It's all about letting go and relaxing. I was watching your arms — you're resisting. Stop resisting. Let the man place you where you need to be. You seemed to be okay when I was spinning you. Was it Dougie? Did he frighten you with his Scottish manliness?"

"Back on the horse!" said Sheila, bustling up behind us. "Can't let that put you off, Evie. Let's get going again — you've done your turn now, so you relax for a bit. Douglas, will you stop doing that, and put the music back on?"

I watched as Catriona, Kirstie, and then Ingrid took their turns in the middle, and a queasy combination of outright jealousy and definite fear began to swill around in my stomach.

On Saturday night, I'd have to do this in front of everyone at the ball, in some weird long fashion-forward dress of Alice's, with Catriona's fearsome mother watching, and with everyone else's engagement at stake.

That was quite scary. But what spooked me was that for the first time in my life, my brain was concentrating on the moves and a new, determined voice in my head was counting the bars.

SEVENTEEN

Max called me in the morning so delirious with excitement that I could barely make him out. He sounded as if he'd been drinking — since he'd got my e-mail the previous night.

"This table. You know what it is?" he demanded. "I mean, you *know* what it *is?*"

"Yeees," I said, thrown. "It's a table, isn't it? I mean, it *is* a table?"

"It's not just *a* table, it's *the* table!" he gurgled. "Evie, you little star, you haven't just got us a big fish, you have found me a whale! A Chippen-whale, if you will!"

He laughed uproariously at his own joke.

I'd taken the precaution of stepping outside to take Max's call, because Duncan had spent the entire morning distracting me with family photographs and artifacts from VIP visits in the twenties. I was easy enough to distract as it was. Right now I was shivering on the terrace, wrapped in my coat and feeling a bit guilty about disturbing the pristine snow around the flowerbeds with my nervous pacing.

"Is it the real thing, then?" I asked, my heart starting to beat faster. "How can you tell without seeing it?"

"Would you like a history lesson?" Max inquired. "You would? Lovely. Now, have you heard of a place called Dumfries?"

"Yes, it's about sixty miles away."

"And have you heard of Dumfries House? The treasure trove of magnificent eighteenth-century furniture, much of it made especially for the Earl of Dumfries by Thomas Chippendale himself?"

I stamped my feet. Picturesque as the snow was, even with a pair of Duncan's jazzy shooting socks on, I was fast losing sensation in my toes. "Can you just e-mail me a link to the Wikipedia page you're reading, please."

"I don't have Wikipedia, you saucy brat. Just years and years of buying old biddies sherry. All *you* need to know is that a quick check of my sources reveals that a certain Donaldina McAndrew was rather pally with the various members of the earl's family, and that various splendid items of furniture were known to have arrived at Kettlesheer around that time. It's not *wholly* unlikely that if Mr. Chippendale was being commissioned to make a substantial amount of furniture for Dumfries House, he might have been prevailed upon to knock up a little something for the McAndrews."

My head swam instantly with visions of messengers galloping across from Dumfries with rolled parchments of plans and wood samples. Donaldina — what a name! — commissioning something to keep up with her rich friend, so the return invitations could be issued. . . .

"So it's worth a lot of money?" I asked, thinking of Ingrid's face when she'd talked about the oil bills.

"Darling, it's worth more than your flat and my flat put together," Max sighed. I could picture his fingers wriggling with excitement. "And it's a major find. No one's seen anything like this for generations. In fact, I might even give my contact at the BBC a call, see if there might be a spare camera crew. . . ."

I wasn't listening. I was too busy being thrilled. "Blimey," I breathed. I'd done it! I'd saved Kettlesheer from being developed!

And yet, I didn't feel anything like that on the table. No history, no glamour. Just wood and polish.

I pushed that thought aside. The evidence

was right there in the book. Max had already known they had something precious hidden in the house — it made total sense.

But still it slipped out. "You can definitely tell it's the real deal from the photos I sent?"

"I'd stake your reputation on it. You said something about written provenance, in a book? And what about the chairs?" There was a horrible slurping noise down the phone. "If there is a whole set of matching chairs . . ."

"I haven't really checked out the chairs." I bit my lip. "Should I tell them, then? So Duncan can prepare himself for having to sell it?"

Because that was another hurdle. Maybe I'd tell Robert first, see if he could make his dad see that, to save the house, he'd have to sacrifice the table. Desperate measures and all that.

"Don't tell them yet. Let me get some buyers lined up, with some nice, tempting cash in hand. Meanwhile, you get yourself in there and look for chairs," said Max, in the manner of someone settling back into an easy chair and lighting a fine cigar. "Find me two dozen rococo Chippendale chairs, and I might even let you go home early on Saturday."

"Ah," I said. "Saturday. That might be a

problem."

"In what way?"

"We're snowed in. It doesn't look good for getting back — the forecast is for even more at the weekend. But probably better that I stay here and carry on looking, right?"

There was a whistling intake of breath from Max as he weighed the advantages to himself. A Chippendale table versus a weekend of selling my photograph frames in the shop. Alone.

For once, I felt in a position of some power.

"And they don't mind you staying?" he asked suspiciously.

"Not at all. In fact," I added, unable to resist, "I've been invited to a ball in the house."

"You've — Why?" Max spluttered, outraged at having been overtaken on the social ladder. "Is it because you've just told them what they're sitting on? Is that it?"

"No!" I protested. "I haven't told them anything yet. I was waiting for confirmation from you before I got their hopes up. They're —"

I stopped myself. Max didn't need to know how much I now wanted Duncan and Ingrid to keep their home. It wasn't very loyal to my boss, but then, he wasn't a very loyal man himself.

"Fine," he said. "But make sure you introduce yourself to anyone who looks like they might have a house full of priceless furniture going unappreciated."

"Naturally," I said. "And if you get any battle reenactors in at the weekend, looking to stock up on swords and small cannon, tell them we can do wholesale."

I slipped back into the house, stamping the snow off my boots at the front door beneath the disapproving gaze of a stuffed elk.

Elk apart, I was slightly disappointed not to find anyone in the hall. I was bubbling with eagerness to tell someone — anyone — what an amazing thing I'd found, and through a notebook no one had seen for nearly a hundred years. If it hadn't been for me making Robert look in that room, and Violet making that note, how would we have known exactly how special the table was?

I couldn't resist going back to the dining room to see if the table felt different to me now that Max had confirmed it was worth squillions. I positively waltzed down the corridor, raising my eyebrows in conspiracy with the bearded Victorian McAndrews along the wall — who must have known too! And then not told anyone.

I'd barged into the dining room, lost in my own vision of Donaldina instructing the famous Mr. Chippendale about table settings, before I noticed that there was someone in there already: Ingrid.

"Oh, sorry," I said, taking in the calculator, the papers, the coffee — not on a coaster! — and her bent head, propped in her hands. "Shall I . . . ?"

"No, don't worry," she said, sweeping up the papers. Not quickly enough for me to miss the red final-demand type on all of them. "This is the only table big enough for our accounts." She grimaced. "Never marry a man who still adds up in pre-decimal currency, Evie."

It was a surprise to realize that Ingrid — fragile, birdlike Ingrid — was the family accountant; but maybe that wasn't such a bad thing, given Duncan's preoccupation with home brew and history. Her stressed air obviously wasn't just down to Janet Learmont's social etiquette lessons.

"Are things . . . ?" I didn't want to pry, but she was hardly hiding the evidence. "Bad?"

Ingrid started to demur, then nodded sadly. "Numbers this big actually stop meaning anything. Maybe selling to a developer isn't such a bad option. I keep trying to tell Duncan, 'Enjoy this ball, it could be the last one,' but he just smiles and says something'll turn up: 'The family won't let us down.' " She pulled a *Grrr* face, then looked exhausted. "It was all right for *the family.* Coal only cost a penny a ton in those days and you had all the maids you could manage queuing up in Rennick."

Robert had seemed so furious at the prospect of the house swallowing up his parents and all their money; he didn't seem so unreasonable now. But why wasn't *he* worrying about this? He was better equipped to sort this out than Ingrid.

"I'm sure it will work out," I said fervently, before I had time to think. "I'm *very sure* there's something *extremely* valuable here."

Ingrid looked up at me, a faint light in her eyes. "Are you . . . ?"

I nodded. "I can't say more at this stage, but not a million miles away."

"Oh!" She glanced down and put her fingertips on the table. "Oh."

"Sorry, but . . ." I moved a council tax bill and put her coffee mug on top of it.

"Oops, yes. Oh!" said Ingrid, her expression brightening. "Speaking of the ball, I meant to come and find you — Robert's organizing another practice for you down at the lodge. Just the youngsters, you'll be pleased to hear — Fraser, and Dougie and Kirstie, and Catriona, of course." She smiled and nodded. "She'll be doing the teaching, I expect; she's been reeling for years."

"Robert arranged a practice — for me?" I felt the blush creeping up my face.

"Mmm. Last night, while you were getting your coat, Catriona suggested her sister, Laura, might step in to dance with Fraser, just for that first dance, and Robert wouldn't hear of it. Wouldn't even let her finish."

She glanced over her shoulder, clearly expecting Janet to drop from the chandelier *Mission: Impossible*-style. "Between you and me, Janet's trying to do some not-so-subtle match-making for Laura. She'd like her to settle down with a nice man like Fraser. Mums, eh?" she added, thinking my dazed expression was over the maternal interfering. "I expect yours is just as bad."

"Worse," I said. "She keeps sending me on speed dating. Sometimes she comes with me, to hurry them along."

To check them out, more like. Mum didn't trust me not to put my wishful-thinking goggles on, after a couple of rather unfortunate misunderstandings.

"Well, that's what reeling's all about!" said

Ingrid. "Speed dating to music! I'm sure you'll leave here with a good few numbers."

I felt a sudden surge of positivity. That did it. Robert wanted me to dance with them, *and* I'd be saving Fraser from some Janet Learmont hostile takeover activity. If it meant defending Alice from any boyfriend poaching, I'd just have to force myself to dance with the most gentlemanly gentleman in Rennick, and indeed in the whole Border area.

And the sooner Max called me back with a buyer for that table, the sooner I could put poor Ingrid out of her financial misery, and make sure of next year's ball.

The moon was so bright, reflecting off the snow-covered fields, that I barely needed Duncan's torch, and the warm glow of expectation tickling my stomach put an extra spring in my step as I crunched through the pristine snow, wrapped up in all my thermal underwear, Ingrid's biggest fleece, and two scarves.

Catriona was already in organizing mode when I arrived. She wasted no time in beginning the lesson once I'd got my coat off, removing the beer from Dougie's hand before he'd even cracked open the can.

"Hamilton House is known as the flirty

reel!" she announced, marshaling the five of us into position in the middle of Robert's sitting room. "Boys on the left, girls on the right. Dougie, I want you to be on your best behavior, please."

"I see you've cleared all breakable furniture out of your sitting room for Dougie's benefit," said Fraser. He was looking like a genial polar bear in a thick white sweater and jeans.

"No," said Robert. "It always looks like this."

"What? Unfurnished?"

"It's called style, Fraser, we don't all have to clutter up our houses with moldy old stuff," said Catriona, before turning her attention to me. "Now, don't take this the wrong way, Evie, but since you're going to need all the help you can get — no offense — I've brought you those instructions I mentioned. As you can see, I've done one for all the reels. Different colors for different people, and so on."

She passed me something that looked like a knitting pattern. I didn't recognize anything from the previous night.

"Thanks," I said. "Why's it called the flirty reel?"

Kirstie leaped in while Catriona's mouth was still open. "It's supposed to have been invented by a right goer who wanted to flirt with her lover and dance with her husband all at the same time. Nothing changes, right?"

"That depends on your partner, missy," said Douglas.

Catriona glared at her. "That's one story. The other is that it's about a tragic young widow searching for her missing husband."

My ears pricked up, and I caught Robert glancing at me, amused.

"But I suppose you believe what suits you," she went on. "Now, the first lady — that's myself — starts, and she ignores her partner . . ."

She turned her head artfully away from Robert, then stepped toward Dougie with a low nod.

". . . she sets to the second man . . ."

"The lover," supplied Kirstie.

Dougie gave her a lascivious wink, then wobbled his knees, while Catriona skipped neatly from one foot to the other.

". . . but then she turns the *third* man."

"Presumably the gamekeeper," said Robert.

Fraser held out his hands and twirled her round in a slow-motion spinning top. Needless to say, she made it look very easy and didn't come anywhere near crashing.

"Then I come round to the top of the set, and meanwhile my partner —"

"Who also has an eye for the lassies," added Kirstie, for my benefit.

"— has started and does the same thing with the ladies."

Robert swung his shoulders at Kirstie, then reached out and grabbed *my* hands, gripping my thumbs, and quickly turned me around. As he did it, he glanced up at me from under his dark lashes. I knew he was acting up, but it still made my chest tighten.

"And then we join hands in a line and step to the side, two, three, four, and then to the other side, two, three, four. . . ."

Catriona carried on talking in her school-teacher voice as we formed one line of boy-girl-boy, then another line of girl-girl-girl, and then did the inevitable circling round.

"So it's just a load of partner-swapping," said Dougie. "Got that?"

"You dance with everyone and end up with the one you brought," I said.

"I know, it's just *impossible* at first," said Catriona sympathetically.

But it wasn't. The flirting story made it a picture in my brain, and the patterns made a shape that I could see, crossing, then turning, then crossing again, like crochet.

Oh, my God, I thought, stunned. This was what it felt like to learn steps.

"Evie? Are you all right? You looked confused," said Fraser. "Do you want to go through it one more time?"

"No," I said slowly. "I think I've got it."

"Don't worry, when we put the music on it'll go wrong," Catriona reassured me. "It always does."

Quite incredibly, it didn't. Even with the music, I still knew where I was supposed to be going, who I was supposed to be reaching out for. Maybe it was because the others were sweet enough to reach out for my hands every time; maybe Violet was discreetly nudging me into place; maybe it was because part of me was instinctively aiming for Robert.

It was fast, it was fun, and after the fifth time, I realized I wasn't even thinking about where I was going next.

We reeled until I accidentally knocked over the one ornament in the whole sitting room, at which point Catriona firmly shunted us into the kitchen to eat pasta served in minimalist white bowls. They were obviously expensive, but seemed joyless compared with the delicate violet and thistle crests of Kettlesheer's service.

Afterward, Fraser and I volunteered to load the state-of-the-art dishwasher, while the others lounged on the sofas, discussing some horsey hunt business. Catriona kept saying, "We shouldn't laugh . . ." but that didn't stop her from roaring with laughter about some girl called Tats McNee. (Tats could have been the horse.)

When I peered round, I saw that Robert wasn't laughing. He seemed preoccupied, but then, Dougie did have his feet up on the glass coffee table, and Kirstie had disarranged the carefully stacked photographic books.

I wondered if he was seeing the reeling in a different light, now that he'd read Violet's notebook and the postcards. Imagining his beautiful golden-haired great-grandmother, dancing with the portly Prince of Wales.

I realized Fraser was talking to me, and jerked to attention.

"You did brilliantly tonight!" he said. "Don't tell her, but it took Alice weeks to work out Hamilton House."

"Really?" I said, warmed by the affectionate pride in his voice.

Fraser paused his systematic plate stacking, and dropped his voice. "I don't want to sound overbearing, but I still haven't heard from her. She is okay, isn't she? You know what she's normally like about returning calls."

I squirmed. I hated lying to Fraser, but I was clueless myself.

As with most men, conversations of this nature came about as easily to Fraser as banjo playing. "Evie, I hope you'd tell me if I've done something wrong. Or" — he hesitated — "if I made a mistake in inviting her up here?"

"Fraser, it's *nothing* like that. She adores you."

"Steady on." He looked down shyly at the cutlery basket, and I envied Alice, having this gentle giant of a man so mad about her. If she was going to stand him up, she could at least put some effort into softening the blow.

"She — she doesn't want to let you down," I went on, my imagination embroidering the scene between historical Major Fraser in uniform and Alice in ringlets, writing a note begging forgiveness for her unexplained absence. "She's just indisposed, with her sprained ankle, and wouldn't want to make you sit out the ball because she couldn't dance."

Fraser looked confused. "Indisposed . . . ?"

Maybe I'd gone too far.

"She's probably knocked out on painkillers," I said. "That's maybe why she hasn't called. I'll be trying to get hold of her myself tomorrow — I'll tell her to ring."

"Would you? That would be awfully kind," said Fraser. "And, you know, I really do hope you enjoy the ball. It's a rather special evening." Sadness jutted his lower lip. "Just a shame we'll be missing Alice."

Awfully. Alice so didn't deserve him.

Eighteen

At eleven, Catriona announced that she needed to get up in the morning for "a very important meeting," and the evening came to a halt as Fraser offered to drive everyone home.

We drifted outside, where the full moon was reflecting off the soft banks of whiteness until it felt almost like daytime. An owl hooted somewhere in the distance, but otherwise everything was still and magical. I breathed in a deep lungful of sharp night air.

"Jeez, it's cold," said Kirstie. "Dougie, get in that car and warm me up. Night, Robert! Thanks for the spaghetti. Sorry about the mess on your nice white sofa. My mum swears by white wine vinegar."

"No worries," said Robert, though I noticed Catriona gave her a death look.

Fraser bleeped his Land Rover with the remote, and Dougie yanked the door open for Kirstie, bundling her in enthusiastically as she blew Robert a kiss off her gloves.

"Good night, Robbie," said Catriona. "You're still on for supper tomorrow night at mine?" She leaned up and went to kiss him on the lips, just as he turned his head to answer Fraser's question about winter tires. She ended up with his cheekbone.

Awkward, I thought.

No, actually, *awkward* was the way she grabbed his chin, dragged his face to hers, and planted a kiss right on his lips while we all watched, complete with *Mmmmmm* noise.

"Night, Catriona," I said. "Thanks for the instructions."

She got in on the passenger side, ignoring the squeals from the backseat. "No problem. Let me know if you need those diagrams explained."

"Do you want a lift up to the house?" Fraser nodded toward the car.

"No, it'd be quicker for me to walk," I said. "By the time you've gone round via the road —"

"Oh, you can't walk on your own —" he started.

"I'll walk Evie back," Robert interrupted. "Take me ten minutes. I'll get my coat."

I turned round, surprised. "You don't have to."

"I do. Can't have you getting eaten by bears in the woods. As I'm sure Cat's mother would tell you, losing one girl from our set is careless, losing two is bad hosting. Wait there." He turned back to Fraser. "You guys get away."

"If you're sure?" Fraser looked at me, then when Robert disappeared inside whispered, "You don't have to be polite. I'm happy to drive you over!"

I raised a hand. "How often do you get to see a night sky like this in London?"

"Never." We both looked up at the inky northern sky, speckled with tiny diamond points, and I stole a swift sideways glance at Sensitive Countryman Fraser, one for the mental scrapbook.

"Right!" Robert was back, jangling his keys. "Let's go."

I waved as Fraser reversed his Land Rover expertly in the snow — not even a tiny wheel spin — and drove off down the track toward the road. Dougie's and Kirstie's silhouettes wrestled in the back. I bet Catriona gave them one minute exactly before telling them to belt up and shut up.

"Brought you this," said Robert, offering me his trapper hat. He'd pulled on a beanie over his own ears and was bundled up in his ski jacket so only his bright eyes and

298

sharp nose were properly visible.

"Thanks." I pulled it on. It was warm but huge, and nearly reached my nose. "Ooh. I can't hear anything."

"Hang on." Robert leaned forward and grabbed the two earflaps, tying them on top of my head. "I save this one for outdoor pursuits. Means when people ask me what I plan to do with my enormous house, I can pretend not to hear them. Only drawback is that I can't wear it inside."

I gave him a look. "You could try *having* an opinion about your enormous house."

He returned my look with extra pointed-ness. "I do. You know what it is. Now, shall we?"

Our feet made satisfying crumping noises in the night stillness, and the moon bathed the landscape with surreal pale blue light, casting shadows under trees.

"Don't you think this is like walking through Narnia?" I breathed.

"Hmm, I haven't skied there," said Robert. "Is it European?"

"No, it's — Oh, shut up," I said.

We walked side by side, our arms swing-ing a few centimeters apart. I was very conscious of how private it felt to be walk-ing alone together at this late hour, in this silent, secret forest. *His* silent, secret forest, in fact. I wondered if Robert felt it too; neither of us spoke for a few minutes.

"Thanks for another dancing lesson," I said, to break the silence. "It was sweet of you to arrange it."

"My pleasure. Thanks for not destroying any of my furniture. I see you picked up Hamilton House quickly enough."

"The story helps," I said. "The husband, the lover, the future lover — and then the husband doing exactly the same. I like things with stories attached."

"Ah, this is about the postcards, isn't it? Our very own transatlantic fairy tale." He said it in a slightly sardonic way, and I glanced sideways. Robert was staring straight ahead, his eyes on the path.

"That's a real fairy tale, though. The chance meeting, the American princess, the love that lasted till Ranald died. Anyway," I went on, sensing he was about to launch into more remorseless bubble-bursting, "the proof'll be in the dancing. It was good of Catriona to come round and teach me."

"She enjoyed it. She likes telling people what to do."

"I'd noticed." I hesitated. "I don't want to mess it up for her."

"Why?"

"*Why?*" The atmosphere between us

300

hummed with something unspoken. Robert couldn't see my face, so I threw caution to the winds. "Because I get the impression that this first reel thing is more of an exhibition dance for you and the future Mrs. Kettlesheer than anything else."

"Ah, that's only if the reel's perfect." He swung his hands.

I really couldn't make out Robert's attitude. Was he being politely vague about his private life? Could he really be as unconcerned as he seemed?

"But that's what bothers me," I went on. "*Your* mother and *her* mother seem to think your party piece in the middle of the Eightsome is going to involve a ring box, so if I crash into a suit of armor and spoil the whole thing, they're going to be pretty — oh!"

The penny suddenly dropped. How had I been so thick not to realize before?

"Oh, I get it!" I was so poleaxed that my feet stopped moving. "You *want* the whole thing to be screwed up, so you're off the hook! *That's* why you insisted on me taking over from Alice — not because you wanted me there, but because you wanted me there to *wreck* it!"

Robert stopped too, a pace or two ahead, and turned back. "Don't be ridiculous. Next

301

you'll be telling me I'm deliberately not getting married so I don't have to inherit."

"You wouldn't do — !" Actually, I didn't care whether he was joking or not. Scalding waves of mortification were sweeping over me.

I'd done it again — let my imagination create a whole scene that not only wasn't happening but was actually the *opposite* of reality! If any snowflakes had fallen on my burning cheeks, they'd have sizzled straight off.

"That's not even funny," I snapped, losing any semblance of self-control. "Catriona expects you to propose! I can't think of anything more ungallant than letting a girl think she was about to get the most romantic moment of her life and then deliberately ducking out of it. Using someone who — someone who isn't a confident dancer at the best of times!"

Had Robert planned this from the moment I'd told him I couldn't dance? Had that spin outside his house been a test, to see how bad I was? Oh, God. And I'd been trying to wrestle him into top hats and breeches, like Fraser. . . .

I pushed away the mortified voice in my head and marched onward. Stupid. My stupid imagination, running wild in that house, casting myself in some imaginary romantic drama. *Again.*

"Wait! Evie, wait!"

I could hear Robert running, but I carried on walking. I had an awful plunging sensation in my chest. I'd never been more embarrassed in my life.

What would Alice do? I thought. She'd be practical. Like Mum. Tidy up. Make lists.

Number one, get back to the house. Two, make a report about the furniture for Max. Three, call Alice and tell her to get herself up here, by helicopter if necessary. Four, leave, in same helicopter.

A hand grabbed my arm and pulled me back. I slipped and tried to keep my eyes fixed on the deep footsteps I'd made in the snow, but Robert pulled me round and I slid, leaving me very close to his face. Close enough to see the faint freckles round his nose, and feel his hot, quick breath in the cold air.

"Evie, that's *not* why I wanted you to stay. Honestly." He tried a smile but it came out crooked. "Look, my *parents* are dancing in this reel — Dad's bound to make at least one major cock-up. I don't need to add any more chaos to the mix."

But I was still smarting. I hoisted my chin. "That's not the point. This isn't just about

Catriona, is it? I don't think you understand what your mum and everyone else is expecting. They need you to be involved. They're struggling. You're right — they don't understand what needs to be done with Kettlesheer to make it work, but you *do*. You could help."

Robert shoved his hands in his pockets. "So what are you saying? That I should just fall in with what everyone expects me to do? Move to some leaky barn that I'll have to patch up as long as I live and then foist onto my own kids?"

"It doesn't have to be like that," I said, thinking of Ingrid despairing over the accounts. "There are loads of businesses you could start, grants you can get. It's a wonderful place! I've only been here four days, and I never want to leave! And that's without any emotional blackmail from anyone!"

Robert spun round and stomped a few steps away, staring out into the trees.

I waited. I thought I'd probably said too much already, but I wasn't sure what to do next. I was in the middle of a forest. A snow-covered forest.

Eventually, he turned back and spoke in a soft, quite angry voice.

"Dad keeps going on about how it's our duty to keep the castle going, because he remembers his father telling *him*. And his father's mother telling *him*. But that's not how our family life was. *I* didn't grow up hearing about how one day I'd have to drop everything and move up to Scotland and be a farmer. Even Dad didn't think he'd have to — I mean, he wore tartan trousers at the weekend and wept tears of pure Macallan at rugby internationals, but you can do that when you're safely in south London and have two uncles ahead of you in the queue, can't you?"

"But you're here now."

"It's a bit late for being sat down at my dad's knee now! I'm thirty-one. I've got my own life, my own career, my own plans." Robert rubbed his hand over his face. "Look, we've had this conversation. I just feel like I keep having it with bloody everyone up here."

"Did you read the postcards?" I asked.

"I did." He looked me in the eye, and though he was cross, I could see something else: panic. "I know what you're trying to do, and it's a sweet idea, but even that's someone else's love story. Not mine. What have I got in common with some rich American princess? Or her landed husband? I'm a self-employed businessman, Evie. This isn't my life."

"But it wasn't Violet's either! She came from New York and —"

"Evie, stories don't do it for me the way they obviously do it for you," he said. "I need something a bit more factual."

"But Violet was a smart cookie too!" I insisted. "Sheila Graham says everyone round here really respected her for the way she kept the house going after she was widowed, kept everyone in work. That's not some airhead, that's a businesswoman. I bet if you went through those rooms, you'd find the most incredible records, a real story —"

Robert raised an eyebrow at my passionate hand-waving, and I stopped, suddenly self-conscious.

"Sheila also said you'd find it different when you wanted to settle down," I went on. "I know that can be scary. But I know lots of people who weren't sure about getting married, and they took the plunge and now —"

"Oh, *God,*" said Robert, and set off walking again. "I preferred it when you were trying to sell me on the house."

I caught his arm. "Robert."

He turned back. "What?"

I screwed up my courage; at least let one good thing come out of my mortification. "Don't let Catriona think you're going to propose on Saturday if you're not. There's really nothing worse than" — my face was burning again — "than realizing you've read the signals wrong. . . ."

"Does that actually *happen* in —" he scoffed, but I carried on.

"And that the reason everyone is cheering is because the man you thought might be proposing to you is actually proposing to someone else."

"Oh." Robert fell silent. "That sounds painful."

"Mmm."

It had been. Jack Wrightson. My ex-flatmate and, I thought, secret admirer. We'd spent many a long night having exactly the sort of long, confessional conversations I felt soul mates should have. He had gorgeous Byronic eyes and long hair, and I'd totally pictured him proposing on the steps of St. Paul's during one of our long chatty mooches around London. I'd even hinted as much to Mum.

Sadly not.

It was still something that was raised at Christmas: "Some people grow out of having imaginary friends as toddlers, Evie. They don't develop imaginary fiancés. . . ."

"How did you get from . . . presumably not much to proposing? If it's not a rude question?"

I sighed and started walking. "Well, when you've got quite an overactive imagination . . ."

Whether it was the forest or Robert, the words tumbled out surprisingly easily. "I've got used to having to fill in the blanks. Supply the romance. You don't know how lucky you are, having a *tradition* to get married to. My family's the least romantic ever. My parents never row and make up, they don't have nicknames, they don't even have a song!"

"A song?"

"You know, like 'Candle in the Wind,' or 'Angels.' "

"Those are both songs about death, Evie."

"Whatever." I crunched faster. "They're shared romance. My biggest fear is marrying a man who gives me power drills for Christmas, like Dad does. Okay, so maybe I overcompensate, and maybe I do want things to be rosier than they are; but honestly, if you'd grown up in my house, you'd be making top-ten favorite historical periods for proposals too."

Robert kindly said nothing.

I stopped, and he stopped next to me. "Catriona's already mentally redecorating the house for when you'll move in together,"

I said. "Please don't make a fool of her, just because you don't know what you want to do with yourself. Do you love her?"

I didn't think so. There were no sneaking glances, no excuses to touch. But then, what did I know?

Robert looked uneasy. "Cat'd make an excellent mistress of a house like Kettlesheer," he said. "And I think she's being pushed into it as much as me. She's a nice girl, I like her. It helps that her dad's the only bloke round here with any money." He arched an eyebrow. "Nothing changes much."

"What if there was something in the house that was worth selling?" I asked eagerly. "Something . . . really important?"

"Is there?"

"There might be."

He looked at me shrewdly. "Then Dad wouldn't sell it."

"Unless you persuaded him that it was worth it, to keep the house." I looked Robert in the eye. "If you found a reason to keep Kettlesheer in the family."

He didn't drop my gaze, and we stood in the moonlight, trying to read each other's minds. Robert's gaze was fierce, and it really felt as if he was trying to drag the thoughts out of my head.

I thought of petite Violet, toughening to survive the Scottish winters, and Ranald, wrapping her in his thick tweed topcoat as they walked back to the lunch hut after a late-autumn pheasant shoot. I didn't know where the image had come from, but it was sharp in my mind.

"You look cold," he said. "Let's get you back to your bed. Come on."

He put an arm around me, initially to move me along, but he left it there as we walked, and it warmed me up. There was no actual physical contact through our many, many layers of clothes, but the gesture was warm.

The woodland was thinning out now, and as we stepped onto the path that led to the house, a cloud moved away from the moon. Clean, cold light flooded Kettlesheer's turreted roofline, leaving it stark against the sky like a film set.

"Fabulous," I breathed.

"All it needs now is a werewolf," agreed Robert. "Or a broomstick."

"Or a family ghost."

"I'm sure we've got one of them," he said. "I'm surprised you haven't found one."

"Give me time," I said. "I've got a few more days. . . ."

Robert smiled, and it reached his unsettling, beautiful eyes.

Stop it, I told myself. *This isn't your fairy tale.*

NINETEEN

I tried to get hold of Alice before breakfast, after breakfast, and on the half hour before lunch, but she wasn't answering her phone. There were things I needed to discuss with her as a matter of urgency — what I was going to wear, for one, and when she was going to call poor Fraser with a decent explanation.

It wasn't as if I had time to run in and out, since I was also supposed to be handing Duncan a preliminary list of what he could expect to sell. To do that properly, I needed to hear from Max about the table, and he was proving elusive too.

Meanwhile, Kettlesheer itself was metamorphosing into a green and gold winter palace. Despite the thick snow blocking some roads, the Ball Committee and its team of volunteers had descended on Kettlesheer with a vengeance, and now tumbling arrangements of ivy and golden apples were springing up everywhere and massive candles were being fastened in every crevice. Ladies in tartan pinnies whisked dusters around while log fires were built in every available grate and scattered with fragrant pinecones.

Deliverymen wheeled box after box of wine through the hall, supervised by Fraser, who'd arrived in his off-duty red jeans to brief the bar staff on the drinks they'd be serving and also to speak with the caterers preparing Ingrid's dinner for sixty.

Poor Fraser kept trying to catch my eye like a freshly kicked spaniel, clearly hoping for some news of Alice's sprained ankle. I was already avoiding Catriona and her Bluetooth headset. She'd cornered me in the dining room while I was trying to get another look at the Chippendale and made me demonstrate the steps of the Duke of Perth reel using eight silver salt and pepper pots being polished by Sheila and Ingrid.

(I got it more or less right, though, as Sheila pointed out, it would have been easier if the condiments had been more obviously male and female.)

The whole morning was very like a reel: me scuttling in and out of rooms, round and behind everyone else, swapping one conversation off against another, and generally trying to avoid everyone other than Sheila and Ingrid.

I couldn't avoid them: they both had lists of tasks for me to help with.

"It's all hands on deck," said Ingrid, who'd taken on a much happier air since I'd hinted about the possible lifeline in the dining room. "Where's my son? He should be up here, mucking in."

"If he doesn't come up to help us, I'm going down to get him," announced Sheila, over the sound of a Jacobean reiver-crushing shield being covered in bubble wrap by two of Janet's elderly foot soldiers. "He *knows* we're run off our feet."

"He's maybe working," I said. "His office is phoning him even though he's on holiday."

"And what am I doing?" demanded Ingrid wildly. "Self-tanning? So much for glamming up before the ball — have you seen my nails? I'm going to fail Janet's inspection!"

Sheila turned to me. "Evie, do you have to go down there this morning for e-mails? Maybe you could persuade him to grace us with his presence."

"I'm not sure I'm his favorite person this morning," I said. "We had a bit of a discussion about the house last night. I think I

314

might have been rather . . . frank."

I'd actually woken up at 6 a.m. with some of the things I'd said clanging in my ears. I'd gone *far* too far. I barely knew the man, and I'd told him what he should do with a life I had no clue about. And oh, God, I'd also admitted my own most embarrassing secret. Not even Max knew about Jack Wrightson and the Invisible Proposal. Yet now Robert did.

Sheila gave me a shrewd look. "Oh, I don't know. I've seen more of Robert round here this week than we usually do in a month."

"It's true," said Ingrid. "Last time he had dinner up here voluntarily was when the river flooded and his electricity went off. And yet . . . twice this week. *And* a trip to the Grahams'."

"Where he's not set foot in over a year, despite repeated invitations."

They turned their combined laser beams on me.

"I think he just enjoys talking to someone from London," I offered weakly.

"But, darling, you *don't* talk about London," said Ingrid. "You only seem to talk about this house!"

"Ladies! What a hive of industry!"

We all jumped as Duncan strode in, his gingery hair wild around his head like static.

315

I slid my notebook off the table and onto my lap, where it wouldn't draw attention to itself. I had a draft list of items to discuss with him, but obviously the table made a huge difference. And beneath my bubbling excitement about it, I couldn't quite shake off that odd sense of . . . wrongness.

"Evie, we must find a moment amidst this fevered preparation to sit down and discuss your discoveries," said Duncan. "When do you think would be a good time?"

"When's a good time for you?" I hedged.

"This afternoon?"

I glanced at Sheila. "Actually, if the main road's clear, I was hoping maybe Fraser might be able to drive me into Berwick this afternoon. Alice's dress still hasn't arrived, and I need to find something to wear."

"Poor Alice. Did she manage to get to the post office?" Ingrid asked innocently. "How is her ankle? It was her ankle, wasn't it?"

"Yes." My neck went hot. "I expect she got her assistant to parcel it up."

Bloody Alice, I thought. These were really, *really* nice people, and I was having to lie to them — and I couldn't even do it convincingly because I was as clueless as they were about why she was being so rude.

"Och, I'm sure he'd be happy to take you," said Sheila. "He's always going on about how that car of his could drive up the side of Ben Nevis."

"This evening, then." Duncan rubbed his hands gleefully. "I must admit, I'm quite excited — it reminds me of opening the first bottle of the year's vintage. How have we done? What surprises will there be? What delights have been revealed?"

"Duncan," I began nervously, "it's really only a preliminary —"

"I'll go and find Fraser now," said Sheila. "Can't have Cinderella going to the ball with no dress!"

"Who doesn't have a dress?"

Catriona had appeared in the doorway, clipboard primed for action and problem radar swiveling.

"Evie's ballgown hasn't arrived yet," said Ingrid. "She was hoping Fraser could run her into Berwick this afternoon, to see what she can find."

"But Fraser's supposed to be moving the trestle tables downstairs for the caterers to start setting up." Catriona's mouth closed, her eyes went blank as her brain worked; then she smiled, plan formed. "I'm sure *I've* got something you can borrow, Evie. The roads are awful — Ollie Jennings nearly wrote off his Subaru last night. You could be gone hours, and there's no guarantee you'd find anything. We're about the same size, aren't we?"

I wasn't sure what to say without being rude to one of us. I was at least four inches taller than Catriona, but whereas she spent her free time riding and breathing country air, I spent mine eBaying and chain-crunching Pringles, and the difference was at least one dress size.

"I've got a couple of stretchy ones," she offered, as if reading my mind. "I can pop home at lunchtime and bring some over for you to try."

"That's *very* sweet of you, Catriona," said Ingrid. "I'd offer Evie something from the trunk we found, but they're so tiny, the old dresses, aren't they, Sheila?"

Sheila nodded. "I'm having to let them out for Ingrid, and you can see what a wee bird she is."

"No, I've ripped enough vintage jackets in my time to know I'm not vintage-sized," I said. "Thank you, Catriona."

What else could I say? It wasn't that I wanted to go to the only ball I'd ever be invited to in someone's old "stretchy" dress, but what alternative was there? I crossed my fingers that somehow Alice's ballgown might still turn up. That was definitely worth another call. She could harass the couriers from her end.

"I'll pop back now and sort that out." Catriona flashed me a satisfied smile and pulled a pen out of the top pocket of her pinafore to jot a reminder on her clipboard.

I noted, with a sinking heart, that she was wearing a pinafore. That didn't bode well for the dresses.

"And I'll go and see if I can raise Robert," I said. It occurred to me that if I called Alice from *Robert's* landline, she might just pick up.

"You do that, hen," said Sheila with a wink.

Outside the sun was bright and surprisingly warm on my face, despite the nip in the air. In the distance the Cheviots were solid white with snow, and the sky above them was pure and clear like pale blue glass.

The second I got any reception at all, I pulled one flap of Robert's trapper hat up and applied the phone to my ear to get my messages.

To my absolute astonishment, the first was from Alice, Queen of Cheek. She must have called in the three-minute window when I hadn't been trying to call her.

"Just me, checking in to see if everything's okay. Have you got the dress yet? And have

319

you remembered to leave some money in your room for the housekeeper?"

"Oh, for God's sake!" I spluttered. She couldn't stop micromanaging even when she'd bailed out.

The second message was also from her. "Meant to say, is Fraser all right? What did you tell him? I hope you didn't tell him anything too outré."

That was it. I phoned her back, ready to leave a ripsnorting message when she didn't pick up.

Imagine my surprise, then, when she did.

"Evie, are you all right?"

I stopped walking. I was right in the middle of the woods, halfway between the lodge and the main house. No one could hear me.

"Finally you pick up," I said icily. "I've only been trying to get hold of you all morning. How are you?"

"Fine," she said. "Apart from this client of Mum's — he's a footballer and he collects turf from famous pitches, can you imagine the mess, they're all over the —"

"That's not what I meant."

"Oh," said Alice in a small voice. "Is this about Fraser?"

"Yes," I said. "It *is* about Fraser."

Maybe it was something about the snow

and the woods that unleashed some unusually fierce home-truth-dispensing instinct, but I was overwhelmed with a vision of Fraser dropping everything to drive me into Berwick with his snow chains, Fraser patiently teaching me to dance, Fraser covering up his disappointment so as not to spoil my weekend, when in fact Alice had just ruined his. Maybe even ruined his lovely planned proposal.

And this wasn't me whipping up imaginary visions; this was real.

I'd always fancied Fraser, but I'd never *liked* him as much as I did after this week. He was a real gentleman, and he didn't deserve to be messed around with like this. Especially if that reason was something to do with Robert.

Oh, God, it was so complicated. Alice always managed to make things so *complicated,* when all I wanted was a nice, straightforward happy-ever-after.

"Alice, there's something I have to say, and you mustn't interrupt until I've finished," I began.

"Oh, actually, while I remember — the dress," Alice interrupted, before I'd even stopped telling her not to. "You might need to get some Spanx —"

"No!" I shouted, then lowered my voice.

"I mean, no, it's not about that, it's about Fraser."

That shut her up.

I swallowed and crashed onward, walking fast as if my feet could somehow give my brain momentum.

"I need to know why you're not coming," I said. "I can't carry on lying to everyone — it's not fair on me or him. And besides which, I think you're making a huge mistake. He is an *amazingly* nice man."

"Don't, Evie."

"Don't what? Don't remind you what you're risking screwing up here? Do you know how his mother is looking at me right now? Sheila's not a stupid woman, Alice. She knows there's something up."

"Don't," she said again, in the *la-la-la not listening* tone that reminded me of Mum.

"Don't say *don't!* That's the problem, no one in our family actually gets past the bloody *don't!*" I spun round, frustrated. "It's Robert, isn't it? Have you had some kind of fling with Robert and you're scared of seeing him? Because if it is that — *don't interrupt me!* — I can totally see why, he's incredibly sexy in that smooth London way you go for, but he's not Fraser. And frankly, he's so completely wrapped up in his own problems that I very much doubt he'd even find time to —"

"It's not Rob. I mean, Robert," said Alice. "We're . . . I mean, he's . . . there's nothing to discuss. Ask him." She paused. Then said, "Actually, don't ask him."

"Well, *that* tells me everything!" I declared.

"No, it doesn't. You're making it sound all dramatic and it's not," she said crossly. "We just . . . had a misunderstanding. That party I met Fraser at — well, I thought I was going *with* Robert, only I wasn't, as it turned out; but it was okay because I met Fraser, but ever since, Robert's always been a bit 'You're not good enough for my mate because you flirted with me,' and then we had a bit of a frank exchange of views about business, and . . ."

I was stalled at the part where Alice had imaginary relationships too.

"We get on fine now," she insisted, "apart from when he tries to boss me around. Fraser says we're very alike, which I don't see at all. I honestly didn't know he'd be there this week. If I'd known, I'd have told you. *Warned* you."

"So why aren't you here?" I demanded. "The only explanation I can think of is that you're trying to let Fraser down gently, and if that's the case, you'd better be really sure you know what you're doing, because there are girls *queuing up* here for him."

"I'm not trying to let him down," she spluttered. "What gives you that idea?"

"I know what you're like," I went on. I wasn't going to bring this up, but I heard myself saying it anyway. "How long have you two been going out? Two years? Isn't this about the time you normally bail? When they try to give you the key to their flat?"

"I do not!"

"It's exactly what you do!" I howled. "Every time! You audit them, and always find a ridiculous problem. Alice, Fraser is a keeper! He's going to be a fantastic father, and a gorgeous, supportive husband, and in thirty years' time he'll be a silver fox and your daughter's friends will have massive crushes on him!"

"Like you do now?" she sniped back.

I stopped spinning and came to a sudden halt by a patch of spiky fern poking through the snow. "Like I — what?"

"I'm sorry," said Alice. "But don't lecture me about bailing out on relationships when you're the one who only has crushes on men you can't have."

"I —"

"Fraser. Max. David Tennant. Don Draper in *Mad Men* who *doesn't even exist,* Evie! Men you can slot into your ridiculous period-costume daydreams where everyone says 'Goodness!' and uses Brylcreem. You fixate on men who won't ever ask you to live in the real world. That's far more of a problem, if you ask me. That and cramming your flat full of other people's junk instead of getting your own bloody life."

It felt as if she'd thrown a glass of ice water over me. I stared sightlessly at the rabbit prints looping across the path. The agonizing thing was, I knew she was right, in her brutal, neat-and-tidy way.

"You call me a control freak," she went on remorselessly, "but if you ask me, you're the ultimate control freak."

"At least I don't make my boyfriends sterilize their toothbrushes if they leave them in my flat."

"Ha!" barked Alice. "As if you have men staying overnight! They can't get past the pile of moth-eaten bears on your bed. And if that's not Freudian, I don't know what is!"

My throat was hot and tight, as if something was trying to force itself out. "I just don't want to be like Mum and Dad!" I wailed, so loud three pheasants launched themselves out of the tree next to me.

"Well, neither do I!" Alice bellowed back. "I'm bloody terrified of marrying Fraser and ending up with beanbag TV dinner trays! In the middle of nowhere! Talking about slacks we like in the Lands' End catalogue!"

We were both quiet. I could hear the traffic in the background at her end; there was no sound in the forest for her to hear at mine. The wildlife had sensibly gone to ground.

I honestly didn't know what I could say next; it was the most honest conversation we'd ever had and I couldn't even see her face.

"Alice, where are you?" I asked. "Are you on your own?"

"The reason I am too scared to come up there this weekend is that I'm afraid Fraser will propose," said Alice haltingly. "Everyone will be watching — his parents, his friends, everyone. I do love him, you have to believe that, but . . . I'm scared."

The crack in her voice made me want to hug her and shake her at the same time.

"You're not scared of anything," I said. "Why are you scared of someone loving you so much he's prepared to spend the rest of his life with you?"

"Because Fraser deserves someone who can *guarantee* he'll be happy. I don't know if I can do that."

"Well, who can?"

"Someone who comes from the same sort of world as him. Someone who knows what to do with a pheasant. Someone who can dance, and bring up happy children with mucky faces, and not care if the dog licks them clean."

"Would you believe me if I told you that the most romantic story I've ever heard was about a pampered American and a Scottish bachelor who —"

"Stop it. You're making it up." Alice heaved a sigh. "It's not like I could have got there anyway, is it? Didn't you say the roads are closed?"

"If you loved him, you'd find a way to get here. He would for you." I stopped, visualizing Fraser driving through snow and ice (admittedly in a horse and cart), doing anything for Alice because he loved her. How long had I tried to imagine a man like that into existence? And failed?

"Fraser is divine and real. If you can't see that, then, yeah, maybe you don't deserve him."

"Evie —"

I couldn't talk to her anymore. I was too churned-up and cross. And jealous.

"I've got to go. I need to talk to Max. Believe it or not, I do have other things to worry about, like my job. And what I'm going to say to all these very nice people to explain why you're too rude to be here."

"Call me later, after fiveish —"

"I'll call you when I can." I hung up and turned to set off again, but my phone rang again.

"I've got a buyer, and better than that, guess what?"

It was Max. *Great.*

TWENTY

"What?" I said heavily. "I'm not in the mood for guessing."

"I've got a TV crew! From the BBC. Remember that runner who booked Leonard Slaine for that terrible 'Sell your granny for cash' program?" Max actually sounded as if he'd had his teeth whitened. He was schlurring schlightly. "Well, he reckons he can get a team together, on the cheap obviously, to follow me as I find the last undiscovered Chippendale in England. He's got a title already: *Max Uncovers the Chippendales!* Or something like that."

I closed my eyes. Max's dream was to break into the closed circle of TV antiques experts. This was an even bigger deal for him than the money. Wheels were being set in motion now, and I knew I should be thrilled, but somehow I wasn't.

"So you scuttle back there and give McAndrew senior the glad tidings," Max

329

went on starrily. "Tell him to settle back and prepare for fame and fortune."

I headed back to the house, strange emotions swilling round me.

It was too much to deal with in one go. Like a particularly toxic party punch of stress — Alice and Fraser, Robert, the table, the looming financial peril of the house, topped off with my own guilty excitement at a real ball — it was making me feel nauseous.

I needed to sit down with Violet's notebooks and just take stock, I told myself. Tune back in to my instincts. Tune back in to the house.

Inside, the hall was a bustling hive of activity, but I pretended to be on an errand and trotted up the sweeping staircase.

When I got to the top, I was struck with a sudden urge to see Violet's beautiful ballroom, before it was filled with dancers.

The clamor downstairs faded away and the velvety silence of the upper floors descended as I turned down the landing toward the ballroom, now helpfully marked with a wooden sign. I pushed open the double doors and held my breath, letting the atmosphere seep into me as I walked slowly across the empty room, drinking in the details greedily.

It was oak-paneled around the five tall windows, each offering a long view of the snow-covered drive. Huge mirrors hung from chains to reflect the candlelight from spidery wall sconces, perfect for stealing glances and checking out rivals, and a row of gold-painted chairs had been set up along the long wall. At the far end of the room was a magnificent organ, its fluted pipes reaching up to the lofty ceiling, garlanded with — yes, feathers and violets, crowned with an eagle. There was no other furniture, just the meticulous slats of the polished floorboards. And the lingering tremors of a thousand memories, triumphs, heartbreaks, surprises, rivalries . . .

My spine elongated as if I were crossing the floor in a corseted ballgown with a diamond tiara balanced in my elaborate hairdo. I couldn't help it. The air was full of ghosts, like the tiny fragments of light that sparkled from the crystal chandelier above me, dancing on the polished floorboards.

I closed my eyes and wished I could open them again and be at one of Violet's glory-days balls, when she had American dollars to lavish on entertaining, and her Ranald to adore, and no clouds on her newlywed horizon. I ached to meet her — she seemed so close all the time, yet tantalizingly distant.

"Believe it or not, this is my favorite room in the house," said a voice from the door.

I jumped.

I saw Robert reflected in the mirror opposite. He was standing in the doorframe, his arms crossed, watching me. I wondered, embarrassed, how long he'd been there.

"Why's that? Because there's nothing in here?" I pretended I'd been looking at the carved panel opposite, and turned round as casually as I could.

"Exactly. I love it because there's never anything in it." His shoes echoed as he walked over, and he raised a hand toward a carved cherub gamboling to a panpipe. "It is what it is. The proportions, the space . . . it's designed for its purpose. Which is dancing."

"Which you don't like," I reminded him.

Robert gave me a funny look. "I didn't say that."

"You did."

"I said I wasn't keen on the *ball.*"

"That's not the impression you've given *me,*" I started, but my brain abruptly crashed with an overload of too many other thoughts, heightened by the still yet charged atmosphere — Robert's crooked mouth, the flash of skin under the neck of his T-shirt, the owlish way he was looking at me, the sudden crackle of connection filling the space between us in this enormous room. I had to make myself look away.

"I bet it's alive when everyone's packed in." My hands were itching to touch something, so I trailed my fingers along the petals of a carved violet. "I think anyone could dance better in here," I added. "It feels . . . as if it's waiting."

"This is the only room that has any real meaning to me," he said. "Not those cases of prehistoric flints or Italian marbles. Violet McAndrew created this room because she loved to dance, and people still dance here now."

I looked up — his dark eyes were watching me, his lips slightly parted. I wondered how like Ranald he was, what he would look like in uniform, with a mustache. I imagined all the McAndrew men, whizzing backward through time in a collage of faces, the eyes staying the same.

"Course, it could just be the snow," he went on. "It is kind of spooky."

I stepped over to the stone windowsill and gazed out at the fairy-tale landscape stretching down the drive. The ballroom had a full panorama of the snow-blanketed park rolling away toward the woods, broken only by faint footsteps across the verandah toward the steps. The trees glittered in the last rays of wintry afternoon sun, which flooded the ballroom with a spectral bluish light. I could see the dust motes flicker in the air like tiny ghosts.

It was so quiet I could hear Robert breathing, and for a dizzying second, it felt as if we were the only people in the whole house. And even though my back was turned to him, I knew exactly how far away from me he was.

"There is a rather different atmosphere in here today," he added, at the same time that I said, "I don't think I've ever seen anything as beautiful as this."

I turned; Robert was close — exactly where I'd known he was — and our eyes met. I felt as if he was reading all the confused thoughts churning round in my head, and I blushed.

"You know, you were very wrong the other night, when you thought I expected to you mess up," he said. "I actually think you've learned it all amazingly fast. Has Fraser managed to teach you the proper fast spin all the girls do up here?"

"God, no," I said. "I've got the patterns of the reels in my head, that's all fine, but I can't make the spin work. I want to, because it looks amazing, but I keep locking up. I don't know what happens, my mind's telling me one thing, and my limbs just go —"

"We've plenty of room here," he said. "Want to give it another try?"

"Oh, um, no, it's fine. . . ." My voice echoed in the empty ballroom, bouncing off the high ceiling.

What was I saying? Of course I wanted to, any excuse to feel his hands in mine. But I had a horrible feeling it would be better in my imagination, where there was less chance of me falling over and possibly injuring him to boot.

"The lack of an audience might help," he suggested.

"Okay," I said, more matter-of-factly than I felt. "Show me what to do." I held out my hands.

"Other way up," said Robert. "Here, look." He took hold of my wrists, positioned them the correct way, and clasped my hands in his, wrapping his fingers round mine.

I shivered, and hoped he couldn't feel it. We'd done this before, but this felt different. More deliberate, more intimate.

"Now, don't *think,* just feel what I'm trying to do with you," he said firmly. "Relax. Now, I'm turning you round. . . ."

His hands tightened, and he raised his

own arms so I had no choice but to rotate slowly toward his body.

"And now I'm going to give you an extra spin, so go with it, that's it, just keep going round, and because I'm a helpful sort of chap, I'm going to position you right in front of the next man in the set. . . ."

All the while he was speaking, Robert was purposefully turning me on the spot, and my feet were obediently following. His voice sounded calm, but in the silence of the room, I could hear his breathing speeding up.

Meanwhile, my own heart was banging so loud in my chest it might as well have had amplifiers.

". . . and there you are." Robert released me with a little push, and I stumbled slightly, and found myself staring at the fireplace, piled with unlit logs and pine-cones. "Ready to dance with Fraser."

I'd done it. No lockup, no embarrassing yelp from my partner. It had been so neat and quick and . . . satisfying.

"When did you learn how to do that?" I asked. "Growing up in Wimbledon and all."

"Oh, once a Scot, you know. I went to a few Highland balls at college, once I learned just what an aphrodisiac a good reel can be. And I had plenty of offers of practice." He grinned at me. "From ladies who liked to be spun so fast they lost their breath."

I caught sight of my own face in one of the mirrors lining the walls: I looked stunned. In a good way.

"Want to try that one more time?" he asked. "Make sure it wasn't a fluke?"

My stomach bubbled with excitement, but I kept my voice cool. "Practice makes perfect."

I held out my hands, the right way up, and he grabbed me again. He spun me faster this time, turning me round and inside out, not letting go as soon as he had before.

"Just trust me," he called out as I staggered, not sure where I was. "You've got to go with it, no point trying to second-guess. Let the man be in charge. Should appeal to your costume-drama tendencies."

"I think I'm starting to get the hang of this," I said as he caught me again and pulled me into another one.

"I think you are too," said Robert. He paused, and we stared at each other, our faces still quite close together. His eyes burned into mine.

"One more go? Fast as you like?" I raised my hands and risked a flirty wink. "So fast I lose my breath?"

But instead of grabbing my wrists to spin me, Robert scooped one arm round my waist and lifted my right hand in the air.

"There's more to the ball than just reeling, you know," he said, setting off in a dizzying circle. "There's breaks for waltzing too."

"Stop! I've done waltzing, this is going to end in tears!" I protested, laughing, but he kept moving, and my feet somehow skittered round between his.

"Don't tell me you haven't imagined yourself in a proper ball situation?" he went on. "Crinoline? Tiara? 'The Blue Danube'?"

"I have!" I protested. Our bodies were pressed close together now, properly close, not the quick hand-grip and touch of the reeling. "But I saw myself on the side, watching from behind my fan."

"You didn't see yourself dancing?" His eyes stayed on mine, and his arm tightened around my waist, guiding me. "That's very sad."

"No, it's perfectly reasonable — I can't dance!"

"What are you doing now, then?"

"*I'm* not doing anything!"

Robert stopped in a long dust-strewn shaft of snow-white light. My feet took a second to catch up, and skidded my body into his.

338

Neither of us moved away.

I could feel his heart beating through the thin jersey, the pulse of his blood in his neck where my hand rested. We were both completely still, afraid to move. He held me, one arm curled round my waist, the other folding my hand into his shoulder, and my breath shuddered in my throat. He was so close I could smell his skin, and it was making me feel weak with desire.

"Evie," he began, his voice low. "I looked at those postcards again, and it made me realize that —"

"Evie? Evie, are you up here?" A voice broke the silence. A very carrying voice.

Catriona.

I sprang out of Robert's grasp as her kitten heels snapped down the corridor outside.

"In the ballroom," I called out, making my way to the door.

"I need to talk to you," Robert started, but I was already pulling the doors open, not wanting her to think we were hiding.

"There you are!" Catriona had come straight from the car; there was still snow dusting her full-length mac, and she was clutching a sports bag. She looked like Darth Vader's hockey coach.

"You went home to get the dresses? That's

339

incredibly kind of you," I said, in a voice that didn't really sound like mine. "I know how *terribly* busy you are today."

God, I sounded like her. I always did impressions of the people I was talking to when I was nervous.

"It's my pleasure — Oh," she said in a sharp voice, "there you are, Robbie. We've all been looking for you. I thought you'd skipped the country."

"Nope, I had a call from work," he said. "I couldn't tell them to wait until I'd put out three hundred gold chairs, believe it or not."

"Yes, well, I was about to send the ladies in here to start the decoration." She thrust the bag at me. "There should be something there that'll fit. Have a try-on, and if you need any alterations, I'm sure Sheila will stitch you up. Do remember, though," she added meaningfully, "the important thing is to be *comfortable* at these dances, not *fashionable*."

"At least you know they'll be preapproved by the dress-code enforcers," said Robert, deadpan, his hands deep in his pockets.

"Oh, you!" Catriona swatted him, but her eyes were steely. "Do you know what Mummy found? In our attic?"

"Your dad?"

"No! Granddad's sporran! The one he wore at the Highland Games when he danced with the Queen Mother." She turned to me. "My paternal grandfather came from a very old Orkadian family. Much older than the McAndrews. Although obviously I don't want to rub Robbie's nose in it, ha-ha! But it would make Mummy so happy if you could wear it over your kilt, Rob."

"Well, as I keep telling Evie, I'm not into antiques!" he said in the same light but steely tone. "Or kilts."

Catriona pulled a *Men!* face at me, and I didn't know what face to pull in return. I settled for a nervous/amused one that I could see, from the mirrors, just made me look stoned.

The light outside had shifted, and abruptly the room felt strange, as if the friendly dancing ghosts had vanished with the sunlight. It was colder, less welcoming. The ballroom belonged to Catriona and Robert, the future hosts, not me, crashing the party in my borrowed dress to rake up the past.

I watched as Catriona snaked her hand round Robert's, slipping it into his pocket.

This wasn't like one of the reels where partners changed merrily from one step to another. This was set long in advance. And there was a lot more depending on it. People's feelings, people's lives. It really wasn't up to me to start whisking it all up, then vanishing while the champagne corks were still being swept away.

A gloomy sense of missing the boat settled on my shoulders. I was here at the wrong time, in the wrong place, yet again. I was used to that — feeling melancholy that I would never wear buttoned boots or live in Victorian Mayfair — but this was a very modern ache, and it hurt.

"I should . . . be getting on," I said. "I'm supposed to be giving your dad my rough report this evening."

"And I need to get on with my team," said Catriona. "That's the trouble with being a perfectionist, I guess! Still, it's good practice for future events, eh, Robbie?" She beamed at me. "Weddings. Don't you think this would make the most marvelous venue for weddings?"

I glanced between them. She looked serene, converting the kitchens and building into holiday lets already, but Robert's eyes were hooded and thoughtful. Somewhere else.

"I'll leave you to it," I said, and did.

TWENTY-ONE

I spent the rest of the afternoon shuttling happily from one ball-related task to another, feeling more Christmas Eve-y as the daylight faded and the lamps went on. I tied gold ribbons, twisted linen napkins into holly-and-ivy rings, and listened to endless stories about proposals. Everyone seemed to have met their husbands at the Kettlesheer ball. It was like a matrimonial eBay.

All this bustling, though, wasn't keeping the castle chill out of my bones. Now that I knew about the oil bill, I could hardly moan about Ingrid keeping the heating turned down, so I excused myself and went back upstairs in search of my last clean cardigan.

But Mhairi had been up and had tidied my clothes again, and not into the same drawers as last time. I looked at the endless chests and cupboards: the room wasn't short of mahogany-based storage space. Ranald must have had a lot of clothes, I thought, starting with the tallboy by the window. How long had Violet kept his shirts and tweeds just as they were, smelling of him, in these drawers?

Maybe Max's television contact was a *good* thing, I reasoned as I rhythmically opened and closed drawers, finding nothing but mothballs and old drawer liners. Maybe they could include dramatizations of Violet's incredible transatlantic love story, from fortuitous bicycle crash to her brave fight for survival, interspersed with documentary stuff about the Chippendale table.

Ooh, yes! My imagination caught fire. And Robert could probably do some kind of deal. They could open a tearoom. Hold weddings in the ballroom! Let it out to other BBC film units to film period dramas . . . yes!

No sign of my own cashmere. I turned to the next likely chest, a long bowfront commode with a pitcher and ewer on top.

And maybe Robert would find some business deal in the romance that could —

I stopped. My eagle eye had spotted a key taped to the side of the top drawer, with a label reading *Bathroom* in faded script. I peeled it off. It was too small to lock the door. What was there in the bathroom that had a lock? A cupboard? A medicine chest?

Positively vibrating with Miss Marple—ness, I hurried into the big bathroom, which had taken on a whole new feel to me now that I knew Violet and Ranald had shared it. The double-ended bath, and the twin cupboards, and the looping brass towel-warmers . . .

No time now for romantic bath speculation. I frowned into the speckled mirror. Nothing. I ran my hands over the dark panels, tapping, feeling for a loose bit of wood. I lifted up the watercolors of High-land scenes on the walls, in case there was a concealed safe. Nothing.

I sank against the rolltop bath, frustrated. Maybe it wasn't *this* bathroom. How many bathrooms were there in Kettlesheer? The enormity of the challenge crushed me, and then I spotted something odd about the medicine cabinet. Slowly I went over to it, and moved aside an old bottle of Listerine and spare coal-tar soap.

In the back was a keyhole.

My hands shook as I pulled out the shelves, then slipped the key into the lock. I had to jiggle it around, but then the whole cabinet swiveled open to reveal a little safe, built into the oak panels. I frowned at the dial, then turned it to 1-9-0-2, the year of Violet's marriage. It swung open.

"I knew it," I breathed. "Ha, Robert. Who's laughing at my panel tapping now?"

I had to admit to a little flutter of anticlimax when I reached in and pulled out not a soft leather pouch of diamonds but another notebook.

It looked familiar. Very familiar. I patted around in the space, just in case there was a diamond or two, but that was it. Nothing else in there.

The light was better in the bedroom, so I went back in and sat on the bed to examine the book properly. Why would you lock up a notebook? Maybe it was a journal! I was desperate to find Violet's proper diary, not just menu lists.

Hungrily, I opened it, and was instantly disappointed. It seemed to be some kind of scrapbook, filled with yellowed cuttings and notes in Violet's madly curling hand. She'd clipped wedding announcements and society details from newspapers and magazines. *Née Maybelle Asquith!* she'd written against one. *In motorcar engines!* against another. *Now in Baltimore!*

I felt a shard of sympathy for Violet as the scent of money and distant glamour rose from the lines. Even if she loved the place, it must have been hard for her after Ranald died, reading about the girlfriends she'd done her London season with making their second and third marriages in New York and London, while she was on her own with five children, difficult tenants, and huge bills that had to be paid with something. Every year that passed, she must have felt more and more left behind with her memories.

I turned a page and came across a draft letter, dated February 17, 1934, and covered in crossings-out.

I lifted the letter nearer the lamp to make out the words better. She was an enthusiastic rather than neat writer. I could actually see her mind working under the scribbles and scratches.

Dear Mrs. Whitelaw Ward *[crossed out]*
Bettina *[written above]*,

I was so pleased to hear that Beatrice liked the charming occasional table I found for you, and that it took pride of place in her wedding gifts! It was, as far as I know, crafted around 1840 and is made from Scottish oak. I hesitate to embarrass the lady who sold it to me, but the family is much envied for its fine collection of furniture, and she can vouch for its authenticity.

There was some scribbled indecision about

pleasantries — Violet obviously hadn't decided which tone to take — but then beneath that were some figures in a more definite hand and a rusty pin.

I turned the page to see what the pin was holding: a wedding announcement between one Beatrice deVille and an Ashton Davis Adams, and beneath that a note to herself.

Angus: for one occasional table: £5.
Table delivered 9/20/35; collected 10/14/35; shipped 10/18/35.
Personal check received from Bettina Whitelaw Ward 12/20/35.
See notebook A for provenance details, supplied.

What? I stared at the paper, wondering if I'd misread it.

I turned the letter over and read it again: *Angus: for one occasional table: £5.* And there was his receipt, and some sketches.

Book A? That was why the book seemed familiar; it was the same as the furniture record. I hurried over to the desk and brought it back. When I flicked through it now, I could see little numbers penciled against the details of the furniture listed, some crosses and some ticks.

I'd thought on first reading that Violet had

given the table to Beatrice; but no, Violet had *sold* the table to Mrs. Whitelaw Ward. *She'd* been the one giving the present; Violet had been the very upmarket dealer in the transaction. And whose table was it? There was no note of any money paid back to the lady mentioned in the letter, just a payment to "Angus" for making an occasional table.

So which had been sent to Beatrice de-Ville? The copy or the original?

Horror swamped me. There was no way of knowing, not without consulting a proper expert — and a proper expert might just decide to go public.

I looked through the notebook to see if there were any more letters.

There were quite a few more. Violet had kept her drafts as copies, and each of them was tagged with details of the piece sold, the price paid to Angus for a copy, shipping dates, and any other details that might affect the price she was asking.

I sank back in the pillows and tried to make sense of it all. Had Violet really been selling off the family furniture almost like a small business? There were transactions covering many years, different items, different letters, but the same breezy tone, treating each transaction as the most marvelous thing, cleverly covering the squalid tang of

349

common or garden retail with skillful charm.

My mind raced. It wasn't exactly unheard-of for families in trouble to hawk the silver. Max had once told me about a grande old dame he'd cultivated for years, taking her out for tea in Chelsea while she dropped wistful hints about the Edwardian tiara she was saving "for a rainy day." Normally he took things like that with a pinch of salt, but in this case her provenance was unimpeachable — she was the daughter of a minor aristo — and he'd had a quick peek at the item in question when she wasn't looking and been sufficiently convinced to hang in there.

Sadly for Max, when the rainy day came and he rocked up at the daughter's house ready to offer his tiara-liquidating services, all he got was the unpleasant job of informing the bereaved family that they'd just inherited a pile of very convincing glass, and that their mother must have cashed it in for ten years of dutiful attention from her Polish companion. To add insult to injury, as he was leaving, two of his competitors were just pulling up in their best black-leather sympathy coats.

I gripped my hair. Was that what Violet had done? Had she even told Carlisle, her son? Was that why she'd impressed on them the importance of saving the house — because if anyone looked round, they'd realize it was all fake? My imagination sketched in the blanks: the furniture shifted upstairs for each ball, a little less coming back down each time. Some pieces reappearing, but not displayed quite so prominently as before.

A cold hand — and for once it had nothing to do with any ghosts, real or imaginary — gripped my throat as the ramifications of what I'd discovered sank in. First of all, I was about to look like a complete idiot in front of Max. What was I supposed to do? Ring him up and tell him to ignore any photographs of furniture, and just focus on the porcelain and silver?

Hastily, I scrabbled back through the notebook. Had Angus copied Sèvres vases too? No. Good. So that at least was safe.

I looked resentfully at the pointless lists I'd made for Duncan. I couldn't show them to him now. Five days of crawling around under tables getting dust up my nose and splinters in my fingers, five days of cricking my neck photographing dovetail joints, five days of listening to Max pronouncing *Chippendale* with a horrible kissy-kissy —

Oh *no.*

The table! The prize table, the Chippendale cherry on the cake that I'd more or less promised Ingrid would solve all Duncan's money worries. If it was a copy, a two-hundred-year-old copy, it was still worth something. If it had been copied in an outbuilding in Berwick within living memory, it wasn't.

Maybe she'd kept it. You couldn't just knock together a table like that. I flicked through the notebooks and papers and letters, my eyes desperately searching for the word *Chippendale,* and right at the back, in the records from 1937, I found it: a transaction with Maribel Edwards Schuster of Long Island.

My heart sank. I'd never realized how true that description was until now: I actually felt my heart fall like a glass paperweight into the pit of my stomach.

Dear Maribel, *[Violet had written on* Kettlesheer *headed paper]*

I am so glad *[underlined twice]* to hear the Chippendale table arrived safely. It is the most divine piece of English history, I absolutely agree! And yes, I can quite picture it in Louise's dining room in Newport with the candelabra I've heard so much about. I hope you enjoy as many magical evenings of hospitality as

And then it stopped.

The handwriting had got tighter as the lines went on, as if Violet was having trouble forming the words. At the bottom she'd noted *MES's fiancé's family in munitions; renegotiate price?* But the usual flurry of exclamation marks was missing. There was no joy in this one, no playful tweaking of the pleasantries. This had been a hard letter for her to write.

She'd pinned some notes from a discussion with Angus: types of wood needed, times, prices. Quite a commission for a little workshop, like building the *Titanic* in a garden shed.

I looked at the dates. December 1937. Not long before the war — Violet would have been in her fifties, handsome now rather than beautiful. Would her three adult sons have been signing up? Would the Schaffenacker Bentleys have been begging her to get on a boat and come home to safety in New York? Were they still penniless? Was there even a home to go to?

Tears filled my eyes. I didn't *want* to think of Violet selling the McAndrews' remaining treasure: the scene of her lavish wedding breakfast, of her ball dinner parties, a link to Ranald's family and his sons' birthright. It must have been such a last resort. The Violet I'd conjured up wouldn't have done that.

But it would explain why I couldn't feel anything on it: no parties, no celebration, no history. How could I, if it had been made just seventy years ago?

Being proved right had never felt so disappointing.

What was I supposed to do? I didn't know who was going to be more devastated to find out it was fake: Duncan or Max. At least Duncan hadn't already mentally spent the money, unlike Max, who was probably lining up imaginary fleets of really rare Dinky model cars and Cuban cigars right now. Not to mention crowing down the Builders Arms to his cronies about finally getting his big TV break.

A crack of hope appeared in my mind. But what if it *wasn't?* What if Violet had done a bait-and-switch, and kept the real thing? But that would make her a crook. Was that better?

I had to tell someone. But who first? I guessed etiquette demanded that Duncan should get the bad news first, but my insides shriveled at the thought of how exactly I was going to do it. Casually informing someone their revered granny was a con artist on a large scale? Hours before dining off the family-heirloom-no-longer? What sort of social clanger was *that?*

I didn't much fancy telling Max either, although there was the chance he could give me three handy tips for confirming the validity of Chippendale tables one way or another. But there was the risk that he might insist on coming up himself, and I shrank at the lurid pictures that summoned up.

I closed my eyes, and Violet herself appeared in my mind's eye. Young and privileged, beautiful and laughing on her way to the ballroom she'd decorated with eagles and violets. I didn't want to see her as a trickster, shilling the family heirlooms to keep the roof from leaking, but it was spirited of her. It showed how determined she was to stay with Ranald's memory once she'd lost him, how enterprising. . . .

Robert. I'd tell him first. He seemed to be supernaturally rational about "the business" of Kettlesheer, as he saw it — maybe he'd be more forgiving of a relative who seemed to share his business instincts.

First thing tomorrow, before anyone collared me to ask where the lists were, I'd go down to the lodge and share this with Robert. I put the letters and notebooks carefully back into the file box and closed the lid.

Then I'd just have to cross my fingers that nothing else happened to ruin the ball for the McAndrews before my news about the table did.

TWENTY-TWO

"You want to talk to me about something so urgent it can't wait until after breakfast?"

Robert ran a hand through his hair, and it spiked up at the front like a newborn chick. He'd obviously just pulled on the first clothes to hand — his feet were bare, and he seemed hungover and a bit sleepy still, as if he'd just rolled out of bed.

This is not the time, Evie, I reminded myself, hopping from one foot to another on the icy doorstep. There'd been another light fall of snow overnight, covering up the tracks like a neat housemaid sweeping the ground clean.

"I've *had* breakfast," I pointed out, my breath making puffs of white in the crisp air. "Janet Learmont's been up at the big house drilling the cloakroom volunteers in hat-and-coat etiquette since cockcrow. But I can make you some coffee, if it helps? And yes, I'd like some too. I *have* just walked half a mile in someone else's wellies."

"Is that some kind of romantic meta-phor?" Robert pushed the door open and stood back to let me and my bag in.

"Ah, no," he said at once. "No, I see you've brought junk *back*. That wasn't the point. I was trying to get *rid* of some clutter."

"We need to talk about it." I hesitated as I entered the kitchen, unsure if we were alone, but it was empty and tidy as ever. Just Robert's laptop on the table next to a bowl of green apples. The same apples that had been there all week. I wondered if they were wax.

He put the kettle on and started to get cups out. "Not more talking. What is it now? Dad's actually Winston Churchill's bastard son?" He frowned, looking for coffee.

"Let me," I said, reaching for the cafetière sitting next to the modern range. No Aga here. "You're going to need a strong one to get your brain in gear for this. Sit down."

Trudging across the park, safely out of range of human ears, I'd rehearsed various approaches of breaking the news of Violet's double-dealings. My imagination had revved into overdrive with the benefit of a night's broken sleep, and I'd had to brush away visions of a shell-shocked Duncan, a weeping

Ingrid, Robert nobly agreeing to marry some bug-eyed heiress to save the castle, etc., etc.

But now, in front of him — and in Violet's old house — they all seemed a bit . . . well, melodramatic. For once, I tried to stamp on my more creative tendencies and present the facts just as they were.

I took a deep breath.

"I think Violet sold the family furniture to keep the house going after Ranald died," I said. "Either that, or she had it copied and sold fakes to half the society families on America's Eastern Seaboard."

There was a moment's silence, and then Robert did a double take.

"Say that again?" He turned round in his chair to look at me properly. His forehead was creased in confusion. "I thought you were going to tell me you'd found a will in a sideboard leaving everything to the Battersea Dogs Home."

I grimaced. "Sorry. I hate to be the bearer of bad news. But here, it's all in these books. The one you found was a record of what was in the house. But I found this other one, with details of how she had it copied and sold."

"Where did you find that?"

"In a secret compartment in the medicine

cabinet in the bathroom."

He did another incredulous double take. "Get out of here. Where was it?"

"Seriously."

"Well, then I owe you an imperial pound of doubloons."

The kettle boiled as I showed him the bookkeeping and the tabs Violet had kept on her old social circle, homing in on their need for upmarket wedding gifts, and the super-discreet operation she'd run from her sewing room.

Robert flicked through the pages while I talked.

"Right," he said eventually, his face giving nothing away. "So, what does this mean? There's nothing for Dad to sell after all?" And the penny dropped. "Mum said you'd hinted that there was something really valuable in the house — I'm guessing it's that big dining table. Don't tell me that's a knockoff too?"

"Well, that's the thing . . . I don't know," I confessed. "I'd need to get a second opinion. Third, too. There's a big difference between a real Chippendale and a fake one."

Robert raised an eyebrow. "How much difference?"

"Several hundred thousand pounds' difference. But if we get an expert up here, and it *is* a fake, then . . . it's going to be quite embarrassing. And, as you say, there's nothing to sell."

He whistled. "Blimey." A pause stretched between us. "But what's your gut feeling?"

I wanted to be cool and professional, but he was gazing at me so intensely that the words came spilling out of their own accord.

"I can't feel anything on it. A table that old, of that quality, should feel . . . I don't know, *alive* with something. Age, experience, something. My fingers tingle when I touch something old. Don't laugh."

"I'm not." Robert's eyes were serious, but that didn't mean he wasn't laughing at me. "And there's no tingle on our table?"

"No." I twirled a teaspoon round in my fingers to break the unsettling eye contact long enough to get my brain under control. "Maybe it's just a bit out of my league."

"Your tingle detector only works on tables?"

I risked a glance upward. He was still looking at me with that half-amused glint. I squashed the butterflies in my stomach: *not* the time.

"Tables, evening bags, porcelain," I said. "Inanimate antique objects only. It's a knack."

"Useful skill to have, clairvoyant fingers."

"Not when you work in London," I said. "You don't want to know where half that stuff's been."

Robert laughed, once, and poured the coffee, pushing one cup across the table to me. He stirred sugar into his own, and flipped over a few more pages of the notebook, saying nothing.

"Say something," I said, unable to bear it any longer.

"Not sure what to say," he replied. "You think they're going to want their money back?"

"Who?"

"The people she diddled. Or didn't." He pointed to the books. "I mean, at least we know where all our stuff is. If we ever had the money to get it back. She left a paper trail of our family valuables, at least."

"It wasn't for her — she didn't have a choice!" I protested. The more letters I read, the more I could see Violet blinking back her furious tears as she packaged up the last consignment of Ranald's childhood. "How else was she supposed to pay the bills? You saw that postcard — Ranald more or less made her promise she'd never leave!"

"I'm not criticizing her," he replied evenly. "How can I? She sold what was hers. I mean, we were planning to do much the same."

"Maybe the table is real! Maybe she didn't bring herself to sell it in the end! There's no final copy of the letter."

Robert's expression softened. "You really want it to be the genuine article, don't you?"

I nodded. "I do."

"Why?"

"Because . . . I like Violet. Whether she was a hustler or not. I don't want people to think less of her. I can understand exactly why she fell in love with this house. It has a character. Your dad's in love with it. You would be too, if you let yourself . . ." I trailed off. I was letting it get too personal again. This wasn't doing my professional appearance any favors.

"But surely," said Robert, "it's better if it is fake, and out of respect for my dead great-granny's cottage industriousness, I decide we do have something in common? Isn't that what you're secretly hoping too?"

I felt something buzzing in my pocket: my phone was ringing.

"Excuse me," I said. "Might be Alice."

Robert pulled an *I'm saying nothing* face as I checked to see who it was — Max. Quickly I sent the call to voicemail.

"Oh dear," he said, spotting my stricken

expression. "That bad?"

"Sorry?"

"Let me guess — the date you're blowing off to come to the ball tomorrow night?"

"No date," I said. Hadn't I made that perfectly clear the other night? Maybe he was just being kind. "My boss. I sent him some photos before I found the second notebook, and he's got a buyer. They'll be gagging to get the table before someone tells you to offer it to a museum. It wouldn't be that hard to" — I hooked my fingers in the air — "*have a change of heart* about letting it go, but you've got to do that before they get a look and work out why you suddenly don't want to sell."

"And you don't want to look like an idiot."

"No," I said. "But I have a feeling this will be the excuse my boss has been looking for to downsize his staff."

"Sorry." Robert sounded as if he meant it.

"It's okay," I sighed. "Do you need an office assistant at ParkIt? I'm not very tidy, but I can do great invoices."

"I'll put your résumé on file." Robert sipped his coffee and regarded me over the top of the mug.

I smiled wanly.

"I assume you haven't told Dad any of this?" he asked.

I shook my head. "I wanted to sleep on it first. I didn't eat a thing at dinner last night. Thank God Sheila was there, talking about clan tartans all night, and whether you should be forcibly put into a kilt."

Robert's face contorted.

I moved swiftly on. "I can stall Max until Monday. He'll be run off his feet selling photograph frames for Valentine's Day. But please don't tell Duncan before the ball. I don't want to ruin it for him." I paused. "I feel bad enough already about, you know, gate-crashing your party."

"You're not gate-crashing, you're invited. How is Alice? Any news on the . . . ankle, was it?" His eyebrow hooked up in a sardonic nonquestion.

"To be perfectly honest, she hasn't called me recently," I said. I didn't want to cover for Alice too much, but I could see what she meant about Robert's high standards when it came to Fraser. He looked annoyed. I crossed my fingers under the table. "She must be in a fair amount of pain."

"To be perfectly honest *myself,* she's gone down in my estimation for this. Fraser's the best guy I know. And your sister . . ." He trailed off. "Well, sometimes there's nothing wrong with a bit of romance. Anyway, are you all set for tonight? Did any of Cat's dresses fit?"

"Yes, I'm going to wear her blue stretchy one," I replied politely. In fact, only one of them had done up — a long navy sleeveless dress, so plain it looked like something Mother Teresa would have rejected as being a touch frumpy. But it fitted, nothing was going to fall out, and the last thing I wanted to do was to draw attention to myself. I'd do that enough with my dancing. "It had a note on the hanger — Caledonian Ball, 2007."

Robert nodded, as if he knew which one I meant. "She catalogues them, so she doesn't repeat."

"She can't *remember?*" I blurted out. I'd have it all imprinted on my brain for the rest of my life. "It was really nice of her to lend me something," I added, in case my face was giving away my shock.

"Very nice," agreed Robert. "She's a very nice girl."

The *nice* hung in the air. *Nice* wasn't really how I'd like my boyfriend to describe me.

"And her notes were helpful. I've been doing the Eightsome in my head all night," I went on, talking quickly as the atmosphere between us thickened with the parallel conversation we *weren't* having, the one about what would happen after the ball, with him and Catriona, "but it's all very well seeing it in theory — in practice, it's so much harder."

"You'll be fine," said Robert. "We'll look after you. You just have to relax."

I nearly laughed out loud. "How can I relax when I'm constantly braced to land in the fireplace and concuss myself?" I demanded.

"You've got to trust us!" He grinned at my nervous boggle, and his eyes crinkled sweetly at the edges, turning his earlier briskness back into something more boyish. "We'll catch you if you start heading toward anything lethal."

"What? Like Janet Learmont?" I joked.

The glint left Robert's eyes, and I bit my tongue. The two conversations had crossed over. "Sorry," I said quickly. "Sorry."

"Don't let that spoil your evening," he said quietly.

"Don't let it spoil yours."

We looked at each other — not romantically, but rather grimly. There were so many things I wanted to say to him, things Alice would have said, knowing she'd be long gone tomorrow, but I couldn't. I wasn't Alice. I could imagine this conversation in thirty different swooning permutations, plus strings, but I couldn't actually set it in motion in real life.

"I'll see you later, will I?" I pushed my chair away from the table, unable to bear it. My voice sounded too bright. "What is it? Drinks at seven, dinner at seven-thirty?"

Robert nodded. "Dad's doing cocktails in the drawing room." His voice sounded kind of forced too. "The Winemakers Club's invented two new ones especially for the evening. And you should know that both involve the Mark I version of his Kettlesheer Gold."

"Oh, my God," I said, thinking of the dancing to come. "Is that safe?"

"If it's not, at least we won't remember a thing about it," said Robert.

He was walking me to the door, and yet again I felt as if time were moving too quickly, sweeping me along while I was still trying to savor each dusty, eccentric moment of this week in someone else's life. Tonight was going to pass just as quickly, I realized; it was already eleven, soon it would be the afternoon, and then dinner and then the ball, and then my time here would have gone, and —

"Thank you," said Robert, jerking me back to attention.

I stopped at the door, half-buttoned into Alice's cocoon coat. "What for?"

"For telling me first," he said. "You're right — I don't think Mum and Dad would react well. This is something I can do. Maybe make it less painful for them."

I wasn't quite sure what he meant. "Er, good?"

Robert smiled back, his large brown eyes full of complicated emotion — regret? amusement? weariness?

"I'll see you tonight," he said, and those simple words sent a skin-shivering thrill through me.

TWENTY-THREE

Several hours, two pots of tea drunk standing up, one polished dance floor, and a flower arrangement so cack-handed it was gently taken off me later, I lay in Violet's vast enamel bath and wondered if she had ever got used to bathing in such magnificence, or if her own bathroom in New York had been as sumptuous.

More sumptuous, probably. According to a note in her desk, she'd had the local plumbers run ragged installing American hot-water innovations. Even now, I had a bare eight inches of water to wash in, but I was taking my mind off that by focusing on the gleaming brass heating rail that pumped a little warmth into the room from some enormous boiler clanking away deep in the cellars.

Cocktails, Ingrid had reminded me before she was hurried off by Sheila to have her final dress fitting, were at seven, "and make sure you eat the canapés before you drink anything Duncan offers you." It was nearly six o'clock: I had an hour to transform myself into a princess, using only one small makeup bag, Ingrid's spare Velcro rollers, and Catriona's stretchy ballgown.

I had at least three paste tiaras at home I'd never been able to wear — until now. Talk about ironic.

I glanced over at my phone, balanced on the towel rail in case it caught some reception. While I'd been rushing around with paper lanterns and suchlike, I'd had a couple of typically bossy messages from Alice. Was Fraser properly warned about my tendency to kick out under stress? Did I have my ticket? Was I wearing clean underwear? (Okay, maybe not the last.) I'd texted back crossly, pointing out that she'd forfeited her right to order me around and that I wasn't a remote-controlled car.

She'd been ominously silent for the past couple of hours, which had led me to wonder if she was, in fact, on a Valentine's date with a third hitherto-unknown person.

That, I decided, would explain a lot.

I was applying the final layer of mascara at the dressing table, wishing I had a maid to flutter around me, beautifying, when there was a brisk double knock on the door.

I took one final look at myself in the mirror before I went to answer. Even taking into account the low-wattage gloom, I wasn't quite as glamorous in real life as I felt in my head.

I'd done my best, but to be honest, I was there last-minute in someone's old dress, and it showed. My soft arms, unlike Catriona's toned biceps, weren't my best feature, and my updo probably wouldn't even stay up till coffee was served. I just didn't have the sort of hair that could be piled with casual elegance, not unless there were trained professionals wielding tongs. As for my evening makeup look — without my full arsenal of slap, I looked all right but not spectacular.

I pulled out the pins and let my hair fall back round my shoulders. At least it was clean. And I didn't have tattoos, and there was no way I could fall out of this dress.

Shaking my head, I went over to the door and opened it.

"Good evening," said Robert.

For a moment, I couldn't speak. Literally couldn't speak.

He was standing inches away from me in full evening dress, tall and spare and comfortable, as if he wore it every day. The outfit was crisp, properly formal — the angled white bow tie, the spotless tailcoat — but everything else about Robert was soft and touchable, from his dark hair brushed back into a quiff to his freshly shaved skin.

He was gazing at me with his dark eyes, appraising me with a faint smile on his wide mouth.

"You look . . . nice," I managed.

"Not as nice as you," he said. "But listen, I've brought you something. Can I come in?"

I stepped back to let him into my bedroom and he brushed past, smelling of cologne and starch. An old-fashioned, formal but sexy smell that I hadn't realized would make my stomach flip over until I smelled it.

"I was going through some boxes this afternoon, after you left," he said. "Cat's dresses tend to be a bit on the minimalist side. Thought you might be able to use these."

I took the bag and sank down at the dressing table. Robert leaned against the four-poster and watched me.

"Can you not watch me, please?" I said. "I feel like I'm about to pull a rabbit out."

"Close."

"Oh!" I pulled out something white and feathery. It was a delicious ostrich-feather

373

shrug, as light as marshmallow, the creamy strands floating on the air as if they were underwater.

"Violet had a selection of fur whatsits," he explained, "but I wasn't sure if you were bothered about that sort of thing. Most of them still had little paws."

"This is gorgeous!" Carefully I slid one arm into the shrug. I'd seen plenty of feather shrugs in antique clothes auctions, but this one was exquisite, a thirties dream of marshmallow backed with Parisian satin and as froufy as the day it was made. As it settled around my bare shoulders, a caressing, tickling warmth spread over my skin.

I admired my new reflection in the mirror: the plain dress was transformed by the halo of pale light round my face, and so was I.

Robert was looking at me through the mirror.

"Are you sure no one will mind me wearing this?" I asked.

"It's been in a box in my sitting room for the last fifty years — I doubt anyone would even recognize it. Violet would be thrilled that her finery was going to the ball again. There's more, though." He nodded toward the bag. "Keep going."

I reached in again, and pulled out a long

pair of white satin gloves with tiny mother-of-pearl buttons running up the insides of the wrists, and a shell-shaped Art Deco evening purse, and a tatty leather jewelry case.

"Don't tell me," I said, pulling on the gloves. "All this turns into two mice and a kitchen boy at the stroke of midnight."

I tried to be light, but my blood felt shimmery in my veins at the thought of sharing Violet's own accessories, in her own ballroom.

"No, three o'clock. I got you an extension for breakfast. Last reel is a three-thirty, so it's cutting it fine. Do you want some help there?"

I had the jewelry case in my hand, and as he spoke I pushed the fastener and opened it. Inside, on a red velvet bed, was a dazzling array of square diamonds. Even in the dim light, they sparkled and glittered against their setting.

"Robert! I can't wear these! Are they real? I mean, shouldn't they be . . ." I looked up, and the words stopped in my throat.

He'd been watching me, amused at the grown woman pulling on ladies' gloves like a little girl, but now his expression changed into something more serious.

"I really don't know. I think it's safe to assume they're not. But even if they are, it's the least Violet can do for you, lend you some of her finery." Robert pushed himself off the bedpost and reached out a hand for the necklace. "Let me help."

I passed it to him and lifted my hair up, exposing the skin at the nape of my neck. It felt chilly, with the feathers tickling it. I *think* that was what was making the hairs stand up anyway.

"She might not think that. Me exposing her secrets."

"She sounds like she was a big girl about that sort of thing. You can tell this hasn't been opened since 1934. . . ." Robert was very close to me. I could feel the warmth from his wool jacket, inches away from my back, and I could hear his breath, moving gently through his nose, as he concentrated on the clasp. "Right, got it. Ready?"

"Yes."

He reached round and put the necklace round my neck. I flinched, partly at the shock of the cold metal on my warm skin and partly at the brush of his fingers just beneath my ear.

Robert's hands hesitated, and our eyes met in the mirror: his dark and bright in the dim light, mine wide and round. Suddenly my lack of makeup didn't matter. The diamonds — crystals, paste, whatever — sparkled on my skin, and suddenly the dress didn't look plain: it looked elegant. And I looked like a duchess, with some bachelor duke leaning behind me, presenting me with a necklace but really thinking about kissing the hollow of my exposed throat.

I swallowed, because the way Robert was gazing at me made me wonder if that was pretty much what he was thinking too.

The moment hung and shivered between us. I didn't dare move, for fear of breaking it. *In this moment,* I thought, *he could kiss me. He hasn't* not *kissed me yet. Until one of us moves, he could still kiss me. If I can just keep this moment perfectly still, I'll have a real memory of Robert in his white tie and his burning eyes, looking like . . .*

As I watched, Robert closed his eyes and slowly, very slowly, leaned forward until his jacket brushed against my back. I couldn't tear my eyes from the mirror, even when I could feel his breath on my skin beneath my ear, then his nose touching my clavicle. My whole body was on fire, but I kept absolutely still, my own breath burning in my lungs.

He hovered there for a second, breathing in the air round my throat; then abruptly he stepped back so I couldn't see his face in the shadows, just his dark shape behind me.

I could see my face, though, in the mirror. My cheeks were flaming red, and my eyes had gone black with desire, darker even than his. It felt as if I were melting from the inside out. It was all I could do to stay upright.

"Sorry," he said indistinctly. "You just smelled so . . . nice."

" 'S fine." My voice sounded faint, even to me.

"Are you ready for dinner?" He retreated back to the bed, then seemed to think better of it, and crossed the room to lean against the mantelpiece. "The dining room looks pretty spectacular. Someone's been in to light the fire, and Mhairi's been bothering the dining table with beeswax all afternoon."

Oh, God, the table.

"Can we not . . . you know. Don't spoil tonight."

"We'll talk in the morning. Well," he corrected himself, "afternoon. No one gets to bed before five, so don't expect signs of life before lunch. Although, as Dougie Graham always says, that depends on how your evening ends!"

"Really?" I said, matching his bantering tone. "Should I watch out for him scuttling in and out of the rooms later on?"

"That depends," said Robert. "Mum said that if the roads are too bad for the taxis to get through from Coldstream, she'll let everyone camp out in the spare rooms, so who knows? You might just get some traditional country-house bed-hopping yet!"

As he said it, we both turned pink, and I had to look down at my gloves.

"What time are you planning to leave tomorrow?" he asked.

"After lunch," I said. "Roads permitting."

"Sure." He nodded. "But I'll see you before you go?"

"Depends how *your* evening ends," I said, then realized what I'd said. "Um, I mean, I don't know how the evening's meant to pan out for the heir, if he, you know, finds himself celebrating . . ."

I trailed off and looked at him. He knew what I meant. If he got engaged to Catriona. We both knew it. I wondered if he had the ring in his tailcoat.

"Don't wish the evening away," he said softly. "It's going to be a big night for everyone."

So that was it; he didn't deny it. He was going to propose to her.

I felt a sudden drop in my stomach, like being on one of those fairground rides that holds you at the top and then plunges you just when you're not expecting it.

"No," I said, pushing it away. "I want to enjoy every moment of tonight." If this was the only chance I was ever going to get to go to a ball and indulge myself in a mad crush, then yes, I was going to wallow in every tiny detail.

Robert extended the crook of his arm with a mock-formal flourish. "Fraser has the honor of the first dance — might I have the honor of escorting you down to cocktails? If you're ready."

"That would be wonderful," I said. "Let me just get my things together."

Quickly I shoved my phone, my lipstick, my powder compact, and some hair grips into the tiny evening bag. The shell only just clipped shut.

"Weren't ladies once trained to travel light?" he observed.

"What do you think all those pockets in your jacket are for?" I gave my hair a last tweak in the mirror and stood up. "Right, then."

Robert smiled approvingly and said nothing as he opened the door for me, and I stepped out into the dark corridor. Then he tucked my arm into his and walked me to the stairs.

■ ■ ■ ■

There was a strange atmosphere in the hall: it was echoey-quiet, but the bustle of the caterers in the kitchens drifted up from the spiral staircase, and the faint chink of glasses could be heard in the drawing room. The past McAndrews on the walls around us seemed to be waiting impatiently for the guests to arrive.

I was sweeping along now, the long dress adding to my sense of stepping back in time. I wanted to savor every single second, as if this were our house and we were heading down to dinner with all the McAndrews of the past, slipping out of the shadows, from behind closed doors.

Out of the corner of my eye, I saw my and Robert's reflection in the mirror as we descended the stairs — him endlessly tall in his white tie, and me punctuated with a puff of ostrich feather at the top of my long navy dress.

I tried to conceal my sideways glance, but he leaned over to me and muttered, "What music's currently playing in your head?"

"What?"

"You've got a soundtrack going, haven't you? You're descending the stairs in time to some kind of soundtrack."

"I am not!" I started indignantly, then confessed, "Something orchestral."

We'd reached the bottom of the steps.

This was probably the last moment we'd get on our own. A mad panic gripped me. *Tell him he's making a mistake about Catriona!* yelled a strange voice in my head.

I pressed my lips together more firmly and felt my deep-red lipstick smear.

"Right," he said, more to himself than to me. "Here we go. Ready?"

Gently I disengaged my hand from his arm, and he looked down at it.

"Much as I appreciate the compliment of being escorted into the party by the Great Prize Bachelor himself, your date's probably in there already," I said. "This is Catriona's night. You're her boyfriend."

Robert held my gaze for a long second, and then said, "No, I'd like to take you in. You're our guest. My guest. And I think it's what my great-grandmother would want."

He held the door open, and I took a deep breath and stepped in.

TWENTY-FOUR

Everyone's head turned as we entered, and for a second, I got an intoxicating taste of what it must be like to be announced at a real stately gala.

Catriona and the Learmonts were there already, standing by the log fire with the Grahams. Janet looked fierce in a steel-gray dress topped with a long clan sash in green and yellow. It was fixed at her shoulder with an impressive Celtic knot brooch, and her hair had been blow-dried into a helmet.

Catriona was wearing a junior version of Janet's ensemble: a long white dress and little gold kitten heels, with her hair in a fancy braided bun and a sash fixed on the opposite shoulder. Another ceremonial detail, I assumed. No idea what it meant.

"Evie!" she said, then peered at me. "Is that my dress? Goodness. Hello, darling!" she added as Robert greeted her and Janet with kisses.

From over Robert's shoulder, I could see Janet giving me the dress-code once-over.

"Sweet," she said, disengaging herself. "You'll have to take your jacket off for dancing, of course. Those feathers could fly off and get in someone's eye."

"Or cause allergies," added Catriona. "You can't be too careful with animal by-products."

"Evie, will you have a drink?" Ingrid appeared at my side and waved Mhairi over with the tray of glasses.

"Ingrid, you look stunning," I said, and meant it. Sheila had adjusted Violet's dress so it appeared made for her — a delicate 1930s evening gown in duck-egg blue, with a swooping bias cut and lots of tiny white crystal beads around the bodice like sea spray. It flattered Ingrid's small frame and made her blue eyes sparkle.

She looked like the Lady of the House. The thirties were her time, from her neat figure to the light curl of her bobbed hair. It was like a jigsaw piece clicking into its setting.

"Oh, candlelight," she said with a blush. "Here, have a glass of champagne."

I hesitated. One glass of champagne, and I got quite imaginative; two, and I started to think it was all actually happening. I didn't want to tip over that line tonight.

"Go on." Ingrid rolled her eyes and angled her shoulder so Janet couldn't see. "I haven't shown you the seating plan for dinner. You might need a glass or two under your belt when you see where Janet's put you."

Champagne or not, my imagination and reality were well and truly blurred over dinner, and after the first course, I didn't care. It was magical.

For a start, everyone around me was in the most formal evening dress, but looked easy and relaxed in it, even Duncan, who was wearing the most ludicrous sporran I'd ever seen. It was the size of a dinner plate and had tiny paws of some description dangling off it. The food arrived on silver platters and porcelain Kettlesheer Limoges plates, carried by white-gloved waiters who might have been local school-leavers during the day, but now looked like spectral Victorians in their black jackets.

I glittered under the candlelight, aware of all eyes on my throat. Conversation bubbled along as our crystal glasses were filled with Fraser's wine, a different one for each course. I'd always imagined myself charming and eloquent when I'd dreamed about dining in some Edwardian romance, but had known deep down that the reality would be tongue-tied panic about which knife to use. Yet tonight, next to Kenneth Graham and Dougie, I found it surprisingly easy. So easy that the time rushed by far too fast.

Too fast, because I wanted to savor each second but also because underneath the chatter was the steady drumbeat of nerves that in two hours, one hour, thirty minutes, I'd have to dance in front of all these people.

Fraser was seated opposite me, and he looked resplendent in the full Scottish rig-out. Alice, I now knew, was out of her tiny mind. Even Douglas and Kirstie had taken on an otherworldly splendor in their evening wear; Kirstie's sash was held in place by something that looked suspiciously like a diamanté hair clip, but from across the table, it didn't seem as if her plunging neckline was impeding the flow of dinner-table conversation with either of the men sitting next to her.

I couldn't see Robert at all. He was right at the other end, and when the coffee came round and the dance cards were distributed on silver platters, I panicked that I wouldn't reach him in time to bag a dance.

"Might I have the pleasure of Hamilton

House?" asked Fraser, his pencil poised above his dance card. The weeny pencil looked incongruous in his big hands.

"Yes, of course." I was about to write his name in when a waitress appeared behind me with a tray.

"Sorry, we gave you the wrong card," she said, putting a new card in front of me. "Could you give me that back?"

"Wrong . . . ?" I started. As she took my card from me, I saw the new one fall open. It already had a dance filled in: *The Eightsome Reel; Mr. Robert McAndrew.*

My skin shivered at the gallantry. I looked up at Fraser. "Hamilton House. Yes, I'd be delighted."

Douglas was equally chivalrous and offered me a dance, as did the charming vicar to my left, and my card was practically full up when Duncan banged his gong with unseemly relish.

"Ladies and gentlemen! If I may crave your indulgence for a moment? Lovely! As the time has now marched on to ten minutes to ten o'clock, it's time for us to make our way to the ballroom for the night's festivities to commence. If those taking part in the Reel of Luck would step to one side, Janet will be arranging us for our grand entrance!"

I glanced across the table, and saw Fraser waiting to catch my eye. He raised his eyebrows in a *Ready?* gesture, and when I nodded, he got to his feet and came round to ease my chair out so I could get up.

Oh, the manners. How I would miss the manners when I returned to normality.

The piper, Terry, had now appeared at the door, his bagpipes splayed over his shoulder like a giant tartan spider.

"Errrr we seyt?" he demanded in a very thick Scottish accent.

"Aye, we are, brave Scot!" replied Duncan with a swing of his sporran.

"I have no idea how historically accurate this is," muttered Fraser, "but Duncan insists on it."

Janet lined us up bossily. "Catriona and Robert, you'll be leading us in as the heir and lady, then Ingrid and Duncan as hosts, and Lady Morag and Sir Hamish, if you'd be so kind, and . . ." She'd reached us. I could tell from the look on her face that it was taking all the self-control she possessed not to shove me out of the line and take my place herself.

"Evie and Fraser," supplied Fraser helpfully.

"I know who you are, dear. Now, Evie, you're absolutely sure?"

"I've been studying Catriona's diagrams all night," I said. "I am a red dot and Fraser is my red cross."

She gave me a reproachful look. "Don't try too hard. If in doubt, let the men move you about. And don't fall over."

"Wise words for us all there, Janet," said Fraser.

She studied him for a minute, to check he wasn't joking, then nodded to the piper, who replied with a blast of warm-up squalling from his pipes.

And then, before I could take in what was happening, he was walking slowly out of the dining room and we were following, very slowly and with ringing ears, as if we were at a wedding and a rock concert simultaneously.

"I may never hear again," I murmured to Fraser as we stepped onto the first stair.

"What?" He leaned down so I could yell into his ear.

"I may never — Oh, never mind."

I took a deep breath. *Help me out, Violet,* I thought. *Steer me, Ranald.*

Ahead of us, Robert and Catriona made a straight-backed couple, taking the turn in the staircase before we did. I could see his eyes fixed straight ahead of him, her hand laid primly on his arm. They were already as stiffly paired as the spouses in the oils they were walking past.

Fraser kept his gaze dead ahead, but squeezed my hand as we reached the top of the stairs and the open doors of the ballroom.

The piper stopped piping and stepped back. From behind the other three couples I could see the paneled room crammed with people who'd dined elsewhere and arrived in taxis, eyes peering curiously past the door to the stairs. In silence — and in slow motion — we walked forward, and a space appeared on the dance floor like the Red Sea parting.

My heart started banging. Literally banging, like it wanted out. *Now.*

Catriona guided us all into the right spots with a regal movement of her head; and then, when we were in a neat square, she turned and nodded to the band, who lifted their fiddles, accordions, guitars, whatever mode of aural torture they had to hand.

Ba-duuuuuuuu-dum!

The reel music kicked in, my hands were grabbed by Fraser and Sir Hamish, and we were doing the circle. No sooner had my brain registered that we'd started than the music urged us back, and we were going the other way.

And then Fraser's strong arm was round my waist and he'd whisked me into the cartwheel, and out again. But he wasn't doing as much nudging as I'd thought he'd need to; somehow my brain was flashing up the patterns from Catriona's book. The music seemed to be helping me along, with fiddle flourishes to indicate when to move into the next step. I stumbled into it, my foot slipping on the newly polished floor.

"And set twice, turn twice!" shouted Fraser, shimmying his knees at me.

"I know!" I said, holding out my arm to be turned.

His eyes followed me round as we turned, and they were laughing — not at me, but with me.

I smiled back. My nerves were still fluttering high up in my chest, but something else was building in me: an odd sense of relief that, so far, it was all going fine. More than fine. Almost . . . fun?

Catriona stepped gracefully into the middle, and we circled round her as she raised her arms and did some extra-Scottishy dancing she'd been saving for a special occasion. I could hear Dougie whooping in the background. She kept her eyes fixed on Robert throughout, and then began her set and turn to him as if this were her actual wedding reel.

A pinprick of envy stabbed me. I dragged my eyes away from them, and lost myself in Violet's ballroom. It was different from the still room that Robert and I had danced in, with the glittering chandelier above us, the sparkling mirrors round the walls reflecting the masses of faces until there seemed to be thousands of people around us. It *smelled* of the past — polish, and old tailcoats, and perfume, and anticipation, just the same as it had been for her, the first time Violet came. I'd never meet Violet, and yet she could have been standing right there by the marble fireplace, watching me.

And then the circle was moving again, and Catriona was setting and turning to Fraser, his warm hand slipping out of mine so he could spin her round with that controled speed I wished I could master.

She was beautiful, I thought, as she moved elegantly into the figure eight. More than that, she fitted in a house like this. Catriona would make it easy for Robert. And wasn't that the most important thing?

And then we were moving again. As the music carried on, I started to relax — after all, I wasn't being asked to do anything so far, apart from watch the other women go into the middle, then form their loops with the men opposite. Ingrid followed Catriona; her steps were cautious but neat, her face a mask of concentration. Then Lady Morag went in, and her dowager image was thrown off as she launched into some wild birling that sent her ballgown billowing and the other dancers cheering round us. The noise seemed to lift us like a football match, and I was just thinking how marvelous it all was — being inside this circle — when I realized everyone's eyes were on me, and Fraser's hand was firmly directing me into the middle.

I was on.

TWENTY-FIVE

I'd never felt more conspicuous in my whole life than I did in the middle of that circle.

The fiddles and drums surged on, and the seven began turning, and I stood frozen to the spot like a dummy. I'd still have been standing there if I hadn't spotted Sheila standing behind the set, frantically making stirring motions with her finger, one way and then the other.

Was that some kind of extra dance? I peered at her, and she rolled her eyes and spun round, much to the confusion of Kenneth standing next to her.

Oh, God, she was coaching me from the side.

In a panic, I started turning on the spot, in the opposite direction to everyone else. It was a bit lame, but there was a cheer anyway, more so when I got bold and raised a hand over my head. Then Fraser's strong hand reached out and caught me for the set and turn, and when he spun me, he swung me so precisely in front of Sir Hamish that I didn't miss a beat.

Sir Hamish smiled encouragingly and turned me with decorous care, and then Fraser and Sir Hamish and I were scuttling round in the figure eight. The lilting music hustled us along, and without warning the tightness started to unwind from my chest. This time, as the circle turned, I spun with one hand on my hip and the other in the air, and when I stepped toward Robert, I was smiling so hard I could feel it on my face.

The *reel* was making me do it. It was taking over somehow, moving my feet without me having to think. There was something so flirty about the set and turn that I couldn't help flashing a cheeky wink from under my lashes as Robert and I swung our shoulders, and I could have sworn when he turned me, he trailed his fingers along the inside of my wrist as he steered me toward Duncan.

My feet and my head and my heart were light. It was so simple, yet so satisfying, to move in time with the music, to feel as if the music was helping me, not trying to trip me up. I stepped back and took Fraser's and Duncan's hands, and we carried on like clockwork.

My heart hammered, but the nerves and the enjoyment were mingling like the most intoxicating cocktail. And best of all, Robert in the middle meant I was free to stare at him, long-limbed and handsome in his white tie. He could have stepped out of any of the portraits in the house, and in just a few moments he'd be turning to me, and holding out his hand with that invitation in his eyes, and . . .

My gaze lingered a second too long. Robert turned faster than I expected and caught me looking right at him. A slow smile spread over his face, and a hot, hot flush erupted deep inside me.

That did it. I didn't think there was any misinterpreting that.

I was so busy trying to cover my confusion that I didn't really take proper notice of the disturbance behind me until a hand grabbed my upper arm and pulled me out of the circle, and a body slid neatly into my place between Fraser and Duncan, leaving me outside.

Whoever it was, her timing was perfect, because on the next beat the circle closed up again and the eight started going around to the left, with Sir Hamish now in the middle.

I staggered backward, nearly tripping on

the person behind me. Who the hell was that? Laura Learmont? Janet Learmont? How far would these Learmonts *go* to make sure I didn't mess things up?

My cheeks burned. *Had* I messed things up? I'd thought I was doing fine.

As the circle turned, a funny ripple effect started on the faces of the other ballgoers. Shocked expressions, confusion, and in some cases amusement flickered up as one by one they got a look at the interloper.

I craned my neck to see who it was, but I was in the wrong place, and painfully conscious that the people who weren't staring at the new dancer in the reel were now gawping at me. All I could see was the flash of a long yellow dress and long arms.

"Well done, Evie. You did yourself proud." A hand patted my shoulder. I turned round to see Sheila flanked by her husband, now looking like a ceremonial bald eagle in a kilt.

"Have I just been sent off?" I gasped. "Who is that? Is that Laura?"

Sheila looked surprised. "No. Can you not see who it is?"

I peered as the new girl set and turned Robert. "No," I began, "I don't — Oh, my God."

The long flailing arms should have given

it away: as Robert tried to spin her, she gave him a nasty thwack in the chest and turned awkwardly to reveal her face to me.

It was Alice. And for some reason, she was wearing a gigantic diamanté eye patch.

"Alice?" I said out loud.

"Indeed." Sheila's voice was dry. "Her ankle seems to be holding up all right. But did she injure her eye at the same time? You never said."

Robert, Fraser, and Alice lurched round each other in the figure eight. Fraser and Robert, I could tell, were using the move as a chance to get a better look at her bizarre accessory. She actually wasn't that easy to look at straight-on; their position right underneath the huge crystal chandelier meant that the diamantés were flashing dazzling beams of light right across the room.

"That? Oh, um, it's her style signature," I improvised. "She often wears one to big events."

"Is that a London fashion?" asked Kenneth. He sounded bemused.

"Yes," I said. "Well, no. Oh, look, Sheila, Fraser's in the middle."

That distracted her instantly, and her clan sash lifted with pride as Fraser took his turn in the center, leaping up and down and making wild shapes with his arms ("He's impersonating a rutting stag") while the men in the room let out weird whooping *Yaaarrrrp*s of approval ("It's traditional").

And then he singled out Alice for her set and turn. Mad as I was with my sister, I had to admit that she and Fraser made a really handsome couple.

Alice's height somehow worked in a ballgown, and she was gazing up into Fraser's eyes, her face rosy with a sort of shy adoration I'd never really seen on her before. Fraser meanwhile looked as if his rugby team had won on the same day that Scotland qualified for the World Cup and the tax on wine and spirits was abolished. Her ridiculous shenanigans of the last few days were clearly forgotten in his undisguised pleasure to see her.

The music shifted up a gear, and he steered her with old-fashioned courtesy; as she turned, her eyes traveled over her shoulder to stay with him as he moved across the circle to Ingrid.

She really loves him, I thought. *And he totally loves her.* In that moment, I realized what Alice had meant when she'd said I only ever had crushes on men I couldn't have. That soul-warming glow I felt when I was near Fraser wasn't a proper emotion; it was just a reflection of what they had. A breathing, caring relationship.

I didn't feel jealous of Alice having Fraser. I was *glad* she had Fraser, and that Fraser had her. I watched them turning their shoulders to pass in the figure eight, eyes following each other greedily.

Then I spotted that Robert was looking at me, and another wave of intense longing rushed through me; it made the crush I'd had on Fraser feel like vanilla ice cream. Melted ice cream, at that.

Sheila nudged me. "Just as well I managed to pick up my mother's engagement ring from Berwick earlier this week." She gave me a stagy wink. "I hope Kirstie didn't get the wrong idea about the box. . . ."

"It could be an expensive night for Janet Learmont," said Kenneth unexpectedly. He nodded toward the reel, and I saw what he meant: Catriona was holding Robert's hand with a proprietorial smile, her neck arched as if she knew everyone around her was whispering about the old tradition.

He wasn't looking at her, though. He was only looking in two directions: at me, or into space.

I saw Janet on the other side of the circle. Her eyes were fixed on the dancing, but she was nodding to a couple of very aristocratic ladies with diamond brooches on their sashes. I could virtually hear the words *wedding registry at Jenners* forming on her pink lips.

The evening was already half over, I thought with a pang. The dinner, the first reel — done. Now it would be downhill fast to "Auld Lang Syne," and then I'd be on my way home, in jeans and Max's car. I wanted to cling to every single moment.

Fraser was the last man to dance, and the band was speeding up as the reel drew to a thundering close, the spectators urging them on. All four couples spun in perfect time, the ladies flowing as if on invisible wheels, the men stepping flamboyantly round them. White hands flew up and were clasped by stronger ones, skirts swirled, hair floated out behind.

And then there was a loud final chord, and it was over. Alice sank into a deep curtsy to Fraser, a graceful action spoiled only when she tried to stand up, not realizing she was treading on her own hem. He grabbed her before she could slip, and turned it into a hug of welcome.

Good job he had strong arms — he'd be doing that a lot over the next forty years, I thought.

As the rest of the crowd swarmed onto the floor to repeat the reel in their own sets of eight, I made my way over to Alice, now explaining herself to a bewildered but happy Fraser.

Robert and Catriona were diplomatically ignoring the tricky conversation going on next to them, and were instead congratulating Duncan and Ingrid and the visiting dignitaries. When they saw me, Robert's eyes lit up, and he reached out a hand to guide me through the crowd.

"Evie! That was some impeccable reeling. Wasn't it, Cat?"

Catriona smiled, as she could afford to now that it had all gone off without me head-butting Duncan. "It was a strong seven out of ten for me."

"Seven out of ten?"

"Well, she didn't finish the reel, did she?"

"Yes, well, I need to talk to Alice about that," I said, grabbing Alice's arm. "Can I have a quick word? Sorry, Fraser, you can have her back in a moment."

I pulled her through the circles of dancers forming as the rest of the guests prepared to repeat the same reel. The room seemed very small now that it was filled with warm bodies, and we had to weave our way out into the empty hall.

"Limp!" I hissed.

"I was *not!* I was very good!"

"No, *limp*. You're meant to have sprained your — Oh, forget it, just hurry up." I came to a stop underneath the portrait of Wyndham McAndrew in his powdered wig and with matching spaniels. "What on earth are you doing with that ridiculous eye patch? You look like Long John Silver, the Studio 54 years."

Alice had only one eye to glower with, but she really only needed one. "What else was I supposed to do? You told them I had an *eye* infection."

"No I didn't." I boggled at her. "Why would that stop you dancing?"

"You tell me! You're the one who left the message." She pulled a *me* face. " 'Alice, you selfish cow, just FYI, you've got chronic conjunctivitis that has laid you up —' "

"Tendinitis!" I roared. "I told them you had an old *dancing* injury that had flared up! Don't you ever listen to anything I say?"

"Oh!" said Alice. "I didn't think it was one of your better on-the-spot fibs. Tendinitis . . . Anyway, it's growing on me." She admired her reflection in the speckled mirror opposite. She still had that peachy glow about her from Fraser's welcome. "Bit David Bowie, bit Lady Gaga."

"Why didn't you tell me you were coming?" I demanded. "I thought the trains had been canceled from Newcastle!"

"Tell me about it. Do you know what time I left Clapham this morning? Six! I've never been on so much public transport in my life. Train, cab, bus, tractor . . . *bigger* tractor. I had to negotiate pretty hard to get here in time." She nodded at me. "And you don't want to know where I got changed. There is a shed with a *very* surprised gardener in it."

I had no trouble picturing Alice urging some poor unsuspecting farmer through the drifts, Dr. Zhivago hat and all.

"And at no point in all this — this cavorting — did you think to ring me and let me know I should do a one-eighty turnabout in my covering-up-for-you strategy?" I spluttered. "It's not like I've spent the last couple of days tying myself in knots!"

Alice grabbed my hands. "Oh, listen, I *am* sorry. You *were* right, that's why I'm here. I *have* been really, really stupid."

She paused, and I basked in a rare moment of Alice apologizing, and in such a beautiful, cinematic setting.

"I thought of what you said about Fraser, and about how he might get the wrong idea and be hurt, and then I thought of you and how lonely . . ." She trailed off, then restarted more diplomatically. "I've been seeing Zoe, the therapist Mum refers sensitive clients to, and she said I had to reset my relationship parameters."

"What does that mean in English?"

"We have to stop believing that we're doomed to be as boring as Mum and Dad." Alice shook my hands for emphasis. "We don't have to be like them! I didn't sleep a wink last night, making a list of pros and cons, and then I got up and thought, *Right,* I'm going to tell Fraser exactly how I feel about him, even the stuff he does that really winds me up, like the sock issue, and —"

"Too much information," I interrupted, but her eyes were shining and she wasn't listening. From the expression on her upturned face, Alice seemed to be hearing my own imaginary strings of emotional climax. There was something in the atmosphere at Kettlesheer, clearly.

"— then I realized that making lists was the whole problem. I don't need a list. I just need Fraser!"

"I'm so happy for you!" I roared, mainly to make her stop talking. "Come here!" And I grabbed her in a massive hug, and we jumped up and down a bit together, which made a lot of secured ornaments rattle.

"So, what about you and Robert?" Alice demanded, breaking free.

"Me and Robert?" I gabbled. "Nothing."

"I'm not stupid, Evie," said Alice in a much more familiar managerial tone.

The blush that gave the pair of us away was sweeping over my neck and up my face like I'd been dipped in dye.

"He was staring at you the entire time you were dancing. Wasn't I right about stepping out of your comfort zone? Good on you! Robert is miles out of your usual league, no offense!"

"No, hang on, he hasn't — we're not —"

She grabbed me by the shoulders, the mad light of zeal in her eye. "Tonight, the Nicholson sisters *do it for themselves!*"

"No, no, no." I shook my head emphatically. I actually preferred Alice buttoned-up and in control. "Robert has a girlfriend. You know, Catriona — um, the girl he was dancing with?"

"So? You were *born* to live in a castle. Think of the space you'd have for your collections!"

I wavered, caught up in Alice's glee, then forced myself to get a grip. It wasn't up to me to decide what Robert's fairy-tale ending was. This wasn't a fairy tale anyway, it was his life. And I didn't pinch other people's boyfriends.

"Don't say anything."

406

"So you *do* fancy him."

"Don't say anything."

Inside the ballroom, the music stepped up a gear into big-finish mode.

"So, what's the next one after this?" Alice asked.

"The Duke of Perth," I said. All eight reels were printed on my brain in letters of fire. "It's the one where you just keep your arm out and everyone turns you round. Sheila says, if in doubt, put both hands on your hips and let everyone else do the hard work."

"Who'm I dancing with for that?" Alice adjusted her eye patch in the mirror.

I checked the card. "Douglas. He's pretty fierce in the turns, but quite exciting once you get — hang on, what do you mean, who are you dancing with?"

"I'm letting you off. Consider yourself excused." She gave me a generous beam. "I won't put you through another seven rounds of that."

My mouth opened.

"No, it's okay," she said. "Just accept before I change my mind." She held out her hand for the dance card.

"But what if I *want* to dance?" I heard myself say.

Alice exploded in raucous laughter, then

nudged me. "You're funny! Come on, let me see who you've landed me with."

I clapped the card to my chest. I had a dance with Robert lined up, a whole eight minutes of being his partner. Everyone else was booked for all eight dances; if she took my place, I really would be sitting out the whole thing like some moldy spinster, and after the dizzying revelation in the ballroom, that suddenly felt unbearable.

"No, I don't mind," I said.

"Well, I don't mind either."

"It's fine — why don't you spend some time with Fraser, now you're here?"

Alice gritted her teeth and — seriously! — began to pry the card out of my hands. "Evie, I appreciate you stepping in to save my bacon and everything, but I didn't hitch a lift with Northumbria's scariest game-keeper just to watch my —"

We were actually struggling in a polite, evening-dressed fashion when I felt a masculine presence looming over us. Well, I smelled aftershave.

"What's going on here?"

Alice and I sprang apart. Robert and Fraser were standing behind us. Fraser was carrying two glasses of champagne and Robert was carrying Catriona's evening clutch. He didn't look thrilled about it, although I noted it was a particularly expensive Lulu Guinness number, a pair of red lips that I had down as a future collectible.

"Evie was just filling me in on my dancing duties," said Alice. She held out a menacing hand. "Weren't you?"

What else could I do? I handed over the card.

"You'll be relieved about that, are you?" joked Fraser. "Did you two draw straws to see who had to dance?"

Robert's expression wasn't so amused. "You're not going to be joining in, Evie?"

I pressed my tongue against my front teeth to stop myself saying anything stupid. "Doesn't look like it," I managed.

He glanced at Fraser, his sardonic eyebrows raised. "We can't have that. Fraser, get your dance card out, let's see if we can't make room for Evie."

"No, honestly," I said, but Robert was trying to get Catriona's bag open, unsuccessfully. "Do you need a hand? The clasp is inside. Here."

I showed him, and our hands touched. A shiver rippled through me as the bag sprang open, revealing Catriona's pared-down essentials. I handed it back before I could look further than the breath mints.

"Thanks." Robert poked about, then pulled something out: a dance card complete with teeny-tiny pencil. "There! She's carrying a couple of spares, in case of emergencies. Right, let's have a look. Who've I got for Hamilton House?"

That was the flirty one. I swallowed.

Fraser looked at me, clearly conflicted about what the polite response was. "Evie, you don't have to," he said. "Not if you don't want to. I know you're not a huge fan of the old dance-floor gymnastics."

Robert's head jerked up. Alice also stared at me. I could virtually feel Wyndham McAndrew's eyes boring into the back of my head.

It wasn't just that I wanted to dance, it was that Robert wanted to dance with me. To dance with *them,* actually. It wasn't about being one person, making a fool of myself while everyone else watched and sniggered. It was about being one part of a team, breathing and moving to the same rhythm.

"I *would* like to," I said.

I don't think Robert realized what a monumental turning point this was in my life. "Fine," he said briskly. "So, how about Hamilton House? I'm supposed to be dancing with my mother, but she won't mind sitting it out. She gets all flustered about the flirting thing. Some of those old goats take it a bit too far."

He was scribbling on the card, then glanced up at me with a wicked glint in his eye. "Watch out for Tam Dalton. He's already met five wives at these balls. He needs an English girl to make up the full Six Nations."

"I can give you a Reel of the Fifty-first," offered Fraser. "Kirstie did block-bookings so her card would be full before Innes Stout got to her over dinner. She prefers to stay down in the disco in the kitchens for as long as she can get away with it. Ah, there's Dougie — now, I know he'll definitely want to have a dance with you, just to make up for the other night. . . ."

" 'The other night'?" Alice cut me a scandalized glance as Fraser handed her the drinks and strode off to find Dougie in the crowds of thirsty dancers now thronging round the drinks table.

"Dougie swept Evie off her feet," Robert explained. "And she fell quite hard for him."

"Not like that," I said.

"Head over heels," he went on.

"Stop it."

"Quite a crash. *Crush,* rather."

"*Stop* it!"

411

I pretended to glare at him, even though I was cheering inside that he *wanted* to make private jokes with me, and the air between us sizzled. Had I been wearing a corset, I would have swooned then and there. Luckily, Catriona's dress was, as advertised, stretchy.

Alice's head swung back and forth. "What did I miss? Or don't I want to know?"

"You missed an interesting week." Robert gave me a private smile and handed over the fresh dance card. "There you go."

"Thanks," I said, and tucked it straight into my evening bag without looking. I didn't want him to see me studying his handwriting or any of the very uncool things I might do.

"Drink?" said Alice, offering me one of the glasses. "Since you're throwing caution to the winds tonight?"

"Thanks," I said, not even looking at Robert's face, and took it.

I'd crossed the line between real life and fantasy now. Maybe if I drank enough champagne now, I'd actually end up back in 1902.

TWENTY-SIX

Fraser was as good as his word and returned with a willing volunteer for the next dance, as well as promises of partners for the rest of my card.

It helped my delusions of Jane Austen that the willing volunteer was a handsome captain from the Border Regiment called Strachan; he was in full dress uniform, and though he didn't say much, when he did he had a proper porridge-and-cabers Scottish accent that gave me a mild flutter.

Cocooned between the Grahams and the McAndrews and their guests, I started out the Duke of Perth nervously; but as Sheila had said, as long as I kept my arm outstretched, there was always someone there to take it. The formality of the opening set reel had evaporated in the warmth, and now the ballroom was crammed with people. No one wanted to sit out a reel when they could be skirling wildly round the floor. There was so little space to maneuver that I was just spun from partner to partner as the music swirled us round like a fairground ride. It was rougher than I remembered — quite violent toward the end — but I never once thought I'd fall with so many hands to catch me.

As Strachan and I worked our way down the lines, setting and turning, setting and turning, the faces became unfamiliar but the smiles were the same, and the hands were warm and guided me even when I went a bit wrong. White ties, kilts, regimental buttons, hunting jackets, bow ties — I could have been right back at any one of Violet's balls, or even earlier. I'd never felt so uncomplicatedly happy as when, right at the end of the Duke of Perth, I suddenly knew what I was doing, and my hands were reaching out to the next partner.

And then it was over, with a final crash of fiddles and drums. Breathless and pink with effort, I let Strachan kiss my cheek in thanks, and then impulsively kissed him back. I'd never actually done that before. I'd imagined it plenty of times, never actually done it.

"Hey, Evie, let me know if you find yourself at a loose end for the last reel," he said with a wink. "Can I get you a drink?"

"Thanks, but . . . I should . . . get some air," I gasped, fanning my face. How was everyone else so cool? I felt like I'd just done a spin class.

I made my way out to the main hall, scanning the crowd for Alice, or Robert. The crush at the champagne bar was seven or eight deep, and all the alcoves were filled with couples flirting or groups of girls gossiping. Sheila and Ingrid had opened up the grand drawing room, and cliques had gathered round the deep sofas and chaise longues, in echoes of the bare-shouldered ladies and black-jacketed men in the old portraits above.

Part of me wanted to sit and people-watch, to imprint as many details of tonight as I could in my memory; but the champagne had gone to my head, and I really needed some fresh air.

Outside the main door, the stone steps were outlined with tiny Chinese lanterns leading down to the drive and, to the left, to the discreet Portaloos that Janet had spent so much of the afternoon disguising that they now looked like a runaway wedding marquee. The gardeners had swept all the snow from the terrace and sanded the drive, but the lawns and flowerbeds were still frosted with a thick layer of white.

Dotted along the terrace were patio heaters, glowing orange in the dark night, for those needing a refreshing lungful of icy Borders air. I stepped down toward the nearest, hugging my feathery shrug around my bare arms.

I wasn't feeling the cold. Something else was wrapped around me, keeping me warm from the inside out. I couldn't pinpoint it — I just felt . . . *happy*. Maybe all those weirdo dance teachers had been right about endorphins and "feeling part of a group." Maybe it was just this house.

Maybe it was meeting a man who made me want to throw caution to the winds instead of sitting at home imagining conversations and scenes I could refine until they were perfect, right down to the period and background music. But still a man I couldn't have.

I leaned my hands against the mossy stone of the terrace wall and let the euphoria mingle with melancholy that this life would soon wear off, along with the champagne and the ballgown.

"Cold? Need my jacket?"

I spun round and there he was, outlined with a faint yellow glow from the windows. Robert's hair was ruffled, and he'd loosened his white bow tie. Now, this was *almost* like

416

one of my favorite daydreams, but I didn't have a clue what he was going to say. My stomach knotted with delicious tension.

"No, I'm fine. Just . . . having a breather."

"Bit different from our practices." Robert leaned next to me, his shoulder close enough to mine for me to feel the heat clinging to his tailcoat.

"A bit." I showed him the inside of my right arm, red and raw from spinning at high speed against wool jackets.

"Ouch!" He touched it with a delicate fingertip, and the contact didn't seem odd. Each time I was alone with him, we seemed to have skipped ahead a few invisible steps. "You'll need to get something on that, it'll bruise."

"No, I'm proud of it. War wounds. And not my fault, for once."

He grinned and leaned against me, a *Get you* nudge. "You're doing really well. You know, someone asked me where the English girl was who couldn't dance. And I said, 'You were standing three down from her in the Duke of Perth, and your husband seemed to be enjoying himself when she reached him.' "

"Joke?"

"Not at all."

"Well, thanks."

We leaned together, watching the moon rising over the hills, turning the snow bluey-white. I wasn't sure whether we could be seen from inside; the heater and the wall partially hid us from view. It certainly felt as if there were only us in the whole world.

"Is it what you expected?" he asked. "Your very first ball?"

"Yes!" I said. "And no. I mean, it's a lot rougher. You can tell it was once an excuse for a good grapple with the opposite sex without getting a slap. And you get to review the whole room, don't you? I think I danced with everyone by the end of that last one. And . . ." I paused.

"And?"

"And I felt as if the *room* came to life. Didn't you? I could feel the floor underneath my feet, flexing as we danced on it."

"It's a sprung floor," said Robert. "Shipped up from London specially. I found the invoices. Good job Violet ordered it while Papa was paying the bills."

There was a luxurious pause between us, filled with echoes of glances and conversations from the last week. I'd told him to look in Violet's boxes, and he had. And he'd seen what I'd seen — a love story worth unpacking.

"Worth it, though," I said.

"Mmm," he replied. "Although I'll reserve final judgment for Hamilton House."

"Why's that?"

He angled his head to look at me. "Because that's the one we're dancing together. Isn't it?"

I shivered at the direct way his eyes fixed on mine, and at once he was shrugging off his tailcoat. "No, really," I started, but he draped it over my shoulders.

This was exactly the way I'd imagined it. I bit my lip, not wanting to say the wrong thing. I'd rather be silent than get it wrong and spend the rest of my life thinking of what I should have said.

"I'm really glad you came," said Robert, leaping into the silence as if he was suddenly aware we wouldn't be alone again.

"Are you?" I said. My lips were very dry, and I couldn't take my eyes off his mouth. I hoped I didn't have *Kiss me* written obviously across my face.

"I am," he said. "Otherwise I'd probably never have found out that my great-grandmother was a master criminal, and that somewhere round here there's a family of highly skilled cabinetmakers I should be turning into a cottage industry. I think that's a good thing." He paused. "It's certainly more interesting than what I thought I knew before."

"And are you . . . going to stay?"

"If I can get the right team together." He carried on looking at me, with a slightly woozy look in his brown eyes. "It's a big project to take on."

Did he mean Catriona? Or literally some management team?

I blinked, then kept my eyes closed, trying to get my thoughts in order. The champagne was jumbling everything up. That intimate glimmer in his eyes — was that flirting, or just the reflection of the lanterns? Did we have a real connection, or was this his final fling, a last flirt in the moonlight with a girl who'd be leaving in the morning?

"Have you spoken to Catriona?" I asked without opening my eyes. I didn't want to see his face. I tried to measure my words carefully, not saying too much. I wanted to keep this gorgeous night of pure romance as a perfect memory; but something in me, some tiny destructive force, couldn't help asking the question I didn't actually want him to answer.

"About?"

"About the perfect reel." Had he proposed or not? She hadn't got that manicure for nothing; that was a *Look at my ring!* manicure. "Not one misstep, unless you count my sister cutting in. Is there some separate tradition that comes into force for midreel partner changes?"

"Good point. Do you think I should?"

So he hadn't yet. I struggled with myself, trying to do the right thing rather than the dramatic, selfish thing.

"I thought you didn't like people telling you what to do?"

Robert said nothing, and I opened my eyes. His dark eyes were still fixed on my face, only now they were burning with a sort of impatience, as if he was only just containing himself.

"Evie," he said quietly, and reached for my cheek with his hand.

Inside I melted, but managed to stay rooted to the spot as his fingers curved around my jaw, as his other arm slipped round my waist. He pulled me into him, and I could feel the warmth of his body through the fine cotton of his dress shirt, and the heat of his breath close to my face.

Slowly, without taking his eyes off mine, Robert tilted his head, and I found myself leaning forward to meet him — again, kind of off-message. He kissed me, tender at first, our lips brushing dryly against each other's, then more urgently; just as it was about to flare into something passionate, he pulled back, leaning his forehead against mine.

I let out a shuddery gasp. Fireworks were going off inside me, hot and cold and shivery. I'd never had a kiss quite like that, and it had barely started.

"I didn't mean to do that," Robert whispered. "I was going to kiss your cheek. Sorry. I couldn't help it. . . ."

I took another breath. I'd be gone tomorrow. He'd be engaged by Monday. I was at a *ball.* This wasn't real, any of it.

"Don't be sorry," I said, and threw caution properly to the winds. I slipped one arm round his neck, tangling my fingers in his thick brown hair, and pulled him close to me, kissing him as if it were the last kiss I'd ever have, wanting to remember every last smell, taste, touch of him.

Robert tightened his hold on me, and we fitted together as if we'd been here before, his lean frame against my softness, my shoulder nearly level with his, his long fingers caressing the curve of my back. For a couple of seconds on the chilly stone terrace, it was just us, him in his evening dress, me in Violet's borrowed feathers, and Kettlesheer's benign presence and the navy-blue February sky.

Then, just as a tiny moan escaped from

deep in his throat, I pulled away. A hunting horn was being blown inside to indicate the next reel. It cut through the silence outside, breaking the spell. I had enough there to base a hundred daydreams on. It was more than I should have taken anyway.

"We should go in," I said.

"I'd rather stay out here," said Robert. He turned and leaned on the wall, looking up at the spotlit façade. He held out an arm for me to nestle into.

I dragged my gaze away from his bare throat and made myself focus on the *now.* "No, you've got reels to dance. Girls to spin." If we stayed out here, I had no idea what would happen; and much as I hadn't warmed to Catriona, snogging someone else's boyfriend at their de facto engagement party was hardly the stuff of Jane Austen.

I tried to smile. "And I've only got a few more chances to reel in your ballroom."

"Is that a euphemism?"

"No," I said. "Please, take me inside."

"They'll be doing some waltzing now. The band runs through its Glenn Miller routine between the main reels." Robert lifted his eyebrow. "Can I tempt you?"

"You know you can't," I said. "You're only

meant to be waltzing with one person to-night."

"I know." He paused. "But I wanted to ask."

"Sorry," I said.

Robert looked at me for a long second, as if he was trying to save the memory too. Then he sighed, and held out his arm, and very courteously led me back inside to the clatter and chatter of the hall.

The rest of the evening passed in a blur of red jackets, black jackets, glasses of ice water brought on silver trays, an old Chinese fan lent to me by Ingrid, and constant, exhilarating reeling. I got everything wrong; I accidentally shoulder-barged a very nice old lady and trod on several toes, but it didn't matter, next to the handful of moments when everything was going right and my feet felt two inches off the floorboards.

My dance with Robert flew round too soon as well. We lined up at the top of a long, long line of other dancers, starting off the Hamilton House reel. The butterflies in my stomach weren't entirely down to him; nerves were joining in for the ride, with every expectant, experienced face turned my way.

"Watch out, this is the flirty one!" said

Sheila, next to me. She didn't need to remind me; it was flirty from the moment we sank into the preliminary bow and curtsy, then stepped forward into the reel.

I could feel Robert's eyes following me as I hammed it up with Fraser and yielded cautiously to Douglas's turn. Whoever had invented it knew something about flirting: pretending to toy with other men only sharpened the thrill of electricity that tingled across my skin as Robert and I joined hands and spun back together in the middle of the set. I loved the amateur dramatics that followed me down the line, winks and playful nods from strangers in kilts and frilly shirts, joined in the rituals of the reel. But Robert's burning glances weren't feigned; they reached right into my heart.

When we finished, I was breathless. When Robert lifted my hand to kiss it, I felt tears prick at the back of my eyelids. If Douglas hadn't hustled us both downstairs to breakfast, I might have cried, it was so perfect.

In the cellar, long tables had been set up in the butler's pantries, covered in white linen tablecloths, ivy wreaths, and silver candelabra, in contrast to the robust breakfast on offer. I spotted Duncan and Ingrid sitting with the Grahams beneath a painting of some McAndrew racehorse; they waved us "young people" over, and immediately waitresses appeared with trays. Normally I couldn't face a full English breakfast, but the constant energy of the reels had made me ravenous, and I devoured the bacon, scrambled eggs, sausage, and soft floury bun, along with three cups of strong tea.

Alice seized the moment when everyone was sitting down and concentrating on their breakfast to announce her engagement.

By which I mean she said to me in a loud voice, "Evie, could you pass me the ketchup?" and then reached out her hand so it was right next to a candelabra, sparkling up the emeralds and diamonds in the ring she was now sporting on her left hand.

I nearly screamed with delight. "Oh, my God!" I yelled, bouncing to my feet. Tea spilled over my breakfast plate, and the lady sitting behind me got shoved into the table with the backward force of my chair. I think I might have got ketchup on Fraser's jacket, but he was very nice about it.

Alice got up too, elbowing Dougie in the face.

"I'm so pleased for you!" I sobbed into her hair as we clung together. "It's all going to be fine. You are going to be so happy. This is going to be the first really glamorous Nicholson wedding. You don't even have to have a fruitcake!"

"I know," she wept back. "I'm going to tell Mum I want a croquembouche!"

We were still hugging and crying and accidentally catching ourselves on people's evening dresses when Catriona came sailing by.

We hadn't seen a lot of Catriona throughout the evening. While the Grahams and McAndrews had booked reels with each other, the Learmonts' more dynamic social obligations meant Catriona, Janet, and Laura "had to" partner the local member of Parliament, a minister of the Scottish Parliament, some judge in an ill-advised pair of trews, and so on.

But now she appeared, just as Alice was showing off her engagement ring, and my good mood cracked.

"Oh, pretty!" she said. "Is it an old one?"

"My grandmother's," said Sheila.

Catriona patted Alice's shoulder. "Aw. Maybe he'll buy you some nice new earrings to go with it," she said in a consoling voice. "I was wondering when there would be a happy announcement — everyone's been saying that was the best Reel of Luck they've seen in years!"

She glanced down at Robert meaningfully.

"The most surprising one, at any rate," said Duncan. "We'll have to check the history books — see if there's a precedent for Eightsome reels danced by nine people! Perhaps it foretells bigamy! Ah ha-ha-ha!"

"Are you going to have some breakfast?" Fraser asked. "We can move up —"

"No, no. I couldn't eat a thing!" she said. "Too much to do!"

Ingrid exchanged a guilty glance with Sheila. "Oh, but even the committee can clock off a bit now?"

"I'm already thinking about *next* year." Catriona tapped her long nose. "Improvements, tweaks. You can't start planning these things too soon. Who knows what might happen in the meantime to eat into my schedule," she added kittenishly.

Robert threw his napkin on his half-finished bacon and eggs and pushed back his chair. "Well, that's me done. I should probably pop upstairs and thank the band, shouldn't I? Take them some beer?"

"So you *did* check your to-do list!" trilled Catriona.

"No, I just thought it would be a nice thing to do." He pressed his lips together and rolled his shoulders back. "Come up with me, Cat. I've barely seen you all night."

Catriona preened. "Well, when you're the

428

hostess —" she started, before Ingrid's shocked expression pulled her up short. "As Ingrid will tell you. Busy, busy, busy!"

Robert said nothing, but suddenly Janet appeared and put her bony hands on their shoulders.

"You two!" she said. "I've been looking for you everywhere! I need to have a little word about . . ." She dropped her voice and looked at the pair of them, her plucked eyebrows arched. "You know what! A certain announcement?"

"OOOOooooOOOooHHH," said Dougie and Kirstie.

My mood finally popped. So that was it. They probably had some kind of fireworks-display announcement outside, their initials in sparklers or something. I felt nauseated with regret, and had to fight my face, which was threatening to crumple.

Robert looked at me; and that, I thought, was a good-bye expression if I ever saw one. I managed a wan smile, and he pressed his lips together.

"Chop-chop!" said Janet. "Almost time for the final reel!"

We watched them weave through the tables to the door, Catriona waving and acknowledging people as she went, in the manner of the Queen.

"When you're the hostess . . ." muttered Sheila. "Not yet, lassie."

"I thought you liked her," I muttered back. "I thought she was the ideal wife for Kettlesheer."

Sheila shot me a look. "Aye, well. You can change your mind."

"So is that another proposal for the night's count?" Fraser asked, cheerfully oblivious. "Will Robert be leading her to a secluded alcove beneath the family tree?" He turned to me. "Did you come across any priceless family engagement rings in your travels?"

Something had stuck in my throat. I think it was a big lump of jealousy and misery, but it might just have been tea cake.

My eyes watered as I shook my head and banged my chest.

Alice pushed a mug of tea at me. "Here," she said. "Cup of tea'll make you feel better."

Our eyes met, and her eyebrows lifted in an *It's not too late!* expression, but I shook my head.

I'd used up my courage outside, in that kiss. Now I had to step out of the dance, and let their real life take over.

"So, last reel of the night!" Fraser rubbed his hands together. "I believe you're dancing with me, Evie! I should warn you that the Reel of the Fifty-first gets a bit fast and furious. You might have to hang on tight, but I'll do my best to keep you on your feet."

Last week, the prospect of Fraser's strong hands wrapped around mine would have sent me into quivers of daydreaming ecstasy. Now I was just dancing with my sister's lovely fiancé.

"Fine with me," I said miserably. "Reel me as hard as you like."

TWENTY-SEVEN

I didn't see Robert again that evening, except across the dance floor.

Catriona had led him down to a group of her own friends at the other end of the ballroom, and our paths didn't cross, despite the room-churning wildness of the final dance, which seemed to throw everyone together.

Fraser hadn't been exaggerating: the Reel of the 51st Division, invented, he explained, by Scottish prisoners of war to remind them of home, was like being trapped in a blender of fiddles. God knows what the German guards thought they were up to; inventing a new form of attack, possibly. I was whirled from one man straight to the next, my arms nearly bounced out of their sockets as our linked hands formed the Saltire cross featured on the Scottish flag across the ballroom.

At one point, as the music whisked into a

final frenzy and the sprung floor flexed beneath us, every single person on the floor was either turning or being turned, skirt billowing or kilt flying. Even before it ended, the crowd was cheering for an encore, and I was glad to have Fraser's protective hands catching mine as I sailed down the room, dizzy with adrenaline and champagne.

It was the purest, happiest moment of my life, filled with nothing at all except the music and the dance.

There was a short pause, in which you could hear everyone gasping for breath, laughing and slapping each other on the back; and then the band launched into "Auld Lang Syne," the signal that the ball was over for another year.

Fraser grabbed my hand and Alice's, and we were suddenly all in a big circle, singing and shaking our crossed arms up and down in time to the music. I had no idea what the words were, but everyone else did, so I just la-la-ed along, not wanting to look too English.

I closed my eyes and thanked Violet for a wonderful night, in her accessories and in her ballroom, and felt a strange sense of peace sweep over me.

And then it was all over, and we were all being discreetly evacuated from the room by Mhairi, in a long tartan skirt.

"Can you believe it's nearly four in the morning?" Alice demanded as Fraser went off to get her coat. "Last time I was up this late, my head and my body were in different time zones. I should be dead on my feet, but . . . I'm not."

"That's because you've just run the equivalent of a half marathon while drinking champagne," I said. "It's how we built an empire. You should go and invade somewhere, quick."

The hall had filled up with people shrugging on opera coats and velvet wraps and — rather spoiling the timeless atmosphere — checking that their cabs had arrived.

"Are you staying here?" She was assessing the piles of unwashed glasses and debris with her unstoppable cluttervision. "There's going to be some tidying up to be done in the morning."

"Committee's job," I said. There hadn't been an announcement, not yet. Robert still hadn't come out of the ballroom. I wondered if he'd taken Catriona upstairs to propose, with a view of the park in the moonlight. I wondered if he had Violet's engagement ring at hand.

The tea cake of gloom returned to my throat.

"So!" Alice grabbed my arms. "When are you back in London? We need to celebrate properly! With Mum!"

"You want me there, don't you? To stop her planning everything."

"Yes! When are you back?"

I let out a long sigh. "I'm leaving after lunch. Max wants me back in the shop, and I've done all I can do here with the valuation."

"Oh." Alice sensed the mood and made a commiserating face. "Like that?"

I nodded. "Complicated. Family stuff."

"Sure you don't want to come back with us? Fraser's got some amazing scotch for a nightcap."

"No. My stuff's here. I should get to bed. Long drive tomorrow."

She looked at me solemnly. "You're really okay? You would tell me? I mean, I know I'm sometimes a bit . . . bossy, but I *am* your sister. I do care."

I patted her back. "I know. Go and celebrate your engagement, Mrs. Graham."

Alice hugged me. "I'm sorry," she started, into my hair, but I stopped her.

"Just go," I said.

I lingered by the staircase for as long as I could, not wanting the evening to end; but

Robert didn't appear, and eventually even Ingrid and Duncan came out, and ushered me up to bed.

I undressed slowly in the silent bedroom, draping the shrug over the back of the dressing-table chair and laying the crystal necklace back in the box. It felt as if the whole room were watching me as I took off the last touches of my Cinderella night, leaving my makeup until last, just in case.

I had to admit, a tiny part of my brain was willing it to be different. Wishing so hard for that gentle tap on the door, the whispered confession that he'd changed his mind, that my ears were actually straining to hear it.

I'd started rehearsing my own protestations when I caught my own pajamaed reflection in the mirror, and pulled myself up short.

This would give me a more painful disappointment hangover in the morning than the champagne would. Robert had given me the one night of fantasy ballroom daydream I'd always wanted. I'd loved it, but now it was over. There would be no tap on my door or knock from the bathroom. Just the faint tick and crack of an old house sitting in an ocean of snow, and then, as dawn broke, the distant cheeps of the birds waking up across the valley.

My Cinderella night was over. But at least I'd had it. That was more than I'd expected for Valentine's Day, even in my most delirious daydreaming.

And the memory of that breath-stopping kiss — that hadn't even been in my imagination.

I didn't hang around in the morning.

When I came downstairs, slowly, because my head was throbbing to the same pulse as my tattered feet, there were already teams of brisk women in overalls swishing down the main hall and hauling bags of rubbish around.

I offered to help, but Ingrid wouldn't hear of it. She was in her velour leisure suit, a pair of large sunglasses fixed to her face.

"You should set off," she insisted, forcing a bacon sandwich into my hand. There was a lot of breakfast left. "Aileen says the roads have been cleared, but it'll still take you twice as long to get to the motorway. And there's more snow forecast for this afternoon."

"If you're sure . . ."

"I'm sure." Ingrid raised her sunglasses; underneath, she looked shattered but happy. "Drive safely, and come back next year."

437

"Really?"

She smiled. "Once you're on the guest list for the Kettlesheer ball, you never leave."

I listened to Ella Fitzgerald singing songs from the Cole Porter songbook on the car stereo all the way home to try to cling to the faded glamour of Kettlesheer as long as I could; but in the cold gray light of London, it felt even more like a dream than it had in the freezing Borders air.

TWENTY-EIGHT

My post-ball, post-Kettlesheer, post-romantic-hallucination melancholy lingered like a bad cold you can't shake off, or even enjoy indulging in bed with cocoa and DVDs.

Max didn't help. I could tell he was of two minds about me and my contribution to his business by the way he kept offering to make me coffee one minute, then quacking on about the outrageous price of skim milk the next.

In the short term, my silver photograph frames and "house-clearance knickknackery" had done a roaring trade over the Valentine's weekend, raking in the shop's highest-ever weekly profit. Even my one-eyed Hitler teddy was sold for fifty quid, and Max grudgingly asked me to look out for more champagne coupes. But in the long term, my big fish had swum away, taking Max's commission — and potentially my job — with it.

He was, naturally, very, *very* disappointed when Duncan called the following Thursday to say that the McAndrew family was terribly sorry to have wasted his time, but they felt unable to part with their Chippendale dining set for sentimental reasons.

More than disappointed, actually. The howl of anguish when he put the phone down was audible in Earl's Court. Of course, Max blamed me, but not for the reason I was expecting.

"I bet you did your full 'Oooh, think of the magnificent occasions this table's seen!' routine!" he raged, systematically ripping up the contracts he'd drawn up for the clients interested. " 'Ooh, you can't sell this! It's part of your family's bloody story!' "

"Well, it was," I said. "Is. You've still got plenty of other stuff to sell, though." I pointed to the list I'd made of the Sèvres china, the good paintings, a barrackload of rusty weaponry — the antiques I was fairly sure Violet hadn't had copied. "And it's photographed, too. You could send those photos I e-mailed you straight to the auction house."

Max glared at me. I noted he'd had his silver streaks topped up, and his teeth were looking suspiciously pearly. He'd clearly invested a lot of time and money in his new HD-ready appearance. Sadly, there wasn't much he could do about his foul expression.

"If you find someone who wants a gross of card tables with a side order of stuffed peregrine falcons in cases, ring me as soon as possible," he said with elaborate sarcasm. "Otherwise, I'm going out for lunch. What was that fairy tale where the princess had to spin flax into gold?"

"Rumpelstiltskin," I said.

"Oh yes. Well, I'd like you to spin Duncan McAndrew's repro Victorian escritoires into a Sheraton side table and a Turner watercolor of the Loch Ness Monster by the time I get back." He added a malevolent leer, which I think was supposed to be raffish, but just came across as camp Bond villain. "I hope you've done your thank-you letters."

Of course I had. It had taken every ounce of dignity I had not to include my e-mail, my landline, and my mobile number.

When Max had flounced a safe distance down the King's Road, I sank onto the chair behind the desk and logged onto eBay. The threat of imminent redundancy, not to mention my mother's continued hints about the state of my flat, had focused my mind regarding my private dealings. So far this month, I was three hundred quid up, and the carpet was visible in my spare room.

The problem was, the more persuasive the sales pitches I wrote, the more I wanted to keep the item. It was a genuine struggle. I was deep into an emotional description of a tatty child's sampler when the bell jangled above the door.

I looked up to see Walter Piven, a dealer acquaintance of Max's, slithering in. If Max was the antique world's Heathcliff, Walter was more of a Fagin type, down to the greasy-brimmed hat that was *his* trademark. He dealt mainly in high-end Oriental stuff, and I only ever saw him when he came round to collect Max's bridge IOUs.

"Evie, it's about those escritoires," Walter began. His eyes kept slipping sideways to the door. "I want to make a cash offer on them."

"Escritoires?" I repeated stupidly. Walter didn't do brown furniture.

"Yes, Max showed me some photos — the ones you were valuing up in Scotland. I want to buy them. All of them." He licked his lips. "For a friend. Who's furnishing a . . . an old people's home."

"That's fantastic!" I began, then remembered Max's rules about keeping cool. "I

442

mean, do you? What sort of price were you looking to pay?"

Walter was so wrong-footed by this unheard-of tactic that he stopped licking his lips and stared at me.

"Maybe you'd like to show me which ones," I said, pulling up the photograph on the laptop. "They were very good examples, some with the original baize."

He leaned forward, but I barely noticed the sudden nasal assault of stale sweat and tobacco, thanks to the pang of nostalgia that rushed over me when the crowded upstairs room popped onto my screen. I wasn't looking at the piled furniture: my eye went straight to the crisp blanket of snow and the forest visible in the corner of the windows. Two doors down was the ballroom, and my bedroom, and —

"I want the whole lot," said Walter. "Two grand. For everything in that room."

I glanced across. He was staring at the screen with a manic gleam in his eye. Not normal. And not at all like the way Max had gripped his head and moaned aloud at the bourgeois tastes of the upper middle classes.

Alarm bells rang in the back of my mind. Had he seen something in that photo that Max hadn't? Had one of those escritoires belonged to someone famous? Was there a

Ming vase hidden behind an elephant's foot?

"If you can have it packed up, I'll send my lad up with the van," said Walter, reaching into his pocket. *The whole room,* he stressed. "Top to bottom."

"Max has just popped out for lunch," I said, peering desperately at the photo. "You might want to —"

"You don't want to make the commission yourself?" He withdrew a tempting wad of actual notes. Red notes. Fifties. "You're the one who did the hard work. What's your cut — twenty percent? Max needn't know."

Now, this was definitely suspicious. No one ever cut deals with me. My head swam at the thought of making some real money, but a sterner voice cut in. *This is Robert's property.*

"I'd need to check with the owners first," I said, playing for time.

"Three grand," blurted Walter, then looked furious with himself.

I reached for my phone, staring at the laptop screen. It was like a Where's Waldo puzzle. "I'm going to call the McAndrews," I said. "Run it past them."

I almost dialed Duncan's number, then chickened out. He'd say yes at once, and now my instincts were telling me that something in there was worth a packet.

Oh, be honest, I thought. *You want to call Robert. Any excuse.*

I dialed his mobile, and it started ringing. My heart started banging to much the same rhythm. I hadn't even had time to imagine this conversation. I hadn't thought through how I'd open the batting, what he'd say, how I'd casually ask about his wedding plans. . . .

"Three and a half," hissed Walter. "Max has really trained you well, the sneaky —"

"Hello?" said a familiar voice in my ear.

My stomach did a slow loop-the-loop, like the Red Arrows aerobatic squad trailing plumes of excitement through my bloodstream.

"Hello, Robert!" I managed. "It's Evie."

"Evie!" He sounded pleased to hear from me. "How are you?"

"Oh, fine, thanks, bit busy, um . . ." I suddenly realized that I didn't *want* to do small talk: I didn't want to hear about the wedding. "I've had an offer for some of the furniture from the house," I said, trying to sound professional. "Are you still interested in selling some of it?"

Just that room, Walter mouthed, sending a jet of halitosis in my direction.

"I might be," said Robert easily. "I have

445

various expensive plans in the pipeline, could do with some cash flow. Which furniture?"

I pushed aside the image of Catriona's expensive wedding needs. She'd be bound to go for the huge marquee, nine-foot cupcake towers, eighteen bridesmaids all St. Tropezed the same shade, the lot.

"The . . ." I almost called it the upstairs junk room. "The room with the . . ." I peered at the screen, trying to find a star item to make it sound better. There was so much stuff packed in that you could barely see the carpet. ". . . table your dad thinks is made out of wreckage from the Armada. Allegedly."

And it was then that I saw what Walter had seen. The carpet *wasn't* carpeting: it was an enormous rug, and the tiny areas visible between the repro writing desks had delicate leaf and star patterns woven into the pile. My pulse banged.

That was what he was after. Not the furniture — the *rug.* I didn't know a lot about them, but my instincts yelled that it could potentially be worth a lot more than three and a half grand, especially if Walter had doubled his offer in the space it had taken me to make one phone call.

I kicked myself. Why hadn't I spotted it?

446

Because I'd been too busy checking the escritoires for hidden love notes and diamond necklaces in secret drawers. Chasing after the imaginary romance instead of seeing what was under my nose.

"The room stuffed full of tables?" Robert said. "Oh, take the money. Please."

"Don't rush into a decision," I insisted, and Walter's expression changed. "There might be items in there that need reassessment."

"Are you angling to come up to Kettlesheer again?" he asked. I could almost see his straight face, his dark eyes glinting as he spoke.

"No, no! I mean, yes, but . . ." My cheeks turned crimson.

"Four grand, and that's my final offer." Walter's toxic breath gusted far too close for comfort.

"Maybe I should drop in and talk it through?" Robert went on.

"Yes!" That sounded a bit keen. "I mean, yes, that's probably a good idea," I said, trying to regain my confident tone in front of both of them. "Why don't you do that? How about —"

There was some background noise on Robert's end. "Hang on," he said, "I've got a call waiting. Don't go away."

As if.

"I won't." I put one hand over the phone and stared Walter down. Forget keeping my job; this was the least I could do for Duncan and Ingrid. Max was always muttering about what some of those rugs fetched — it might make up for the table.

"What's it really worth?" I demanded. "It's the carpet, isn't it?"

Walter's eyes went sideways. "I don't know what you mean."

"Come on," I snapped, anxious to get this brokered before Robert finished his other call. "We can bring you in as an expert. Just tell me."

The shop bell jangled, but I ignored it. If it was Max, it'd do him good to see me playing hardball for once. "Walter? I can easily advise him not to sell." I raised my eyebrows. "Did Max mention the important table? The one that's *staying in the family* after all?"

At that, Walter seemed to choke on his own tongue. "And I thought Max was a coldhearted, self-interested . . . I'll double your cut. Just get on with it!"

"It's not for me," I hissed. "It's for them! It's my duty to get the best price for the client!"

"Good," said a voice.

Walter and I spun round.

Robert was standing next to an Art Deco globe drinks cabinet, one hand resting on the top. He swiveled it casually, as if choosing his next holiday destination. My skin went chilly, then very hot, and finally settled on a buzzing warmth.

But Walter, like Max, was no friend to the casual browser, and gave him a dismissive glare, then turned back to me. "Okay, so it's probably worth a bob or two. They don't need to know that. Get it at the right price, and if we split the profit on it three ways, we're still quids in."

"They deserve to know what it's worth," I said.

"Philistines like them don't *deserve* a priceless Persian carpet!" Walter roared, finally losing it. "They're using it to line their junk room! You might as well let them use *straw!*"

I gestured to my phone. "I think they've come off hold. Um, hello? I can offer you five thousand pounds."

"No, I'm going to take private advice," said Robert into his mobile. "But thanks for your professional honesty."

Walter gripped hold of the desk as if he was about to keel right over, then gave me a piercing glare. "I'm going to talk to Max," he whispered furiously, pointing a nicotine-stained finger right in my face.

"Do," I said. "And I'll tell him how you were going to cut him out of the deal."

Walter let out a strangled squeal, then gathered himself sufficiently to stalk out of the shop, tipping his hat down so as not to meet Robert's amused gaze. He tried to slam the door behind him, but it was set up to release slowly to spare Max's nerves, and he had to haul it shut, which rather spoiled the effect.

The bell jangled, and Robert and I looked at each other. I could feel an involuntary stupid grin playing at the edges of my mouth — not so much at Walter, but because my chest felt full of bubbles. My mouth went dry and my mind went blank as all the blood rushed elsewhere.

"So, we have another unexpected valuable in our midst?" he inquired.

"If Walter Piven's sniffing around, then yes," I said, grabbing on to the facts. "I mean, I'm assuming Violet didn't know any backstreet rug-weavers in Jedburgh . . . ?"

"It's all cashmere golf sweaters, as far as I know." Robert helped himself to a chaise longue. "Any chance of a cup of coffee? I hear it's a specialty of the house."

■ ■ ■ ■

I don't think I've ever made coffee so fast, or cared so much about the state of the cups.

Robert sipped it politely, and if he was suffering clutterphobia surrounded by so many sewing boxes, he didn't show it. Instead, he chatted about the "big family conference" that had erupted shortly after I left.

"Fraser sorted us out in the end," he said. "Put me and Dad in the dining room with a good bottle of wine and told us not to come out till we'd cleared the air. I mean, obviously we had to send out for more wine. It took hours. Went through the lot — why he thought I needed a qualification to fall back on, in case people stopped needing storage; why it drove me mad that he didn't even ask if I wanted to do law; why I was never *ever* going to play cricket, but how that didn't make me a bad son. . . ."

He rubbed his face. "Anyway, we've basically reached a compromise — we're giving it a three-year trial. Kettlesheer Gold. He's going to have his distillery in the stables, but I'm going to run it and get some specialists in, so it actually makes a profit. I'm looking into grants. And insurance."

"Wow. That's brilliant news," I said, delighted for Duncan as much as for Robert. "So you're moving up there?"

"Not yet." Robert looked for somewhere to put his cup down, and settled on a gramophone. "I've got things in London that I don't want to give up yet." He looked at me, his dark eyes searching mine. "It's not going to be straightforward, working with Dad, but I think keeping a little bit of space is important. I don't want us to fall out and ruin everything."

I smiled. "You've changed your tune."

"Well . . ." He looked away, slightly embarrassed. "Hindsight's a wonderful thing, but I think I'd just got too close to it all. Looking at it through your eyes made me realize, yeah, I'm pretty lucky." He reached into his pocket. "I've got a present for you."

Robert leaned over and handed me a small tissue-wrapped parcel, tied up with a tartan ribbon. "Sorry about the packaging," he added. "Bit twee, but Mum's already started looking into packaging for Kettlesheer Gold."

"Family business, eh?" I said, unwinding the tissue paper. I didn't mention Catriona. I wanted this to be our moment.

Something heavy and silver dropped out of the tissue into my palm, about the size of a drumstick with a decorative end to it, topped with a solid thistle.

"Wow, thanks!" I said. I had absolutely no idea what it was.

I looked up. Robert was watching me with a grin.

"Go on," he said. "Pretend you know what it is."

"Of course I know what it is. It's a . . . reeling aid?"

He swung himself up from the chaise longue and held out his hand for the silver stick. "It's a porridge spurtle," he said, waggling it around an invisible pan. "For stirring porridge. I found it among Violet's belongings — it was a subscription wedding present from the tenants on the Kettlesheer farms. She kept it in the original box, with the note. I thought since you were so good at stirring us into action, it was an appropriate thank-you present." He handed it back, his eyebrow raised. "And, of course, I know how much you like sentimental knick-knacks."

"But I didn't do anything!" I protested, touched and thrilled to have a tangible memento of a woman I now felt I knew better than my own great-granny. I might even

453

start eating porridge for breakfast.

"You did. You made us look at stuff we'd been doing our best to ignore for years. And I don't just mean the dining table."

"Oh, come on. You had to tell your dad you don't like carrot schnapps at some point," I teased.

"No. Not that." Robert glanced down, then up at me, and I flinched at the direct honesty in his eyes. "Catriona and I have decided to go our separate ways."

"Oh," I said faintly. "I thought . . . at the ball . . . the announcement?" Was that what I'd seen, when Robert had led her away? Was that not *Will you marry me?* — but instead *Good-bye?*

He looked at me as if he were reading my mind. "Oh, you missed that. Managed to turn it into her taking over from Janet next year. Bit hairy — Janet had already called for hush — but I think we managed to cover things over. Until afterward." He rubbed his head ruefully, as if massaging away a tension headache. "The ball really brought home to me that there are more important things in a relationship than finding a good managing director."

There was a momentary awkward silence.

"I'm sorry." I wasn't sure what the correct reaction was, but inside I was flipping about with joy. I hoped my face was more sympathetic.

"Don't be too sorry," he said. "We parted friends — maybe that was the problem. Did you know Cat and her sister have already set up some kind of dating agency for luckless Border farmers?"

"I did, actually, yes. She's sent Alice her business card about organizing her and Fraser's 'wedding experience.' She can get owls to drop the rings at the altar, apparently."

"Well, there you go." He managed a small smile. "She's already dating some point-to-point champion from Berwick. Strong thighs. Drives an Aston Martin. Totally her type."

"And are you . . ." I began at the same time he said, "I was wondering . . ."

"No, go on." I nodded encouragingly, twisting the spurtle round and round in my fingers.

"I was wondering," said Robert with a faint hesitation, "now you're such an impeccable reeler, if you'd like to go to another ball with me? There's one in London, in May. White tie, tiaras, your usual requirements for a night out. Fraser was talking about taking a party, and —"

"I'd love to," I said at once. "Any excuse

for formal wear. I mean, not that you have to wear formal wear, it's just that you look so amazing in tails and . . ."

Shut up, Evie.

"That would be lovely," I finished. "May it is."

"Ah, well, May's a while off. I thought you might consider a few practice evenings. Informal dress is fine."

Robert reached out and took the silver spurtle from me, laying it gently on the desk. The bubbling sensation in my chest went into slow motion as I watched him take my hands in his, as he had done in the ballroom. Only this time, he held them as if I were some precious porcelain *objet,* not as if he were about to hurl me across the room backward.

"I'll try to make sure Alice doesn't cut in," I said, tingling at the warmth of his fingers interlacing with mine.

Robert half-smiled. "Ideally, I'd like you to be my partner for the whole evening. If you don't mind?"

I gazed up into his huge brown eyes. I didn't think I'd ever get bored of looking into them. They didn't even need adorning with a top hat, or repositioning in the Napoleonic Wars. They were . . . perfect as they were.

"I'll clear my dance card," I said.

"Good," he said softly, and leaned forward.

I met him halfway, breathing in his familiar, intoxicating smell, feeling his warm lips brushing against mine as his hair tickled my face. There was no rush this time, no panic to imprint every stolen moment into my memory. This was real. This was actually happening to me.

Behind us the bell rang above the door, and I thought I heard Max come in, but I didn't really care. I wasn't taking any lectures about what was valuable from anyone. Not today.

■ ■ ■ ■

GALLERY READER'S GROUP GUIDE SWEPT OFF HER FEET
HESTER BROWNE

■ ■ ■ ■

INTRODUCTION

Evie Nicholson, an assistant antiques dealer in London, has a fascination with what others might consider "old junk." When her sister, Alice, offers Evie the chance to value items in her friend's family castle in the Scottish Borders, it's the opportunity of a lifetime.

Kettlesheer Castle appears to hold many wonders — none more intriguing to Evie than the castle's attractive young heir, Robert McAndrew. But when she discovers the late Violet McAndrew's notebooks, Evie uncovers a scandal that could financially ruin the McAndrew family. On top of this upsetting discovery, Evie is forced to take her sister's place in the McAndrews' annual Scottish Reeling Ball, learn a complicated dance routine, and sort through her feelings for Robert — all in the course of two days.

TOPICS AND QUESTIONS
FOR DISCUSSION

1. Max's motivations for being in the business of antiques are very different from Evie's: "To succeed in antiques, you've got to ignore the item and focus on the *person* you can sell it to" (p. 12). If you were looking to buy or sell an antique item, with which dealer would you rather work? Why?

2. At the beginning of the novel, Alice and Evie are two sisters at odds. How does their relationship change over the course of the novel?

3. Although Evie and Alice's mother never actually appears in the novel, each sister speaks to the effects she's had on their lives. Did you find the girls' relationship with their mother to be typical? In what ways do their relationships mirror your own relationship with your parents and in what ways is it different?

4. What do Evie and Robert think of each

other when they first meet? Do you think either of them expects to fall so deeply for the other?

5. What were your feelings toward Catriona? Did you like or dislike her character? Did you feel sorry for her when she didn't get the proposal she so expected?

6. When Evie doesn't "feel" anything from what is supposed to be a very valuable and historical table, she tries to ignore her suspicions. Did you think something was wrong with the table? What were *your* initial suspicions?

7. Evie's impression of Violet changes when she finds out Violet is selling off the castle's antiques and replacing them with duplicates. What was your reaction to this scandal? Do you admire Violet for doing everything in her power to keep the house? Were you appalled to find she'd sold off the family's most valuable treasures?

8. The beauty of the fallen snow outside the castle catches Evie by surprise. In what ways does nature have an impact on the novel, particularly on the individual characters?

9. Evie is entranced by the candlelit ball, which she says is straight out of a Jane Austen novel. What are some other references or comparisons to Jane Austen

novels in *Swept Off Her Feet*?

10. Although Evie has spent her entire adult life avoiding dancing in any form, the magic of the reeling ball takes charge as she finds herself easily moving with the music. Can you picture the ball through Evie's eyes? Discuss what you imagine the reeling ball looks like.

11. Did you find yourself surprised when Alice showed up at the McAndrews' mid-first reel? Or had you anticipated that she would show up all along? Did you think it was fair of Alice to take her sister's place after having pressured Evie to fill in?

12. Robert and Duncan have very different opinions on how to run both the castle and Duncan's proposed brewing business. Do you think the compromise they reach at the end of the novel will be successful? Why or why not?

13. Evie's crush on Fraser disappears when she finally realizes the strength of her feelings for Robert. How are her feelings for each man different? What do you think would have happened with Fraser if she had never met Robert?

14. Max groans when Evie mentions using eBay to sell antique items, and Duncan brushes off her need for an Internet connection, telling her to use her eyes and

brain instead. Are there other examples throughout the book in which the generations differ in their opinions on technology?

15. Despite having always wanted to attend a romantic ball, Evie is unsure when Alice presents her with the opportunity: "It was my absolute dream, actually happening. So what was holding me back? Fear. Fear of being the one part of the dream that didn't match up" (p. 249). In what ways has Evie overcome her fears by the end of the novel? Which other characters had fears of their own that they had to conquer? Were they successful in doing so?

16. If *Swept Off Her Feet* were to be made into a movie, which actors and actresses would you cast to play the main characters?

17. Max tells Evie to look out for Kettle-sheer's many assets — the famous table, beautiful silverware, paintings — but Evie's drawn to far more personal treasures in the house, such as the daily household book of Lady Violet and her love letters. Which are, ultimately, the most "valuable" to the McAndrew family? What would be the real treasures in your family?

18. Evie loves history and is always looking

for ways to make the past come alive around her, whether it's buying vintage clothes, or imagining Ranald and Violet following the reel she's learning, in the very same ballroom. Have you ever done anything to "connect" with your family's past?

19. To begin with, Evie has a very romantic view of what life would have been like as a noblewoman in a Scottish castle. Do you think her view changes over the course of her stay?

20. Scottish reels are often danced in "sets" of four couples. Who would you invite to make up your ideal "set"?

ENHANCE YOUR BOOK CLUB

1. Visit an antiques shop with your reading group and explore the shop's unique treasures. Can you imagine the history of each object, like Evie does? Which objects do you think Evie would have found the most interesting?
2. Evie feels a deep connection with Violet and Ranald as she wanders through their castle. Which items around your home would you want to represent *you* in one hundred years? Ask each member of your reading group to compile a list, then compare lists to see which items are similar and which are different. Why did you choose the items on your list? What special significance do they hold?
3. When Evie and Max have trouble selling an item in Max's store, Evie often turns to eBay. Ask the members of your reading group to search eBay for antique items. Who can find the best bargain? The rarest

object? The oldest piece of furniture?

4. If your reading group is feeling particularly brave, why not try to learn a Scottish reel? For instructions, go online to the Scottish Dance Archives at http://www.dancearchives.co.uk/instructions.htm. If you'd rather skip the dancing but still want to experience the music of the Scottish reels, try looking for recordings online or at your local library.

5. Can't get enough of the Scottish dances and customs featured in *Swept Off Her Feet*? Visit the following websites:

All forms of Scottish dancing, from the very formal to barn dances: http://www.scottishdance.net/

Royal Scottish Country Dance Society — the official body of the formal side of things: http://www.rscds.org/index.php

The Strathspey Server — everything you ever wanted to know, and more: http://www.strathspey.org/index.html

6. To learn more about Hester Browne and her books, including her bestselling The Little Lady Agency series, visit her author page at http://authors.simonandschuster.com/Hester-Browne.

ABOUT THE AUTHOR

New York Times bestseller **Hester Browne** is the author of *The Finishing Touches* and The Little Lady Agency series and was named by Sophie Kinsella as one of her "favorite picks." A devotee of vintage-clothes hunting and cryptic crosswords, she lives in London. Visit www.simonand schuster.com/hesterbrowne.

The employees of Thorndike Press hope you have enjoyed this Large Print book. All our Thorndike, Wheeler, and Kennebec Large Print titles are designed for easy reading, and all our books are made to last. Other Thorndike Press Large Print books are available at your library, through selected bookstores, or directly from us.

For information about titles, please call:
  (800) 223-1244

or visit our Web site at:
  http://gale.cengage.com/thorndike

To share your comments, please write:
  Publisher
  Thorndike Press
  10 Water St., Suite 310
  Waterville, ME 04901